ALSO BY NELL FREUDENBERGER

The Newlyweds

The Dissident

Lucky Girls

LOST AND WANTED

LOST AND WANTED

·

Nell Freudenberger

ALFRED A. KNOPF
New York 2019

THIS IS A BORZOI BOOK PUBLISHED BY ALFRED A. KNOPF

www.aaknopf.com

Knopf, Borzoi Books, and the colophon are registered
trademarks of Penguin Random House LLC.

Grateful acknowledgment is made to Random House, an imprint
and division of Penguin Random House LLC, and Curtis Brown, Ltd.
for permission to reprint an excerpt of "This Lunar Beauty"
from W. H. Auden Collected Poems by W. H. Auden. Copyright
© 1934 and renewed in 1962 by W. H. Auden. Reprinted by
permission of Random House, an imprint and division of Penguin
Random House LLC, and Curtis Brown, Ltd. All rights reserved.

Library of Congress Cataloging-in-Publication Data
Names: Freudenberger, Nell, author.
Title: Lost and wanted : a novel / by Nell Freudenberger.
Description: First edition. | New York : Alfred A. Knopf, 2019. | "A Borzoi Book."
Identifiers: LCCN 2018017575 | ISBN 9780385352680 (hardcover) |
ISBN 9780385352697 (ebook)
Subjects: LCSH: Domestic fiction. | BISAC: FICTION / Literary. | FICTION /
Contemporary Women. | FICTION / Family Life.
Classification: LCC PS3606.R479 L67 2019 | DDC 813/.6—dc23
LC record available at https://lccn.loc.gov/2018017575

Jacket image: Nebulae in the constellation Cygnus by Haitong Yu / Getty Images
Jacket design by Abby Weintraub

Manufactured in the United States of America
First Edition

For Michael Friedman

The past has no existence except as it is recorded in the present.

John Archibald Wheeler, "Beyond the Black Hole"

ENTANGLEMENT

1.

In the first few months after Charlie died, I began hearing from her much more frequently. This was even more surprising than it might have been, since Charlie wasn't a good correspondent even when she was alive.

I should say right away that I don't believe in ghosts—although I've learned that forty-five percent of Americans do—at least not in the sense of the glaucous beings who appear on staircases, in abandoned farmyards, or on the film or digital records of events that absolutely did not include, say, a brown dog in the lower left-hand corner, or a man standing behind the altar in a black hood.

Charlie died in Los Angeles, on a Tuesday night in June. I was in Boston and I didn't know; we hadn't spoken for over a year. People talk about a cold wind, or a pain in the chest, but I didn't feel anything like that. On Wednesday at about noon, my phone rang. Or rather, I happened to be looking through my bag for my wallet, and I saw that the screen was illuminated: "Charlie." I grabbed the phone and answered before I could think any of the obvious things, such as *why pick up right away* or *it's been more than a year* or *what are you to her anymore?*

"Charlie?"

I heard a shuffling, something lightweight falling to the floor. Empty boxes, maybe.

I said her name again, and then I lost the call. I called her back, but no one picked up. I felt foolish and unaccountably disappointed. I vowed that if she tried again, I wouldn't pick up. I would wait a few days before deciding whether I even wanted to call her back.

2.

I became Frederick B. Blumhagen Professor of Theoretical Physics at MIT in 2004, just after I turned thirty-three. This was the year after Neel Jonnal and I published our AdS/CFT model for quark gluon plasma as a dual black hole in curved five-dimensional spacetime. I was subsequently invited to every physics conference and festival from Aspen to Tokyo to Switzerland, and accepted as many as I could get away with, at least of those that didn't ask me to speak on the subject of Women in Science.

Five years after Neel and I gave birth to our eponymous model, the Clapp-Jonnal, I gave birth to Jack. I'm what is called a single mother "by choice," which means that I decided to give up on the fantasy that a man with the intelligence and ambition required to interest me in the long term would arrive at the perfect reproductive moment, and be willing to give up a certain measure of professional success to contribute to the manual labor involved in raising a child. (Charlie's solution—finding a man who seemed to have no ambition other than to be with her and raise the child—struck me as workable, if you could be attracted to a person like that.)

Before Jack was born, I published two books for a general audience on topics related to my research: the first a collection of essays on quantum cosmology, and the second, more successfully, on black holes. Both books were published internationally, and *Into the Singularity* even spent a brief moment on several best-seller lists. It sometimes amuses me that the people who seem to envy the small amount of name recognition I've accrued—because I have the ability and the inclination to put what we do into words the nonscientist can understand—are the same people who dismiss that work for its lack of seriousness. I would much rather talk to laypeople who read the books and get excited about primordial black holes or the potential of the Large Hadron Collider than to Vincenzo Goia down the hall, and so I tended to do a fair amount of speaking about the books, at least before Jack was born. I am, as people are always noting, extremely busy. All of which is a long-winded way of saying that I didn't *need* Charlie.

I didn't need her, but when I got a call the next morning from an L.A. landline, all my resolutions melted away and I picked it up immediately. I believed it was my old friend finally calling me back.

"Helen?" It was Charlie's husband, Terrence.

"Oh—hi! Charlie called yesterday, but it was a really bad connection, and I tried her back, but—"

"Charlie's dead."

I'm ashamed to say that I laughed. I'm told that this isn't an uncommon reaction.

"What?"

"It happened late Tuesday night."

Tuesday, I thought, Tuesday, and was relieved to discover that it was impossible. This was Thursday, and Charlie had called me yesterday.

"We knew it was coming. But this was how she wanted it—no drama."

The idea that Charlie would want to do anything—least of all dying—without drama was ludicrous, as was this sudden phone call in the middle of the morning. It was eleven o'clock and I was in my office, peer reviewing an article for *Physical Review Letters* on ultrahigh-energy debris from collisional Penrose processes. I thought of how Charlie used to laugh at the titles of my papers. I always said it was just a matter of getting past the unfamiliar language. If she could read Shakespeare, she could read physics. This particular paper suggested that subatomic particles orbiting near a spinning black hole might collide more forcefully than previous calculations showed, possibly even powering ultrahigh-energy cosmic rays.

"What do you mean?"

I knew Charlie was ill. Charlie had lupus. They had diagnosed it eight years ago, just after her daughter was born, when her suppressed immune system allowed the previously dormant disease to flare. But even before that, for as long as I'd known her, Charlie had believed something was wrong with her. The diagnosis, when she described it, wasn't a tragedy. It was a relief to know what it was, and to be able to get treated. She'd been waiting her whole life to find out. There was no question of *dying*.

"I got a call from her phone yesterday," I told him.

There was a pause.

"What time?" Terrence asked, and for a moment I thought there was a note of hope in his voice. As if it might be possible for me to convince him.

"At about noon."

"Because her phone is missing," Terrence said. "There've been a lot of people in and out—the health care aides especially. The coroner and the men from the funeral parlor. And then a few different sitters for Simmi, and our housekeeper—but she's absolutely trustworthy." Terrence sounded fierce, as if I had accused the housekeeper. He took a breath and continued. "We sleep—we've been sleeping—together, and Simmi fell asleep next to her mother on Tuesday as usual. I moved her to her own room, and I think she knew when she woke up. I was sitting there, and she didn't cry when I told her. We had breakfast. She didn't ask about the body. It was only when I started looking for the phone, and couldn't find it, that she went crazy."

"Terrence," I said. "I can't—"

"Yeah."

I was the maid of honor in their wedding ten years ago, on the beach in Malibu. I thought then that Charlie's parents, an art dealer and a psychiatrist who still lived in the Georgian house in Brookline, where Charlie grew up, felt the same way I did about Terrence. Still, they didn't show that they were disappointed to find their daughter marrying a surfer whose brother had served a three-year sentence for possession with intent to distribute, whose mother smoked menthols behind the catering truck before and after the ceremony, whose father was nowhere to be seen.

The couple was blindingly attractive. Terrence had his Irish mother's green eyes and his black father's hair, twisted into short, beach-friendly locks. Charlie had her mother's incomparable bone structure. There was a lot of talk about how beautiful the children would be. There was no talk about Charlie's disease, because at that time no one knew she had it.

"I didn't cancel her phone service until this morning," Terrence said. "We wanted to trace the phone, but she never set that up. She said she'd do it. It takes, like, three minutes."

Terrence hesitated, and other noise took over. In my office there was the whir of dry heat being forced through the empty ducts. On Terrence's end, the hysterical rise and fall of children's television.

"There's something I need—from her email. They make it almost impossible to get into email on the computer, if you don't know the password. But the passcode on the phone is 1234. I once showed her an article about how it's everyone's first guess—but she never changed it. Maybe she figured she didn't need to email it to me, since I could always get in on the phone."

I was having trouble following Terrence, but I didn't want to ask him to repeat himself. What was it he needed? At first I thought of a will, but the only copy of a will wouldn't be locked in a deceased person's email account.

"I might have to hire an actual lawyer."

"That's crazy."

"Yeah, so . . . whoever has the phone—they must've pocket dialed you."

"That makes sense." I said this to be kind to Terrence. I didn't believe it. What were the odds of being called accidentally by a thief who stole a phone, even if the passcode were easy to guess? You didn't keep a stolen phone and start using it. You wiped it clean and sold it right away.

Terrence coughed. "Charlie wanted me to—reach out to you. She didn't want me to get into the medical details with everyone, but since you understand this stuff—it was the encephalitis that did it. She was doing chemo."

"Charlie was?"

"Chemo's not just for cancer."

"I know that."

"Yeah, so, we stopped that three weeks before—we decided to stop it, because it wasn't helping. She was worried about her hair."

"She would have looked fine without hair."

"She didn't lose any."

"That probably made her happy."

"I think it was her chief concern." Terrence let out a sound between a sigh and a choke, and I was sorry I'd ever thought badly of him.

"Terrence, I don't—is there anything I can do? I know it must be . . . with Simmi and everything."

I hadn't seen Simmi since she was a baby, but I thought that if she were anything like her mother, she would survive. In fact, that was the piece of it that made the least sense, because the central fact about Charlie was her resilience. It wasn't so much that Charlie couldn't die, but that the Charlie who was dead couldn't be Charlie anymore.

"She's lucky to have you, though." I didn't mean to relate it to me and Jack, or to suggest that just because Simmi had two parents, it was okay that she had lost one of them. But I'm still afraid Terrence might have taken it that way.

"Me?" He sounded incredulous. "I'm no substitute."

"No, of course, but—"

"She's just waiting for her mother to come back. Now I think that's why she didn't ask about the body. If she saw a body—"

There was a pause in which I heard the television again. It was so loud. Had he put it on to distract his daughter while he called their friends? Or had she turned it up herself, to drown him out?

"There's going to be a memorial in Boston next month," he said. "Her parents will let you know."

I asked if there were anything I could do to help, and Terrence politely declined—naturally, he was eager to get off the phone.

"People are posting on her wall," he said.

"Okay."

"You can memorialize her fucking Facebook. But you can't get what you actually need."

"I'm so sorry."

"Yeah," he said. "Thanks." And hung up.

I went to the missed calls from yesterday: one incoming, followed by two outgoing in quick succession. I touched the number and the screen obligingly responded: "Calling: Charlie . . ."

But it was as Terrence had said. The mobile customer I was trying to reach was no longer at this number. No further information was available.

I was alone in my office. I got up and locked the door. I put on my wireless headphones, clicked on the German Requiem, and turned off the lights. I sat with my back against the couch and put my head on my knees. This is what I did when my grandmother died in 2005, and it had helped. But this time I felt as if I were watching myself do it, as if it were a performance. I couldn't cry. I got back up, turned off the music, and sat down at my computer. If tears came, fine; if not, I would work until my 1:00 p.m. seminar.

I tried to focus on a grant proposal for a postdoc who'd just gotten a job at Harvey Mudd, and then opened my email. I wasn't checking for anything; do we even "check" anymore? It was just a reflex, like rubbing my eyes or stretching. But there it was, incredible and absolutely real, in its narrow, rectangular box, slotted between a message from the PA at Jack's school and a solicitation from Greenpeace—Charlotte Boyce. I stared at it for a moment to be sure. The time was 10:57 a.m., this morning. I clicked:

That was it. It was in reply to a message I'd sent three weeks earlier, asking how she was, but there were no words, nothing but those tiny pictures. It was not impossible to believe that a message from Charlie might have been delayed for three days, and she was certainly capable of sending a goodbye like that. Or it might have been a fake, a hacker—except what motivation could such a person possibly have?

If it were someone else, it would be better not to respond. But there was no "if," I had to remind myself—whoever it was, was someone else.

3.

In my line of work, I do get asked about the paranormal; everyone who brings it up does so in the same shy, half-joking way, as if they assume they are the first. I'm always tempted to give a lecture about Newton: the debate among historians as to whether he belongs in the supernatural past of the Sumerians and Babylonians, or as a shock trooper of the Age of Reason. I come down with the latter group. The fact that Newton owned an enormous collection of alchemical and religious manuscripts has no bearing upon his invention of differential calculus or its brilliant application in the *Principia*. What I normally say instead is that it isn't that magical things are necessarily impossible—only that they must be confined to environments we haven't yet observed.

I couldn't bring myself to look at Charlie's Facebook, but I did google the rules regarding deceased persons' accounts:

- If Facebook is made aware that a person has passed away, it is our policy to memorialize the account.
- No one can log into a memorialized account and no new friends can be accepted.
- Depending on the privacy settings of the deceased person's account, friends can share memories on the memorialized timeline.
- Anyone can send private messages to the deceased person.

The last rule seemed the strangest to me: Facebook actually sanctioned the idea of private messages to the dead. The messages existed somewhere on the internet, but no one other than their authors were allowed to read them. Such letters to the dead must always have been written; it was just that in the past, the writers had nowhere to send them.

I went through the emails I'd saved from Charlie. I generally erase personal email at the end of each year, and there were only a few that had wound up in permanent folders, including one in which we worked out the logistics for the last time we'd seen each other, the Christmas Jack was four. I had almost given up looking when I found another, in a folder I might have intended to discard. This one was older, from just after Simmi was born:

> I have currently checked into a hotel for a couple of days to try to finish my NBC pilot, the first draft of which is due this week. I am having a VERY tough time trying to write and be a mom— and also I've had all these weird health issues post-pregnancy (they first thought I had lupus but now hopefully just arthritis— typing that makes me feel ancient—along with an acute thyroid problem). We just hired a nanny, but somehow managing that, along with the constant mental checklist (is the baby eating enough? did she nap? for how long? is there enough food in the freezer? diapers? formula? etc.), seems to preclude the kind of sustained concentration it takes to invent the characters and world of this pilot. I have less than a month to write a script from an idea that wasn't mine in the first place, and that takes place in another time period—New York City society in the "roaring twenties"—a period of American history about which I know (& dare I say care?) relatively little. No wonder so much of network TV sucks. Anyway, hoping that being away from the

responsibilities of the baby will allow me to fall back on some
of my old tricks—like pulling all-nighters, say?—so that I can at
least crank out a draft.

I printed it out, and then didn't know what to do with it. That
"dare I say care?"—it was so Charlie. She didn't pretend to care
about things she didn't care about, and she cared passionately
about the things she did. It could be a seventeenth-century poet—
Marvell was her favorite—or a TV show about aliens; if she loved
it, she would defend it against any attack. She was the same way
about people, especially her father and her older brother, William.
With her mother, Adelaide, her attachment was more fraught. And
for a while I was included in that charmed circle of loyalty. She
might tease me: once she convinced nearly everyone we knew that
I was a member of the Greek royal family, and that my real first
name was Iphigenia, that I went by Helen only to remain incog-
nito at school. (I learned of this several months later, from a Greek
woman on my intramural soccer team, who said that she had to ask
because she was actually a distant relation herself, through Princess
Olga Isabelle, Duchess of Apulia.) Charlie made fun of me, but she
also comforted my heartbreaks and disappointments, and encouraged my ambition in a way that made me feel I really could do
the things I imagined doing when I was that age. People used to
joke about Charlie and me being lovers, and maybe they really did
wonder; it was something harder to describe than that. We were on
each other's side in a way that felt permanent, and so it hurt more
than it might have otherwise, when she decided to shut me out.

In the days after Terrence's phone call, I heard from college classmates. They wrote to me because they'd gotten the news about
Charlie's death and remembered how close we'd been. I directed
those in the L.A. area toward a woman named Ellie, who was
organizing a meal train for Terrence and Simmi, and the others
to the scholarship fund I'd learned that her family was setting up
in Charlie's name. I was always anxious, in these correspondences,
when I revealed the fact that I hadn't seen Charlie during the last
years of her illness, and that we had communicated only intermittently. I thought it would seem as if I'd abandoned her when
she most needed friends; under the circumstances, I didn't think I

could explain that she was the one who had abandoned me, if only because she refused to talk about the illness that was increasingly taking over her life.

As it turned out, no one even asked me. Was that because losing touch with one's classmates from twenty years earlier seemed natural, or because it seemed natural to have lost touch with someone who was now dead?

I did get a call from Neel. He'd heard online, like everyone, but at least he'd picked up the phone.

"It's a weird impulse," he said. "The meal train."

Neel's need to dissect every bit of convention, to expose the contradictions in other people's behavior, had always been exasperating.

"I think it's pretty standard, across cultures. Don't Indians bring food when someone dies?"

"Well, yes, but we're always cooking," Neel said. "You have to eliminate us from the data set."

His sense of humor, on the other hand, was so perfectly calibrated with mine (we had all the same references) that I liked talking with him better than with almost anyone else.

"People need to eat," I said.

"Yeah, but do you think we do this to avoid thinking about what happened?"

"Have you been thinking about her?"

Neel and Charlie had gotten along beautifully in college—unexpectedly, too, because their core beliefs were so different that it could easily have gone the other way. During the brief time Neel and I were dating, they acted almost like brother and sister, teasing each other and often ganging up on me as well. I'd meant to reconnect them once he moved out to Caltech, but I'd never done it.

"You remember that time we went to her house?"

"In Brookline?" I knew which house he was talking about, and it was possible that I asked that question just to stall. It's hard for me to think about that weekend without losing my composure, even now.

"No, on the North Shore. To see Swift-Tuttle."

"But it was too cloudy."

"The first night was too cloudy," he said. "But we saw it the second."

"Are you kidding?"

"No."

"We didn't stay two nights. We got drunk and went swimming."

"It's strange that you don't remember the comet."

That was another thing about Neel—he could never let a subject drop.

"I do remember it—we saw it at Harvard, at the CfA in January."

"You're thinking of Hale-Bopp in '97," Neel said. "After we both got back to Cambridge. It was Swift-Tuttle in Gloucester. I bet Charlie would remember."

"Yeah, well."

There was a long pause, and then Neel asked how Simona was doing. I told him briefly what Terrence had said about Simmi—I thought that Neel, who didn't have any interest in children, could hardly understand—and then we shifted to the safer subject of Caltech LIGO, where Neel had been working for the past eleven years. The Laser Interferometer Gravitational-Wave Observatory, an international collaboration of more than a thousand scientists, was dedicated to detecting the gravitational waves that Einstein posited the existence of in 1915. People describe these waves as "ripples in spacetime," with analogies about bowling balls on trampolines and people rolling around on mattresses, and these are probably as good as we're going to get. The problem with all of the analogies, though, is that they're three-dimensional; it's almost impossible for human beings to add a fourth dimension, and visualize how objects with enormous gravity—black holes or dead stars—might bend not only space, but time.

When Charlie died, LIGO's massive gravitational wave detectors were about to make their first science runs. LIGO isn't an observatory in the traditional sense, but rather a pair of L-shaped interferometers—detectors with concrete arms two miles long, down which beams of light bounce between the most high-tech mirrors in the world. The fifty-year-old project had been one of the most technically difficult in science; now that the machines were finally operational, no one knew how long it would take to detect a gravitational wave, but Neel believed it was only a matter of months. The interferometers were located in remote parts of Louisiana and Washington State (there was also one in Italy), and there were teams of LIGO scientists at universities all over the world: in the U.S., Caltech, Columbia, and MIT were the most significant. As LIGO got closer to a detection—which everyone predicted would earn them a Nobel—I was glad Neel wasn't on the East Coast but three thousand miles away at Caltech. We'd been competitive from the moment we met each other, as college freshmen, and now that we weren't working together anymore, I found that rivalry more distracting than inspiring.

In our discipline, we're taught to think about time with a flexibility that transcends the ordinary experience of it. The conventional wisdom was once that this kind of abstract thinking came more naturally to a twenty-year-old than to a forty-year-old. Einstein thought that a scientist who hadn't achieved a breakthrough by age thirty never would, and that was basically true before 1905. But in the last century, the age that great scientists do their best work has steadily increased, so that the average Nobel Prize–winning physicist is now forty-eight. People give various reasons for this— students earn their doctorates later, rarely before twenty-five; there's more to learn before you can do original work. I have sometimes wondered whether our more advanced age influences the science that is being done today—whether our conclusions, especially with regard to cosmological time, are different because we are older.

I met Charlie on the first day of freshman orientation in 1989, when our proctor organized a game of "Two Truths and a Lie" for the students on our floor. The point was to get acquainted by offering three pieces of information about yourself, among which a falsehood wouldn't be immediately obvious. We sat in the common room of a suite whose inhabitants had already decorated it with a rubber Bart Simpson, a lava lamp, and a velvet Elvis.

I hadn't visited Harvard before I arrived there from California. I'd seen plenty of pictures, but in my head the august professors I had read about were lecturing in front of green chalkboards in the hot, run-down classrooms of my public high school in Pasadena. I, a Harvard student, was still sitting at an undersized desk pushed together with others to accommodate as many students as possible, struggling to ignore the muffled shriek of Def Leppard or Poison from someone's concealed headphones, the drone of a decrepit and ineffectual air conditioner. I knew Harvard was going to be different, but until I walked into the Italianate brick-and-sandstone freshman dormitory for the first time, right in the middle of Harvard Yard, it had seemed impossible that it would really look as perfect as it did.

Our Freshman Proctor was an energetic grad student in biology named Lynn who had sought me out the moment I arrived, and kindly invited me to the first meeting of a group she was starting: Women in Science at Harvard (WISH, naturally). I knew better than to join a group like that (at the time I couldn't even see the need for it) or evince any enthusiasm for her game. As it happened, though, Lynn called on me first, and so I didn't have much time to think. I pretended a sort of world-weary patience, and began:

"I like the Pixies." (This was true, although I liked several less respectable bands more.) "I'm from California. And . . . I'm a witch." I thought this was clever, since it revealed nothing important, and made it clear that I wasn't even trying to play the game, telegraphing my disdain for the kind of enforced socialization that I thought I'd left behind in high school. Harvard wasn't any more inclined toward this type of activity than most of its students, and after a week of word games, trust falls, and ice-cream socials, we were left to fend for ourselves.

A skinny white kid in a dog collar and Doc Martens gave me a knowing look. "You're not really from California," he guessed. "Otherwise you would've said where."

Charlie went next. She said that she had lived for a year in Paris, that her mother had been a model, and that she didn't like to lie. Her tone was calm and self-possessed, not bragging but simply stating a series of facts.

Lynn the proctor contributed something to the effect that honesty was a wonderful quality, but that for the purposes of the game, Charlie needed to give one false statement.

"I did," Charlie said.

The proctor was confused, and so Charlie looked around the room.

"Are you people going to guess?"

"You didn't really live in Paris?"

Looking at Charlie, it was hard to believe someone in her family wasn't a model. She was nearly six feet tall, with skin the color of—Charlie once pointed out the way brown skin is described almost exclusively in relation to food or spices, things you can eat, and so I won't use that type of analogy. She was a medium-skinned black woman, thin, and at that age, gangly. Her eyes were large and far apart, and her mouth was perfect, as if she'd drawn around it with pencil, even on the rare occasions when she hadn't. On that warm September day, she was wearing flared white jeans and a sleeveless top, of a sort of lime-green brocade, with leather, cork-bottomed sandals. Her hair was pulled back into a smooth chignon, and her ears were decorated with square diamond studs.

"I did live in Paris," Charlie sighed. "But it's not true that I hate to lie. I love lying. It's so liberating."

In our era at Harvard, there were various, distinct types: the international students; the children of immigrants; the scattering of anonymous valedictorians from all across the country, like me, the only ones from their high schools. And then there were the kids from New York: the rich ones, nearly all white (with some Saudi royalty thrown in), whose fathers and grandfathers had gone to Harvard, who belonged to the final clubs and the Hasty Pudding. Having begun in public school in Brookline, spent the year in Paris, and then finished high school at an elite boarding school in Connecticut, Charlie managed to have friends from this set without belonging exclusively to it. Then there were the graduates of the specialized New York City public schools, brilliant math and science grinds from Stuyvesant, Bronx Science, and Brooklyn Tech—mostly Asian, with a smattering of black and white nerds—and the culturally sophisticated, mostly Jewish crowd from Hunter and LaGuardia.

I would have said then that Charlie and I—an upper-middle-class black girl from Brookline and a work-study white science nerd from Pasadena—didn't fit into any category, and that that's why we were eventually drawn to each other. Now I think that the twenty-some eighteen-year-olds in the room that day must have been equally uncategorizable, each with their secret, disjunctive parts. I think that the boxes we used to sort them were nothing more than comforting fictions, like Bohr's atomic model, which is so pretty and so sensible—its particles orbiting the nucleus like a miniature sun and planets—that it's still the definitive representation. This is in spite of its incompatibility with everything we now know about the very tiniest pieces into which the world can be broken.

4.

It was about a month after I got the news about Charlie that Jack said he'd seen the ghost. Our house is more than a hundred years old. I bought it in 2005, with the money my grandmother left me. A narrow blue Victorian in Cambridgeport, a five-minute drive from MIT, it had a front porch, a hexagonal tower, and a German couple already installed in the rental unit downstairs. The Germans rode off together every morning on their bicycles to their studio, where together they were making a documentary film about the few remaining Wampanoag tribespeople on Chappaquiddick.

Once—this must have been soon after I joined the faculty at MIT—I came home from work and found the Germans passionately kissing in the front hall. The blond bulk of him obscured her narrow frame entirely, such that I thought for a moment he was leaning against the door in some kind of despair. He stepped back when he heard me, revealing his black-haired, blue-eyed wife.

"Excuse us," he said, and their expressions were as if I had surprised them in their house, rather than the other way around. They looked at me with barely concealed pity, as if I must feel so lonely. This surprised me, because at that time I was the furthest thing from lonely.

(When a group of physicists publishes a paper, we will sometimes parenthetically note a related topic that we plan to explore later. After we published our model, Neel left to join the LIGO effort at Caltech, under Kip Thorne and David Reitze. For four years Neel and I emailed each other almost daily, a correspondence that ranged from particle physics to the incredible machines Neel's team was building in Washington and Louisiana. We didn't only talk about physics, but about the politics of his lab and my department, the politics of our country, the books we were reading, the people we were dating, what we ate for lunch. It was the most indirect and the most exciting conversation of my life, and by the time I finally asked Neel the two questions I most wanted to know—

1) whether he was ever coming back to Cambridge, and
2) whether he had changed his mind on the subject of children

—I was thirty-six. There was a kind of relief in getting his answers. In general I like to know the facts.)

That was when I decided to have a baby. People said I was crazy to give up so soon. Thirty-six was so young, and anyway, they all knew someone they hadn't thought to set me up with until now. Was I interested in coffee, dinner, a hike? I smiled and nodded, but I had already picked out the father online. The number of PhD students in physics among the candidates was striking—a qualification that apparently signals intelligence to the general population—but I'd skipped over these quickly. I was familiar with the characteristic quirks of such people, and anyway, I was looking for genetic product that would complement rather than enhance my own strengths. The father I selected was a rock-climbing graduate student in musicology, cryobank handle "Papageno," who had grown up on a farm in Washington State. Papageno was six feet two inches tall, with sandy hair and blue eyes. In his childhood photo (the only type the site permitted) he grinned at me as if he knew he'd done something wrong, and also that I would forgive him.

I sat across from wasted, adult specimens in bars and restaurants—once, in a canoe—and tried to be polite, then went home and stared at the gorgeous boy on my screen. I wasn't *giving up;* by having a child, I was releasing myself not only from these pointless encounters, but from the pressure to settle for someone who didn't meet my standards. In the meantime, I would get pregnant. I've never waited so breathlessly for anything as I did for that package from California, vacuum-sealed vials that produced the love of my life.

I don't know whether this is something other parents feel—it's not something you would bring up on the pavement outside the elementary school, where the conversation turns more naturally to the ways our seven-year-olds are unmanageable. I can participate in those conversations, complain about Jack's baroque rituals at bedtime, or tell a story about the time he wandered off as a toddler and relieved himself on a stranger's front porch, but all the time I'm doing it, Jack's physical presence inside the building is exerting a kind of force on me, impossible to ignore.

It isn't so much that I'm excited to see him at the end of his day as that my body longs to be with his. The need to pick him up and caress him seems to be increasing just as it gets more difficult to do so. Sometimes, especially right after he wakes up in the morning, or when we're reading together in his room at night, he'll still sit on my lap, lean back against my chest, and allow me to put my face in his hair. In those moments there is a surge of contentment so intense that I can hardly see the page in front of me.

I did worry about sex before I had him, whether I would ever have it again. The surprise was that for the seven years since his birth, this alternative physical intimacy has taken the place of the other kind. I'm still introduced to men, and twice this has led to brief, sexual relationships. (My sister refers to these people, who haven't risen to the level of boyfriends, as persons-of-interest, or POI.) But I've never gotten to the point that I wanted to introduce any of these persons to Jack.

The Germans have a child now. When I run into them in the hall, the father likes to tell stories about things the little girl has learned to do—climb the stairs, for example, or sing a German song about the moon—while his wife gently teases him for his pride. They tell me as a fellow parent, as if there's no difference between us, but it's now that I've begun to envy them. Some nights I see them sitting on my porch, drinking wine with the window open to the living room, keeping their voices low while she sleeps. I imagine they're talking about her, their plans for her. I would like to talk with someone about Jack that way.

5.

I was surprised when Adelaide Boyce called me. I had considered sending Charlie's parents a note when it happened, and even went into a fancy paper store—a place I thought Addie might herself patronize—to buy a card. But the very elegant and contemporary cards at that shop seemed ridiculous to me, and I couldn't do it. What would I write? Something about condolences? About them being in my thoughts? It was true that they were in my thoughts, but in a haphazard way that had more to do with my own guilt than with Charlie. I daydreamed about accidents that might befall me, about Jack finding me dead.

Addie apologized for calling me at work, said she didn't have another number. She would be happy to call back if now wasn't a good time.

"Of course, now is fine," I said, glancing at the clock. I was supposed to meet a graduate student in twenty minutes. "I'm so sorry—"

"Yes," Addie said crisply. "Thank you. We're all trying to focus on Simona now—without her, I'm not sure what we'd do."

"Is Simmi . . . here in Boston?"

"She and her father are staying with us while they wait for the house in L.A. to sell. Perhaps longer."

"It's good that Terrence can take the time."

"He works for his brother's business now," Addie said. "Apparently they're just getting off the ground on the East Coast, and his brother thinks he could be useful here. The Brookline schools are wonderful, and Simona could be registered from our address, even if Terrence decides to rent a separate apartment for the two them."

"That makes sense," I said, although I thought that Charlie's mother could have told me that Terrence and Simmi were going to live on the International Space Station and I would have accepted it just as readily. It had to do with the way she said things.

I first heard about the Boyces in bits and pieces, the way we all exchanged information about our families in college. I knew Charlie's mother had grown up in a socially prominent Philadelphia family, had been a model in Paris in the early sixties, and then an art student in New York, where she'd met Carl—a wounded Navy corpsman on his way home from Vietnam—at a concert in Washington Square Park. They married in Philadelphia, and moved to Boston so that he could go to medical school at Tufts. Addie got her PhD in art history while the children were small, eventually opening a successful gallery in the South End, specializing in contemporary African painters. She had run the gallery until Charlie's older brother, William, a chess prodigy, began having discipline problems in school—at which point she sold it to stay home with the children. By the time William and Charlie were in college, she served as an advisor to the boards of two different museums, and ran an after-school art program for children in Roxbury.

Carl was from much humbler circumstances in Baltimore—his father was an orderly in a municipal hospital; his mother cleaned houses and took care of other people's children. He had enlisted right out of high school and chosen hospital corpsman training; he shipped out after twenty weeks to South Vietnam, where he was assigned to a battalion of marines as a combat medic. He often said he was lucky to have been hit by shrapnel after eleven months, sent home to recover at the VA hospital at Wilmington, where he first became interested in psychiatry. He was in medical school in '71, when Charlie was born, and eventually rose to become chairman of psychiatry at Tufts. In the eighties, he occasionally appeared as a "relationship expert" on television, once even on Oprah's show.

In college I believed that Charlie simply came from a more interesting family than other people I knew. My own seemed to me almost comically dull by comparison. It took me a long time to see that although the Boyces were genuinely dynamic and accomplished people, it was Charlie who made them fascinating; she was able to tell a story in a way that appeared to impart information, distracting you with well-chosen details, but ultimately hid more than it revealed. This was maybe especially true of the way she presented her mother.

"The memorial is the eleventh," Addie said. "You should get a card next week. That's why I'm calling, actually—Carl and I wanted to ask if you would consider saying a few words. Her brother will speak, and one of her cousins. A friend from childhood. But we'd like it to remain informal."

I was overwhelmed and grateful that Addie still considered me a close-enough friend of Charlie's to speak at the memorial. At the same time, I was well aware that this was an event planned by Charlie's parents for their family and friends. As far as I knew, Terrence hadn't been involved in any of the arrangements, including the decision about who would speak.

I struggled not to say the wrong thing. "Thank you," I told Addie. "It's going to be hard to—there's so much I'd like to say about her."

"Yes," Addie said, a little impatiently. "I feel I should tell you something about her death, unless Terrence has already shared those details with you?"

"He said it was encephalitis, a complication of the lupus? And I know she was doing chemo—"

"Encephalitis was the official cause," Addie said. "It should be what was written on the death certificate. It would be, if she'd been fortunate enough to die in Oregon, Vermont, or Washington State. There is actually legislation in the pipeline in California—but all of that will come too late for Charlie."

As a child I'd had a habit of interrupting an explanation to say that I'd understood, until I noticed that it was a practice that endeared me to no one. In this case I kept quiet, although I did understand almost immediately that Addie was talking about assisted suicide. Something Charlie had said to me once made this easier to believe than it might have been otherwise.

"They have a new name for it—aid-in-dying. Forgive me if I've lost patience with the names we have for everything now. Terrence didn't mention it, I take it?"

"No—he said it happened more quickly than they expected."

"Well, yes—if you overdose on barbiturates, it does tend to be quite quick."

I had a vertiginous feeling, the taste of bile in my throat.

"I have no problem with the legislation. I would vote for it myself—I will vote for it, when Massachusetts gets around to it. But you have to understand, we had decided on hospice-at-home.

We'd hired a team. I had just come home to get things in order here, and then Carl and I were going back to L.A. There was going to be time for her friends—all of her friends—to say goodbye. Her brother would have come out and we would have been there with her when it happened. And Charlie never suggested that this wasn't what she wanted. Terrence says that she changed her mind, that Charlie wrote to us about her reasons for this . . . change of plans. An *email.*"

"He did say there was something—"

"A letter that we never received. And has since been mysteriously lost."

"I guess they make it hard to access the account."

"There is always a *they* making things difficult," Addie said. "I did try to teach my children that. But the point is that you have to anticipate whichever obstacles that entity may choose to put up in front of you, and have a plan in place to circumvent them. Were those my daughter's wishes, I am quite certain—"

Addie's diction was always formal; Charlie would often imitate it. But now this manner was so heightened that it was as if Addie were doing an impression of herself. When she paused there was a silence into which, if I were a different kind of person, I would have known how to inject some kind of comfort. Instead I just waited until Charlie's mother recovered herself.

"In any case, none of this is relevant to the memorial. Except that there are those among our guests who will have religious objections to the path Charlie took—the path she appears to have taken."

"I don't have any objections."

"I assumed—but you understand that this isn't something that can be mentioned, even obliquely."

"I understand."

"Well I'm glad, Helen. You're still on Putnam Avenue?"

"Yes."

"So you'll have the invitation next week."

When we hung up I remembered Jim, who was waiting for me in a conference room at the library. He wanted to talk about his upcoming summer research fellowship at Brookhaven. That day MIT was as quiet as it ever is, since most people had already left for the summer. The only sounds were footsteps on the linoleum outside my door, a pair of voices retreating down the corridor. The venetian blind threw a gridded shadow on the white wall. There was still enough time to meet Jim, if I hurried, but I just sat there, staring at the screensaver, onto which I'd downloaded an image one of my favorite colleagues, the chair of STS, had forwarded.

It was his own photograph of the largest telescope at the Observatorio del Teide on Tenerife—the white dome with a yellow moon hanging behind it—which he and his team were planning to use in their tests of Bell's Inequality. I've never worked on quantum entanglement, which Einstein once dismissed as "spooky action at a distance." It's a real phenomenon, though, one that has less to do with communication than with a shared history that causes a pair of particles, even once they've been permanently separated, to behave as if they knew what each other was thinking.

6.

PLEASE JOIN US TO CELEBRATE THE LIFE OF
C H A R L O T T E   A D E L A I D E   B O Y C E

THE MEMORIAL CHURCH, HARVARD UNIVERSITY
SATURDAY, JULY 11, AT 10:00 A.M.

The invitation included a photograph framed inside a piece of heavy gray-blue card stock. It was a close-up of Charlie laughing: I recognized it as one of a series taken by a photographer before she went to L.A., when she still thought she wanted to act as well as write. It wasn't that the laughter was fake; you could see Charlie had hit it off with the photographer, and was really amused by something he or she had said. (Something about her expression made me think the photographer had been a man.) But this was her social, extroverted persona, and more than anyone I've ever met, Charlie had two distinct selves, one private and one public. You had to come fairly close before you could see the other one, much less capture it on film.

The card had been tucked into the corner of our dry-erase calendar for several days, but Jack hadn't mentioned it. That in itself suggested to me that he understood. On the Thursday before the memorial, I picked him up from soccer camp, and we walked home from the park through the humid afternoon. At home I gave him peanut butter crackers and a banana. A Lego catalog had come, and he paged through it, leaving crumbs in the binding. There was something called a "hydroponic space station" that he'd been eyeing for months.

"You can build all this," he said. "You can buy it."

"Remember I told you about my friend Charlie?"

"Uh huh."

We were sitting at a green-and-yellow laminate table that I'd had since college, in our small kitchen, where I've hung two spider plants from the ceiling in rope baskets. Sun was coming in around their leaves, making patterns on the table.

"There's going to be a memorial."

"I remember."

"I don't think we've ever talked about the memorial."

"I mean—I remember *her.*"

"That's right," I said. "She came to visit when you were four."

"No," Jack said, in a new wounded way he has. Now that he's seven, all of a sudden there are times when he's able to correct me, when he's observed a physical object or a situation more carefully than I have. This is normally true of things that he's more interested in than I am, such as the route of the ice-cream truck, or the progress of the new construction along Mem Drive.

"I *saw* her," he insisted.

"Where?"

"In your office."

I thought I understood. "Are you thinking of Rose in my office?"

Rose was one of the Knight Science Journalism fellows this year, who was interested in an article I'd written on NASA's Wilkinson Microwave Anisotropy Probe. She had come to talk with me on a day when Jack was hanging out in my office after school. Rose was both younger and less glamorous than Charlie in that photograph, but she was a tall Nigerian woman with short hair; I thought she was the only person Jack might have seen in my office whom he could have confused with Charlie.

"Rose?" Jack said incredulously. "I know Rose. She got me the CMB with googly eyes."

I had told the Knight fellows that Jack was curious about the cosmic microwave background. Sometimes it feels like I end up regretting every anecdote I allow myself to tell about my son at work. Anyone would be attracted to the brightly colored map of the early universe created by NASA's WMAP—an especially pretty golden satellite that spins around the project's home page in animated form. A basic version of the concept—that the satellite took a picture of light left over from the Big Bang, teaching us a lot about the history of the universe—is possible to explain even to a six-year-old; it didn't signify anything exceptional about my child that he was interested. Nevertheless, Rose had managed to find a cosmic microwave background stuffed toy (an item that could have been procured only in the immediate vicinity of MIT) and bring it in for Jack, and so naturally he remembered her.

"So who did you see in my office who looked like Charlie?"

"Not your work office," Jack said. "Upstairs."

I was lost. "Here?"

Now Jack finally looked at the picture on the calendar. "She's pretty."

"Yep."

If he doesn't want to answer a question, you can't push him. I waited, and sure enough, he continued.

"She was sitting at your desk, and I said, 'Hi.' I scared her." He smiled, as if at a real memory. "She—" He jumped a little in his chair and opened his eyes wide, a parody of adult surprise.

I have always thought that if there were ghosts, they would be unlikely to act as purposefully as they do in popular representations. It didn't make sense to think of incorporeal human beings who nevertheless retained all of the preoccupations of the living. If they appeared among us, I thought it would be in the manner of subatomic particles, appearing and disappearing according to the energy transfers of quantum mechanics; and further, that our ability to perceive anything about them would be severely limited, just as all interactions between classical and quantum systems are limited.

"When did this happen?" I asked Jack, and then reframed it,

because his grasp of time is still evolving. Sometimes he'll say "yesterday" to refer to something that happened recently. When he was four, "yesterday" meant anything that had happened in the past; sometimes to distinguish one day from another, he would say, "that other yesterday."

"Was it when you were in first grade? Or before that?"

Jack looked frustrated at my inability to understand. "It was *now.*"

"Now?"

"Last week."

"I think you might have imagined that, Bug."

But Jack had gone back to the catalog. I thought later that it might have been better to explain, then and there, why it was impossible for him to have seen Charlie the previous week, in our home, what it meant that she was dead. But something prevented me from doing this, and I said nothing. And so I have to conclude that a good deal of what happened later was my own fault.

7.

I spent one evening going through boxes of old photographs in my closet, until I found the one I was looking for. It was a shot of me and Charlie at her wedding. She had worn ivory chiffon, a sleeveless column with a high, pleated neck, the kind of dress only Charlie could pull off. I was wearing a sage-green, strapless dress she had helped me choose. My expression is giddy—I was more than a little drunk—but Charlie is staring into the camera in a serious way. Maybe it's the contrast in our expressions, but looking at this photo, now framed on my desk, I have the strange feeling that something in it is alive. Charlie seems to look through time, as if she knows what's going to happen and has something very urgent to say, if only I could concentrate hard enough to hear it.

By the time we graduated, Charlie maintained that she couldn't stand the smugness, the insularity, or the poverty of the academic lifestyle, and that she'd always known she was going to L.A. This might have been true, but it was also true that if Charlie had wanted to apply to the Yale School of Drama, or the Henry Fellowship at Oxford (things she had claimed to want up until that point), it would have required a letter of recommendation from her thesis advisor, the man we referred to as "Pope." With his heavy eyebrows, long nose, and dark, wavy hair, Charlie said he resembled the black-and-white engraving of the eighteenth-century satiric poet Alexander Pope reproduced on her handout from Comp Lit 96: Cross(pollinat)ing the Channel: Poetry of the Augustan Age. Professor Pope was a great lecturer, the most famous professor in Harvard's Comparative Literature Department; like her mother, Charlie was a Francophile, and she took Pope's seminar on French female writers of the Enlightenment—*Du harem, aux salons, à la Révolution*—the following year.

Honors-track students in the humanities had a one-on-one tutorial every year after their first; most junior tutors were graduate students, although full professors would sometimes accept an especially promising student, if their research interests dovetailed. Charlie had decided to apply for a junior tutorial with Pope on the eighteenth-century playwright and epistolary novelist Françoise de Graffigny, whose work she read in the original. She told me privately that she hoped she could continue with him as her senior thesis advisor. The fact that an academic career, whether in theater or physics, would require at least one powerful mentor was clear to us even as undergraduates. Pope was the one who had told Charlie about the Henry Fellowship—whose recipients spent a year at Oxford, furthering their studies in their chosen field—because he was one of three people on the nominating committee.

All of this worked out as Charlie had planned, and it wasn't until well into the first semester of our senior year that Charlie confided in me about her problems with Pope. Even then it was with characteristic world-weariness that she told me her professor had literally *gotten down on his knees* one day during their tutorial in his office and confessed his uncontrollable attraction. At this point she was deep into her thesis about Choderlos de Laclos's novel, *Dangerous Liaisons*. Charlie had chosen Laclos in part because she already knew she was playing Mme. de Merteuil in Christopher Hampton's play; when race was not a theme, student directors at least seemed to feel more comfortable with what was then called "color-blind casting." Her thesis was about the ways that twentieth-century dramatic adaptions of the novel reflected the cultures in which they were produced.

By the time we were seniors, Charlie had been paying her dues in the Dramatic Club for three years, waiting for a starring role in the annual student production on the mainstage at the Loeb, which normally housed the American Repertory Theater. She had played Lucienne in Feydeau's *A Flea in Her Ear* and Miranda in *The Tempest* in smaller Harvard venues. The big show our junior year had been *Six Degrees of Separation,* and Charlie had read for both Tess and Ouisa, the part Stockard Channing played on Broadway and in the movie. The director, a friend of hers, later confided that her auditions were excellent for both parts, but that casting her in either would have been "too confusing" for the audience. Charlie told me this in a matter-of-fact way, and went on that semester to play the stepdaughter in Pirandello's *Six Characters in Search of an Author,* in the smaller black-box theater attached to the main-stage. The difference between the two shows was in degree, not in kind, she joked, and didn't make a big deal about it. Even if she were thinking it, she could hardly have been the one to suggest to the director that a student production might make its mark with this kind of unconventional casting, or that there might have been something productive about confusing the audience in this way.

Pope knew about her role in the play, of course, and began attending rehearsals, sitting in the back of the theater as if he didn't want to be noticed. Charlie's friend Brian, an especially talented classmate who would go on to start his own innovative theater company in New York, was thrilled that one of the foremost experts on Laclos should take such an interest in his production. He would approach Pope after the rehearsals, ask earnest questions about lighting, or the range of implications in the word *lenteurs.* In the private tutorial Charlie attended in Pope's office every week, Pope mocked her friend the director's flamboyant mannerisms, and also told Charlie that watching her onstage affected him so strongly that he had to remain seated for some time after the lights came up. That was the kind of thing he said; the meaning was always clear, but could conceivably be interpreted a different way, if it were someday repeated.

Throughout the semester, Charlie had thought about switching thesis advisors. There was a more junior, female adjunct who had offered to take her on. But because she wasn't feeling well—was skipping an increasing number of classes in order to save her energy for rehearsals—dropping the thesis altogether was a more attractive option. What Charlie's immunologist had identified as chronic fatigue syndrome was making it hard for her to complete even an ordinary amount of schoolwork, much less a book-length paper. Without the thesis, her chances at securing any of those postgraduate fellowships were almost nil; but as Charlie reasoned then, she would've needed Pope's approval for the Henry, the fellowship she wanted most. She told me then that no fellowship was worth approaching him for a favor.

Charlie went to L.A. after graduation, hoping to act, but was disgusted by the number of roles that her skin color (what casting agents referred to as her "look") eliminated. She was living on her cousin's couch, in a small apartment in Echo Park, hostessing at an Italian restaurant frequented by industry types on La Brea, and in desperation, she told me later, she'd emptied her bank account and checked herself into a hotel (a strategy she would repeat on and off after Simmi was born), where she spent three nights finishing a *Law & Order* spec script. I could picture her in a modern Los Angeles hotel room, clothes strewn across the bed and the floor, the small space smelling of her perfume, lemon and vetiver, ordering meals from room service and leaving the trays in the hall.

This was the kind of extravagant behavior that had always thrilled and shocked me about my friend, as it seemed to contradict everything I'd ever believed about work and success. As it turned out, that script got her her first staff writing job on a WB drama about teenagers, from which she moved on to one show after another, eventually rising to become a co–executive producer by the time she was thirty-five. And so my doggedness, and Charlie's daring, returned almost equivalent results in our respective fields, where we were both successful early.

The difference was in the way we responded to the inevitable cooling-off that accompanied our mid-career period, especially after our children were born. I put my head down and worked, taking on committees, evaluations, grant proposals. When my sabbatical came, I chose conferences and workshops carefully, attending only the most prestigious, eliminating anything that might be construed as fun. Incredibly, I believed that this dutiful plodding was one of my strengths, for which I would someday be rewarded. Charlie had no such delusions, and maybe that was the reason why, even before she got her diagnosis, she seemed to fall into a kind of despair.

8.

I went out to L.A. just after Jack was born, to see my parents and to speak at a particle phenomenology conference at Caltech. The conference wasn't strictly necessary, but I wanted to prove to myself that things wouldn't be so different, now that I had a baby. I discovered quickly, though, that a simple cross-country trip with a three-month-old required an enormous amount of planning. I had decided to nurse exclusively, and had been stockpiling milk a few ounces at a time in plastic bags in my freezer. Only I couldn't take any of it with me without risking losing it, either in security or because it might defrost. That meant that I had to get up several times the first night in L.A. while Jack was sleeping, in order to pump enough milk for a bottle to leave with my parents while I'd be at the conference.

Why was I—a single mother with a demanding career—nursing to begin with? Why, for several months at least, did I prepare my own baby food, freezing it in BPA-free rubber trays? I'd read several studies that suggested the immunological benefits of breastfeeding were exaggerated, and the number of nights Jack and I order pizza now has certainly undone any of the good that organic strained sweet potato and amaranth cereal did in his babyhood. I would've denied it at the time—would have said something breezy about how nursing was just simpler than mixing bottles in the night— but the fact is that I like doing things the hard way. I'd turned down an epidural at the birth for the same reason: not because I thought the anesthesia would be any danger to Jack, but because I wanted to prove something to myself.

As the date of my trip to California approached, I resisted calling

Charlie. The last time I'd heard from her at any length she had been struggling with childcare, and nothing more serious than arthritis; it seemed to me that she had less reason to be out of touch than I did, and that it was just a symptom of the haphazard way she did things. Once she had told me only the day before that she would be in New York for the weekend; could I come down from Boston? It was petty, but I resolved to do the same thing with her, and held out until two weeks before my visit, when my desire to see her took over and I emailed. This time she wrote back right away, with enthusiasm, saying that she couldn't wait to see me; I should bring Jack and come anytime.

At the conference I talked about supersymmetry-breaking and the consequences of the Large Hadron Collider for Neel's and my model. This was in September 2008: the conference had been organized to coincide with the inauguration of the world's most powerful particle accelerator at CERN, the European Organization for Nuclear Research, in Geneva. I had beautiful slides of the facility: the underground tunnels where the scientists sent beams of protons in opposite directions, examining the exotic by-products of their collision, as well as of the detectors, especially the five-story, fourteen-thousand-ton magnet called the Compact Muon Solenoid Detector. Some people hear "Compact Muon Solenoid" and stop listening; when I sent Charlie an image of that spectacular multicolored clockworks, she had written back: "the rose window of particle physics," with appropriate awe.

What no one had known—not the conference organizers, not me when I accepted, and certainly not the team of physicists in the lab in Geneva, who spent their time replicating the extreme conditions we believe existed at the universe's birth—was that a massive explosion would shut down the Collider just days after its debut. A faulty connection between two of the superconducting magnets released six metric tons of liquid hydrogen, destroying the vacuum in the beam pipe and contaminating two thousand feet of it with soot: a totally unanticipated disaster. In Geneva they went ahead with the Collider's inauguration—the speeches, the food, and the customary champagne—but the fact was that nobody could be sure that the repairs would be successful. I couldn't help thinking that if Congress hadn't stopped funding for the Superconducting Super

Collider (an appropriately Texan name for a machine that would've been located just south of Dallas), we would have had energy levels three times what the Large Hadron Collider could provide here in the U.S. already. What did it mean, I asked the audience, that the richest and most powerful country in the world had stepped away from funding high-level scientific research?

This question looks naive from where I'm standing now. But in the year Jack was born, the year Obama was elected, the decision to defund a cutting-edge research facility on which American taxpayers had already spent two billion dollars seemed more like an aberration than a sign of things to come. When I finished my talk, there was a message on my phone from Charlie, asking if I wanted to stop by that afternoon. I begged off a lunch with the conference organizers with excuses about my new baby; called and asked my mother to give Jack the one bottle I had; and reparked, next to a hedge. I covered my chest with a scarf I'd brought for the purpose, held both shields with one arm, and texted Charlie back with the other. Like every woman I've ever talked to about it, I hated pumping: the indignity, the surge of hormonally triggered sadness, the primitive machine's repetitive wheeze. To me it always sounded as if it were saying, *Give it up.*

Once I'd zipped the plastic bottles of milk into the insulated cooler bag, though, there was an enormous sense of freedom. In the gloomy auditorium, I'd given an optimistic speech about the potential once the Collider was repaired. I'd done it in a different time zone, traveling alone with an infant. In the clothes I'd chosen for the presentation, a black suit and gray silk blouse, I felt that I looked as good as I could possibly look under the circumstances. My mother texted me that Jack was asleep, but that she would give him the bottle as soon as he woke up. I had another three hours until I absolutely had to be back.

Charlie's house was a white, Spanish-style three-bedroom in Los Feliz, about twenty minutes from the Caltech campus. It was nothing like as luxurious as the one she and Terrence eventually bought in Santa Monica, to be closer to the beach, but it was designed in a way that made it seem bigger than it was, with a path that wound around a small, free-form pool, up terra-cotta tiled steps, past a lemon tree and a bed with birds of paradise, to the front door.

Charlie met me at the door, screaming as she grabbed me. Then she called to Terrence, "Helen's here!" and stepped back. I hadn't seen her since Simona was born, but she hardly looked different. She was wearing a white tank top and jeans, and appeared to have lost all the weight from the pregnancy. Nothing about her face or the way she moved suggested that she was ill.

"You didn't bring him!"

I explained about the conference and my parents. I said that maybe I could bring Jack by before I left, but that I had to seize the opportunity to socialize when I could. I asked if I could store the milk in the fridge, and Charlie took me into the kitchen, small but with brand-new stainless steel appliances. Everything was very clean and modern, and even the colored wooden blocks on the floor looked as if they'd been arranged by a stylist. I remembered Charlie telling me that Terrence was obsessively neat.

"You don't use formula?" Charlie asked, as she made room for the milk. "It makes it so much easier."

"I would," I said. "But I produce a lot."

"Oh, I made enough," Charlie said. "I just couldn't deal with it. All that measuring and storing. And I never know when I'm going to be home from work."

Terrence came into the kitchen with Simona, now sixteen months old. The few times I'd met him before the wedding, I'd found Terrence aloof and inscrutable; Charlie said that it was only shyness. His skin was lighter than Charlie's, but not so light that you would necessarily assume he had a white parent, except for his very striking light green eyes. He had an especially strong, square chin, and his hair was in the same short dreadlocks I remembered from the wedding. In his track pants and faded T-shirt, he still looked as though he spent a lot of time at the beach, but without sacrificing the pleasures of fatherhood; as he bent down to hold the baby's hand, his tenderness for her was obvious.

Charlie stretched out her arms to the baby, but Simona sank down to her bottom and crawled.

"*Walk* to Mommy."

"Hey," Terrence said to me. And then to Charlie: "She knows when you're showing off."

"Of course I am," Charlie said, picking her up. "How could I not?"

Simona's hair, what there was of it, stuck out in a little cloud around her head. Her eyes were giant, a variegated hazel color somewhere between her mother's and her father's, and she was wearing an expensive-looking playsuit with a pink crocheted top and creamy linen bloomers. It was clean, too—maybe Terrence had just changed her into it? Jack never went more than an hour without spitting up on whatever I'd put on him.

"Hat," she said suddenly.

"She can talk!"

"That's her big word," Charlie said.

"She has seventeen words," Terrence put in.

"Who's showing off now?" Charlie smiled at her husband. "Is it okay if we catch up a little?"

"Sure," Terrence said. "We have major plans. We're going to the farmers' market. Want to take a ride in the car, Sims?"

The baby made a sound like "heh," assenting.

"Hopefully she'll nap on the way back," he said, taking Simona from her mother with one practiced arm.

Charlie leaned over and kissed him. "Thanks."

"Nice to see you," Terrence said, holding up his free hand.

"Can I make you a latte or something?" Charlie asked.

We sat outside and dangled our legs in the pool. It was close to eighty degrees in September, desert heat. The smell in the air reminded me of being a kid in Pasadena, sitting on the curb of our suburban block with my sister, our feet in the runoff by the drain. There was the same insect drone. You could hear the cars going by Charlie's house outside, but the hedge gave it a separate, protected feel. A vine of brilliant pink bougainvillea began in a clay pot and grew over the wrought-iron fence.

"It's beautiful here."

"Terrence did most of it," Charlie said. "He loves plants and all that—I keep telling him he should go back to school for landscape architecture. You can make a fortune doing that out here, and I'd be able to help him make a lot of connections."

"What does he think?"

"Honestly?" Charlie said. "He doesn't really want to work. His brother's starting this surf company, and he may get involved in that."

"He's still really into the surfing?"

Charlie glanced at me. "You sound like my parents."

"That's not a criticism! It's just—I don't know anything about surfing."

"He once told me that he wasn't white enough for the white kids at his high school, and he didn't sound black enough for the black kids. He said the beach was the only place he ever felt like everything about him was right."

"That makes sense."

"And when he's not surfing, he just wants to take care of Simmi and cook. I get it, because that's exactly what he didn't have. His mom was single—I mean, not by choice." Charlie hurried on: "They never had enough money, and they were always moving. That's why he's obsessed with the house, keeping everything so perfect. Which is better than the alternative, I guess. But sometimes I feel like he's like a nineteen fifties housewife—a fifties housewife who surfs. It's a huge stress for us. Or for me, anyway."

"Because of money?" I was surprised that Charlie was confiding in me right away, and also ashamed in the same way I'd been in the kitchen. For me this visit had been loaded with anxiety about how I would appear to her, but Charlie wasn't thinking of it as a competition; she was treating me as a friend. She actually seemed desperate to talk to me.

"Not really," Charlie said. "I moved up a peg to co-producer on this new show—the one about Vegas—and I make enough, at least for now. It's more like, what's he going to do when she goes to school? And counting on me as the breadwinner is risky, at least long-term. The schedule when we're shooting is really punishing. I feel fine now, but . . ."

"Because of the arthritis?"

Charlie shook her head. "It's lupus now, officially."

I looked at her. "You didn't tell me."

"I only found out a few months ago—I haven't really told anyone, except my parents."

I didn't know what to say. I put my hand on hers, on the warm stone tile. She squeezed mine and let go.

"It's kind of a relief to know. The treatment is clearer, for one thing."

"Do you feel okay?"

"I do, yeah. It's called a flare, with lupus—that's what happened after I gave birth. I was so sick—rashes all over my body, fever. And the steroids blew me up like a bicycle pump—really disgusting. But then it went away, and I've been basically okay."

"Is it an issue if you get pregnant again?"

Charlie nodded. "I'd have to go off the methotrexate, first of all. And even though some lupus patients actually do better when they're pregnant, that wasn't true for me. A second pregnancy could make things a lot worse. It's probably not going to be possible, my doctors say."

"I'm so sorry."

"That's the thing. I'm not. I'm sorry for Terrence because he'd like two or three. I love her to death, but I don't want another. Even if I weren't sick."

It sometimes seemed that every parent I knew had at least two, if not three, and I'd read the term "singleton" in the parenting books with distaste. The idea that Charlie didn't want another, in spite of the fact that she was married, was reassuring.

"What I want is to run my own show."

"What would it be about?"

"Black physicists on the Manhattan Project."

"Where on earth did you get that idea?"

Charlie smiled. "Yeah, I know. I'm going to try to get you a consulting gig if it happens."

"I could use a consulting gig."

"Careful what you wish for, though. Because this industry is so much more fucked-up than you can imagine."

"I've heard it's a boys' club."

"There's that, of course," Charlie said. "But casting directors are usually women—white women. When I first got out here—back when I was still trying to act—people told me to go for everything. But if it doesn't say black, that's not what they're looking for. They'll be like, 'Oh, it's not an ethnic role. And I'm like 'ethnic'? And then you go to a call for black actresses, and there are three times as many people there, because there are one-thousandth the number of parts, and they'll be like, 'Can you do it more sassy?' Which means that they want you to, you know, roll your neck and snap your fingers."

"Is it better now that you're writing?"

"Not really. I was in a meeting with this guy at Sony the other day, he's a really big deal. And not uneducated—he went to Stanford, I think. And he says this one character—Tyrone, naturally—is more ghetto and he wants me to write that."

"And I say, I can do some research, and I make a joke about how I watched *The Wire*."

"And he totally doesn't get it—he's like, 'No, no, not like *The Wire*.' Because this isn't for cable and he wants people to be able to understand—'without turning on the fucking subtitles. Write from your own *experience*.' And I'm like, '*Oh okay*, yeah—*my* experience. Got it.' But that's what you have to say if you want to work."

"Jesus, Charlie."

"The mean streets of Brookline," Charlie said. "But enough. Now tell me about you."

9.

I went home that weekend with my baby, happy to have seen Charlie with her family, hopeful that our friendship was entering a new stage. I did a little research online, and learned that lupus affects men less often than women, and white women less often than black women, who inexplicably tend to contract it earlier, with greater risk of life-threatening complications. It's a disease that can lie dormant for decades before suddenly flaring, that is sometimes ignored or misdiagnosed, but that produces persistent, excruciating pain in the people it attacks most severely.

I had those facts, but on another level, I didn't understand. Charlie had complained about everything in college: the rooms we were assigned; the boys we dated; the deadlines we were expected to meet. She complained about authority figures, the university in general, and especially about her parents. I assumed that if her illness were really life-threatening, she wouldn't hesitate to complain about that, too. The very obvious explanation—that the things

Charlie had always made a fuss about were not her real grievances, that those were the ones she'd always kept quiet—didn't occur to me. That was the kind of observation about people that came easily to Charlie, and that I often failed to make in my own life, especially after I stopped sharing it with her.

As our children grew up, Charlie and I fell more and more out of touch. The less I communicated with her, the more I looked at Facebook, and eventually at Instagram. Charlie posted photos and videos frequently, mostly of her daughter. There was Simmi onstage in a white ballet outfit; Simmi playing the guitar; Simmi doing a cartwheel on an actual balance beam. She was (as everyone had predicted she'd be) an extraordinarily pretty child, and she appeared to excel at anything performative. When I allowed myself the consolation that Charlie and Terrence pushed their daughter too hard, I would be confronted by a picture of Simmi on a boogie board in Malibu, Simmi eating an ice pop by the pool.

Just before he turned four, Jack had a series of health problems. First his adenoids were swollen and needed to be taken out, a minor procedure complicated by a bleeding disorder he'd inherited from my father. A few months later he had an episode of croup, something I thought he'd outgrown in infancy. The third time we went to the ER in the middle of the night, Jack was admitted for three days, and diagnosed with asthma. The attending pulmonologist gave me a nebulizer, vials of albuterol, and prescriptions for two different steroids, assuring me that at least ten percent of American children now suffered from asthma and that the rates were higher in other parts of the world.

Did these statistics comfort anyone? In the hospital, Jack and I read books, did puzzles, and were visited by Child Life volunteers who brought craft projects—plant a cactus in a clay pot, decorate a mug for Valentine's Day—or, once, escorted us to a playroom for a magic show by a clown named Looney Lenny. In the playroom were bald children undergoing chemo, children with cystic fibrosis, a boy who couldn't speak or focus his eyes, ten years old, in a wheelchair and a diaper. (There but for the grace of God, my maternal grandmother would always say.) Because of his comparative health, Jack was Lenny's assistant, turning a scarf into a flower, and discovering a plastic dinosaur behind Lenny's ear.

The thing I liked best about the hospital was the way that time seemed to stop there. I could ignore department meetings, student email, and articles for peer review. Sometimes I forgot to look at my phone for hours. At night I would climb into bed with Jack, being careful of the monitor (they attached it to his toe with surgical tape), move the gray cord, and rest my arm over his hip, to avoid making breathing more difficult. When he was getting oxygen, he would sleep with the mask, and I could hear the air whistling inside it. The pediatric nurses came often, and I preferred them to the doctors; they were so calm and unsurprisable. They opened the door in the dark, or slipped through the curtain in their scrubs and soft shoes. They were almost all heavy and maternal in shape, full-breasted and -hipped, with delicate hands that unceremoniously manipulated their equipment. I was terrified by the prospect of going home and having to operate the nebulizer myself, count the breaths per minute. In the hospital I knew that if Jack stopped breathing, even if I'd dozed off, someone would be with us in an instant.

10.

I have always liked to get up early, even before I had Jack. In my twenties I could do it without an alarm. I would simply think of the hour I wanted to awaken, and usually my eyes would open ten or fifteen minutes before that.

Those early mornings are the time I can do physics; in my office, everything else takes over, and while I can sit with a colleague and hammer out an idea—the way I used to do with Neel, my closest and best collaborator—I have to have done the real work beforehand, alone at my desk.

In the case of the Clapp-Jonnal model, my most significant insight came between 5:00 and 5:30 a.m. I wasn't technically at my desk but sitting with my back against the couch, looking at a preprint Neel had emailed me, if not actually reading it. I was drinking coffee and thinking about garden hoses. Specifically I was thinking of a hose my father had invented (but unfortunately never patented) sometime in the late eighties. Neither of my parents was a scientist, but my father was a mechanical engineer and a hobbyist inventor. He worked on a screened porch separated from our small living room by a set of French doors. My father's hose was made of flexible fabric that crinkled when it wasn't in use, then swelled to its full capacity when you turned on the tap. It was that swelling—the finite diameter of the hose, by comparison with the water flowing in one potentially infinite direction—that suggested the crucial geometry.

I was living near Porter Square in Somerville then, and I put on my running shoes. I shoved the piece of paper with the equations I'd scribbled into the armband with my phone—as if I could've forgotten them! It might have been faster on the T, but I couldn't have stood there waiting. I ran right down Oxford to Harvard Square, past the Science Center, where I'd taken Physics 16 as a freshman and had felt grateful to know right away where I belonged. I ran south to the river in a light drizzle, over a glistening carpet of red and yellow leaves, past cars with early commuters inching forward with their lights on, and arrived at Neel's apartment in Peabody Terrace, where he was a resident advisor to married students, just before six.

Neel was living with a girlfriend at the time, and I remember that Angie answered the door in a white terry-cloth bathrobe. There were things between me and Angie, having to do with my collaboration with Neel, Neel's and my brief undergraduate romance, Angie's perfectly symmetrical Japanese face, my red hair, big nose, and habit of interrupting, but that morning I put my arms around her: "Good morning—I'm sorry it's so early—we did it!" I think that's what I said. Neel was standing in the hallway leading to their bedroom in a T-shirt and boxer shorts, squinting at me, and when I thrust the paper at him, he had to go put on pants and find his glasses. Angie stood at the counter and made coffee while Neel, now dressed, sat at the kitchen table and went over it.

"Stop staring at me," he told me at one point, but I couldn't help it—I couldn't wait to hear what he thought. I knew he was as excited and hopeful as I was, and also that there was a part of him that hoped to prove me wrong—so that he himself could be the one to dream up the final piece of the puzzle we'd been working on since we'd returned to Harvard as postdocs.

It took us two pots of coffee and three hours of refining. (Angie went to one of her classes at the Design School; we barely registered her.) I skipped a department meeting, and Neel didn't go into his lab, but by nine we were on the phone to Arty Hofmann, our advisor. That five-dimensional AdS/CFT model—the Clapp-Jonnal—was born that morning. We joked that if only it had been a 3+1 model, we might have called it the "Clapp-4-Jonnal." (Jokes about physics are maybe not quite as amusing for non-physicists.) We decided that it didn't roll off the tongue like Kaluza-Klein, but was nowhere near as bad as the Friedmann-Lemaître-Robertson-Walker metric.

We picked up frosted doughnuts on the way to campus. I remember that the sun had come out, as if it knew. I was thirty-two, and I tried to save the feeling as we walked to Arty's office to show him our work. It was the way people describe falling in love but it was so much better than the reality of that. The model gave me a kind of happiness that didn't depend upon anyone else; it could be carried with you. I thought that this was what religious faith must be like, the peace in knowing that there was something beyond the world you knew, and that your own inner experience would indeed endure.

Neel and I met when we were freshmen in Arty's Inflationary Cosmology lecture course. Both of us liked to work in the Cabot Science Library, at the shiny wooden communal tables, their undersides blistered with gum, but we did it at different times of day, me in the early morning and Neel in the middle of the night. Because of our oppositional schedules, we might never have gotten to know each other if Arty hadn't suggested we work together on a problem related to Gaussian functions. We began meeting once a week in his office in Jefferson. Arty was on leave that semester and often away; Neel and I were charged with watering his plants.

I tend to be slow to notice my own feelings. It's easier for me to identify deviations from a baseline than it is to speculate about motivations. For example, I observed that I was spending an unusual amount of time preparing for my meetings with Neel. I would think about what I was going to wear the night before; I would leave time to shower and wash my hair.

These aren't things Neel would have done whether or not he was interested in a woman. He always wore a dark-colored T-shirt and corduroys. If it was cold, he wore one of two sweaters: maroon with a single black stripe, or beige wool (hole in left elbow), and put a Salvation Army peacoat over that. Neel was skinny and only about five foot nine. He went to the barber as infrequently as possible, as an economy measure, and so his thick black hair varied between almost military and mad scientist. He wore rimless glasses over his best feature: beautiful, heavily lashed dark eyes.

One day I wore a sweater my sister, Amy, had given me for Christmas. It was black with a white mohair collar and cuffs, more appropriate for a holiday party than a study session in February, and on the way from my room in Thayer, I regretted choosing it. The sweater had looked nice with my hair in the spotty mirror of our cold and unpleasant bathroom, but it was too dressy for a weekday, and it called attention to itself with the soft white collar in a way I didn't like. I'd almost gone home to change it, but I have always had an anxiety about being late, and I decided that Neel wouldn't notice anyway.

Neel was sitting at Arty's desk when I came in.

"You're dressed up," he said, barely looking up.

I thought it was presumptuous of him to sit there; I never would have done it myself, especially when there were two other vacant chairs.

"I'm going out after," I told him coldly.

Neel looked up, surprised by my tone. "Sorry," he said. "I wasn't being critical."

"You weren't?"

"I guess I was."

"So, what's wrong with my sweater?"

Neel took off his glasses, considering.

"You look like a poodle."

"A *poodle*?"

"With those furry things." Neel touched his own neck and wrist. His wrists were thin and knobby, with black hair on them. Where did he get the idea he could say things like that?

"It was a present from my sister. I like it."

Neel nodded. "It looks expensive."

"Did you water?" I demanded, and when he shook his head, I took the pink plastic can into the bathroom and filled it. Then I came back and tended to Arty's plants, acutely aware of Neel the whole time. When I finally did sit down, I launched into a detailed description of the solution to the fifth problem from Arty's set, because I could see that Neel was only on the second. I was conscious that I was showing off—Neel was slightly less mathematically inclined than I was, though much better at designing an experiment—and once he stopped and asked me to repeat something.

"So it's like a Hegelian synthesis," he said, after I had explained.

We had a joke about one of our classmates, who had made a pretentious reference to that philosopher in section one day.

"Totally," I said. "You hit it exactly."

Neel smiled at me, and I had the uncomfortable feeling I sometimes get in conversation with another person, as if the fundamental part of myself has evaporated—not in the sense of being gone, but as if it has undergone a phase transition and is hovering over my actual body as a vapor. That's the best I can describe it, as if my consciousness and my physical person are suddenly separated.

It's unbearable to be with other people when I'm in this state, and so usually I get up to go to the bathroom, where I can lock myself in and recalibrate. That's what I did then, excusing myself. I rested my forehead on the inside of the cool metal stall and counted prime numbers down from 997; for some reason this usually helps. I waited ten minutes, but my panic (or whatever it was) didn't go away, and so I went back to the office and told Neel I had to go.

"Where are you going?"

"Out to dinner with . . . a friend. What are you doing?"

"I'll be struggling with number three," Neel said. "But have fun."

Charlie wasn't in her room when I got home, and so I called another friend, Elaine, and begged her to go for a drink with me. We went all the way to the South End, only because I was afraid of running into Neel. I could've said that I'd changed my plans, but I wanted him to think I was out on a date.

Elaine listened patiently as I described how arrogant the guys in the physics department were.

"At least there are male human beings in your department."

I had dragged her away from an anthropology paper she was supposed to be writing, and so I offered to buy our drinks. When I opened my wallet to pay, there was a folded piece of paper stuck in the pocket in front of my university ID.

"What's that?" Elaine asked.

I read it quickly myself, and then I showed it to her—although I didn't want to. I wanted to keep it absolutely private forever, because it scared and excited me so much. On three separate lines, in almost illegible printing, it said:

> The sweater is ugly.
> The sweater is charming.
> The sweater may be ugly, but you make it charming.

"What's that supposed to mean?"

I explained our joke about Hegelian dialectics.

Elaine shook her head. "It doesn't work. Those are opinions, not logical propositions. Also, Hegel didn't even use that formulation. He borrowed it from Kant, and it was popularized by Johann Fichte. And why does he keep trashing your sweater? It's not *that* bad."

That was why I liked Elaine: she was honest and intellectually rigorous, unlike so many people you met in the humanities. But it's strange how you can ignore even your smartest friends, when you start to fall in love.

11.

The morning of Charlie's memorial, I woke up early with a dull ache in my stomach. I tried to go over some preliminary data from the Gaia satellite just released by the ESA, but I couldn't focus. I was thinking that if I hadn't already had coffee—I keep an electric pot on my desk so that I don't have to go downstairs and risk waking Jack—I would have gotten back into bed. My phone was next to me, as it so often is now, and it pinged with a new message. When I glanced down, I saw that it was from Charlie Boyce.

Luvya lady!

Beyond this cryptic and almost offensive salutation, there was nothing. If someone was texting from Charlie's phone, they weren't hoping to sell pornography or prescription drugs. I couldn't remember a specific instance in which Charlie had written "Luvya lady!" although she did use the abbreviation "luv" in her electronic communication, and would sometimes greet me, "Hi, lady." Yet there were probably thousands of women who might have used the same formulation.

Who IS this? I wrote back, and then sat there staring at the phone, willing it to ping. A moment later it did, twice, with a message from Amazon alerting me that my package with Lazrwhite electric toothbrush heads and two other items would arrive tonight before 8:00 p.m.

I could still feel my pulse in my ears a few minutes later, when I heard Jack in the living room. I put on my slippers and went downstairs, where I found him crouched over whatever he was building, the rest of his Legos scattered on the floor. His ant farm had come with him from his room, maybe to keep him company, although I'd warned him several times about the consequences of dropping it.

"Good morning, sweetie," I said.

"Hi."

"What are you working on?"

"Train station."

"It looks like South Station."

Jack was concentrating, his tongue protruding slightly between his lips.

"Are you trying to make a dome?"

"Yeah."

"Can I help?"

We worked on the dome for a while, Jack getting down on his stomach and resting the side of his body against my hip. The ants went about their own enterprise with silent intensity.

"Today's the funeral," he said suddenly.

"Memorial—it's a little different. A memorial is supposed to be a celebration of the person's life." I realized as I said it that nothing about the service in the church at Harvard was going to correspond to Jack's idea of a celebration.

"Will she be there?"

"Who?"

"Your friend."

"Oh. You mean, will her body be there? No, definitely not."

Jack didn't say anything, but he was visibly disappointed. "Will we see the coffin?"

"Nope."

According to the psychologist at Jack's school, we're uncomfortable with the idea of death in our society, and for that reason often avoid talking about it with children. It was therefore good for them to experience the death of someone they didn't know well, to prepare them for the deaths of loved ones later. I heard this back when I attended all the workshops the school offered, in an attempt to do as much exemplary parenting on my own as two people might have accomplished working together.

But the death workshop wasn't especially illuminating. I'd been showing Jack dead leaves, worms, and insects ever since he could talk. We'd prodded a dead raccoon with a stick. This wasn't some kind of acclimation process, but rather science, and although I wouldn't have said it to the school psychologist, I didn't feel the need to use Charlie for the same purpose. Society aside, I've always thought that most normal people are afraid of death.

Einstein famously was not; there is the letter he wrote to Michele Besso's family, after his friend's death: *So he has departed this strange world a little ahead of me. That means nothing. People like us, who believe in physics, know that the distinction between past, present and future is only a stubbornly persistent illusion.*

I have always wondered, did this comfort the Besso family? Did it comfort his wife, Anna, to whom Einstein had introduced him? Did she believe, as Einstein did, in a sublime order of which even the most gifted people—people like Einstein and her husband—could only perceive the dim outlines? Did she think of her husband's illustrious friend when she wondered what to do with his leather boots, or held his glasses in her hand and gasped at their sudden strangeness?

"Where is the coffin?"

"There's no coffin. She's being cremated—that's what most people do now, because there's really not room to bury everybody. The body goes into a machine that turns it into ashes. We call them ashes, but they look more like pieces of bone. Sometimes family members scatter the ashes in a place that the dead person loved."

It's rare that I say something he finds interesting enough to make him stop playing, but now Jack looked up.

"Where do you love?" he said.

"You mean, where would I want my ashes scattered?"

Jack waited.

"Well, you know—I'm not going to die for a very, very long time. I told you my friend was sick, but I'm completely healthy."

"Yeah I know. But I mean, *if*."

I hesitated only a moment. "A lake in Switzerland. It's the bluest water I've ever seen."

Jack fit a tiny helmet onto a tiny yellow biker, and looked as if he were going to cry.

"But I told you—you don't have to worry." I tried to put him on my lap, but he squirmed away. How had we gotten into this before breakfast?

"My grandmother lived to be ninety-seven, and you know your grandma does all that yoga—she's also going to be alive for a long time."

But I couldn't make Jack smile. He has his donor's blue eyes and general coloring; a tow-headed baby, his hair has gotten steadily darker each year, stopping at the sandy color I remember from that photo on the website. His large, oval-shaped head is similar to my father's, but his nose and pointed chin are like mine. So far his own father's height is not in evidence, and the contrast between his big head and slight frame is striking. Especially when he's unhappy, his face tends to look a little older than it is.

"What is it, Bug?"

He hesitated a long time, but finally spoke. "I'm scared I won't be able to find it."

I did take him in my arms then. I put my face in his hair and closed my eyes.

"I'll leave you a map."

I could tell that he liked that idea, because I felt his body relax. When he has grievances against me later, at least I'll be able to say that I talked to him like an adult, that I tried not to lie. We sat there like that for a while, before Jack decided that he wanted French toast.

"No problem," I said. Breakfast is the only meal I enjoy preparing. He wiggled away and started playing, and I got up to go make it. On my way to the kitchen, he called out to me.

"I want mine at that place in California."

"What place?" I asked.

"You know."

"Zuma Canyon?"

"Is that where we had pizza?"

"It's where we went hiking—with the waterfall."

"I mean the place with the colored balls."

"Chuck E. Cheese's?"

"Right!" Jack said happily. "Right in the pit!"

"Okay. But you'll have to tell your own children about that."

"Yeah," he said. "I'll give them a map."

12.

Luvya lady, I thought, as we crossed Harvard Yard. What it meant depended upon the punctuation:

luvyalady

Luvya, lady!

Luvya,
Lady

It was a hot July morning. The campus felt empty and still, as if those three-hundred-year-old buildings had breathed a sigh of relief in expelling their messy human occupants. Oaks and honey locusts threw sharp-edged shadows on the grass, and across the radial paths. The bells in the steeple would ring at nine.

"You know I'm going to have to get up and say something," I told Jack. "You'll just sit right there until I'm finished."

"But I won't say anything."

"No, of course not. You don't have to."

"Will Simmi?"

I was surprised that he remembered the name. "No."

"Why not?"

"Because she's only a little older than you."

"But it's her mom." He looked to make sure he'd gotten that right. He and Simmi had never met.

"Still." I wanted to stop talking before we reached Memorial Church, where I could see Charlie's mother, Adelaide, standing on the columned portico, calmly greeting family and friends. Not everyone would be composed enough do that, I thought, but it didn't surprise me that Addie was. She looked perfect, in a gray summer dress and black, short-sleeved lace jacket. Charlie's father and her brother, William, were standing on either side of her. I didn't see Terrence or Simmi.

"Helen," she said, when we reached the front of the line. She took my shoulders in her hands. The face that had once put her in magazines, with its high cheekbones and wide-set eyes, was only slightly aged, with a smooth brow and delicate crow's feet. I didn't know what she'd done to herself, if anything, but it didn't look false or unnatural; it was only uncanny that the twenty years since I'd last seen her seemed to have had so little effect. Her hair was done in a smooth, dark bob; her lipstick was plum-colored. Apart from the serious way she said my name, there was no visible sign of her grief. I had the same feeling I'd always had around Addie—that she saw obvious errors in the way I'd arranged my appearance, and yearned to fix me up.

"I've been thinking of you, and Dr. Boyce." It was awkward, even apart from the odd formality of "Dr. Boyce," but that was the way I'd referred to him when Charlie and I were students. Addie glossed over this gracefully.

"Carl and I were so glad you agreed to speak. We realize that her friends are mostly in Los Angeles now." Addie looked down at Jack.

"And who is this? He's just a couple of years younger than Simona, I think?"

"Jack." I nudged him, and he said hello very quietly, forgetting to extend his hand. He was wearing a navy-and-white checked shirt with a collar, which seemed to emphasize the narrowness of his frame. His hair hadn't been cut for a while, and was starting to curl at the ends.

"A little more than a year," I said.

Addie nodded. "Simona's tall for her age." She put a hand on Jack's shoulder. "She's inside with some other children. She'll be so happy you're here."

Carl finished speaking to another guest, and then turned to us, squatting down first to talk to Jack. He'd gained weight since I'd seen him last, and he wore his mustache and beard neatly trimmed; his head had been bald and shiny as long as I'd known him.

"Hi there," he said. "You must be Jack." Even in the midst of his grief, it had occurred to Carl that my son—whom he'd never met— might be uncomfortable or frightened at a gathering like this, and he took steps to remedy that, bringing the conversation immediately to his level. "I bet you've been to Harvard lots of times."

Jack's eyes lit up. "For the bouncy house."

"That's what he remembers from Reunion a few years ago," I explained. "They had one for the kids."

"I never understand why they don't get one for the grown-ups," Carl said, making Jack giggle. "Lord knows we need it." Then he straightened up and gave me a forceful hug. "Thank you for being here."

I started to protest—of course I was here, but Carl continued: "And thank you for speaking."

"I wasn't sure what would be right to say."

Carl shook his head, dismissing that worry. "There's nothing to say," he said. "It's just about being here, being together." There was another couple Carl and Addie's age waiting next to me, and Charlie's brother, William, was surrounded, so Jack and I proceeded with the other guests into the church. Awed by the white columns and the red carpet, the sudden shift from bright to dim, Jack took my hand. Long windows glowed on either side of the nave, but the light didn't penetrate very far into the interior. There was low conversation everywhere, and then children's laughter. Several of them ran out of a side chapel and down the aisle, chasing each other. I recognized Simmi in a navy dress with white polka dots, and then Terrence stopped her gently, putting an arm around her shoulder. It had taken me a moment to recognize him because his hair was shaved close to his skull; either he'd started losing his hair in the seven years since I'd seen him, like his father-in-law, or he'd purposely cut off the dreadlocks. He looked like a different person in the conservative dark gray suit, guiding his daughter down the side aisle toward one of the forward pews.

"There's Simmi," I said to Jack.

"The laughing one?"

"She's with her dad now."

"She shouldn't be so happy."

I don't shush Jack often, but I did then. The raw heartlessness of children continues to surprise me. Much is made of their sensitivity and purity—and those things are true of Jack—but I've been fascinated to observe that we aren't born with empathy, that our own needs and wants radically trump those of all others, at least until we learn to feel otherwise.

I thought it would be better to find Terrence after the service, or maybe I was only postponing it. As Jack and I were making our way down the aisle on the other side of the church, I heard my name; when I turned around, I saw Charlie's college boyfriend, Kwesi, standing next to his English wife, Alison, whose name I remembered because Charlie had called me in tears when they got married.

Kwesi and I hugged each other.

"You're in London now?"

Kwesi nodded. He was wearing a beautiful brown suit, and his hooded eyes were the same under the same round, wire-rimmed glasses. Even in school Kwesi had been a calming presence—someone you might seek out when you missed the company of adults. Of course there had been adults at Harvard when we were undergraduates, but they had remained mostly in their offices and lecture halls. In our residential houses, we had advisors, but all I remembered of them was that they'd periodically hosted afternoon tea. It wasn't a place for people who believed they needed guidance or mentoring outside the academic realm.

Kwesi told me the ages of his children, young teenagers, and I introduced Jack, who this time held out his hand to both Kwesi and Alison. I was proud of him.

"I saw that you're going to speak," Kwesi said.

"Yes."

I was worried that he was going to say something that began, *She was so . . .* something that would sum Charlie up, turn her into a character. I felt like that would be even worse in front of this strange woman, his wife. But Kwesi didn't do anything like that.

"I remember the first time my parents took me to a Ghanaian funeral," he said. "I was amazed. The coffin was in the shape of a stack of American dollars, because he was a businessman. Funerals are almost like weddings there, and equally expensive. People dance."

"It's a carnival," his wife said. "Unimaginable until you experience it." She was sharp-featured, petite, with a confident, intelligent way of speaking, and I had the strange thought that Charlie would be disappointed not to have met her.

"No one is required to"—Kwesi seemed to search for what he wanted to say—"to sit quietly in their grief."

"You've been to more memorial services than Ghanaian funerals," his wife pointed out, needling him in a gentle, marital way.

"True," Kwesi said, "and I've always been more comfortable at this type. But I have a great deal of admiration for the other."

I was afraid that Jack wouldn't want to stay in the pew when I went up to make my speech, or that I would become too upset to speak, or that I wouldn't feel anything and that would be apparent in my voice. I was used to public speaking, even used to talking about things that mattered to me a great deal. But at a physics conference, you knew there would always be a conversation after the presentation, sometimes even a collaborative working-out of ideas that continued after that was finished. There was always the next conference, the next paper; nothing was fixed forever. How could I tell just one anecdote about Charlie?

William had begun to speak. Back when we were in college, Charlie's parents were frequently in a state of panic about William, who was three years ahead of us, ran the radio station with a bunch of his stoner friends, and tended to sleep through his classes. This was in spite (or perhaps because) of all the chess tournaments as a child, Charlie often explained. Although they didn't always get along, the glamour of William's life wasn't lost on his sister. As a young adult, William preferred cards, and in the summers—when other students got jobs in their hometowns, or went off to spend a few weeks building houses in Haiti or Honduras—William went to Vegas as a prop player. He came back rich in the fall, ready to commence partying again.

Since college William had put his talents to work for a hedge fund in Manhattan. He had acquired a very sociable Chilean wife, and adorable, undoubtedly chess-playing twin boys. It was a turn toward convention that I'd seen in other Harvard students who had been disaffected with the university for one reason or another. William had been as reticent and sardonic as Kwesi was earnest and outgoing, and although Charlie had once been in love with Kwesi, I knew her perspective had been more like her brother's. If either of them had felt discriminated against at Harvard, they would never have said it. Once I'd forwarded an image from the "I too am Harvard" social media campaign—a girl holding a sign that said, "No, you can't touch my hair"—to Charlie, who didn't keep up with Harvard news or attend reunions; she had heard of it, but had expressed amazement at the amount of activism around race on campus these days. "Maybe this is totally gen X of me," she wrote back. "I mean, more power to them. But I can't imagine us doing any of this, back then."

William said that he'd chosen to read a poem that his sister liked. He himself had always been more interested in poker than in poetry (this got a laugh), but his sister had helped him understand it.

This like a dream
Keeps other time
And daytime is
The loss of this.

Like William, I'd never had the patience for poetry, but I liked this one. I liked its short lines and the way it seemed easy to understand, at first—it was about the moon—but how the "this" of the poem kept slipping away.

For time is inches
And the heart's changes
Where ghost has haunted
Lost and wanted.

Later I checked Auden's dates to see whether "time is inches" could be a reference to relativity—based on another poem of his, called "After Reading a Child's Guide to Modern Physics," he seemed to take a dim view of our discipline—and discovered that it could. At the time, though, I just sat there listening to William, who was so changed from the college student I remembered—saying that love was particular even though it was directed at the same person, that we hadn't lost just one Charlie but as many as the number of people who were seated here today.

William's black shoes descended the steps from the chancel on silent red plush, and there was a space that applause might have filled in any other setting. A middle school teacher spoke about Charlie's multifarious artistic talents, and then the chaplain got up to read from the Second Letter of Paul. When he was finished, it would be my turn. I had prepared my remarks, but I didn't want to deliver them. Sometimes at work, our team would identify a problem in the question we'd asked rather than the solution we'd devised. It wasn't that I had too much to say, but that I didn't want to say anything. And that wasn't because I didn't love Charlie, but because I couldn't believe that she was really dead.

Jack had been patient but he was starting to fidget; it would be a disaster if he needed to be taken out just as I was starting to speak. (This was the kind of single-parent problem, purely to do with logistics, that I hadn't fully considered in advance.) I looked around, but I wasn't the only one: two other children in our immediate vicinity were looking down in their laps, their faces vaguely glowing. I muted all sounds and handed Jack my phone: he was immediately perfectly still and absorbed in a game, almost as if I'd switched him off.

There was an Amen, and then I patted Jack on the shoulder and walked up the side aisle to the pulpit. The chaplain made way for me, a scientist and a nonbeliever. I looked at the faces and tried to keep Charlie in my mind; it normally helps me to remember that speeches only last a short time, and you always feel that you could do a better job, if you had it to do over again. There were Adelaide and Carl in the front row. Charlie's father was crying, making no attempt to hide it: his son's speech had moved him. But Addie's face was more upsetting; in place of her earlier composure was a fierce tension—she was almost vibrating. Behind her Terrence was bent over Simmi, buried in his chest; I couldn't see either of their faces. Don't think of losing Jack, I told myself—don't think of that.

I was glad I'd chosen something lighthearted to say. It was a story about the time Charlie had made a plane turn around. This really happened. We were on our way to New York for a graduation party. Not only would I never have flown anywhere for a party except under Charlie's influence, but I would have always allowed enough time at the airport to make missing a flight impossible. Because I was with Charlie, we were late, and when we arrived the plane had just begun to taxi away from the gate. Charlie burst into tears, and to my amazement, told the ground crew behind the desk that if she didn't get on the plane, she was going to miss her grandmother Althea's funeral, at Calvary Cemetery in Queens.

The point of the story was Charlie's unbelievable chutzpah, her skill as an actress, and the joke in the reference to Charlie's grandmother Althea, who had been very much alive then, on an Elderhostel cruise down the Peruvian Amazon with her new boyfriend, Chester. I had been concerned that the story was slightly transgressive—the lie, the pushiness—but I had gotten the tone right and it had more than gone over. I saw Charlie's father laughing, and even Addie seemed to have relaxed a bit. Jack hadn't heard a word of what I'd said, but at least he was quiet, and I had only a few sentences to go.

It was at that moment that I noticed someone had come into the narthex; maybe he'd been standing there, a silhouette against the wall, and the usher had taken the opportunity to seat him during the pause in my remarks. It wasn't a disruption because he didn't make any noise. Possibly no one saw him come in but the usher and me. Now he sat down in the last pew, in the sunlight streaming through an arched picture window: Professor Pope.

I'm rarely at a loss in front of an audience. I've said foolish things, not-thought-out things—but never nothing. In this case the congregated guests must have attributed my sudden hesitation to strong emotion. In fact, that wasn't wrong. I couldn't believe that he could simply walk into the church and sit down, uninvited, that rather than questioning his connection to the proceedings, the usher had hurried to find him a place. He was looking at me along with everyone else, but only because I was speaking. He wouldn't remember who I was.

Afterward I thought of what I might have said to call him out, without disrupting the ceremony. I could have said that Charlie learned how to survive in Hollywood here at Harvard, where racism and sexism were enshrined in ways equally difficult to disrupt. I could have talked about her unfinished thesis, "Dramatic Liaisons: Reflection and Refraction in Twentieth-Century Stagings of Choderlos de Laclos," and said that when she most needed a mentor, Harvard's distinguished faculty had failed her. The memorial was invitation-only, but Widener Library opened at ten o'clock. Since it was now quarter to eleven, it was entirely possible that an interloper might have walked down the stone steps of that historic building, from one of its most coveted offices on the top floor—a perk of his distinguished chair—before crossing the Yard, a distance of perhaps five hundred feet, to the church. Pope nearly eighty, Charlie forty-five. Pope alive, Charlie dead.

In the end I said only what I'd planned, that Charlie had an imagination and a will like no one I'd ever met, that when she wanted something, it seemed she was able to shift the ground in front of her. That no one who had met her could have ever forgotten her. That was all true of Charlie, but I had to struggle while I said it not to look at the man in the back, whose presence had made me stumble.

Then I left the pulpit. The chaplain stepped forward and asked everyone to please rise for . . . some hymn. I returned to the pew, took my phone from Jack, and showed him the page in the book. He was interested in where the music was coming from, and because I had turned around to show him the organ, I couldn't resist looking again.

Pope looked older at this distance, thinner and slightly stooped. His hair was still thick and full, but now pure white. No one could consider him a threat, and yet there was his hand, the color of putty, lifting the crimson hymnal from its place behind the pew. His hand could grip the book, his legs could raise his body up—those powers remained to him, while all that was left of my friend was empty space.

13.

Space, as I like to tell Jack, is anything but empty. Four years after I went to California to see Charlie, and to talk about the Large Hadron Collider's debut at CERN, the physicists there had a triumphant success. Scientists had been looking for the Higgs boson since Peter Higgs's team had theorized its existence in 1964, but the particle remained elusive. When evidence for the Higgs appeared in the new Collider at CERN, it was widely celebrated as the first groundbreaking advance in the physics of the new century. Neel's efforts to record gravitational waves were just as important, but at that time, the LIGO collaboration had come up with nothing.

The Higgs discovery happened in 2012, when Jack was four. We were spending a week in California with my sister. Amy and her husband, Ben, kindly offered to take the kids to the beach in Santa Monica while I sat at my computer, waiting for confirmation that the elusive particle had indeed been found. Or not found, exactly. (I explained this to a journalist who asked me to put it in terms anyone could understand.) I said that the Higgs was the final piece in a puzzle called the Standard Model—an organizational chart, I said, that describes the most fundamental particles of matter, as well as how they move and interact. We arrange the particles—quarks, leptons, and bosons—according to electric charge, as well as more exotic properties like "color charge" and "spin"; since the Higgs has none of these properties, it couldn't actually be seen. It could only be identified by its after-effects: the more familiar particles it left behind in the frigid subterranean racecourse of the supercollider. I told the journalist that the Higgs is important because it creates a field, producing profound effects on the particles around it, while remaining invisible itself; for that reason, it has sometimes been called the "God particle"—a designation most physicists dislike. I have always thought that if a name makes people interested enough to learn more, it's probably doing more good than harm.

The day Jack came home from school and asked where exactly hell was located, I told him that it didn't exist, but that there was a very cool laboratory more than five hundred feet under the ground, where I would someday take him to visit. So *that's* where bad people go? Jack asked. That was too good not to repeat to Neel, who said that all of LIGO Caltech now knew about good physicists going to heaven and bad ones going to CERN.

Neel and I became friends freshman year, but he didn't meet Charlie until she and I started rooming together as sophomores. We were living in a three-room double under the blue bell tower in Lowell House, a luxurious space that she'd secured for us with a note from her immunologist. Charlie missed more classes because of illness than anyone I knew; in general she suffered from tiredness, headaches, and stomach pain. Because of her chronic fatigue syndrome, Charlie spent a lot of time in bed, reading magazines. Her bed must've been the same iron-frame, extra-long single that they issued to all Harvard undergraduates, but she'd added a featherbed, a white comforter, and a plethora of white-on-white decorative pillows. On the walls she'd hung film and theatrical posters, all framed—Charlie believed in framing—Audrey Hepburn in *Charade*, Charlotte Gainsbourg in *Oleanna*, Pam Grier in *Jackie Brown*. The top of the dresser was covered with a vibrant scarf, on which she arranged cosmetics and perfume. There was also one relic from her childhood, also framed: a yarn sampler onto which one of Charlie's aunts had embroidered A. A. Milne's "Cottleston Pie" in green on a patterned yellow ground. I couldn't imagine how long it would have taken, the words as well as the animals in the style of the original illustrations: Pooh, Eeyore, and Piglet, even Christopher Robin with a rainbow umbrella. Carl's sister had made it in honor of Charlie's birth, and put her initials at the bottom: PWB '71.

"You know most of those immune disorders are imaginary?" Neel said, the first time he visited our room.

"Please don't tell her you think that," I said, but I shouldn't have bothered. Charlie had an answer for everything. She walked in just as Neel was finishing the tour of our expansive suite—thankfully, once we were already in the living room.

"Nice place," Neel said. He had a fierce sense of justice, coupled with his almost insane economy, and if Charlie had been white, and as adept at securing special privileges as she was, his disdain for her might have been immediate. As it was, he reserved judgment.

"Thanks," Charlie said. "I went to see the dean of student services."

"He just gave you this room?"

"We may have exchanged some *services,* but that's what his office is for—right?" Then she winked. She was one of those people who could actually pull off winking.

Later, after everything had happened with Pope, I wondered if she regretted talking that way. If everyone else went up to a certain line with a joke, Charlie would be sure to cross it. This was true of her humor, her sophistication, her clothes, and even her intellectual life; she at first seemed to prefer French to American literary theory, the more impenetrable the better—de Beauvoir, Irigaray, Cixous, and Kristeva—and then made a move toward black American feminists: bell hooks, Audre Lorde, Barbara Christian, and Hazel Carby. It was maybe a frustration with all of that theory—she was not interested in debates between black and white feminists—that pushed her toward popular culture. She admired Addison Gayle on blaxploitation and Barbara Creed on slasher films, but what she really loved was a period drama, anything set in another place or time. She was obsessed with the first film version of Christopher Hampton's *Dangerous Liaisons,* and especially with Glenn Close's extravagant Merteuil; the film was what led her eventually to Laclos, with such unfortunate results.

"Your roommate seems a little unbalanced," Neel told me, soon after they met. We were sitting on the mattress in the minuscule room he rented from the Grossmans, a retired couple in Somerville. He was the first of my friends to live off campus, to save money and because he chafed at the restrictions and ponderous tradition of dorm life at Harvard. Apart from the mattress that served as bed and couch, Neel had only a desk and a dresser (provided by his landlords) and his many piles of books. He didn't smoke inside, but the room smelled of the Drum tobacco he rolled himself. It was a corner room on the first floor, with a separate entrance. I would knock at the door under the gingko tree, waiting for Neel to let me in. Although the atmosphere was dank (it seemed always to be overcast when I was there), there was a window onto the Grossmans' yard, where you could see a storage shed with a padlock and, in the fall, the gingko's yellow foliage. If Neel cracked his window during that season, you could smell the rancid odor of the round, rust-colored fruits. The gooseneck pharmacy lamp standing on the bare boards, the white paint peeling off the steam pipe in long, bark-like strips, the Grossmans' narrow dresser with its cut-glass knobs, inside which Neel's corduroys and wool sweaters had a temporary home: the scarcity of his possessions may make it easier for me to recall the visual details. Or it may be that the intensity of my feelings for him at that time allowed me to preserve this extraneous information—somewhat like the massive Higgs particle that announced its presence in the Standard Model long before it was discovered, as a medium for the less spectacular particles it affected.

"You don't know her," I told him. I began by defending her, which only encouraged Neel to argue. I wonder now if I secretly wanted him to point out her flaws.

"Does she really read all those fashion magazines?"

"It's for her classes, actually. They do feminist readings of magazines and TV shows and stuff."

"Uh huh," said Neel, not bothering to hide a smirk. "What's her family like?"

"Her dad's a psychiatrist in private practice, but he used to run the department at Tufts medical school. And her mother started an art gallery. Now she's on the board of the Museum of Fine Arts—and she runs a free after-school program for kids."

"So they're these very high-culture black people and she embraces anything popular, television, media, in order to annoy them. She wants to be an actor for the same reason. But"—Neel raised his index finger, a parody of our professor, Arty Hofmann—"she does it through the prism of academia, so she's not escaping at all."

I had to admit that this did seem like an accurate assessment of Charlie, one I hadn't come to myself in spite of how much time I spent with her. As my friendship with Neel developed, we continued to talk this way about people, especially Charlie. Sometimes, sitting on his mattress and engaging in this glorified form of gossip, I knew I was betraying my friend and felt guilty. I didn't read fashion magazines, not out of any discipline or intellectual purity, but because they made me feel unsophisticated and ugly. I was aware that Neel was giving me a sort of compliment, and also that this compliment was at the expense of my friend, and maybe women in general, but it felt so good to receive that I overlooked that part of it.

This kind of conversation extended to our love lives as well. During those times that Neel had a girlfriend, I knew about her from the beginning: her irresistible attractions, her humorous foibles, the thing he had identified that he guessed would doom them in the end. I shared the same information about my romantic life with him. I sometimes found myself on a second or third date—drinking at Shays, at a concert in the drained swimming pool under Adams House—distracted by the thought of how I would describe the interaction later on, to Neel. Sometimes, sitting and talking on that mattress, it seemed as if we'd outsmarted not only other people, but love itself.

Neel's and my friendship was of a very collegiate type. We studied together, drank together, hugged each other each time we said goodbye, but in the first three years we spent together at Harvard, we never went beyond that. Later, when we did get together for real, we would speculate about what had taken so long, but I don't think we really figured it out. I wonder now if it was the way we talked together that had kept us apart. It was so safe, so empowering, that neither one of us wanted to give it up for the real thing; we wanted to hold up that potential against which everything else could be compared.

At the end of one of my evenings in his cold and uncomfortable apartment, it was a pleasure to return to the spacious, overheated room I shared with Charlie in Lowell House. She was always awake. If she wasn't shut in her room with her boyfriend, Kwesi, she would be puttering around our messy common room in a white silk bathrobe with multicolored butterflies. We would make Swiss Miss hot chocolate, dumping two or three packets in the mugs we'd stolen from the dining hall, until the surface of sludgy liquid was swimming with marshmallows, and talk until the early hours of the morning.

Charlie had been with Kwesi—straight-A philosophy concentrator, varsity soccer player, and president of the Black Students Association—since freshman year. (Kwesi would go on to win a Rhodes and teach at the London School of Economics.) Through Kwesi, Charlie was able to move between the black and Latino–centric social world of the Radcliffe quad, and her mostly white friends from boarding school, the Hasty Pudding Club, and the Signet, an arts club where she sometimes ate lunch on Thursdays. In our day, housing at Harvard was "semi-random," which meant that you could list your three top choices on your housing form; the fact that black and Latino students often chose the less convenient houses at Radcliffe in order to remain together—this strikes me now as one of the most quiet and effective protests I've ever witnessed—embarrassed the university, and no doubt led to the institution of complete randomization a few years after we left.

Charlie and Neel didn't get to know each other well until our senior year, but each of them seemed amused by my description of the other. When I was with Charlie, the whole style of Neel's off-campus apartment seemed pretentious, and the things he said—he was planning to teach physics to children in rural India after graduation; he was a Marxist-Leninist—absurd. Charlie made fun of his clothes (which he did actually have the money to replace, had he chosen to) and his hand-rolled cigarettes (which she purposely misidentified as cloves).

When I was with Neel, though, it was the other way around. Neel even suggested that Charlie was tolerated by her black friends because of Kwesi, but that there were people who dismissed her as a snob, a Black American Princess, and worse. I defended her—how could you please everyone?—but Charlie and Neel were the two best talkers I'd ever known, and I found myself susceptible to their arguments. I sometimes consoled myself with the thought that this was the way a scientific mind worked, constantly doubting, open to revising its ideas if new evidence presented itself. But the fact was that Neel and Charlie did just as well academically as I did, and they weren't constantly changing their minds, or finding that their own ideas shifted under the influence of powerful fields created by two equally magnetic friends.

14.

I had suggested we get the kids together. I'd done it because I didn't know what to say to Terrence after the service, but I hadn't expected him to agree. I didn't think he considered me a good enough friend, maybe even of his wife's, to want to talk to me about her now, and I couldn't imagine what use Simmi would have for a new playmate, especially a shy younger boy, just after her mother's death.

But Terrence had taken my number at the memorial, and texted me two weeks later to arrange it. He and Simmi showed up on a Sunday morning at exactly the appointed time. We half hugged at the door, and then I led them into the living room, where the four of us stood in uncomfortable silence. Or rather, the three of us; only Jack was perfectly content, watching Simmi. Recent events, not to mention her age and costume (she arrived in leopard-print tights and a tank top with a sequined star on it), clearly fascinated him. Terrence was wearing jeans and a white T-shirt that said *Zingaro* in fancy black script. The clothing made him more recognizably himself, but the change from the man I remembered was still striking, perhaps only because of his close-cropped hair. It made his face less boyishly handsome, more angular and dramatic. There was a tattoo I couldn't make out on the inside of his left arm.

I suggested that Jack show Simmi his room, but Simmi sat down cross-legged on the floor and started looking at an old issue of the *MIT Technology Review*. There couldn't have been anything there to interest her, but she turned the pages systematically, as if it were a hurdle she had to cross before moving on to whatever business was at hand.

"Simmi," her father said, and Simmi looked up, but at me rather than him. Her hair was secured in two very neat French braids; it seemed like an unlikely skill for a father to have, and I wondered if Addie had done it. Simmi's features, like Charlie's, were perfectly regular, but her face was wider, heart-shaped like Terrence's.

"Are you an astronomer?" she asked, her eyes on me.

"No. But I do use data—information—that astronomers and astrophysicists collect."

"So you study stars?"

"Not usually."

"What do you study?"

"It's a little hard to explain, but I mostly study forces. Like the way the very smallest things we know about move around, and also the very biggest things, like stars and planets."

Simmi looked impatient, as if I were intentionally being difficult. "So you know what stars are *like*."

"Yes," I said. "I think you could say that."

"Is there, like—" She slapped our hardwood floor twice with the palm of her hand: "ground?" Her face had an intensity that made me uncomfortable. Terrence had been frowning out the window, but now he gave me a kind of warning look.

I thought Simmi noticed that and was trying to keep all my attention on her.

"No," I said carefully. "A star is just a hot ball of gas."

"Because of the nuclear fusion reactions in its core!" Jack was showing off for our guests, but Simmi ignored him.

"Isn't it too hot for people on stars?" she asked.

"You're right, it's much too hot. In the middle there's hydrogen—that's one of the two ingredients in water—and helium, like what's inside balloons. The tiny pieces of hydrogen crash together to make helium, along with light and heat. Some of the stars we're looking at are so far away that the light we're seeing is thousands or even millions of years old."

"The speed of light is the fastest thing in the universe!" Jack said. "Faster than Power Rangers!"

"It's like a fire pit," Simmi said. "Like hell."

"No, it isn't," Terrence said firmly.

"There's no hell," Jack said.

Simmi focused on him for the first time. "How do you know?"

"He's right, baby," Terrence said. "Everybody knows that."

I could see the next question on Simmi's face, the obvious one that I wondered myself as a child, when I'd heard my own grandmother talk about meeting her parents in heaven—how could there be one and not the other?

"Most astronomers do think there are other solar systems like ours out there," I said. "Maybe even with planets like Earth. They could just be too far for us to get to."

But Simmi had turned back to the magazine, examining a glossy and somewhat frightening portrait of Elon Musk standing in an empty airplane hangar, leaning on one of his cars.

Jack had also lost interest in cosmology and was shifting from one foot to the other. "Do you want to see my room?"

I could tell Simmi wanted to say no, but her father accepted for her.

"Go on, Sims."

Simmi uncrossed her legs and stood up reluctantly.

"Do you like Legos?" Jack asked eagerly.

"Not really." But her tone was truthful rather than harsh. "My best friend in L.A. is Piper," we heard her say as they walked down the hall. "She's nine already."

"My cousin is nine," Jack said gamely. Then they went into his room, and shut the door.

I looked at Terrence. "I'm not sure I did the best job answering that one."

He shrugged. "It's her grandmother. She said that maybe Charlie was 'smiling down on us' from a star."

"Oh—"

"You have no idea, the conversations we've had about that one."

I agreed with Terrence that the idea of Charlie smiling down from a star—in addition to sounding vaguely out of character—was unlikely to comfort a child who had just turned eight. On the other hand, there are all kinds of platitudes I've heard myself repeating to Jack that I never would've expected, comforting banalities I must've been told so many times that they had been hard-wired in there.

"I can imagine," I said.

Terrence expelled a breath, said nothing. He sat down, not on the chair itself, but on one upholstered arm. He ran his hand over his head, as if feeling for the missing hair, then interlaced his fingers. On his left hand was the simple platinum wedding band.

Apart from the few words we'd exchanged at the memorial, we hadn't spoken since the phone conversation when he'd first told me about Charlie. That was two days after she died, the day after I received the wordless phone call, which he'd dismissed as a pocket dial. I didn't think he would be able to do the same with the symbols that had come over email the next day, or the text on the morning of the memorial itself—but sitting across from him, I felt it would be wrong to bring those things up.

"I made some coffee, if you want?"

"I'm good, thanks."

There was a ridiculously long silence, in which Terrence seemed to be studying his fingernails. They were either clipped or bitten very short.

"What's Zingaro?"

Terrence looked up. "Oh, it's our company—mine and my brother's. We make wooden surfboards."

"What does it mean?"

"Gypsy," he said. "It's a British word for an Italian Gypsy."

"I've never heard it before." There was the sound of the children's voices from Jack's room. They at least had overcome the initial awkwardness.

"Charlie would be glad we're doing this," Terrence offered suddenly. "I mean, a playdate. She'd talk about you."

"Really?"

"Yeah. Like when there was an article or something—I think she had a Google Alert on your name. She told Simmi how you were a famous scientist and everything."

"I don't know about that," I said, but I was pleased. It was one thing to hear it from Charlie, who tended to flatter people, another to think that Charlie cared enough to follow my career remotely.

"I think she also wanted Simmi to know there's another kind of famous," Terrence said. "Not just pop stars and actors—you know?"

"It's impressive that Simmi remembered."

"She's something," Terrence said. "She could read when she was three."

"Me, too," I said.

Terrence glanced at me, but didn't say anything. Was I trying to impress him? And even if I were, would this be the way to go about it? I know better than to bring up the spooky stuff my parents have told me: that my first words were a full sentence, spoken at eight months—"Candle makes light"—and that I seemed to read from a book ten months after that, a Jane Austen novel that was lying open on the bed. *The parson is coming to dinner,* I supposedly said, startling my mother, who was ironing. In third grade, Mrs. Katz made me stand in front of the class while she threw addition and subtraction problems at me. I'd been rude, she said, claiming that I "already knew how to add and subtract," and she wanted to teach me a lesson. I got them all, up to four digits, and was surprised when it turned out I had to sit through addition anyway.

Jack does not manifest the unusual abilities I displayed early. His report card, which doesn't yet have letter grades on it, is always good; although he professes to dislike math, his evaluations in that subject and in science are often excellent. His teachers' most frequent complaints are about the sloppiness of his homework, and his disinclination to speak up in class. These are issues I struggle to help him with, since I had the opposite problem as a child; I was so eager to please, not only to show what I knew but to be allowed to move on to whatever was coming next, that I couldn't shut up.

Terrence walked in a circle around our small living room, then paused at the shelves to look at my books.

"Do you know the author Robert Lanza?"

"I don't think so."

"He's a scientist, too, more of a biologist. He has this theory about where the energy goes when someone dies. Because of the Second Law of Thermodynamics."

"Mm," I said. It's strange that people are often moved to make the most far-fetched nonscientific arguments to scientists, rather than to the type of audience that might be more receptive.

Terrence became more animated, gesturing with his left hand: "He says that we all exist in our own bubbles of spatiotemporal reality. And that when we die, all that happens is that the bubble pops. The people left behind experience your death, but you don't. Or another way to think about it is that the universe is like an infinite collection of shows on cable, and when you die, you just start a new series." He came the closest I'd seen to a smile. "Charlie liked that."

"I should check it out."

"You should."

There are different degrees of fringe science, usually undertaken by the kind of person who begins with a real career and goes off the rails: people who post their unconventional ideas on the alternative preprint server viXra all the way down to the unhinged, profanity-fueled climate-change-denying blogger. I once spent some time answering a sociologist's questions about what made these propositions non-science. One clue is that in pseudoscience, every piece fits neatly inside a theory and the scientist is never wrong.

"I think you're doing such a great job with all this," I said. "Simmi really does seem okay."

Terrence made a skeptical noise.

"As okay as could be expected."

"In public," he said.

I was sorry then that I hadn't been more receptive to whatever it was—popular science, literature, or quackery—that had gotten him through the last few months. Why did I have to be so critical, Marshall, my most recent POI, would demand. When I'm honest I have to admit that he wasn't the first person-of-interest to mention it.

"I guess I'd have some coffee," Terrence said. "Just black." He stayed in the living room while I got it, scrolling through his messages. But he thanked me genuinely when I handed him a mug.

I realized I hadn't heard the kids in a while. "They're quiet."

"I'll check on them," Terrence said immediately.

I went back to the kitchen. I hadn't thought of lunch, but luckily there were apples and bread. I started to make peanut butter sandwiches.

"They're upstairs," Terrence said when he returned. He retrieved his coffee from the living room, and joined me in the kitchen. "He's giving her a tour."

"It's pretty much what you see. I don't think Simmi's going to be impressed."

Their most recent house in L.A. was white stucco. I'd looked it up online when they bought it. There was a gunite pool, outlined in blue-and-white ceramic tile. Charlie had sent me a picture of the living room, which she'd decorated with mirrors and patterned fabrics, Moroccan in character. Her taste in home décor was dramatic and over-the-top, what she liked to call "barococo."

"Simmi spends time with my mom," Terrence said.

"Where's your mom?"

"Where she always was. Palms—near Culver City."

"I know right where that is. We were all the way out in Pasadena."

"Private school?"

"Nope. But the high school there is pretty good, especially for science and math."

"Mine wasn't. But we had a gifted and talented program—it was called GATE. I tested into it, actually." Terrence glanced at me. "But then things weren't so great with my mom, and I basically stopped going."

"She's okay now, though?"

"She married a cop, this retired guy with a pension. Now she paints dolphins and sells them at a craft fair in Altadena. That's what she's been doing for twenty years."

"That sounds okay."

"I just mean, Simmi's not spoiled."

"I didn't think that—I just—Charlie sent pictures of your house. It's beautiful."

"I hope someone else thinks so—we're selling it. It was always too much space for us, and now . . ." Terrence's voice trailed off.

"Yeah."

"We left all the furniture, because the broker says it's easier that way. She's saying the owners are 'relocating to Europe.'"

"Why?"

"It sounds better than 'Someone died here.'"

"Oh—right."

Terrence eyed the sandwiches on the counter. "I don't think we can stay," he said. "I promised Addie."

I felt a kind of panic. Should I mention the messages? It was possible this would be my only chance. Terrence had said Charlie would've wanted them to play together, but he might consider once to be enough. And who knew how long they would end up staying in Boston? Wouldn't it be better to say something now?

"Addie said you might be in Boston for a while."

"That's the plan." Terrence's tone was gently ironic. "She had a plan beforehand, too."

"The hospice care at home?"

Terrence looked surprised. "Yeah. But, you know—that was exactly what Charlie didn't want: everyone parading through our house. And then *getting in their cars*—that's what she said. That everyone would come, and then they'd get in their cars and put on their headsets, and call other people to say how hard it had been to say goodbye. How guilty they'd felt for actually *wanting* to get out of there. And then the other friends, the people they'd called, would be like, 'Yeah—don't blame yourself. It's so hard.' And then they'd all go out for drinks to comfort themselves. And all the time she would be there, dying."

"She said that about me?"

Terrence swallowed the rest of his coffee. "With you it would've been on the phone."

"She thought I wouldn't come?"

He shook his head, in frustration rather than denial. For a second he looked like he was going to throw the mug against the wall. It was a mug my friend Vicky had made in a pottery class, which I now saw clearly for the first time. Painted a speckled turquoise color and heavily glazed, it was hideous.

"I'm sorry."

Terrence put the mug down lightly in the sink and shrugged. "She said that's how she would act, too, if it were someone else. She just didn't want any of it."

"I get that."

"We'd just seen Carl and Addie—they were out in May and the visit almost killed her." Terrence laughed humorlessly. "Charlie felt like she'd said goodbye then, but she knew they'd be devastated. Her idea was that she'd write a letter—to try to explain."

"And that's what you can't get."

He gave a sharp, affirmative nod.

Maybe because of Terrence's reticence, or Addie's formality, the full force of Charlie's decision hadn't hit me until now. She had denied her parents the opportunity to be with her in her death. She had written a letter to explain—but the letter had gone missing. If I were Carl or Addie, that would undo me, too. I would have all kinds of doubts, and I wouldn't hesitate to blame anyone who could have borne responsibility, especially if that person had been the one who had taken my place at my child's deathbed.

"She didn't show you the letter."

"She said she'd email it." Terrence was leaning back against my kitchen counter. Now he closed his eyes and pressed his thumb and forefinger into their sockets. "We didn't have *time*. It was—it was crazy. We would start things, and then there would be something else to talk about. Money, or the different palliative care doctors. The one at Cedars versus the one at UCLA. What we were supposed to say to the nurses. And then everything for Simmi, keeping it as normal as possible—which wasn't very normal. I kept making lists, and then starting them over. She was going to handle her parents on her own, and so I let her do it." Terrence looked at me, almost imploring. It was like my usefulness as a potential ally had just occurred to him. "She *did* do it—I'm sure. It must be in her drafts."

"And if you had the phone, you could get it."

"It would be easy."

"Someone has it," I blurted out.

Terrence looked at me as if I were a little simple. "Yeah," he said. "I told you—it was stolen."

"But I mean, they're using it. I got an email, too."

"You mean, after that phone call?"

I picked up my own phone from the table, and searched for the message. My hands felt slower and clumsier than usual; I could feel him watching me as I looked at the screen. When he took it, though, it was with less urgency than I would've expected. He looked at the screen, and sighed, as if it confirmed what he'd expected. He scrolled down to be sure.

"That's all there is," I said.

He handed back the phone. "This is common, as hard as it is to believe. I run the website for Zingaro, and so I read a lot of tech blogs. A spammer can spoof the 'from' address without even having access to the account."

"Except that it was right after you told me—the same day. And then I got this, a few weeks later." I showed him the text—*Luvya lady*—but didn't mention which morning it had come.

Terrence was nonplussed. "It's possible someone's screwing with you, whoever took the phone. But it could also just be standard-issue spam. It may have gone to a bunch of people in her address book, and you're the only one who told me."

"But if a spammer can get in—"

"Not in. It's the difference between holding a book open in front of you and actually reading. Getting in officially is another thing."

"There's a lot of security?"

"I'm still on part one of the process," Terrence said drily. "Google needed my driver's license, her death certificate, a copy of an email she sent to me—so I got to, you know, go through lots of our emails—that was fun. Part two involves a court order. If I even get that far."

"Jesus, Terrence."

Terrence shrugged. "It's not Google's fault. They have to do it, or people would break into accounts this way all the time."

"They could make it easier for you, though. Given the circumstances."

"So could her mother." He shifted his weight from the counter and faced me. "That's the thing about this family—you know? Birth plans, life plans, estate plans—they can't even fucking die without a plan."

There was a pounding on the stairs, and then the children were in the kitchen.

"We're hungry!" Jack said. "Is Simmi staying for lunch?"

Simmi looked at her father. "Can I?"

"Not this time."

"Please," Simmi said.

"We're having lunch at Nana's."

"Okay," said Simmi, "but I want to come another time."

"Okay, sweetheart," Terrence said, not looking at me.

Jack had seated himself in his customary place at the kitchen table. He picked up the sandwich I put in front of him, but didn't take his eyes off Simmi.

"Come anytime," I said. "We'd love that." I didn't think Simmi would want me to hug her, and so I touched her shoulder. She seemed to tense under my hand.

I turned to Jack. "What were you showing Simmi upstairs?"

Unaccountably, Jack looked nervous, and Terrence was suddenly attentive.

"Jack?"

"Your office," he said in a small voice.

Normally my office is off-limits, but I held off getting angry for Simmi's sake. "There's not much to see there."

"No telescope," Simmi said.

"I don't really use telescopes," I told her. "But I know lots of people who do. If you'd like, I can take you to see one."

"Simmi?" Terrence said.

"Thank you," Simmi said.

The way she looked at me! They weren't her mother's eyes—they were almond-shaped and a much lighter color. It was the expression, almost as if she were daring me to do something. Or as if Charlie were, from inside there.

Terrence was collecting a backpack Simmi had been carrying with the most recent Disney princesses on it—the ones who were supposed to be Scandinavian feminists—with their waist-length hair and impossible proportions.

"Can I walk with Simmi to the sidewalk?" Jack said.

I nodded and the two of them went out of our apartment, down the steps to the front door together. Terrence and I followed them more slowly. We stood in the hallway outside my tenants' apartment. The children had left the door ajar, and I could see our next-door neighbor, Marjorie, through the screen, scraping the sludge of mustard-colored pollen from the uneven sidewalk with a rake.

"I used to get angry at Charlie," I said. "Why wouldn't she call me back? And then I'd wonder why I cared so much."

Terrence was looking at the messages on his phone. He seemed to have a lot of them, but when I said Charlie's name, he looked up.

"That's why she didn't call you."

"I know. I just—love her."

Terrence put the phone back in his pocket, and left his hands there. He rocked a little on his heels, and looked past me to the children, who were talking to Marjorie. She had stopped raking and was showing them something in the elm tree outside her house—a bird's nest, maybe. They were all three looking up.

"You're, like, the only person who's said that."

"What?" I asked.

"Daddy!" Simmi called. "Come look!"

"Without the *e-d*," Terrence said.

Then he skipped two steps and hurried down to the sidewalk to look where his daughter was pointing.

15.

That night I opened the email that had come right after Charlie's death. I looked again at the little pictures, and even pressed reply. Then I felt foolish. I decided to call my sister in L.A.

Amy teaches mathematics at a private girls' day school in Pasadena that she hopes her daughters will someday attend at a reduced rate. Her husband, Ben, is an engineer for the city. As kids, Amy and I fought so much that our parents decided to give us separate rooms. Since there were only two bedrooms and I was older, I began sleeping on the enclosed porch that had always been my father's workshop.

I made a fuss about being "kicked out" of my room, but everyone knew I was happy on the porch, with all the batteries, the rolls of copper wire, the slide rule, the coffee cans that were labeled to identify their carefully sorted contents: nuts, bolts, nails, washers. My sister, by contrast, demonstrated certain obsessive-compulsive behaviors that could be controlled only with absolute order and a strict routine. It was difficult for her to sleep anywhere but that dark little bedroom, where she performed various bedtime rituals: flipping the light on and off, executing twirling maneuvers (to "unwind her string"), touching the rows of stuffed animals arranged on whitewashed, plywood shelves my father had made when he was unemployed.

As adults my younger sister and I are as close as any siblings I know. There are certain facts we don't discuss:

1. Helen and Amy are both very smart.
2. Amy is prettier than Helen, and has a husband and children.

3. Helen is more successful than Amy and does more interesting work.

4. Helen and Amy's mother loves Amy and her children more than she loves Helen and Jack.

5. Helen and Amy's father is a little in awe of Helen and tends to brag about her to his friends.

Amy and I sometimes marvel at other siblings who let their differences get in the way. What, after all, is the point?

That night I told Amy about Terrence and Simmi's visit. I said that they seemed more eager to befriend us than I'd expected.

"Why wouldn't they be? I mean, if they're planning on staying in Boston?"

"Just, I don't know—Terrence and I don't have that much in common. And Simmi's older than Jack."

"About a year, right?"

"That makes a big difference when the girl is older."

Amy acknowledged that. "What did they play?"

"They kept going up to my office. Simmi was looking for a telescope—she's interested in stars."

"That's cool."

"Adelaide said something about her mother looking down from a star."

"Oh dear."

"Yeah."

"But she doesn't really believe that—at eight?"

"I'm not sure. Jack thinks he saw Charlie."

"What do you mean?" Amy asked.

"Just before the memorial. He saw the photo on the invitation and said he remembered her."

"That's possible, right?"

"He said he'd *just* seen her—in my office, upstairs."

"Could he be remembering a visit or something?"

"He's only met her once. He was four—they were here for Christmas. I doubt he remembers."

"So you think he told Simmi that?"

"What?"

"About seeing her—in your office."

I was silent for a moment. "I didn't think of that."

"She might have been talking about telescopes, but maybe she just wanted to go up there, see the ghost for herself."

I didn't want to be guilty of manufacturing a comforting fiction, like the one Addie had told, or of allowing Jack to do it. On the other hand, I wasn't sure that Jack thought of what he'd told me as a story about ghosts—or as a story at all. He had said only that he'd seen the woman in the picture, upstairs in my office.

"There's a photo of her on my desk—now. Not when he said he saw her, though. Maybe they were just playing a game."

"Maybe," she said. "Have you gotten any more messages?"

I had told Amy when I got the call from Charlie's phone, as well as the email and text message. She hadn't suggested an explanation, but like Terrence, she refused to countenance that anything out of the ordinary was going on. That annoyed me, but I didn't know why. What did I want her to say? That there was a ghost who was trying to contact me? I didn't believe that either. I just wanted her to admit that it couldn't be a string of coincidences.

"No—but I got three of them. What are the chances they aren't connected?" I meant it rhetorically, but Amy wrote her thesis on probability, and she doesn't get many opportunities to talk about it with people who understand her.

"Very high, I think. Just assign variables to each independent event and you're in business."

"Thanks. But they're not independent. I would use a PBA."

"Nooo—you would use a Poisson distribution. It's exactly like the classic analogy with postal mail."

Amy was warming up. I sometimes think about how infrequently my sister must find a high school senior who is genuinely interested in probability or statistics. By contrast, my students are the best in the country, and have already determined that they hope to make a life in physics. It's a question of sorting the merely capable from the ones who are extraordinary.

"You receive about four letters a day from different sources. Some days more arrive, some days fewer—occasionally you may not receive a letter—but the probability mass function will peak at four."

"If they're independent events," I said.

Amy sounded impatient. "Of course they're independent."

"Luvya lady?"

"Was there a link to nymphosonlinenow.com?"

"Why, yes—there was! Now why didn't I think of that?"

"I'm just saying—it's possible you see a pattern that you wouldn't otherwise," Amy said. "Because you're grieving."

"I think the word 'grief' is sort of like the word 'diversity.' It just flattens out the problem."

My sister sighed.

"And how do you explain the emoji?" I continued. "There was a flower—a tulip—a wink, a syringe, and a Swedish flag."

"A series of random digital images?"

"Not random—Charlie's a big winker. And she was sick, and she was always very into fresh flowers."

"What about Sweden?" Amy asked.

"I don't know." I had an idea about what the flag meant, but I couldn't say it out loud to anyone, least of all my sister.

Amy would say I'm more competitive than she is. I would say that she has given something up. I still think about the fact that my undergraduate thesis was beaten out for a Hoopes Prize by Krzysztof Kapusniak's "Angular Analysis of D+—Op+ Decay" and Jonathan Lieberman's "Gamma Rays as Standard Candles." I didn't work with Arty for my undergraduate thesis, but with a quantum field theorist, Emre Aksoy, who reassured me at the time that it was his fault I hadn't won the prize. He'd gotten a better offer from Princeton and was leaving, and Harvard wasn't giving him any parting gifts.

I followed Emre to Princeton for my PhD, in spite of the fact that string theory was really the only game in town there at that time. Emre said it kept us humble, and on the defensive, and that those were good positions from which to do science. I think there's a part of me that likes being in the minority—a particle physicist at Princeton in the nineties, a woman in this field at all. This is simply a personal preference, in the same way that I prefer running or swimming to team sports, and has no bearing on my genuine desire for more equity in the discipline.

Although I tend not to speak publicly on the subject, I have sometimes written about physics institutions and their problem with women. Recently I wrote a short blog post about hearing Chien-Shiung Wu speak soon after I arrived at Harvard in 1989. At the time I didn't know who she was; I was a freshman studying in the Cabot Science Library when I ran into one of my teaching fellows, who excitedly informed me that I had the chance to hear one of the three greatest women in twentieth-century physics speak right that moment, and that I would regret it forever if I didn't go.

The lecture took place in a small auditorium in the Chinese Department, where there was standing room only. Wu began her talk not with physics, but with the story of her life. She was seventy-seven years old at the time, wearing a gray silk jacket with a high collar. She said that she'd left China at twenty-four to pursue a PhD at the University of Michigan, but had chosen Berkeley over Michigan upon arrival, after hearing that women weren't allowed to use that university's front entrance. She described her struggles to secure an academic position as an Asian woman in America, followed by her recruitment onto the Manhattan Project by John Archibald Wheeler and Emilio Segrè. Segrè had remembered Wu's thesis on the decay of radioactive uranium isotopes just in time to avert a crisis at the new B reactor at Hanford, Washington (where one of the LIGO interferometers is today). Her sensitive work during the war, as well as political events in China, prevented her return home in the fifties; her parents and her brothers were killed in the political convulsions of the Cultural Revolution, and she never saw them again. As we sat listening to the thin but still strong voice of the brilliant woman on the stage, my teaching fellow leaned over and whispered: "She gave up everything for science."

As I write this, Wu has been dead twenty years. Had she won the physics Nobel in 1957, she would have been only its second female recipient. Her very difficult experiment undermined the physical law of conservation of parity: the idea, according to one biographer, that "the world reflected in the mirror appeared no less possible than the world in front of it." Wu conducted her famous experiment using cobalt; when a radioactive cobalt nucleus decayed, conservation of parity dictated that it should shed electrons both with and against the nucleus's spin. In fact, the electrons showed a marked preference for moving against the direction of spin. The idea that nature did indeed have a left and right preference—called "non-conservation of parity"—earned Wu's theoretical collaborators, Chen Ning Yang and T. D. Lee, the Nobel in 1957; in spite of the fact that the Nobel can be given to three scientists at once, Wu wasn't included.

When I was pregnant with Jack, I swam at MIT's Z Center. As I grew larger and more unwieldy, I no longer had to compete for lane space; I was given a wide berth, almost as if I were contagious. But I've rarely felt more productive and alive than I did pulling the two of us through the water, thinking about the rippling pattern in the images then being collected by the WMAP satellite. Those ripples were left over from the shivering movement of the very first light in the universe, like tiny footprints in spacetime. I swam my twenty laps, trying to imagine the moment when that remnant heat was released, the journey it had traveled to reach our satellite today. I didn't experience pregnancy brain (whatever that is) but published my second-most-cited paper with two collaborators near the end of month six.

After my sister and I hung up, I looked at the email again. The Swedish flag couldn't be an accident. It made too much sense. And so, breaking that down:

 = Charlie's favorite flower, or: an example of the kind of luxury most people don't bother with, which to Charlie was essential.

 = Don't worry.

 = The medications she had been taking, or perhaps, the last one of which she'd availed herself.

 = The Nobel Prize in Physics.

 = Remember: it is a race and you don't get points for anything but performance. Or in other words, do it for me.

I didn't actually write those explanations down, but that was the way I thought of them. I thought for a good amount of time, with the cursor hovering impotently around "reply." But once I decided, I wrote and quickly sent:

I know you're there.

Ghost or thief or explicable internal glitch, how much damage could I do with a single sentence?

16.

Exit Charlie, she used to say sometimes, when she was going out. When she was in *The Tempest* our sophomore year, she would say *Exeunt omnes,* which she explained was Latin for when everyone— including the freshmen pressed into service as Reapers, Nymphs, and "strange Shapes"—left the stage together.

I have enough colleagues at Harvard that I'm there at least once a month. One afternoon in early September, I went to see Arty at his office on Oxford Street; it was a meeting we'd scheduled knowing that each of us would soon be swamped with a semester's worth of work.

Normally I wouldn't have gone through the Yard, but I had a little time before our meeting, and I'd promised to buy Jack a certain type of eraser, popular among his classmates. I parked in front of Arty's office in Jefferson and crossed the old quadrangle, where I hadn't been since the memorial service. It didn't occur to me until I was right outside Thayer Hall that I'd done it because I wanted to look up at the first room Charlie and I had shared. The two blank third-floor windows produced no reaction in me, but when I jogged left around the southern edge of the building, avoiding a knot of tourists in front of the John Harvard statue, I heard her voice in my head, very clearly: *Lough Derg.*

For a moment the words meant nothing; then I knew. The year we lived in Thayer Hall, Charlie had written a term paper on something called "The Black Hole of Lough Derg." Unlike its astrophysical corollary, this was an actual hole—a pit in the ground in Northern Ireland popular among medieval pilgrims because it was reputedly an entrance to the underworld. Sleeping in that damp, cold recess overnight was supposed to shorten your time in purgatory. "They really believed that they might be bound to wheels of fire, or hung by their necks from fishhooks for years at a time," Charlie told me. "They were terrified. Isn't that amazing?"

Charlie learned about Lough Derg in an undergraduate Shakespeare lecture about Hamlet meeting his father's ghost on the ramparts of Elsinore. She did think at one point about writing a Shakespeare thesis, but Pope advised her to choose the "relatively untrodden territory" of Laclos. That was a valid argument, and Charlie was flattered that he would take an interest. This is maybe an opinion I've developed since becoming a teacher myself, but most of us are humble. Or at least, most of us aren't arrogant in the way my father's parents assumed when they called him "professor"— poking fun at him, because he said he wanted to go to college. It's more like the arrogance of priests, robed in humility, the secret belief that one has dedicated one's life to something pure. And the concomitant idea that this entitles one to little leeways, pleasures, indulgences, small things in comparison to the great work: the life of the mind.

My own mentor has won almost all of the big prizes, including the Wolf and the Kavli, but he would be the last person to feel any such entitlement. The university has bestowed on him even more honors, as well as time, money, and a parking space a few steps from Jefferson's entrance—which normally sits empty. I'm sure that this must annoy his less decorated colleagues, and also that Arty is unaware of this fact, as he cheerfully preaches to them (as he has done to me) about the benefits of doing physics while walking. Even though he lives in Newton, about six miles from his office, he often commutes on foot.

The first time I met Arty, I thought he reminded me of my father. I was a nineteen-year-old redhead from Los Angeles, and while that provoked different reactions in the other faculty members I encountered (dismissal, mild flirtation, or embarrassingly chummy encouragement), Arty was the only one on whom my physical person seemed not to register. Arty himself is unremarkable-looking, with a large, boyish face; gray hair that he wears too long; large, square glasses; and a habit of raising his shoulders toward his ears. His smiles are sudden and slightly out of his control, in a way that could be either charming or off-putting depending upon your point of view.

On that afternoon in September, after I bought Jack his erasers,

I went to Arty's office in Jefferson. He'd asked me to come and discuss a paper one of his postdocs had coauthored on Advanced LIGO detection of black-hole binaries in globular clusters. It was a fashionable topic: when LIGO detected a gravitational wave, it would be the biggest news of twenty-first-century physics, and theoreticians everywhere were scrambling to get in on the action, even before a detection had actually occurred. I was sorry to see through the window in Arty's door that the postdoc had arrived already; he was sitting with his back to me, wearing a T-shirt and a knit ski cap; his bike lock was clipped to one of his belt loops. In general I don't care what people wear—you can do physics in a bathing suit, if you want—but it was seventy-three degrees outside, and the air-conditioning in Jefferson has never been such that you need to put on outerwear indoors.

"Helen!" Arty said. "Come in, come in. Meet Jason. You both have classical Greek names."

This was typical Arty, awkward but effortful. He has told me that the most difficult part of socializing in a group for him is the need to come up with "topics," by which I think he means topics outside of the physical sciences. Arty carries the kind of suppressed excitement that you sometimes find in people who've just fallen in love, an almost maniacal focus on one thing, and a just barely concealed desire to turn any conversation to that subject.

Jason stood up. "It's great to meet you," he said. His T-shirt said, *I'd rather be lost in the woods,* and he had heavy muttonchops, with a soul patch, that may have been intended to distinguish him from less style-conscious colleagues.

"I can't remember who Jason was," I said.

"The captain of the Argonauts," Arty supplied. "Husband of Medea, the sorceress."

"The one who kills her kids."

Jason smiled. "And Helen caused the Trojan War."

"She was the scapegoat," I said. "I don't think she caused it."

"My wife is a chef," Jason said, "which is sort of like sorcery. But we don't have kids, thank god. Are you married to a physicist, or—"

"I'm not married. But I have to pick up my son after this, so we should start."

Jason looked slightly taken aback, probably by my tone, which can sometimes be a little short. Arty swiveled his screen toward us and started in happily:

"We were looking at redshifted chirp masses before you came in—red is high metallicity here and blue is low."

After I started working as Arty's research assistant during my final undergraduate year, and we began spending more time together, I realized that it wasn't my father he reminded me of so much as myself. If there were a way to strip us of our genders and synchronize our birth dates, Arty and I would be people with the same frame of reference, the same interests, and the same way of relating to other human beings. It's just that being female makes it more difficult to blurt out whatever comes into my head without seeming rude or crazy. Whereas people generally find Arty's eccentricity winning—if not a sign of genius.

We sat down and Jason began explaining the way that previous studies had relied on simplified globular cluster models and assumed a static mass for the black holes in each group. Jason's team used a Monte Carlo approach to generate more realistic models of dense star clusters in the Local Group. The idea was that those clusters would be a likely place for black holes to exist in revolving pairs—and to collide with each other, producing the powerful gravitational ripples that LIGO's interferometers could detect. The paper was impressive, and I began to like Jason while he was talking about it. I've been aware recently that I'm getting older, and making the kind of judgments I used to despise in my parents, as if complicated facial hair could predict whether or not someone was serious about his or her work.

"He reminds me of Neel," Arty said, when Jason was finished. "When you were first working with me."

"Really?"

"Who's that?" Jason asked politely.

"Neel Jonnal," Arty said. "Her collaborator on the Clapp-Jonnal."

"Oh, yeah—of course. I never knew his first name."

"He's at LIGO now," Arty said.

Jason's expression changed. "Really? Lucky bastard—I'd love to be there." He looked from me to Arty. "How long do you think before they get a detection?"

"Neel thinks soon," I said. "But he tends to be optimistic."

"Is he at one of the sites, or—?"

"Caltech," I said.

"Wrong!" Arty said, grinning in the way he does. "Or soon to be wrong—he's coming back."

I must have been staring at Arty; I couldn't help it. What he'd said didn't make sense. Neel and I had emailed about one of my grad students just last week, and he hadn't said anything about coming to Cambridge, even for a visit.

"Coming back to Boston?" I said. "But not permanently?"

Arty nodded, still smiling.

I didn't have to ask which university, since the only LIGO team in Boston was at MIT. My first thought was that I must have overlooked a message in which Neel told me this momentous news. From the time we were undergraduates we had talked about our eventually landing at the same university. It had happened temporarily here at Harvard early in our careers; the result had been some of the best work of our lives, not to mention the adult friendship we had now. That had tapered off a bit when I had Jack, but there wasn't any reason it couldn't pick up again now that he was older and Neel was moving back. As a LIGO research scientist, he'd be attached to MIT's Kavli Institute rather than holding a professorship like mine, though that distinction hardly mattered. We'd attend the same lectures and colloquia; be at the same department-wide events; run into each other at the coffee shop. I just couldn't understand why Neel hadn't told me.

Arty seemed to know what I was thinking. "He must be under orders to keep it to himself before it's official," he said. In addition to the American detectors in Louisiana and Washington, and the Italian site outside of Pisa, the collaboration also included teams in Germany and Japan. There was even a project in the early stages in India; the more interferometers there were, the larger cross-section of the sky they could survey. If Neel had wanted a change of scene, there were plenty of places he could have gone; instead, he had chosen the one lab that happened to be at my university.

"He'll be supervising some of the preparations for India, too," Arty said. "IndiGO, they're calling it, for LIGO-India—that's clever. I once met a man in a restaurant in Athens who'd made a fortune in indigo—the blue stuff. He'd been orphaned as a teenager and just shipped out to Bombay. He ended up as the Greek ambassador there—fascinating guy."

"They're moving one of the Hanford interferometers to India," Jason said. "Not building a new one, right?" He seemed accustomed to Arty's digressions, and what was necessary to get him back on track.

Arty nodded. "Somewhere in Maharashtra, as far as I understand. Oh, and he's getting married over there, so that's convenient!"

It was as if a wave passed through my body. A dizzying swish, such that if you told me I had been squeezed in one direction while being stretched in the other, according to the principles of relativity, I would have believed you. That's where the metaphor falls apart, though, because real gravitational waves aren't something we feel.

"*Neel* is getting married?"

"He didn't tell you that either? Don't let him know I put my foot in my mouth!"

"Married to whom?"

Arty shook his head. "I don't know, I can't remember. He did tell me, I'm sure, but we were also talking about their NSF funding, that whole saga, and . . ."

If we'd been alone, I might have pushed him. But Jason was eager to get back to his chirp masses. We returned to his paper, and then I talked about the possibility of primordial black holes—black holes created during the Big Bang—actually becoming dark matter, as suggested by a recent paper from Johns Hopkins. I talked while Arty nodded and smiled, and once got up to modify an equation of Jason's on the whiteboard. Both of them had forgotten Neel's move, and his upcoming marriage. I could keep up with the numbers they were tossing back and forth, but at the same time there was another data set preoccupying me, one with which neither of them was likely to be familiar.

Last year was the first in which unmarried Americans outnumbered married ones; and yet, even with all of these single people, we still don't have a word for the person who was your most important person—if you don't wind up with him or her. Neel was that person for me, and so the person he'd chosen took on a mythic dimension—was she also a physicist? Or a pianist, or a kindergarten teacher, or a director of marketing? Did the fact that they were getting married in India mean that she was Indian, as Neel's parents had always hoped for him? Was she younger, or the same age we were? Was she okay with Neel's well-established position on children? Was she pretty?

We had to wrap up before three, when Arty was teaching his famous Inflationary Cosmology lecture. Arty was one of those rare professors who could remain interested in explaining his work to each new generation of students, and there was no doubt that his lecture would be packed as usual. The three of us walked outside together, and Arty observed that I'd taken his parking spot.

"I always do."

"Why not walk, in this weather?" he teased me.

"I have to get Jack," I said. The truth, which Arty knew well, is that I can't stand walking—it's so slow. "When he's older, we'll bike."

"How old is he?" Jason asked, to be polite.

We chatted for a minute about Jack. I told them that it was now possible to buy your child a Cosmic Microwave Background stuffed toy.

"Now I remember," Arty said suddenly. Jason and I both looked at him.

"She's a cardiothoracic surgeon," he said, bobbing his head as he does whenever we've reached some kind of conclusion. "From Mumbai, I believe. She's been working with Doctors Without Borders—wonderful organization. But now she's got a new job here, at the Brigham."

Understandably bored by details about people he didn't know, Jason was pulling out his bike. I noticed that Arty was looking at me anxiously, as if even he could understand why this news might be upsetting. It seemed important to reassure him, not only for his sake.

"That sounds exactly right for Neel," I said. "Someone smart, but practical."

Arty smiled at me, relieved. "Exactly."

17.

My own parents didn't get married at first. When they moved in together, in Manhattan in 1965, my mother was a receptionist at the hair salon at Lord & Taylor (a job she says she got only because of her long red hair, which she used to iron straight). My father was working his way through college, and neither one of them had any interest in children. They insist that I wasn't an accident, but a gradual change of heart, and that they had my sister to keep me company.

I was born in '71 and then Amy arrived in '73, after which they decided to move to California. My father left Con Ed in Manhattan for a construction management job in L.A., and my mother stayed home with us. When I was five, they got married in our backyard, "for you girls," not because they had any newfound faith in the institution. Doing it the other way, the marriage without the children, has never made sense to me—or that's what I said to the few friends with whom I discussed Neel's engagement. What it really made me feel was that there was some magic I'd never experienced, which might make two people decide to yoke themselves together in that official way, for no practical reason at all.

The day after I went to see Arty, I taught my first seminar of the semester, for second- and third-year undergraduates: Introduction to Special Relativity. When I checked my phone afterward, there was a text message from Charlie. I did not believe, and yet my breathing and my heartbeat sped up. My skin was hot, then clammy. The message read simply—*Where does the universe END?*—not the kind of question that normally interested Charlie, but employing capitalization just the way she did, to reproduce her own animated manner of speaking. The following evening there was another email, blank except for the attachment: an article in which I was mentioned as one of ten female physicists "to watch." It was nine years old and of course I'd seen it at the time; it was as if "Charlie" had just noticed it.

My first thought was that Terrence might believe me now. There was no ghost, but there was someone who was, as he had said, screwing with me—it wasn't an anonymous spammer. I thought that if a health care worker or a delivery person had really picked up Charlie's phone and guessed the lazy password, my name would've been easy to find in her contacts. I wasn't under any delusions about being famous, but there had been times since the books were published that I had been recognized—usually in a bookstore, by a clerk who was excited about science, and once on the playground with Jack. A woman had approached me and said, "Are you Helen Clapp?" and we had talked for half an hour, while our children climbed and slid together.

There is a certain kind of person—usually male, but not always—who makes physics into a hobby, who reads all the popular books and makes an honest effort to understand. Sometimes all these people want to do is show you how much they know, but many of them (the woman on the playground included) are really curious. It doesn't have to do with education, necessarily; there are just some people who get pleasure from considering abstract questions about forces and cosmology. It hadn't occurred to me before, but sitting in my office after the seminar that afternoon—having just met eleven students with that type of brain, who'd also had the luck and drive to make their way to MIT—I thought it was possible that the person on the other end didn't know whose phone they'd taken. Even if you had come into the house to provide some service, seen a phone on a counter, and pocketed it, there was no reason to assume it belonged to the dying woman upstairs—in fact, "Charlie's iPhone" didn't suggest that it belonged to a woman at all. And if she'd really used 1234 as a passcode, anyone who felt like it could've gotten in; Terrence was just fortunate that there hadn't been a credit card or other financial information stored there.

I had thought that I would call Terrence right away, to tell him about the message. By the time I got home, though, I'd changed my mind. If it was shocking for me to receive these things digitally, how much more disturbing would it be for him? Simmi had suggested to her father that she wanted to see Jack again, and I hoped that the next time we got together, I could bring it up in a natural way. I took screenshots of the two messages and emailed them to myself. Then I went back to work. My responsibilities that day were mostly bureaucratic—having to do with the resumption of classes—and I completed them with only half my attention.

I didn't answer the text about the end of the universe, but I did think about it. Having a child Jack's age challenges me to put what I do into the most basic terms, something I always tell my students is a valuable exercise. As far as universe formation goes, I am partial to Andrei Linde's "balloons producing balloons producing balloons" model: the idea that there are many universes pressing up against each other, each having expanded from a tiny region of space. There is also Paul Steinhardt's Cyclic Universe: growing, collapsing in on itself, and being born again as a new entity. Neither of these were ideas I could explain in a text message, however.

What I used to say—that we don't know for sure where the universe ends, because none of us was around to see its beginnings—is not exactly true anymore. Ever since the Wilkinson Microwave Anisotropy Probe's data was published, in 2012, we have actually been able to see a real picture of the oldest light in the universe. This brightly colored pattern—the googly-eyed version of which usually rests against Jack's pillow alongside a hypoallergenic polar bear named Bruce—is like any temperature map. The fact that there are an equal number of hot and cold spots confirms the simplest and most beautiful version of inflation. We now know that our universe is almost certainly 13.77 billion years old, and that it expanded more than a trillion trillion times in the first trillionth of a trillionth of a second of its life. The tiny variations created during that wild beginning are the seeds of the galaxies we see today.

That's what I would have told Charlie about the universe's origins, if it had really been Charlie asking. She had a way of nodding when I talked about physics, in college or even after we lived on separate coasts. Her eyes would get just slightly wider than usual, and she would do a convincing impression of someone who was really paying attention. Once we were at the Museum of Fine Arts in Boston seeing Alfred Stieglitz photographs with her mother—this might have been in our sophomore or junior year—and Adelaide had given us a little lecture about Stieglitz's landscapes (which I'm ashamed to say I later reproduced, almost word for word, on the exam for the class I took to fulfill my Literature and Arts B requirement). Charlie listened to her mother in the same way she listened to me talk about neutrino mass parameters, and then joked with me later that she found Stieglitz's bare tree branches as boring as O'Keefe's flowers.

"I can't really get interested unless there are people in it," she said.

18.

N:

    Arty told me your news (both parts). And then Mark over at LIGO basically confirmed (the move, not the wedding . . . I'm going to take that on faith). Belated congratulations, although I have to admit I'm surprised. If I were accepting a job at Caltech, for example, I'm pretty sure you'd be among the first to know. I can promise I'll be more forgiving about your other big announcement, especially if you give me some details. And I promise not to spread them around among your new colleagues. I'd advise against making a confidant of Arty in the future—he's utterly reliable in every department except secrecy. Actually I think that's part of his fundamental decency . . . it probably never occurs to him why anyone would *want* to keep something a secret.

    What's going on in L.A.? Is everyone going to drink each other under the table at that hole on Figueroa in honor of your departure? Or do you not get a going-away party when you're moving within the cabal? I'm busy here with the electroweak paper I mentioned (my postdocs are the best I've ever had) and with Jack. He's still obsessed with Legos, and now that he's outgrown his asthma, he's getting pretty good at penalty kicks, too. They say he needs to volunteer more in class discussions, but I tend to be more and more on his side. Talk is cheap, which I guess is something you realized a long time ago.

    Cheers,

    H

I wrote that on the evening of the day I met with Arty, but it was more than two weeks before I received a response. At the time I didn't know what was going on at LIGO; even Arty didn't know, until a physicist at the University of Colorado started speculatively tweeting about it. It hadn't occurred to anyone that the LIGO scientists might detect a powerful gravitational wave even before the machines were officially taking data, during one of the final test runs—but that is exactly what happened. As it turned out, Neel got my email just a few days before LIGO detected its first gravitational wave. The scientists were thrown into a frenzy of activity, confirming and reconfirming the data, and for months afterward—until they published their historic paper the following February—all of those in the collaboration must have put off answering a lot of email. Because I couldn't have known about the detection, I simply assumed that Neel was silent because he was afraid his more personal news had hurt my feelings. That made me furious—or maybe what made me furious was the fact that I couldn't disabuse him of that idea until he deigned to write me back.

> H:
>
> I feel like I owe you an apology, though you're hardly the last to know. I've told basically no one about things with Roxy, including my brother—admittedly, I try to make that a general rule where my family is concerned. I've only just broken the news to my parents, who are thrilled, of course. She's not a Telugu Brahmin, but I think they'd lost hope that I would ever get married at all. Roxy's family is Parsi—a tiny minority in India, famously successful in business. There's also a strong tradition of service, and that's what she's generally been up to since medical school. (She got her MD at Stanford—we were both in California for years, but didn't meet until last year in Mumbai.) She's been on a two-year stint with Doctors Without Borders, running a clinic in eastern India, but now she's ready to come back to the States.
>
> Meanwhile, how are things in the infinite corridor? Am I throwing myself to the lions with Mark and his group? I have to admit, I've gotten used to the weather and am a little trepidatious about coming back to Cambridge. (Roxy's a baby about the cold, which I find funny given her general steeliness. We're getting married in February in India—short notice, but I hope you'll come.)
>
> I have something else to discuss with you, which I'll keep to myself until I see you in person. Both interferometers should be up and running anytime now, and recent developments have made me especially optimistic. As it is, 2016 is shaping up to be a momentous year for me and for the universe in general, and I'm glad we'll be in closer proximity to exchange notes.
>
> Xo
> Neel

19.

A few days after I received that reply, I went to retrieve Jack from a playdate. It was a beautiful fall day, and so I took Arty's advice and walked. The air smelled like burning leaves. I wasn't thinking about Charlie at first, but about my graduate students Jim and Chendong, and their analysis of the latest Planck satellite data. I walked from my office in Building 6 out to Mass Ave., where the mother of Jack's playdate had asked me to meet them at Darwin's, the popular sandwich shop. There was a plate-glass window, and a glass door that kept swinging open and closed in the lunchtime rush.

That was when I saw her. In profile, through the glass, dressed in white, gesturing to the girl behind the counter. And this was in character, because Charlie would never pass up an opportunity for conversation with a stranger. I sometimes thought she enjoyed talking to people she didn't know more than those she did. The girl was laughing. She passed Charlie a brown paper bag; then she moved, reflections shifted, the window was a pattern of light and dark shapes. I took a step back—it was not like what you sometimes heard, people mistaking a stranger for a lost loved one in a crowd. This was real and I was frightened.

The door opened, and I was standing in front of Adelaide Boyce, blocking her path. I almost laughed, I was so relieved. Charlie's mother was wearing white, more of a knitted cape than a sweater. She was alive and very real, buying bread from a store. Nothing could be more normal.

"Helen!"

I almost said that I'd thought she was Charlie. I might have said it in the past, even if it wasn't true, just to please her.

"What are you doing here?" she asked, even though we were in Cambridge, and she was the one who was well outside her Brookline neighborhood.

I said I was picking up my son from a playdate.

"I won't keep you, then. But how *are* you?"

I'd mistaken Adelaide for her daughter (I saw now) because she'd styled her hair differently. I'd never seen Charlie's mother with anything but straight hair, with a heavy fringe of bangs. Now it was short and natural (though without any gray), just the way Charlie's had been in that photograph. It made her face look older, in spite of the fact that she was wearing a good amount of makeup, especially around her eyes.

I said that I'd been working a lot.

"What are you working on these days? I'm still recommending your book on cosmology to everyone."

"Thank you."

I had the strange urge to tell her that Neel was coming back to MIT. I thought she would remember him, but only from the article in *Science* that Charlie had shown her, when our model was published. I had received a handwritten note from her then, congratulating me on my achievement, and again when each of the books came out. Addie kept track of Charlie's friends, especially the women; she bought my books for her own friends as Christmas presents. When our classmate Sarah, a cellist, first performed with the BSO, Addie bought a subscription.

"We're doing some exciting work related to the Large Hadron Collider, in Geneva," I said. "But the further along you get, the more meetings you have to attend—it sometimes seems like my whole life is meetings."

"I can believe that," Addie said. "I'm just coming from a meeting myself—my lawyer at Ropes and Gray. I've known him forty years. You realize whom you trust, at times like this." Addie tilted her head and looked at me. "You have a will, don't you?"

I must've looked startled, because she put her hand on my shoulder. "I know. I'm being a nosy old woman, but you have to do it, once you have a child."

"I should."

"I'll email you Robert's information. You don't have to call him, but just promise you'll call someone."

I thought that if Adelaide had been driven mad by grief, this was the form it would take: the frantic organization of other people's lives.

"Anything is better than nothing," she said.

"Charlie didn't have a will?"

"Of course she did—financially, her affairs are quite clear. Carl saw to that." Addie laughed shortly. "I'm asking Robert to advise us about the family's options regarding the other matter."

I glanced at Addie. Was she testing me, or trying to ascertain how much Terrence had said? "About the letter?"

"I'm not sure there ever was a letter."

"Terrence thinks there was something," I said.

Addie looked grim. "As he's told us many times. In which she explains everything. But I know my daughter—and however bad things may have gotten, I don't think she would have gone so far as to obtain the drugs illegally for that purpose."

"Terrence mentioned that there was a palliative care physician—at Cedars Sinai or UCLA?"

I saw an edge of doubt in Addie's expression; suddenly the doctor was slightly more credible. Like my own parents, but probably for different reasons, Charlie's put great faith in elite institutions. You only had to mention one, and suddenly everything you were saying became more legitimate.

"They've decided to stay on with us, at least for the time being," Addie continued.

"Terrence and Simmi have?"

"It was very last-minute—a scramble to get her enrolled. Thank goodness there was space."

"She'll be in school in Brookline?"

"Cambridge, actually—at BB&N. It was too late for public school, and we thought a smaller environment might help her this year. It's hardly convenient, but it's the best school that had room. And Carl and I wanted to do it."

I wondered what Terrence had wanted; I thought it was probably hard to turn down thirty-five thousand dollars in tuition for your child.

"It's a lot for Terrence to manage at this point—her grief and his own." Addie indicated the busy sidewalk. "You see people just going about their days, and—" The left side of Addie's face twitched suddenly, a tic. She shaded her face and looked back into the sun for a moment, as if she were orienting herself. "Well," she said, turning back to me.

"I can't imagine what you and Carl must be going through."

Addie's face didn't change, but I suddenly felt the hypocrisy in that familiar statement—the way it magnifies the other person's pain, and at the same time seals the speaker off from it.

"Oh, no—you can," she said. "Any mother can." She put a hand firmly on my arm and kept it there. "You think about things."

I nodded. I hoped Addie wasn't noticing my discomfort. Under normal circumstances, neither she nor I tended to touch other people in conversation.

"The sun, for example."

"The sun?"

"The sun aggravates the disease," Addie said. "When she was diagnosed, we might have convinced her to move back east for that reason."

"Her career was there, though."

Addie looked at me thoughtfully. "That's what Carl says. He's very reluctant to assign any blame—which is of course a lovely thing about him. His responses to things are always . . . healthy."

"I don't think anyone could have convinced Charlie to move somewhere she didn't want to move," I said, "even if it would've been better for her." I was trying to say something that would absolve Charlie's mother of any guilt she might be feeling, however misplaced. I stopped because I had the feeling that Addie had been through every what-if scenario already, and that she was hardly listening.

She removed her hand from my arm. "Perhaps not—in any case, we're concentrating on Simmi now. Charlie and I did talk about that before she died. Of all the friends she had, she said you were the one she hoped could become more a part of Simmi's life."

I felt almost ashamed of how happy this made me. It was like being asked by Addie to read at the memorial.

"Terrence mentioned that you got the children together."

"It went well, I think."

"It's so important that Simmi has people in her life who were purely her mother's friends."

I nodded. The kind of closeness I'd had with Charlie was something no friendship since had replicated. But the next thing she said startled me:

"Terrence is young, and someday there will be someone else."

"Not for a long time, I'm sure."

Addie went on, dismissing this. "The point is who that person will be. Simmi's only eight. You can imagine that, too, I think—knowing you won't get to choose who mothers your child." She looked as if she was going to continue speaking, then changed her mind. "You go get your boy. I know it's a trip across the river, but Carl and I would so love to see you—you and Jack. I'll be in touch."

I told her that we'd love to come, and Adelaide kissed me once on each cheek. Then she turned away from me, merging with the stream of pedestrians headed for Kendall Square. I went into the shop, where I saw Jack, his friend Miles, and Miles's mother, along with her three other children, seated at a wooden table next to the window.

"We saw you!" Jack said.

"I just ran into a friend."

"The lady from the funeral."

Miles's mother looked alarmed. Evelyn was at least five years younger than I was, carefully made up and dressed in the sort of stylish exercise clothing that is now worn outside the gym as well, her blond hair pulled into a neat ponytail. Somewhat unconventionally for our Cambridgeport public elementary school, she wore a large diamond cross around her neck.

"Jack and I went to the memorial of a friend of mine over the summer," I explained. "That was her mother."

"She was young, then." Evelyn's voice was sympathetic.

"My age—we were in college together." I found that I wanted to talk about it, but that when I did there was a nagging uneasiness. Was I turning it into conversation—what Arty would call a "topic"?

The children were ignoring us, playing with the paper wrappers from their straws. They bunched them up and then dribbled water on the compressed tubes, watching them expand.

"She had children?"

I thought that Evelyn's appearance—the wholesome prettiness coupled with the ostentatious display of faith hanging around her neck—belied the gentleness of her sympathy. It seemed real, without being at all intrusive.

"One."

"It's unbearable," Evelyn said.

To my dismay, I started to cry. I'd hardly cried at all about Charlie and it seemed absurd, here among the people enjoying pesto and arugula sandwiches, with someone I hardly knew. It was maybe the fact that we didn't know each other, and that she still bothered to go beyond ritualized sympathy, that moved me. Evelyn must've noticed that I was struggling to regain composure, because she looked away, wiping the face of the youngest child with a paper napkin.

"We have a group at church. Harper, be *still*. I joined after my mother passed. That was two years ago, and I'm still going."

"Thank you—but I'm not religious."

"It doesn't matter. It's congregational, very relaxed. We welcome everyone."

"Well, and Miles should come for a playdate at our house soon." I was thinking that it would have made Charlie laugh, how her death was getting me multiple invitations to events that took place in churches.

"I like Miles's house better," Jack said. "There are so many kids."

I found myself crying more. It was as if, once it had started, it could happen at any time. I decided one night to make shrimp for Jack and me; he had seen them at the fish counter and been curious. I cleaned them, then followed a recipe carefully—I didn't want to waste them—and as I put them in the pan I remembered a phone call from Charlie. This was when Jack was about two. She'd said she was coming up from New York, where she had gone to take a meeting about a possible feature, and I had bought groceries to cook for us. When she called to cancel, I told her about the shrimp in a joking way, but she knew I was annoyed.

"Shrimp!" she said. "Now I feel twice as bad."

Shrimp! I thought, and suddenly the pan and the stove and the window to the right of the stove blurred and my shoulders started to shake. Jack was drawing at the linoleum table, and he looked up, alarmed.

"I'm just sad," I told him, but it took several minutes for me to stop.

"I don't want shrimp," he said. "Yuck."

"We have to eat them!" I turned them angrily, one by one with a pair of tongs as the recipe dictated, suddenly frantic at the possibility of overcooking.

"Why?" Jack asked, his eyes wide and frightened.

Another day I was blow-drying my hair. I don't do this very often; I don't have the patience to do a good job, and I tend to get dizzy from holding my arms above my heart. This time I gave up, sat down on the side of the tub. I left the dryer on so that Jack wouldn't hear me. Charlie had been the one to show me how to separate my hair into top and bottom layers, and to do the bottom first, starting with the ends.

"You have this easy hair, and you can't even blow-dry it," she'd said to me once, the first time she'd seen me doing it. I said something to the effect that I thought it looked okay, and she had sighed and taken the brush and the dryer out of my hands.

"Me fixing your hair is like Einstein fixing my toilet."

"You're the Einstein of hair?"

"I have certain God-given abilities," Charlie said.

I thought that if I hadn't blown my hair dry, or decided to make shrimp, I would never have remembered those conversations. Was it just chance, what I got to keep of her?

I tell my students that cosmic background radiation, which is now giving us so much information about the origins of the universe, will be gone in a trillion years. The photons that we can see now with the help of satellites like the WMAP are slowly lengthening, and will eventually stretch beyond the wavelength of visible light. If there are astronomers still looking then, they'll have to rely on other sources of data—hypervelocity stars, for example.

The photo on my desk sometimes seems to be alive, and is sometimes very flat, as if there is a glare on the plastic frame.

20.

Something kept me from calling my sister to tell her the news about Neel. I waited until Amy called me with a worry of her own. My sister is always happy to listen to me talk about my work, but in practice we use our weekly phone sessions mostly to compare notes about our parents or our children. Sometimes she talks about Ben, and their arguments about money. If I go on a date, she always wants to hear about it. This is true of my married friends in general: they revel in the details of any romantic interaction, in the way people who once visited the place you're traveling enjoy comparing their memories with your contemporary snapshots.

When Amy called me I was in my office, but my postdoc Vasily had just left.

"I'm worried about Dad," Amy said. My sister was in the car with the children, as she always seemed to be—I could hear "Let It Go" in the background. "He seems anxious."

"Anxious?"

"He gets into a panic these days, especially about time. He's always worried about being late."

"What does Mom think?"

"That's the thing—I don't know if she even notices. It's almost like they don't hear each other anymore. Like Dad will say to Mom, 'The check engine light is on,' and she'll say, 'I'm taking Bess to buy sneakers.'"

Bess was my nine-year-old niece; her sister, Avery, was six.

"He says, 'Don't forget we're going to see *The Man Who Knew Infinity* at seven-forty. We should be out the door by seven-ten,' and Mom is like, 'Did you see, I got your new kind of yogurt?' It's like there's goodwill on both sides, but a complete lack of attention."

"Did you see it, too?"

"I'm the only one who sees it!"

"I mean the movie."

"Oh." My sister paused and told one of the children that they couldn't repeat the song again. "Yeah, on Netflix—I like Jeremy Irons, but the math was very vague."

"You wouldn't really expect them to go into detail."

"Maybe that's just the way it is after you've been married forty-five years."

I'd been waiting for an opportunity: "Neel is getting married," I said.

"Your Neel?"

"Yep. She's a heart surgeon."

"You just found out?"

"Arty told me—Neel told him first, which I still can't quite . . . anyway, I had to email him and ask. She's Indian, but her name is Roxy."

"Roxy?"

"She's from some kind of fancy family in Mumbai. She works for Doctors Without Borders."

"That's such an amazing organization," Amy said.

"Yes, I'm aware."

"Sorry."

"Don't you think it's weird he would've told Arty and not me?"

"Well, I mean . . ."

"I was pretty hurt, actually."

"How do you feel now?"

I was thinking about how I felt, trying to get it right, but Amy must have mistaken this analysis for emotion.

"Like someone's cutting your heart out with a scalpel?"

"No."

"That was a joke."

"They're going to live here. He's coming back to MIT."

"Oh god," Amy said. "In your department?"

"Not teaching—but yeah."

Amy hesitated. "What's she going to do?"

"She'll be at the Brigham. And also traveling the world to aid people in need, I guess."

I could hear the specific sound of L.A. traffic in the background, both louder and more resigned than the Boston variety.

"You didn't say how you felt," Amy said.

"Excited."

"Excited?"

"Like something's about to happen." There was a pause, some static in our connection.

"You worry me," Amy said.

21.

At 9:30 on Saturday morning, the bell rang. It was about an hour before we had to leave for soccer, but Jack was already wearing his shiny yellow uniform, his black knee socks, and shin guards. I was upstairs and I called to him that he could answer the door.

"Hey, little man. You got a game?"

I recognized Terrence's voice, but I was still getting dressed. Who showed up unannounced on a Saturday morning? I hadn't done the laundry yet, and I ended up in a pair of not-totally-clean jeans and a plaid shirt. I was hoping that this might looked relaxed in a Hollywood kind of way, rather than just sloppy.

"Hey," I said, coming down the stairs. "Welcome."

"Sorry," Terrence said. "We were right in the neighborhood, and Simmi wanted to see if you were home." Terrence didn't look much better prepared for company than I was. He hadn't shaved, and the beard coming in had a lot of gray in it. The hair on his head was growing back dark and even, though; it made me think that cutting off the dreads had been a gesture of mourning rather than a defense against balding. There was a purple shadow at the corner of each eye, and he looked as if he'd lost weight, even since the last time we'd seen him.

Simmi, on the other hand, was full of energy. "Let's go play," she encouraged Jack, and started immediately up the stairs. Jack looked at me.

"Jack's room is down here, honey."

Simmi seemed as if she was going to argue, and I thought of what Amy had said. If Jack had told her about seeing Charlie in my office, it would explain Simmi's eagerness—not only to play upstairs, but to be in our house at all. Today she was wearing navy-blue joggers with a sparkly tuxedo stripe, red Converse high-tops, and a T-shirt that read *J'aime Paris*. She'd stopped midway up the stairs, her feet on two different steps, looking down at her father and me.

"I'm sorry," I said. "But it's a mess up there—you'd better stay downstairs." Simmi descended reluctantly, and followed Jack into his room. I offered Terrence coffee.

"I just had one."

He seemed as if he'd had several. He stood in the open entrance to our small living room, hands in his pockets, bouncing slightly on his toes. His clothes, from the thin blue surf sweatshirt—the style self-consciously retro, the logo in Japanese—to his gray suede sneakers, seemed to come from another time, when he had had the leisure to pay attention to them.

"You decided to stay for the school year," I said.

"The semester, at least."

"That's good."

"We were actually just at an open house, on Trowbridge. That's why we came over here this morning."

I tried not to look too surprised. Addie hadn't mentioned anything about Terrence and Simmi moving out.

"You're not staying in Brookline?"

"No."

I waited, but no other information was forthcoming. I thought I should use this opening to bring up what Jack may or may not have said to his daughter.

"I think Jack may have been a little confused about the memorial. Because he didn't really know Charlie. She was here once when he was four, but that was the last time. I'm not sure he remembers." When I'm nervous, I tend to circle around a subject. "He recognized the photo on the invitation, though."

Terrence nodded, but he looked distracted. "What's up with the people downstairs?"

"What?"

"In the apartment—are they friends of yours?"

"No—I mean, not from before. I like them well enough. They've lived there since I bought this place."

"Oh, okay."

"Why?"

"I was just thinking about the apartment."

I looked at Terrence. "You mean . . . for you and Simmi?"

"But it sounds like they're dug in, so—"

Addie had said she hoped I would be involved, and I couldn't help wondering if this was her idea. Charlie used to say that it had been a mistake for her to choose Harvard, that she should've gone farther from home, where her mother would be less able to meddle in her life. At the time I'd thought that was a little unfair to Addie—who clearly did everything she did for Charlie out of love—but I had to admit that sending Terrence and Simmi to ask about the apartment qualified as meddling. At the same time it flattered me that Terrence would entertain the idea. Did he really think we should live in the same house?

I waited for him to explain, but instead he went to the window, looked out at the street in an appraising way.

"Addie . . . ," he began.

I waited, but he didn't continue. "I ran into her, actually."

"Where was that?" Terrence turned from the window to look at me, but there was nothing accusatory about his tone or his expression. It was true that he looked very tired, but the stubble that extended down his sideburns to his beard, and shadowed his upper lip, gave him a rougher, more grown-up kind of beauty than he'd had in the photos Charlie used to post of him—with his stylish hair and washboard stomach, looking like an advertisement for his brother's store. Now he was handsome in a way that was more approachable; I thought later that might have been what made me speak without thinking:

"She said she was seeing her lawyer downtown."

I knew it was a mistake as soon as I'd said it.

Terrence expelled air through his teeth. "And I could've told her what he was going to say for nothing. It's technically still illegal, yeah, but it's on the fucking ballot. California's going to go for aid-in-dying next month, just like Washington and Oregon."

I offered Terrence a chair—he had perched on the window ledge—but he shook his head impatiently. In contrast to the last time he'd been in my house, when he was measured and a bit aloof, he now seemed eager to talk, albeit in a manic way. I'd seen my students in the same state, usually from lack of sleep.

"If she thinks her daughter wouldn't have chosen it on her own, then maybe she didn't know her as well as she thought she did."

"She thinks you were—influencing Charlie?"

"I was the one who kept her from doing it, for months!" Terrence glanced toward the hallway that led to Jack's room, then lowered his voice: "It's against everything—I mean, that's not how I was raised—okay? My mom's full-on Irish-Catholic. But you know Charlie. Not even God's going to get in her way."

"Yeah."

"And that's the funny thing, right? Because that's her mom all over. They're *exactly alike.* Addie's all about the plans she made and the people she hired, but she's not going to sit there and talk about pain. And if you don't see it—if you don't actually sit there with her, you know, the eightieth time she tells Simmi that no, she can't come watch gymnastics, or Daddy better have lunch with you, because Mama has to stay in bed, again—well then it's hard to totally get what's happening."

"I never saw her like that."

"Well, it sucks."

"I can imagine."

Terrence was nodding madly. "Even you can imagine. Anyone with the empathy of a squirrel—"

I felt a little offended, but Terrence seemed barely to register my presence. "Not Addie, though. She's like, 'Oh my god, my daughter's death didn't go according to plan. It must be because of this trash she married.'"

"But why would you—"

"Yeah," he said. "Yeah, exactly. What possible motivation do I have? It actually would have been good for Simmi, I think, having her grandparents there when it happened. But I was just following orders, and Charlie said her parents wouldn't have let her do it the way she wanted. And she was right about that."

He paused and looked to see whether I was following. "You know they made us get a prenup?"

"No."

"I'd never even heard of that—didn't know what it was. But Charlie was getting those staff writing jobs, show after show, at least before she got sick. There was no reason to think she wasn't going all the way, you know? An EP credit, then her own show. Everybody loved her out there."

"Addie made you get the prenup?"

Terrence smiled. "That's what you'd think, right? But it was him—Carl. He didn't grow up with all this stuff—the fancy house, the fancy school. He grew up more like me, not that he'd ever admit it."

I didn't contradict Terrence, but I'd never known Carl to conceal anything about his background. If anything, he used to play up his origins as a scholarship kid, especially if I mentioned my work-study jobs. He would tease his own daughter for being spoiled—but gently, with some pride. Addie's family was part of a long-standing Philadelphia elite, but it was Carl's practice, and his television work, that had paid for Harvard.

"Like they thought I'd try to *steal* from her." Terrence shook his head, disgusted. Then, more quietly: "Like it wasn't going to last."

"Yeah."

"Charlie said she wouldn't sign the prenup—*I* was the one who finally convinced her. I didn't want them to think I'd talked her out of it."

"I understand."

"So now the only thing we own in common is the house. She insisted on that. The rest's in trust for Simmi—not that it's so much. Charlie liked to spend what she earned."

"I'm sure Carl and Addie know that."

"Okay," Terrence said. "But then why's she seeing a lawyer?"

"I don't know."

Terrence got up and started toward Jack's room. Then he seemed to reconsider, turned back to me. "That's why I have to get out of there."

"But you wouldn't want this apartment."

"What's wrong with it?"

"No, I mean—it's nice. But it's even smaller than this one. And compared to your house in Santa Monica—"

"We haven't sold the house yet," Terrence said shortly. "I don't have a ton of cash. And I won't take anything from them, beyond the tuition. It was Addie who suggested this."

Terrence seemed to soften a little, and I thought that my guess had been right.

"She remembered that you had a tenant—it was actually the first thing that we've all been able to agree on. Simmi loves the idea."

I also had a guess about why Simmi loved the idea, but I couldn't say so. I didn't want to suggest that my son, or our household, was psychologically or emotionally unstable, since I thought that was exactly what Terrence was trying to escape; maybe he had even considered that his in-laws' grief was compounding his and Simmi's own. And if I were going to keep Jack's fantasy about the ghost to myself, it occurred to me that I should do the same with the new, scientifically oriented messages from Charlie's phone. It was my role as a mother—and maybe even as a scientist—to help keep everyone's feet firmly planted on the ground.

I thought of them in the apartment downstairs. I thought of the kids running up and down to visit each other, of spontaneous trips to the park or to a movie. I thought of the practical advantages, of being able to call Terrence—who seemed to be working a very flexible schedule—if I was going to be twenty minutes late for the sitter, and of being able to take care of Simmi in turn. And I thought of Charlie. For the last several years—maybe since that visit when Jack was four—I'd wondered whether she put any stock in our friendship; eerie messages aside, now both Addie's and Terrence's behavior gave me hope that she had.

"Their lease is up in December. I haven't talked to them, but Andrea's pregnant again—they might be planning to move." I thought I had to say something about money. I was doing fine financially, but I needed the income from the apartment to keep up with the mortgage payments on the house. "I wish I didn't need to rent it. I mean, I wish I could just offer it to you."

Terrence looked a little offended. "I wouldn't do that. And our house in L.A. is going to sell. We'll want something permanent again, eventually, but it'll be simpler. I just need an interim option, and I'd rather not explain the whole situation to someone, again. Also, it's got to be flexible. I mean, we wouldn't run out on you. But I'd have to be able to leave if it's not working."

He was standing in the framed opening between my living room and the hallway that led to Jack's bedroom. I thought of seeing Terrence with the baby, seven years ago in Los Angeles, and it was as if time had skipped from that moment to this present one. I felt Charlie's presence, as if we were both looking at this scene and wondering at it.

"I'll just talk to my tenants," I said. "See what they're thinking."

"But you'd be okay with it?" His tone was hopeful, if still a little guarded. He laced his fingers together and stretched them so his palms faced outward.

I thought that it wasn't so crazy. What had he called it? An "interim option"—two people brought together by a tragedy, helping each other out.

"We'd love it," I said. "Jack would love it." I realized it was 10:30. "I have to take him to soccer, but I can talk to them as soon as we get back. I can probably let you know tonight."

"Great," Terrence said, with feeling. "That's great."

22.

The game went well for Jack. He scored one goal and assisted twice. When he got into the car afterward, his cheeks were flushed; his skin blushes easily, like mine. He had an orange wedged between his lips and his tongue, his teeth in the weedy flesh. I rarely allow him to sit in the front seat, but I let it go for once.

"Nice job out there."

"Mmph."

I kissed his head before pushing the button to start the car; his hair was damp, pieces of it sticking to his forehead, and his whole body had a grassy, sour smell. "The goal was terrific, but the way you passed it to Leo was even better. You were using your head."

"Mmph?"

"I mean, that was good thinking. I know you're not allowed to head the ball."

I didn't play team sports as a child, although I ran track in high school. In college I switched to long runs along the river, with a friend or on my own, because it was easier to fit into my schedule. My parents were always proud of my academic success; what was clearly the most important thing to them had by that time become so for me. But when I chose Jack's father, I told myself that I was looking for something different. I wanted someone with the potential to be satisfied—to be happy. And I see that in Jack, especially when he's building something, or coming off the soccer field—the pure delight in being himself in the world.

Jack took the orange out of his mouth. "Will they be there when we get home?"

"Who?"

"Simmi and her dad."

"Oh—no. Of course not."

"Because Simmi said they might live downstairs."

I'm careful not to overshare with Jack, and I thought Terrence might need some practice in this area. I could imagine how in his situation, on the other hand, it would be tempting to make Simmi his confidante. There could be nothing worse than his daughter siding with her grandparents against him.

"Günter and Andrea live there," I told Jack. "I don't think they're leaving."

"But if?"

"Would you want Terrence and Simmi to move in downstairs?"

"Yes!"

"How come?"

Jack looked at me as if I were an idiot. "Because I *like* them."

I noted that he'd said "them," rather than "her"; normally he was indifferent to adults he didn't know. "Well, that's good to know."

"Except you have to tell her she's wrong."

"Simmi? She's wrong about what?"

"She says"—Jack rolled his eyes in a way I'm afraid he's learned from me—"that there's something called a 'say'-something. I don't know what you say. 'Aunts,' I think. You build a machine, and then you say it—and then you can talk to dead people."

"You say 'aunts'?"

Jack looked embarrassed, as if I might attribute these ludicrous ideas to him. "I told her that's not what real scientists do."

I had a moment of clarity. "Are you talking about a séance?"

"Yes!"

"Oh. Um, yeah—you're right. We don't do that." It was easier to keep a straight face because I was driving. Some of Jack's worst tantrums occur when he thinks I'm making fun of him.

"I told her that." He rolled down a knee-high sock and peeled off the Velcro to remove the shin guard. "She said you use a machine. She's in third grade."

"Well, actually—there were some physicists who built a machine like that."

"Really?" He sounded distraught.

"At Berkeley in the seventies. They called it the metaphase typewriter—it didn't work, though."

Jack cheered up: "You have to tell her that."

"Well, but if that idea makes her feel better, for now—then maybe it's okay?"

"But it's *wrong*. You can only talk to people who are alive."

"That's what I think, too."

"Is there a machine for talking to people who are alive?"

I did laugh then. "The phone?"

"Or the internet."

"Right."

"Even if they're in China."

"Yep."

We pulled into our driveway just as Andrea was letting herself in, her stomach protruding from an unzipped jacket. She looked up and waved; I lifted my hand, but I felt a nagging worry. Andrea and Günter had never said anything to me about moving once they had a second child; as far as I knew, they put any extra cash they had into their films. I thought it was completely possible that they might sacrifice space and comfort for their growing family to filmic space for the Wampanoag, to whom they felt an almost religious devotion.

"Even if you don't know *where* they are," Jack said, "you can find them."

23.

Although its name sounds absurd, Berkeley's Fundamental Fysiks Group was composed of real scientists. After the Second World

War, government funding poured into physics departments all over the country, nuclear and solid-state physics most of all. Graduate programs were suddenly oversubscribed, and there was no time to sit around dreaming up exotic or speculative ideas. The way that Einstein and his circle had made their extraordinary advances, meeting at cafés or in one another's homes, playing music together and excitedly debating their vexing *gedanken* experiments, seemed more like a romantic movie than the real, historical past. Musical soirees and European coffeehouses were replaced by giant American lecture halls. The order of the day, as my colleague David Kaiser writes in his history of the Fundamental Fysiks Group, was "shut up and calculate," Richard Feynman's famous phrase to suggest that rigorous mathematical labor—not philosophy—was the path to understanding the quantum world.

The Fundamental Fysiks Group was a casual gathering of ten scientists who met once a week to discuss those more philosophical ideas, beginning in 1975 in Berkeley. Kaiser suggests that the FFG's open-mindedness toward parapsychology and ghosts, combined with their minor celebrity as members of the counterculture, helped to keep quantum entanglement—the "spooky action" between distant particles that Einstein refused to countenance—on the map. It turned out that spooky action, at least, was right: pairs of subatomic particles like electrons can be "entangled" in such a way that observing one of them instantly influences the other, even after they've moved far apart. The observer is important because these quantum particles exist as probabilities; they don't have a fixed position or momentum until a scientist pins one down by measuring it. By measuring one, she instantly influences the other, simply because the pair of them once interacted with each other.

The uncertainty that is the defining feature of the quantum realm—the role of chance in the behavior of tiny particles of matter—made sense to scientists in the seventies. Randomness seemed compatible with events in the larger world. With far-fetched experiments like the metaphase typewriter, the members of the FFG hoped to push the idea of entanglement even further, to elucidate human consciousness. Instead, entrepreneurs have used entanglement to devise encryption systems for financial and other data. The fact that entanglement today is working out for banking and information technology rather than for parapsychology must disappoint those among the group's members who are still living.

A few days after our conversation in the car, Jack asked me to tell him about the scientists who had tried to invent a machine to talk to ghosts. I explained that an American physicist named Nick Herbert, along with a group of friends, hoped to be able to reach the spirits of the dead, in particular Harry Houdini. I told him that people had been designing instruments for this purpose throughout human history, but that this had been the only attempt I knew of by real scientists. First, Herbert had obtained a sample of thallium. He chose that element because it was a readily available radioactive material—and maybe also because it sits right between mercury and lead on the periodic table, elements associated with alchemy. Herbert and his friends were fascinated by the ideas of Evan Harris Walker, a physicist and parapsychologist, who believed that the brain is actually a quantum mechanical system. Walker thought that leftover human consciousness—what you might colloquially call a "soul"—persists after a person dies, and sometimes inhabits a living body. He speculated that the soul could dictate human behavior quantum mechanically, just as one entangled particle can influence another from a distance. The Fundamental Fysiks Group considered it unethical to try their consciousness experiments on human subjects, and so they invented a machine, through which those dead souls might be tempted to speak to the living.

Jack wasn't interested in any of this history, of course. He just wanted to know how the machine was supposed to work. I explained, without much hope of him understanding, that thallium is a radioactive element, which means that it can decay. When that happens, it releases tiny, energetic particles. We call radioactivity a typical quantum event because it's uncertain—you can't predict exactly when this energy will be released, or in what form. You can only give an average interval between the decay of individual thallium atoms. Herbert hooked his thallium sample up to a Geiger counter, and the Geiger counter to a teletype machine. (How my father would have loved tinkering with the metaphase typewriter, if he'd been in Berkeley in the seventies.) If the thallium atoms decayed at the average rate for that element, as measured by the Geiger counter, the teletype machine printed one of the most common letters in English—*E* or *S*. When the rate departed from that average, a statistically rarer letter, like *J* or *U*, was printed. I explained to Jack that the FFG invented this complicated machine mostly for fun, and that the word "metaphase" is actually meaningless in physics. The idea was that the scientists might induce the dead to enter the machine and spell out messages to the living: they proposed to contact a recently deceased colleague, who'd known the inner workings of the experiment. It was never clear to me why, if the dead could enter human minds and influence behavior, they wouldn't simply encourage a pair of hands to type out a message on an ordinary typewriter—but I also have to admit that the Fundamental Fysicists were probably enjoying themselves a lot more than we do in our symposia and colloquia today.

Jack and I looked at an FFG member's website, and I showed him a sentence the metaphase typewriter had created:

WIRN OF ACERIONINE SE IND BE B WHAD ATHE OROVESSOUNDRO

He laughed, because there's nothing so amusing to children as the failures of adults, and even a second grader could see that the "words" were nonsense.

"The machine printed a common letter when the thallium released particles at a normal rate, and an uncommon one when the rate was more unusual. It worked the way it was supposed to," I told him. "It's just that there aren't any ghosts floating around out there, trying to talk to scientists." I said this on purpose, to clear up any confusion that might have been brought on by Charlie's death, and Jack really seemed to understand.

He nodded, and said, "Right."

I talked to Andrea, and as I'd guessed the last time I'd seen her, she and Günter had no plans to leave the apartment. I was afraid Terrence would be even less inclined to seek me out once I told him, but in fact the opposite was true. He'd texted right back that it wasn't a problem—he was looking around and would certainly find something soon. We made plans to get the kids together after school, and then we began texting about them, first in brief, and soon at greater length. He was one of those people who put each thought in a different bubble, and sometimes there were six or seven of them chiming into my phone at the same time. I always wrote back, always with the same feeling of eagerness, a feeling that I had no desire to examine, or to discuss with my sister.

I was scrambling a little that semester, between the Relativity seminar and a Physics II survey I was teaching for undergraduates. I had my postdocs and my graduate students to advise, including two who were close to completing their theses, and I'd been invited to speak at a conference outside Vienna just after Christmas. The physics institute at Pöllau wanted me to talk about my second book, *Into the Singularity*, which was being reissued, an invitation the German publisher encouraged me to accept. It occurred to me that going to the conference in January would preclude another big trip in February—to India, where Neel was getting married.

I told Vincenzo Goia, my colleague down the hall, that I was going to Pöllau, and that I could stop in at CERN on the way home, which would be useful for our current project: a paper about exploring electroweak symmetries in the Large Hadron Collider. It shouldn't have been an especially difficult paper to write, but Vincenzo and I often disagree about language. My colleague tends to sprinkle his written work not only with Italian, but with French and German words as well, possibly to impress the postdocs with the (admittedly impressive) number of European languages he speaks fluently. Vincenzo thinks of himself as an especially stylish writer of physics papers; if there is anything that writing the trade books has taught me, it's that the words we choose have real consequences for the version of reality that we're describing, and that it's almost always best to go with the simplest possible option. According to Vincenzo, this preference is symptomatic of a certain American obstinacy on my part.

I shouldn't have been thinking of anything but the paper and my academic responsibilities, but the reissue of *Into the Singularity* activated a part of my brain that had been dormant for a while. I'd made a kind of promise to myself when I had Jack that I would put aside writing for a lay audience, at least until he was in high school. I would be on sabbatical in the spring, though, and it didn't seem worth rearranging our life in order to travel somewhere for just a couple of months. I thought I could use those months instead to start work on a new book: an astrophysical history of precious metals. I would be betting on the idea that LIGO would record not only the gravitational waves from colliding black holes, but from pairs of neutron stars, exploding in what is called a kilonova. The most massive elements in the universe are created in kilonova explosions; without them, nothing heavier than iron would exist on our planet.

I thought I would call the book *Kilonova: A Cosmic History.* I hoped the subject would have an element of human interest, in the sense that the metals created in a kilonova explosion—gold, silver, platinum, and uranium—are the most precious materials on Earth. (The gold in any wedding band, for example, came from a long-ago stellar explosion, millions of light years from Earth.) The fact that their cosmic infrequency is what makes them valuable, and even beautiful, I thought added a philosophical element to the science. I thought I could point out an irony as well: that these explosions create not only human wealth, but also the most powerful weapons we use to fight for it.

This was in October, and like everyone, I'd heard the rumors about what was going on at LIGO. The first clue was in Neel's email—*I have something else to discuss with you,* he had said—and when I saw the tweet from Bob Wertheim at the University of Colorado, I knew. Everyone was furious at Wertheim because the scientists on the project were taking such dramatic measures to keep the detection quiet until they could be sure. LIGO had had several false alarms in the past, but all of the information that was leaking out of the collaboration suggested that this was the real thing.

If the rumors were true, LIGO's first detection of a gravitational wave had happened even before the billion-dollar experiment had officially started, during one of the final test runs. Ten milliseconds apart, the two interferometers had recorded a major gravitational wave signal. All the work the scientists were doing was to confirm the signal as the first record of a gravitational wave, as well as the first direct evidence that black holes actually collide in space. A confirmed signal would surpass even the Higgs discovery, and the three architects of the project would almost certainly win a Nobel Prize.

I couldn't pretend that a book about kilonova explosions wasn't motivated at least in part by my excitement about LIGO; just like Arty's student Jason, I wanted in on the action. I knew I would have to rely on Neel for some of the inside information—although, when I'd first conceived of the idea, I'd never imagined that we would do more than exchange a few emails about it. I'd assumed that Neel would remain at Caltech, working on an exciting project that hadn't yet come to fruition. Instead, Neel would be arriving in the department of the university where I occupied a chair just as the LIGO team had its moment in the international spotlight. I was envious in a way I knew Neel hadn't been when I'd been awarded the Blumhagen professorship—he had always preferred pure research to teaching—or when my second book made the *New York Times* best-seller list. Like most of my colleagues, Neel considers writing about physics for non-physicists too boring to contemplate.

If we hadn't been communicating about his engagement, I would have called Neel as soon as I heard the first rumors. The science was exciting enough that I wouldn't have let professional rivalry get in the way under any other circumstances. It even occurred to me that Neel might be offended that he hadn't heard from me. The fact that it wasn't official, and that everyone at LIGO was trying their best not to spread information before they actually published their results, gave me an alibi, but it wasn't the reason for my silence. He would arrive in Cambridge just before the holidays, with Roxy, and I would let him tell me then.

24.

Jack and I went trick-or-treating with my friend Vicky, whose son Dylan is on Jack's soccer team. Halloween is a big deal in our neighborhood, and by the time we got home, Jack had substantial loot. I made him a grilled cheese to soak up some of the sugar, and then we sat on the blue rug in the living room while he sorted it into piles by color.

"Dylan said he's going to wear his costume every day now."

"He was the Flash, right?"

Jack nodded. "In case there are bad guys."

"I don't think there will be bad guys."

"But bad guys are real."

"Well, yeah—I mean, there are bad people out there. They don't turn into giant lizards, or climb up the sides of buildings like they do in your comic books."

Jack had stopped listening. "Who started Halloween?"

"I think it was the Irish."

"Why?"

I hesitated for a moment, thinking how to put it. "They believed in—spirits back then, and so people chose a night to go out in costumes and scare them away."

"You mean, ghosts?"

"Right."

Jack was examining a package of gummy worms. He looked up in surprise. "Grown-ups did?"

"I think so."

"But not anymore."

"That's right," I said. I thought this was mostly true, at least among the grown-ups I knew.

"Then why—"

"Have you heard of wishful thinking?"

Jack shook his head.

"People want to believe in ghosts because they miss people after they die. They're something we imagine to make us feel better."

Jack had taken off his hood, but he was still wearing the black ninja costume. He traced the curved plastic blade of the sword on the rug next to him. "What's your favorite candy?"

"Peanut butter cups."

"Not Milky Way?"

"I like the name of that one, but you know peanut butter's my favorite."

Jack examined his orange pile. I could see him counting. Then he carefully pushed a peanut butter cup across the rug.

"Hey, thanks."

He nodded and chose one for himself. There was a pause, in which I thought I was doing a good job hiding what were suddenly strong feelings. Jack peeled off the wrapper, a little at a time.

"Are you going to be sad forever?" he said.

. . .

It was several weeks before we saw Terrence and Simmi again. At MIT the campus had the frantic energy typical of November, as if everyone, students and faculty, were competing to see who was the busiest, who had the most to get done before the holidays. It wasn't yet truly cold, but wind coming off the river made you glad for the warmth of the labs and lecture halls, especially as the afternoons bled earlier and earlier into night.

On one of those short fall afternoons I was sitting in my office when I got another message.

Are you writing a book?

It felt eerie, but it was three o'clock on a Friday, and so it was reasonable to guess that I'd be at work. I tried not to overthink my response. The point was to keep a channel of communication open:

I'm busy these days with my students, and with a paper I'm co-authoring, but I do have an idea for another book. Not sure if you read the earlier ones? Are you interested in physics?

Along with the article on scientists to watch, these messages seemed to confirm that their author was someone interested in me specifically, perhaps someone who'd read my books. If that were true, it only reinforced my instinct not to upset Terrence further by telling him about the messages—at least not yet. Under these circumstances, I would be much better at convincing the thief to return the device than Terrence would, or indeed even than the police. What police department was going to spend time on mysterious (but ultimately nonthreatening) messages sent from a phone stolen in another state?

I imagined handing Charlie's phone to Terrence. I thought I could see the look of gratitude and relief on his face. I imagined myself telling him that I hadn't looked at any of its contents— although it did occur to me that I now knew the passcode. If I somehow were to recover it, would I have the discipline not to invade Charlie's privacy? What were the rules regarding the privacy of the dead?

The phone was silent for about twenty minutes. When it pinged again, I reached for it eagerly—but this time it was Chendong, asking if she could stop by to talk about figure 2 in the electroweak symmetries paper. I agreed, trying to suppress my disappointment. It struck me that I was anticipating messages from "Charlie" the way I did when I met a new person-of-interest: my ordinary life buzzed with possibility every time I looked at my phone. I put it away and looked purposely out my window, but already on that dark afternoon it had the quality of a blank screen, reflecting my blurred image back at me.

25.

Chendong and I got embroiled in the paper until just before five, when it was time for me to leave to get Jack from aftercare. He was in a buoyant mood because Terrence and Simmi were coming over. I'd invited them for dinner, but Terrence had insisted on bringing it; he'd said that he missed cooking at his in-laws', and wanted to make a lamb stew. They arrived at six, Simmi in a new silver parka, preparation for her first Boston winter. Terrence's only concessions to the fall weather were a cap with the now-familiar cursive Z on it, and a lightweight down vest he was wearing over his T-shirt. He was carrying bags from Whole Foods.

I have an aversion to fancy supermarkets, not for any of the valid reasons people dislike them—the expense, the hypocrisy of consumerism dressed up as environmentalism, the pretense that food is art—but because they make me feel inadequate as a mother. I was never going to make homemade lamb stew for Jack. Charlie had been a good cook, of a different kind than her husband. She didn't like recipes, but could look in an empty refrigerator and whip up something elegant—frittata, or salade niçoise.

Terrence had bought two full bags of ingredients, perhaps because he didn't trust me to have anything on hand. He went straight to the kitchen, while the children went to Jack's room, and so I was able to sit in the living room and finish an email to Chendong. Then I started filling out paperwork related to the conference in Pöllau. Soon wonderful smells began coming from the kitchen.

The children didn't come out when Terrence called that the stew was ready, and so I said I would get them. The door to Jack's room was shut, and when I went in, I saw that none of the toys had been pulled out. I called again, but the bathroom door was open; there was nowhere they could be hiding.

Terrence had come into the living room. "Where are they?"

"I'll go up and check." He followed, and I was conscious of his footfalls on the steps behind me. It had been a while since I'd brought a man upstairs, and I was glad that I'd made the bed that morning. I looked in the office first, since that's where they'd gone the last time, but it was empty. Terrence and I went into my bedroom, where there was a light behind the closed door. An unidentifiable clicking sound was coming from inside.

"What are you guys doing in there?" Terrence asked, with strained cheerfulness.

I have a walk-in closet, an addition of the previous owners, where plastic shelving units from the hardware store take up most of the space. These are crowded with old journals, years of tax returns, Jack's artwork, medical records—less organized than stacked into piles to be dealt with later. Seated on the floor next to this jumble were both children, seemingly uninjured and wearing all of their clothing. These happy circumstances didn't seem to alleviate Terrence's worries the way they did mine.

They looked up, equally guilty but wearing different expressions: Jack embarrassed, Simmi sullen and defiant. Maybe she was nervous about having disobeyed my instructions about staying downstairs. On the floor between them was an extensive assemblage of supplies: a shoebox, black and red wires from Jack's Snap Circuits kit (which they'd successfully connected, illuminating a red light that they'd fed through the side of the box), and the metronome that normally sat beside the keyboard in Jack's room. For some reason, Simmi was holding two of our plastic drinking cups in her lap.

"Simmi?" Terrence asked. "What are you doing?"

To my surprise, it was Jack who answered first. "Science," he said shortly, not looking at Simmi's father. Simmi hugged the cups to her chest, concealing their contents with her hands.

"This is Helen's bedroom," Terrence said. "She asked you to play downstairs."

"It's okay," I said quickly.

"We're not *playing.*" Simmi's voice had a disobedient edge to it, the way Jack's sometimes does when he knows he has done something wrong and is trying to cover it up.

Terrence sounded more exhausted than stern: "You do not talk to me that way."

This is something I've said to Jack myself, but I find that it doesn't work—since it's clear to both parties that the child has just done what the parent insists he or she does not do. Terrence looked from one child to the other. Jack seemed to waver, but Simmi glared at him, and he was silent.

"Can you explain?" I said, kneeling down. "What's all this?"

This was all Jack needed. "It's a metaphase typewriter," he said eagerly. "We set up the circuit here—see—and here's the thallium—" He turned the box gently, so that I could see. It was impossible that the children could've obtained a radioactive poison like thallium, but the dirty clay-like lump was convincing enough to make my pulse speed up. "Jack—what is that?"

"Our radioactive source," Jack said, but he sounded uncertain.

"But what is it really?"

"Surf wax," Simmi said, and I laughed a little in relief. "It was in my backpack." She looked at her father. "We used to go to the beach a lot after school."

"But it worked," Jack said, attempting to change the subject, as I'd noticed he often did when Simmi talked about her life in L.A.

"Okay," I said. "You guys figured out that surf wax conducts electricity. So what does the light do?"

"Nothing," Jack admitted. "That's just to show that we're doing a science run."

"Is a 'science run' a real thing?" Simmi asked me.

"It's when a machine is collecting information," I said. "Data."

"See," Jack said, gaining confidence. "And then we turn on the metronome."

I had bought the metronome with the electronic keyboard in an ill-fated attempt at piano lessons in kindergarten. Physicists tend to be musical (Neel can pick out anything on the guitar, and Arty is a proficient cellist), and I've always regretted my lack of ability in this area. I had hoped that his donor's genes might predispose Jack toward music, but he had demonstrated very little interest.

On the other hand, it was nice that he was using the metronome for something.

"When the metronome clicks, Simmi—"

"Shut up," Simmi said.

Jack stopped, surprised.

"Simmi," Terrence said. "You can't talk to your friends like that. I think it's time for us to go."

"Fine," Simmi said. "I don't care."

Jack made a small sound of protest, but didn't say anything. Simmi unfolded her crossed legs.

"But first you'll help clean up. And apologize to Helen and Jack."

"Sorry."

"It's okay. I can take those for you." I leaned forward to collect the cups, but Simmi hugged them toward her chest, one in each arm, as if they were dolls. Terrence seemed to notice them for the first time.

"What's in there?"

Simmi's hair was twisted into two knots on either side of her head, making her look younger than usual. "Just some toys and stuff," she said.

"Give them here," Terrence said, as if he didn't believe her. Slowly, Simmi obeyed.

Terrence took the cups carefully. Maybe he thought the children were actually playing with dangerous materials. His expression when he looked inside was perplexed.

"Scrabble?"

"See," Simmi said, crossing her arms over her chest. "It's nothing."

But Jack couldn't keep himself from explaining: "When the metronome clicks, Simmi throws a letter out of the cup. Then we use the letters to spell the words."

Suddenly, I understood. The Scrabble tiles replaced the teletype machine in the metaphase typewriter. The metronome was the Geiger counter. This was the part that impressed me, because the children had understood the concept of measuring intervals between events—if not the necessity for radioactive events to happen at uneven intervals, in contrast to the clicks of a metronome.

"What words did you get so far?" I asked the children.

"Nothing," Simmi said. "It's stupid."

"Maybe it's just the beginning," Jack suggested.

Simmi looked scornful. *"Hrik fax?"*

"A fax is a thing," Jack pointed out.

"Not anymore."

Terrence laughed. He seemed to have mellowed a little, given that the kids weren't misbehaving in any obvious way. I began to hope that we could salvage dinner, proceed toward the lamb stew as if nothing had happened.

"But what does it do?" Terrence asked.

"You can talk to people who aren't here," Jack began. I gave him a sharp look—but if anything, all this was my fault. If I'd spoken to him as soon as I understood that he might be talking to Simmi about seeing her mother's ghost, we could have avoided this moment.

"What people?" Terrence asked.

Jack looked at me helplessly. Even he knew better than to tell Terrence whom they had been trying to contact.

"There was a little confusion," I began.

Simmi was looking out the window. It was already dark, and all you could see was the street lamp haloed against the black trees outside my window. The look on her face could have been mistaken for boredom, if she hadn't been holding herself so perfectly still. Terrence watched her with a concerned expression.

"It's just a game, okay?" she said suddenly. "We didn't think it would actually work. Or at least *I* didn't."

"Me neither," Jack said quickly. "Because we didn't have real thallium."

"It wouldn't work anyway," Simmi said. "Obviously."

Jack looked confused. "Then why did you say we might be able to talk to your mom?"

Terrence made a short sound, a strangled groan. Simmi looked at him, frightened, then turned back to Jack. "I *didn't*," she said fiercely. "I was just doing it because there's nothing to do here. All we do is sit around inside, playing with Legos. I want to go *home*."

"Okay, Sims," Terrence said. "Okay." He put an arm around her and she looked as if she would break free; then she made a sudden move and put her face against his chest. He wrapped both arms around her. She wasn't audibly crying but her small body shook; he bent his head over hers, and for a moment I saw them again the way they'd been at the memorial—in the midst of a group of mourners, but also alone. The difference in their sizes seemed to emphasize her suffering as well as his ability to comfort her. Jack stood in the lit closet doorway, watching them with an unreadable expression.

Terrence straightened up and gave me a questioning look. I shook my head, as if I were just as perplexed as he was. It struck me later that it is possible to lie without saying anything at all.

"Maybe we're all hungry," I suggested. "We could go down and eat—"

"I'm not hungry," Simmi said immediately.

"I think we should probably just head out," said Terrence.

"But the stew—"

"Don't worry about it. Freeze what's left and you'll have another meal." He didn't sound angry, but he wouldn't meet my eyes. The only light was from the closet and the street. Terrence put his arm around Simmi.

"It was his idea," she said suddenly. "He wanted to find his dad. I told him you just Google for that. But . . ." Simmi shrugged, as if the ignorance of second graders was beyond her.

"Did not." When Jack is trying not to cry, he pulls on his ears.

Simmi glared at him, and turned away on one foot in a way that momentarily undermined my sympathy for her. *Whatevs,* her mother used to say. I followed them down the stairs to our front hall, but Simmi had already gone out, and was heading down the second flight to the outer door.

"I'm sorry," I said to Terrence, who was collecting their jackets from the Shaker-style bench just inside the door.

He gave me a half smile. "Not your fault—it's like this all the time. Just usually in private." He glanced down the stairs. "Hold up, Sims." He put a hand briefly on my shoulder. "I'll see you," he said, before hurrying down the stairs after his daughter. The door downstairs locked automatically behind them, and I closed and locked our apartment door. Jack had come down from my bedroom, and was sitting three steps from the bottom of the stairs.

"Like what all the time?" he said.

I went to sit with him, and he made room on the step.

"You understand why Simmi was upset?"

"Because of her mom."

"Right—she really misses her."

What would Terrence think if he found out that I'd known all along that my son believed in ghosts—that in fact he believed he'd seen Simmi's mother in my office several weeks after her death— and that I'd kept that information from him, perhaps in an attempt to make him like me?

"That's why you really can't talk about things like ghosts, even if you're just playing a game."

"Okay."

"You understand?"

Jack nodded, lifting the hallway carpet with his toe, a dark red runner with a pattern of yellow triangles, flipped over the edge to reveal the rubber mesh pad. It was clear that something else was bothering him.

"Simmi said you were trying to use the machine to find out about your dad."

Jack scowled at me. *"No."*

It wasn't that I hadn't thought about talking to Jack about his donor; if anything I'd overthought it. I'd been waiting for him to ask, not about the mechanics of his conception—we'd covered that years ago—but about the man himself. I was going to show him the profile with the childhood photo of "Papageno," and explain what musicology really was. I thought we could go to the rock climbing gym in Somerville and learn about that passion of his father's, too.

I looked at Jack's face now, and I knew how naive I'd been. Any child his age would've started thinking about his father and long- ing to meet him. A career and a few hobbies were hardly going to satisfy him.

"We don't have to talk about it now—"

"I don't want to talk about it," he said. "Not ever."

"But we will have to later. Because I'm afraid you don't understand—"

Jack looked at me with such fury that I stepped back, startled.

"I *do* understand," he said. Then he got up, slipped past me, and hurried down the hall to his room.

26.

Jack said he didn't like the stew, and so I put on a movie to get him to eat. I watched half of it with him, and then let him stay up a little later while I cleaned the kitchen. I was just about to tell him it was time to get ready for bed, when someone knocked on our door.

Jack looked up from the screen. "Can I open it?"

It was our tenant Andrea. Her stomach ballooned under a tight, red-and-black striped sweater. She was very pale, her eyes shadowed as if she hadn't been sleeping, as if the baby were taking its health and vitality from her. She looked from Jack to me, smiling uncertainly.

"I hope it's not too late? I have some questions about the lease, but maybe now is not so good?"

"It's okay." I turned to Jack. "Can you do your own shower?"

Jack nodded, but he was watching Andrea with uncharacteristic excitement, as if she'd promised him a gift of some kind.

"What time is it?"

"Nine," I said. "Past your bedtime."

"Nine exactly?"

"It's eight-fifty-eight," I told him. "Go take a shower."

"I won't take your time," Andrea said, when Jack was gone. "Only some friends from Germany are moving to Brooklyn. They've bought a house—they would like to rent us half. We like it here, but New York is better for us, for our work, and this is a way we can afford to be there. And with the baby and Emilia, too, it will give us more room."

Emilia was their toddler, now almost three.

"I know we've signed the lease already. Only you asked us if we are moving? So we thought, maybe she has some other tenant."

"I'm not sure," I said. "But if you'd like to get out of the lease, of course we can figure something out." As soon as I said it, I wondered if the events of this evening had changed Terrence's mind about the apartment.

"Oh thank you!" Andrea said. "This is wonderful!"

"There is someone who might be interested. But in any case, it's no problem. What a great opportunity for you guys."

Andrea was nodding joyfully, as if it were all settled. "And so, in two months we can relocate?"

We talked for five, or maybe ten more minutes, and then agreed to meet on Saturday with her husband to finalize the details.

When I went upstairs I found that Jack was in the bath instead of the shower. His head was partially submerged, his eyes closed, and I had to tap his shoulder to get him to sit up.

"Why are you getting your hair wet?"

"I like the sound under there," Jack said, rubbing his eyes. "Is she moving in?"

"Who?"

"Simmi!"

Whatever animosity there had been between them seemed to have evaporated over the course of the last hour, at least on Jack's part. He was looking at me with barely concealed delight.

"You mean because of Andrea?"

"Aren't they leaving?"

Of course he'd been listening in. "I think so."

Jack beamed at me. "It worked," he said. "It wasn't the way we thought—but that's what you always say, right? You do an experiment because you're looking for one thing, but then you sometimes find something else."

I laughed. "Sometimes, yes."

"Like, we thought it would talk to us. But instead—"

I closed the lid of the toilet and sat down. "Jack, what do you mean?"

Jack looked away. He was old enough to understand when I told him he wasn't supposed to have a certain idea, but not old enough to keep it to himself. His voice was quieter, a little coy. "The ghost *made* them leave."

"Jack—there's no ghost!" I struggled to modify my tone. "Andrea and Günter want to go live with their friends in New York."

Jack didn't look at me. He was playing with a set of floating rubber vehicles in primary colors, toys he has outgrown but still refuses to give up.

"We know enough to know that magic things like ghosts aren't possible in our world," I said more gently. "It doesn't mean they couldn't be possible elsewhere, in a different kind of universe." This is the explanation I normally give adults, when they ask questions about the megaverse or extra dimensions, concepts that have been (to my mind) irredeemably perverted by Hollywood.

"Of course they're elsewhere," Jack said.

I decided to let this go for a moment.

"But, Bug—we do need to talk some more about what Simmi said. About you wanting to find your dad."

Jack stared at his own face, distorted in the stainless-steel dial underneath the faucet, which you turn to open and close the drain. His expression, as usual, was serious and older than his age, with his firmly defined brow and protruding upper lip. His head seemed especially large and heavy, held up by the thin, wet stalk of his neck.

"Do you remember when we talked about getting sperm from the cryobank?"

He nodded, but still didn't speak. I had always used the correct words for body parts, as the books told me to do. In fact, it had been much easier to answer Jack's questions about his origins without having to go into any of the details about conventional reproduction.

"And I said your donor was anonymous? That just means that we don't get in touch with him, and he can't get in touch with us."

Jack mumbled something.

"What, sweetheart?"

"Some do. Simmi has a friend with two moms, and she said she met her dad."

"Her biological dad—right. But that's not the kind of donor I picked."

Now he looked at me, startled: "Why *not*?"

I thought about several answers, and decided on the real one. In contrast to what my sister thought at the time, I didn't choose an anonymous donor because I wanted to keep Jack from identifying his other parent.

"The anonymous donors are the best. I mean, they have the best DNA. You remember what that is?"

"My recipe," Jack said.

I thought he might ask why again, why did I think the anonymous donors were better than the ones who'd agreed to one visit. I was nervous about this, because I didn't have what you would call experimental proof. It was just a theory. I wanted the kind of person who would complete the transaction and move on, rather than the type who wanted to see the results of what he'd done.

But if Jack wanted the answer to that question, he didn't want it from me. He made a bridge with his legs, and floated the red rubber truck underneath it. His wet hair looked darker than usual, slicked down around his ears, and his vertebrae made a knobby ridge down the middle of his back. When I asked if he wanted help getting out of the tub and into his pajamas, he scowled and hugged his knees. And so I left him in the bathroom, closing the door behind me.

27.

I called Terrence as soon as I'd dropped Jack at school the following morning to apologize. I said it was my fault for telling him about the metaphase typewriter.

"No problem," Terrence said. His voice was neutral, if not warm, not any different than usual. "She's okay. Every day's a new start with them, you know?"

"Yeah."

"How's Jack?"

"He was a little quiet this morning."

"He didn't want to talk about it," Terrence guessed.

"I tried to be very clear with him last night—no ghosts. I think he gets it, but I'm so sorry if he suggested that to Simmi." I didn't go into any more detail. Assuming Simmi had kept Jack's supernatural encounter from her father, I didn't want to make things worse by bringing it up.

"Yeah, no—I'm sure the science project was a joint effort," Terrence said. "But I was talking about the stuff with his dad."

I hesitated for a moment. I'd been worrying lately about the absence of men in Jack's life, and had even made an effort to find him a male babysitter, without success. I would have liked for him to spend more time with my father and my brother-in-law, Ben, but they were all the way across the country. I'd even introduced him to Arty, who was willing but comically hopeless with children—including, he'd confessed to me, his own.

Now, suddenly, I was talking to a man who'd grown up without a father himself, who was easy and natural with children, interested in Jack, and who might be prepared to move in downstairs.

"We had a talk about it last night," I said. "It was good, I think."

"It's kind of hard to know about those talks," Terrence said. "You know?"

"Yeah."

"You plan it all out in advance. And you think you've had this big moment together, like you're all connected and they totally get it—and then they're like, 'So, can we get doughnuts?' And you realize they haven't heard anything the last ten minutes. The little brain in there is going: *doughnut, doughnut, doughnut.*"

I laughed. I'd thought the metaphase typewriter might scare Terrence away forever; instead he was joking with me in a way he never had before. I was uncomfortable, but this was the moment. I just had to blurt it out.

"Weirdly, the apartment just got free."

"Yours?"

"The tenants are moving to Brooklyn."

"Oh."

"I didn't know if you were still—" There was a long silence in which I felt as if I were in tenth grade again, asking Adam Hurwitz to the semiformal. He had said that his family was going out of town, and then shown up with Sophie Anastopoulus.

"Yeah," Terrence said. "Yeah, we are."

"Oh," I said. "Okay. Great!"

"Yeah?"

"Yeah," I said. "Jack'll be thrilled. You should come see it, though, make sure."

"The main thing is that it isn't here," Terrence said.

If not flattering, it was at least definitive.

He came to see the apartment the following afternoon, while I was at work; I thought it was better for him to see it when I wasn't home. Andrea showed him around, and he texted me afterward to say that it was perfect. He especially liked the backyard, which is bigger than it looks from the street. We agreed that they would move in just after the holidays, while I was in Europe.

Normally Jack and I spend Christmas at my sister and Ben's, a ten-minute drive from my parents in Pasadena. The children, who see each other only once or twice a year, fall into a rhythm immediately; the cousin affinity I've heard described by other parents is maybe even more intense for him, as an only child. Bess, who is two years older than Jack, bosses him and her sister, Avery, around, and Avery and Jack happily obey her. I like going back to California, too, if not quite as much as Jack does; I've lived in Boston eighteen years now, but I still associate Christmas almost exclusively with the wide, palm-edged boulevards of my childhood, the terra-cotta-tiled roof of my parents' church, where we would go for a carol service on Christmas Eve. The smell of the car's heater, the first time we turn it on each winter, fills me with incredible nostalgia; it seemed to me that in Los Angeles, we'd only ever used it on that one evening.

Still, there's always the moment when my mother tells me that I look tired—can't I take a break for a few months, and take care of myself? There's the moment when I have to interrupt some holiday activity to take a call, and my sister picks up the slack with my son, something she seems to do more naturally than I manage to do with her daughters. And the moment when one of my nieces climbs onto her father's lap after dinner, puts her head in the hollow of his shoulder, the look on Jack's face when this happens. Every Christmas I suggest that we might host in Boston the following year, and am greeted with the reflexive financial argument from the adults (six plane tickets as opposed to two) and the now-reflexive argument from Jack: *I like it better here.*

This year would be different, though. Because I was going to Europe for four days just after Christmas, Jack and I would go to California the week before. We would fly back on the twenty-sixth with my parents, who had agreed to take care of Jack while I was away. That made the holiday feel slightly more balanced than usual. Although I wouldn't have said it to any of my family members, I was looking forward to staying in an Austrian hotel on my own for three nights, to talking to a European audience genuinely interested in physics, in an institute housed in a medieval castle. And I was looking forward to the following semester, in which I had a break from teaching; I would be returning to that luxurious schedule, and to having Terrence and Simmi in the apartment downstairs.

I was Christmas shopping with Jack at the mall in Porter Square when the next message arrived. In general I do everything online, as close to the holiday as I can reasonably complete it, but Jack likes to go to the toy store and choose gifts for his cousins himself. I'd been trying not to let the phone distract me when I was with him, and so I'd left it in my bag; now I tipped the bag slightly to read the illuminated screen while listening to Jack debate the merits of various boxed crafting activities that the girls in his class enjoyed. The toy store became more segregated by gender every year, much more so than when I was a child.

Do scientists believe in God?

More than any of the other messages, this one made me want to call Neel. During our years working together at Harvard, we'd had a running argument about Einstein, and when Walter Isaacson's biography came out, two years after we published the Clapp-Jonnal, we both read it. If we had a difference of opinion, it was about Einstein and free will; Neel regarded Einstein's determinism as an extension of the "cosmic pantheism" he'd gotten from Spinoza. There was an intricate and beautiful order to the universe, and we were smart enough to perceive only glimmers of it. The appreciation and investigation of this divine symphony, however, was the noblest of human pursuits.

My feelings were a little different. I loved the way Einstein detached Judeo-Christian tradition and the idea of an anthropomorphic God from morality, but I thought he was a little quick in his rejection of free will, which I fundamentally didn't understand. Neel had once spent several hours arguing that Einstein's determinism was really just a profound faith in science. Everything, including human behavior, was governed by "causal laws." I thought that this was nonsensical, as well as morally dubious, since it seemed to me to absolve human beings of all the responsibility for our actions.

I wrote back to my correspondent immediately, as I had the last time:

> **Some do. A lot of people think Einstein did, but if you read his letter to the philosopher Eric Gutkind, you'll see that he didn't think very highly of organized religion. He called himself a "religious nonbeliever" because he definitely thought there was more out there than just us. He said he had "unbounded admiration for the structure of the world so far as our science can reveal it."**

For the first time, I got a reply to my reply:

> **Is the earth going to crash into the sun?**

I had a sinking feeling. The questions had seemed, until this moment, quirky but smart, the product of a perhaps eccentric, but sincere reader. This disassociated rejoinder made me revise that assessment: I thought it suggested someone who wasn't mentally stable. Instead of offering the reassuring answer to that question, with an explanation of angular momentum, I decided to move on to the question of the phone:

> **There's a reward for this phone. $500. I'll transfer it to you via PayPal if you email me a receipt from the post office.**

This was met with a winged stack of money, which I took as an indication of interest. I wrote back:

> **But I need the receipt first.**

The next question seemed obvious: Why should the person at the other end trust me to pay them, if they actually put the phone in the mail? I thought I would simply tell the truth. They couldn't be sure that I would pay, but since the old phone had little value in itself, and was clearly valuable to me, it was a reasonable chance to take.

But there was nothing. I waited a few minutes, giving whoever it was a chance to consider, and then tried what I'd decided was a last resort:

Otherwise, the owner has told me that he'll file a police report.

This turned out to be a tactical error. Whoever was on the other end went silent, and I didn't get another message from Charlie's phone for almost two months.

GRAVITY

1.

I looked at the phone immediately upon waking; the action was there before I was fully conscious, even if I'd taken ten milligrams of melatonin before bed. I'd read about psychological dependence on technology, and I thought that might be my problem. I turned the sounds off at night, but it was as if the pinging mechanism was inside my body. Someone was plucking my guts as I slept.

I reached for it Thursday morning, and was disappointed to see an empty home screen. When I checked email to be sure, there was nothing from Charlie's address. I was scrolling through the rest—an update from Vincenzo, a few newsletters, my cell phone bill—when I saw the unfamiliar address: roxanaaslani@msf.org. It only took me a second to identify it:

> dear helen—i'm SO thrilled to have the chance to write you, finally. i'be been looking forward to meeting you for so long. i think—hope!—N has told you how muhc I admire your books—i've listened to him go on & on about LIGO and GW in general, but honestly it wasn't until i read YOU on black holes that it clicked. Am writing this in the airport, mad rush before we get on the plane—but wanted to let you knowa bout a get together we're having in cambridge, w idea of meeting each other's east-coast based friends before the wedding—do say you'll come? we've rented a space—belly @ kendall sq., 7pm on 12/11. Hope to see yousoon! xx roxy

I read that seven or eight times, then put the phone down on the unused side of the bed. I could hear Jack playing downstairs. Each time he dumped a box of Legos on the wood floor, it sounded like a catastrophe. December eleventh was a week from tomorrow, and Belly was the fanciest bar in the vicinity of MIT. I thought that the idea of "renting a space" would be anathema to Neel. I couldn't even imagine him saying those words. He had written that he had an idea to discuss with me, and I realized as I lay there that I had actually imagined this exchange occurring in a specific place, at the Muddy Charles, in the summer, with plastic cups of beer in front of us, the view of the river the only luxury—not that any luxury was necessary when you were talking about the most profound descriptions we have of our universe with a person you'd once passionately loved. But it was the beginning of winter, and the only place I was likely to hear what Neel had to tell me was at the engagement party his fiancée had organized.

2.

It didn't occur to me to make up an excuse. I knew that I wanted to go, and also that I couldn't go alone. I briefly considered Marshall, but we hadn't spoken in months, and arriving with an ex felt desperate. I probably knew a good portion of the people Neel was planning to invite; all I had to do was treat it like a work event and find someone else who was going. I texted Sonja at LIGO, who was brilliant and especially sociable for a physicist, also possibly an alcoholic; I thought that if I stuck by her, it would seem as if I were having a good time no matter what. Sonja wrote back to say absolutely—she was so curious about Neel's fiancée that there was no way she'd miss it.

I dislike choosing clothing, and have trouble determining what goes with what or what is flattering. Charlie used to say that the "clothing node" hadn't been activated in my brain. When I have a stubborn wardrobe question (this happened more often before Jack, when I was doing the publicity for my books), I go to my sister. Amy is hardly an expert, but she's better than I am; more important, she's willing to be patient with the whole neurotic process. In this case she suggested a dark blue lace dress that she'd helped me select for the wedding of our horrible cousin Janine.

"Is it too dressy for this?"

"How did she describe it, exactly?"

"A party so they could meet each other's 'East Coast–based friends.'"

"But not an official wedding event."

"I don't know."

"Are you going to the wedding? Because maybe you should save the blue dress for that."

"It's in India."

"Jack could come stay with us."

"It's in February—I will have just gotten back from Geneva."

"Is that why you're going to Geneva?"

"No! I have to go to Pöllau for my paperback's reissue. And I'm stopping in Geneva at CERN on the way home."

"Uh huh. I just think the wedding might give you closure."

"Nothing's open."

Amy laughed. "Okay. The blue dress for this, then."

I was already wearing the dress when Sonja texted me, at ten minutes past six on the night of the party. She was coming down with the flu and she had a conference the following week. She thought she had to take some Tylenol Cold and go to bed. She hoped I "wasn't going to kill her." That remains one of my least favorite locutions, presuming your disappointment, allowing you no way out—but Sonja at least was perfectly correct in the way she wrote even casual communication. She used appropriate punctuation, and clearly reread before sending. The way Roxy's email was written was more intimidating: the combination of haste and guileless friendliness, along with the distinguished address from Médecins Sans Frontières. She was so busy saving lives, and becoming Neel's wife, that typos were inevitable.

Jack's sitter, Julia, had arrived and was giving him mac 'n' cheese in the kitchen. I was doing my makeup in the upstairs bathroom, the phone balanced on the side of the sink. Unlike clothing, makeup calms me down. It's the same every time. I have a steady hand—Mr. Ryshke, my AP Chemistry teacher, once said that I could be a surgeon, a fact I recalled just recently—and I especially enjoy doing my eyes. When Sonja's message came, I continued doing them, rubbing pale shadow under the brow, a darker color in the crease. I lined them carefully with black powder and an angled brush (something Charlie taught me) and admired my work in the mirror. My eyes are hazel, and my hair has darkened from its orangey childhood shade to a more subdued auburn color. I also have what my mother used to refer to as "a good figure." She would say this in a slightly accusatory way, as if I had purchased for myself some extravagant and unnecessary item. I have always felt that my nose is too big, and there are now impossible-to-cover lines in my forehead, exacerbated by reading too much in insufficient light or without my glasses. There was no way I could go alone.

Jack screamed an inquiry about ice-cream sandwiches from the kitchen, and I gave permission. I considered what I would tell Julia, if I could plausibly send her home with only an hour's pay. My phone pinged and I glanced at it reflexively: maybe Sonja had changed her mind. But it was Terrence—he was wondering if Jack and I would like to meet them for Thai food in Central Square.

Old friend having a party tonight.

I wrote this without thinking. I wanted Terrence to know that my friends had parties, that we didn't sit around all the time doing equations together. A moment later it occurred to me that Terrence was, in fact, the perfect person to bring to the party. He was much better-looking than Marshall, but no one could say I was bringing him out of defensiveness. I was spending time with the bereaved husband of my friend, a person who was soon to move in downstairs.

I added:

Physicist I worked with on big project—his engagement party.

Neel?

I was surprised. By the time Charlie met Terrence, my relationship with Neel was years in the past. Even if she'd mentioned our collaboration, she would hardly have bothered to go into detail about a friend of mine whose name wouldn't have meant anything to Terrence.

Did Charlie mention him?

Y

In what context?

Gloucester

Until Charlie died, I hadn't thought about her aunt's house on the North Shore for years. Now the weekend we'd spent there seemed like the fulcrum on which the past had tipped into the present. Of course there was no way to say that to Terrence.

Right—he came up for the weekend once.

I waited for a response, but none was forthcoming. I couldn't help myself:

Should be some interesting people tonight—if you want to come?

The gray dots appeared, then disappeared, then appeared again. I was surprised by how much I hoped he'd say yes.

Not free till 9.

I gave him the details, and he said he thought he could be ready by 9:30. I said that I would pick him up. Then I stood in the bathroom with my phone for a half an hour, pretending to look at the news, worrying that Terrence would reconsider. Finally, at 8:45, I went down to say goodbye to Jack, who was watching a movie with Julia.

"You look nice," she said, with the condescending generosity of people her age. When I got in the car, it occurred to me that I hadn't asked Terrence for the address, but I found that I didn't need it. It had been twenty years since I'd driven to Charlie's childhood home, but I remembered the way.

3.

As soon as we arrived at the bar, I saw that I'd made a terrible mistake. The restaurant was one of those Cambridge establishments that aspired to a more cosmopolitan style: Scandinavian in feeling, it had a black-and-white tiled floor, brick walls, and a beamed ceiling. Bottles shone behind the lacquered wooden bar. There was a sign on the door that said "private party," but instead of elegant people in cocktail attire, it looked like a department happy hour. Even those I didn't know were dressed like scientists, which shouldn't have surprised me. Those who belonged to Roxy were likely to be in medicine or nonprofits. Why had I let my sister talk me into blue lace?

"Do you want a drink?" asked Terrence, who managed to be

both stylish and appropriately casual, in a black long-sleeved T-shirt with a sports jacket on top. I didn't want him to leave me alone, but I also hesitated to take off my coat, which would be necessary when we left the vicinity of the door. I hadn't yet said hello to anyone, and so I was thinking that it was still possible to leave.

"I'm afraid this is going to be boring for you. We don't have to stay."

"I go to bars all the time," Terrence said, misunderstanding.

I remembered Charlie telling me that Terrence didn't drink, maybe in the context of my own habits, which are moderate. If I have more than two drinks, I inevitably forget to stop. Charlie, who took pride in being able to hold her liquor, liked to tease me about it.

"I'm getting sparkling water," Terrence said. "You want something?"

I asked Terrence for a beer, then took off my coat and put it awkwardly over my arm. At least the room was crowded enough that no one was looking at me.

"When did you stop drinking?" I asked when Terrence returned. I was scanning the room for Neel and Roxy.

"I never started."

"Never?"

"My brother went in for possession when I was eight, so."

I had been listening with less than half my attention. Now I looked at Terrence.

"To jail?"

"I was eleven when he got out, and he was all into being clean. All I wanted to do was be like him. For a while we went to this church with a girl he knew. Then that didn't work out, and that's when we started surfing."

"And he's still okay?"

"Better than okay," Terrence said. "He sent me to college. Community college, not Harvard."

"It's not necessary to go to Harvard."

"Yeah, well—my brother didn't go anywhere. But now I work for him."

"He's the one who owns the surf shop?"

Terrence nodded. "He started by renting boards out of his truck. Selling weed, too, but only until he got Zingaro off the ground."

"I was thinking that wasn't the same brother."

"Only have one."

Vicky tapped me on the shoulder, and I introduced her to Terrence. Vicky can be a little overpowering—her voice is pitched high, and she has a habit of standing too close when she speaks—but she's excellent at her job in the development office, which involves soliciting alumni and other donors to MIT's endowment. Charlie sometimes had a tolerance for my very nerdy friends—she found them so awkward as to be charming—but I suspected Terrence wouldn't feel the same way. Vicky, in any case, seemed more interested in talking to me. She clearly assumed I knew much more about Neel and his fiancée than she did, and started asking me questions about the wedding. She was interested to know if I planned to have my palms painted with henna, and whether Neel was going to ride a white horse.

It was while I was straining to hear Vicky, and Terrence was looking around the bar as if he wondered how he'd come to be there, that I saw Roxy for the first time. Naturally I had image-googled her. She was like those pictures, and also not. She was wearing a sweater with the sleeves rolled up, jeans, no makeup. She was talking animatedly to Mark from MIT LIGO, whose team Neel was now joining, holding not a drink but a package of tissues in her hand. Her long, wavy hair was pulled up in a rubber band. She looked like a student arriving for an early-morning lecture, except for her face, which was wakeful and bright, absolutely engaged in whatever she was discussing.

She must've felt me looking at her. She turned and gave me a smile of recognition, excusing herself from Mark immediately, and making her way to our side of the bar. Had she looked me up as well?

"You're Helen!" she said. "I would kiss you if I didn't have this rotten cold. Neel wanted to cancel, but I said no—everyone's schedule is madness this time of year, and when will we ever manage to get all the people we love in one place again?"

Her voice was British in pronunciation but Indian in warmth

and tempo. I introduced her to Terrence and Vicky, accidentally furthering the impression that Roxy and I had a preexisting relationship.

"You're from Mumbai?" Vicky asked. "Are you also a physicist?"

Roxy laughed. "God, no. I'm a doctor."

"What's your specialty?" Terrence asked.

"I'm a cardiologist," she said. "I've been working with Doctors Without Borders for a bit now."

"Oh, I know someone in the office in Delhi," Vicky said. "I'm in development at MIT."

It turned out that Roxy knew him. "He's a Parsi," she said. "Like my family. Do-gooders." She managed to say this in a self-deprecating way, as if she were slightly skeptical of her own noble impulses. "There are hardly any of us left, so we all know each other. Speaking of Parsis, some of the few remaining on the planet have just arrived—my aunt and uncle from New York. I have to say hello." She put a hand on my arm. "It's so loud here—would you come to our place afterward? Please? We're having just a few people, so we can actually talk."

I glanced at Terrence, and said I'd have to check with my babysitter. As Roxy left us to greet her aunt and uncle, I saw Neel for the first time. He was crossing the room to say hello to his new relatives, wearing a dark green sweater with a collar sticking out of it. He looked as if he'd tried too hard, as I knew I had. His hair had been recently cut.

"That's your ex?"

"Yeah."

"Did he hang out with you and Charlie much? I mean apart from that time in Gloucester?"

"While we were dating, yeah. Then Neel and I worked together, but that was much later."

Terrence was watching Neel, who was talking animatedly with an elderly Indian woman wearing a raw silk tunic and a great deal of jewelry. I couldn't tell what he was thinking from his face.

"We built these two models," I explained. "For some reason it's what we're both best known for, even though I'd say we've each done more interesting work since. That was when we were closest, actually—much more so than when we were dating in college."

I stopped myself; Terrence wouldn't be interested in my relationship with Neel.

"What's a model?" he said.

"It's a sort of guess about the way something works—subatomic particles and forces, in this case. A way things could be."

"Like an alternate reality," Terrence suggested. There were so many people that we had to stand very close to hear each other; he put his hand on my elbow, moving me out of the path of a boisterous man carrying drinks.

"More like an explanation of a part of this reality that we don't understand yet."

For some reason, Terrence nodded eagerly at this. "I think about that a lot."

I might have been more focused on this comment if Neel hadn't been making his way toward us, having done his duty with Roxy's relatives. Or, it occurred to me, maybe it wasn't a duty; maybe he genuinely enjoyed Roxy's family, who seemed to lead fascinating lives in Mumbai.

"I'm going to get another soda," Terrence said. I almost asked him to wait—I didn't want to be alone with Neel—but I saw on his face that he didn't want to talk to a stranger who'd known Charlie. I let him go, and then Neel was there. He gave me a hug that smelled like his old apartment: tobacco and Dr. Bronner's. His sweater was cold, and I knew he'd been outside, smoking.

"Congratulations," I said.

"Thanks. But it's a weird thing to get congratulated on. Maybe in twenty years someone should congratulate us—but now?"

It was such a perfectly Neel type of comment.

"Well, then, on the events at LIGO I'm not supposed to know about."

"That," he said. "That deserves congratulations. But I'm not supposed to talk about physics tonight—I promised Roxy."

"We just met. She's terrific."

"She is." Neel had a habit of closing his eyes when he was uncomfortable. I only remembered it now.

"Is it strange to be back?"

"Not really. I'm on TeamSpeak with these guys every day. I'm going to be working with Martina on frequency dependent squeezing."

From the bar across the room Terrence met my eyes and lifted his glass, asking if I wanted another. I felt a rush of gratitude, not only for the drink. I nodded yes.

"Is that guy—?"

"That's Terrence."

"Terrence—Charlie's Terrence?"

"He's here for a bit, with his daughter. They're staying with Charlie's parents."

Neel seemed to search for what he wanted to say. "I keep thinking about this one night we hung out together."

"You mean the three of us?"

"No. Just me and Charlie—maybe the only time we did that. At the Plough and Stars."

It wasn't a place I'd known either of them to go. "When was that?"

"Senior year—I just ran into her. I was taking Jazz, remember?"

"Of course—with Graeme Boone. You were so into that class."

Neel nodded. "My TF's trio was playing that night, and so I went. I asked Charlie if she'd come to hear them, and she said, no—she didn't know anything about jazz. I said she should take the elective—I was always proselytizing about it—and she said she would take it if she were me, but she just couldn't stand the idea of being a black girl learning jazz history from a white professor at Harvard."

"I can see that," I said. I was almost sure that Charlie had never mentioned anything about that extremely popular jazz elective to me. "Are you sure she was by herself?"

Neel nodded. "Absolutely. We ended up getting a bunch of drinks."

"Because normally she had a thing about not sitting by herself in restaurants. I think that's why she liked meeting me places—I'm always on time."

"But she'd been there by herself for a while, that time," Neel said. "I had to drink fast to catch up."

I looked for Terrence, who had gotten the bartender's attention. She was young and blond, leaning in to ask him something—in spite of the crowd of scientists eager to be served. Terrence seemed to answer her courteously, but with little interest.

"How's he doing?" Neel asked.

"Okay, I think, given everything. He's moving into my down-stairs apartment."

Neel turned to me. "In your house?"

"Our kids are friends, and they needed something temporary. And my tenants wanted out."

"That was nice of you."

"They're paying rent."

"Maybe 'nice' isn't the right word—involved. That's involved of you."

What did he mean by that? That I wasn't involved in other people's lives in general? That I was selfish or cold? I couldn't keep the defensiveness out of my voice:

"I miss her."

"Yeah."

He asked about Jack, and I told him how interested my son was in science now. I mentioned his ant farm, and also the snap circuits kit. I said that he was still playing soccer, and wanted to try out for the travel team. I didn't say anything about his carelessness with homework, which I sometimes think is because the work is too easy, and other times worry signals academic struggles ahead. Nor did I mention the conversation we'd had in the bathtub, about my failure to provide him with a father.

"I thought I didn't want him to grow up, when he was little. But it's more fun as they get older—harder, but also more fun."

Charlie once told me that she didn't like the way Neel looked at me when I was speaking. She had said it was like I was "an interest-ing thing in a museum." I thought at the time that she misunder-stood him, because I believed that that expression (which I could recall as soon as she put it into words) was evidence of his serious desire to understand me. I saw that look on his face now.

"Did Roxy tell you about later, at our place?"

"I'm not sure I can."

"But maybe?" There was gray in the part of his hair.

"Maybe," I said.

"I hope so." He gave me another careful hug, and then released me. I went to find Terrence at the bar.

"We can skip the after-party," I told him. "This is bad enough."

Terrence shrugged. "Up to you. For me it's that or sitting in the guest room listening to my mother-in-law cry through the wall."

I looked at him. Charlie's mother crying was a startling thing to imagine. "Addie cries?"

"I put on headphones," Terrence said. "But, yeah."

4.

Neel and Roxy's new apartment was across the river in Jamaica Plain, nothing like what I'd expected. It was a brand-new building (there was still a sign advertising luxury condos for sale) with a large, empty lobby, a doorman behind a shiny black desk. They were on the sixth floor, and the apartment itself was mostly empty, too, except for a black leather couch, a large flat-screen TV, a travertine dining table. Everything looked both plain and expensive, the light gray wooden floors, the blue enamel kitchen cabinets. The only constants from the Neel I'd known were the abundant books and the general scarcity of other possessions. There were large windows, through which you might be able to see the Arnold Arboretum during the day. Now the windows were dark, alternating with framed collages that combined vividly colored vintage Bollywood poster art with Chinese urban street scenes. The artist was from Singapore, Roxy told me. She was setting out dark blue porcelain bowls on the low table in front of the television: olives, almonds, candied ginger.

I excused myself to get a drink, which I planned not to consume. If I had another, I didn't trust myself not to reveal how uncomfortable I felt in Neel and Roxy's new home. I made my way across the room and took the empty seat beside Terrence, whose prohibition on controlled substances seemed, inexplicably, not to extend to weed. He was sharing a joint with Neel's old friend Dan, a molecular chemist. I felt a surge of love for Dan, who was over six feet tall and becoming fat. He had wild hair and terrible posture, but his expression was the same one I remembered from when I'd known him well. When Neel and I were working together, we would often go out for a meal with Dan. Neel and I would make passionate arguments on one subject or another, and Dan would sit there eating: tolerant and slightly bemused. Dan had always placed less faith in talking than Neel, and had lower expectations about people and the world in general; he was funnier than Neel, and it was more relaxing to be around him.

"Your friend is knowledgeable," Dan said. "I'm telling him about the stuff we used to cook up in grad school."

"I only remember you guys doing that the one time," I said. "And nobody actually tried it, thank god." I turned to Terrence. "More important would be his small molecule immunotherapeutics—cancer drugs."

"That was also worthwhile," Dan acknowledged. "But it's been more thoroughly publicized." He called to Neel across the room, patting the place next to him. "Come here, my little monkey," he called, but there wasn't really room for Neel on the couch. He came over anyway, and settled on the floor at the conjunction of two leather sectionals. He stretched out his legs and grinned at Dan:

"Dude, I'm not your monkey."

Roxy made her way across the room and sat on the coffee table, facing Terrence. She shook her head at Neel.

"What are you doing down there?"

"I'm so comfy," Neel said. He'd had a good smoke, I could see, and was ready to talk. He kept looking from me to Roxy, Roxy to me. I thought that for an apartment like this you needed money, and that the money would have had to have come from Roxy's family. Neel wasn't the kind of man who minded that; in fact, I thought he probably appreciated the irony that some people who'd stayed in India over the past generation could now support those who'd immigrated to America. Where he was sitting, he was so close to me that if he'd leaned just slightly in one direction, his shoulder would've been against my leg. I could have reached out and touched his hair.

By contrast, Roxy seemed perfectly sober. She was asking Terrence about surfing with what seemed like real interest. Could she really learn? Even if she was not at all athletic? Where could you go around here, or on the East Coast in general? What did he like about it?

Terrence had taken off his jacket and was leaning back into the couch. He began in his laconic way, intensified by the weed, to describe a point break he'd surfed with his brother in Peru—the longest left in the world. For the first time that evening he seemed to be having fun.

"I'm going to tell you a secret," Neel said suddenly, turning away from them.

I could tell that he finally wanted to talk about LIGO. "Do you really have a detection?" I asked.

Neel put one arm on the couch next to me. He was still skinny, his face a little sallow from too many hours in the lab. His features had always been very open and pleasant, handsome even, but he was nothing like as good-looking as Terrence. I'd always thought that the thing that brought Neel and me together was conversation—about our work and everything else. We loved talking, and words in general, more than any of the other physicists we knew.

"September 14, 2015," Neel said. "Two-fifty a.m., Pacific Standard Time." He raised his eyebrows theatrically. "Where were you?"

"I don't know," I said. "Asleep, probably."

"Me, too. And then that morning I was running late, and so I called into the weekly telecon. I'd already looked at the logs and saw that there was a candidate event, lots of speculation—but I mean, we weren't up and running yet. This was ER8—the last engineering run. The first advanced science run had been postponed a week, because they were still tweaking. So there weren't supposed to be any blind injections."

"What's a blind injection?" I asked.

"Sometimes the technicians insert a false signal in the data stream, to test the way we would respond to an actual detection. September is storm season, lots of microseism that interferes with the machines. It was just a frustrating time to be getting off the ground. Both sites were having trouble locking, and so that's why we weren't taking data yet. Blind injections would've been an unnecessary distraction, but that's what everyone assumed it was. The alternative was too exciting to wrap our heads around, at least at first."

"So you're sure?"

Neel tapped his left hand on the couch twice. "I get on the call, and I'm still sort of waking up, haven't had coffee, and I hear Alan talking to Mike—Mike Landry, at Livingston—and he's like,

'Mike, can you say that again?' And Mike says—" Neel lowered his voice. "He says, 'This was not a blind injection.'"

"Wow."

Neel smiled.

"When are you publishing?"

"Not until February."

It was hard to know what was more exciting—the fact that Neel's team had actually detected a gravitational wave, or that they'd achieved the first direct observation of a pair of black holes merging.

"It's amazing." I could hear the stiffness in my voice. I imagined Neel could, too, and was enjoying it.

"I thought we would do it," he said. "Just not so soon."

"Wait a minute," Roxy said, catching the end of that. "You're telling people now?"

"Helen isn't 'people.'"

"Well if you are, I don't see why I can't." Roxy turned to Terrence. "Neel has discovered gravitational waves."

"Me and a thousand other people," Neel said, reaching up to shake Terrence's hand. "We didn't really meet."

Terrence introduced himself and congratulated Neel and Roxy on their engagement.

This time Neel didn't speculate about the nature of marriage, but just nodded seriously. He seemed even more earnest than he might have been, had he been sober. "I don't know what to say," he said. "Charlie was extraordinary."

"Thanks."

Roxy was the only one who didn't understand what was going on.

"My wife passed away earlier this year," Terrence said.

Roxy turned all of her attention on him. I notice that she didn't react, or say anything right away. In other words, she wasn't concerned about how her own reaction would appear to others.

"From what?"

Terrence hesitated a moment. "Complications from lupus. Encephalitis."

"That is terrible," she said. "You poor thing."

"It's been really rough—but we're managing."

"You have children?"

"One—she's eight." He seemed much more comfortable accepting Roxy's condolences than he did Neel's, either because she was a woman or because she knew how to give sympathy in an inherently professional way. I could imagine that doctors got inured to death, but I could also imagine the opposite—that you would become obsessed, start to think about nothing else.

"What did you discover?" Terrence asked Neel, maybe to change the subject.

"It's boring," Neel said.

"It isn't," Roxy said. "It's, like, the *one time* your work isn't boring." It was both skillful and generous, the way she suddenly turned everyone's attention to Neel, teasing him, and gave Terrence a break. Neel needed only a little encouragement.

"Like I said, there are more than a thousand of us on the team," he said. "And no one 'discovered' anything."

"We're talking about gravitational waves," I told Terrence. "Einstein predicted them. He basically saw that the laws of motion that apply here on Earth—classical Newtonian laws—don't work on other scales. Not when you're talking about tiny things, subatomic particles, or giant things like stars and planets. He figured out different rules, especially for gravity, because of the way that large astronomical bodies curve spacetime. Before Einstein, we didn't know that space and time are one thing, like a fabric. The waves Neel is studying are like ripples in that fabric."

"But can you surf them?" Roxy asked.

Terrence smiled.

"I think it would be more like them surfing you," Neel said, "if that makes any sense."

"It doesn't," Roxy said. "You should always let Helen explain."

"I've been reading about spacetime," Terrence said.

"In Helen's books?" Neel asked politely.

I knew what Neel thought of my books. They weren't inaccurate; it was just that there was no reason to write them.

Terrence shook his head. "An author named Robert Lanza. He says that time is just a human invention, and so there's no real past, present, and future. Everything is just *nows*. So even after your body dies, your consciousness is just in another now. Einstein said that, too."

"I think Einstein said just the opposite," Neel said. He had a way of jumping in and correcting people, as if he expected they would also take pleasure in being contradicted, as soon as they realized he was right. "He believed that the universe has an objective reality that scientists study. A lot of people say he was religious—*God doesn't play dice,* and all that—but his notion of God was really just physics. He thought there was a sublime order in the way the universe is arranged, and he was awed and inspired by that. But he thought the idea that we outlive our physical body was ridiculous."

Terrence was looking at Neel in a way that worried me. I realized that I wanted them to like each other, maybe because of how much I cared what each of them thought of me.

"I think Terrence is talking about a version of the anthropic principle—an explanation for why our part of the universe is so perfectly calibrated to support human life." I addressed this to Dan and Roxy, since Neel obviously knew what the anthropic principle was, and I didn't want Terrence to think I was talking down to him.

"Philosophy," Neel said, "not science."

"Lots of scientists you respect embrace it."

"Yes, okay," Neel said. "But that's a very weak form of the anthropic principle—Penrose's or Susskind's. Not a biologist like Lanza who writes scientific best sellers, and fancies himself another Einstein. No offense, Helen."

"None taken. I don't fancy myself another Einstein."

Neel smiled. "I meant the best sellers."

"Only one of them was on the best-seller list. For about ten minutes."

"Go back to the black holes," Dan said. "What happens when they crash into each other?"

Roxy nodded. "Yes, please."

Dan winked at her. "I used to go for moo shu pork with these two guys all the time, so I had to learn how to distract them. Otherwise they're at each other's throats."

Neel picked up two olives from the bowl on the table, and

moved them along two ellipses, one clockwise, the other counter-clockwise, getting closer and closer to each other with each rotation. "The black holes are inspiraling, like this. They're attracted by each other's enormous gravity, and also pushed apart by angular momentum, and so they circle each other for centuries, getting just a tiny fraction closer with each rotation. Finally they come together with the most terrific noise you can imagine." He smashed the olives together, then popped them into his mouth. "If you think of the energy of the sun, and then multiply that by a billion trillion, that's how much energy is released—more than anything since the Big Bang. But it's released as sound, not light. If it were possible for a human being to be close enough, we could actually hear the sound. The combined black hole is still wildly spinning after it comes together. It releases wave after wave of energy as it goes around—each one slightly less powerful than the last. The sound becomes quieter and quieter, like a bell." Neel drew the wave in the air with his right hand, its amplitude diminishing as it got more distant from the source: "That's the ringdown."

"That was pretty good," I told him. "You should write a best seller."

"That's why for most of the twentieth century, we thought we'd never be able to measure a gravitational wave," Neel said, ignoring me. "Finally we have machines sensitive enough to do it. You can translate that incredibly quiet vibration to an audible register, and the computer spits out an actual, billion-year-old sound: a rising tone—we call it a 'chirp.'"

For the first time, Terrence looked astonished. "This thing with the black holes happened a *billion* years ago?"

Neel nodded happily. "And now our detectors can hear it."

"What's the point?"

I didn't know whether this was a challenge or not. Terrence's way of talking was so casual, so Californian, that it was sometimes hard to tell.

"Ah," said Roxy. "Now we're getting to it."

Neel took a drink from a bottle, some fancy microbrew. "It's less about a practical application than it is learning more about the universe. Combining our data with data from traditional, light-based astronomy."

Terrence looked skeptical.

"Scientists have been dreaming of finding these waves—hearing them, I should say—for a hundred years."

"You never know, though," I said. "Lasers came out of pure physics. Not to mention MRI machines, the microwave, and a lot of today's encryption technology." I wasn't sure if I was defending Neel, or my profession in general, but it was important to me that Terrence understand that what we did had real-world applications.

"Not to mention the atomic bomb," Neel said.

"What I'm saying is that you do the science for its own sake, and things develop from there."

"How much does it cost?" Terrence asked.

"The interferometers?" I asked.

"All of it," Terrence said.

LIGO's total expenditures to date was a number I happened to know, and I thought it might sound less preposterous coming from someone who wasn't directly involved. "One-point-one billion."

"So far," Neel added.

Terrence looked at us. Then he exhaled sharply and shook his head.

"Okay, it's a little nuts," Neel admitted. "But what's so cool—at least to me—isn't the detection. It's the future. It's like until now we only had one sense—we could look up at the stars, but that was it. Then we learned how to measure X-ray and radio waves. And now all of a sudden we have ears, too. We can *hear gravity.*" Neel looked around at all of us in wonder. "All of this means that instead of building these really expensive and time-consuming machines on Earth, we can let the universe do more and more of the work for us. Black holes are actually the biggest particle accelerators in the universe—they're spinning these tiny pieces of matter around and around faster than anything we could ever build at CERN. And they're totally free."

Terrence looked at Roxy. "Imagine what her organization could do with that much money."

"True," Neel said. "But I just read that they spent 445 million making *The Force Awakens,* and our government's defense budget was 601 billion this year. So, you know, money doesn't always flow to the noblest cause."

Terrence nodded, as if in agreement. "Sometimes it flows into black holes," he said.

5.

I drove Terrence back to Charlie's just after midnight. In college I'd gone home for Thanksgiving my first year, and then saved money by spending the next three with Charlie's family. My father was an only child, and my mother had a half sister; sometimes our paternal grandmother would come from St. Louis, but in general when I was a kid, the meal was a quiet affair, very much focused on the food. I had been amazed by the long table and tall, elegant chairs—rented, I learned later—the garlands of gold leaves, the bottles of red wine on the sideboard, and the catered meal. The Boyces were upper middle-class, but with two children in college they didn't normally behave this extravagantly. The Thanksgiving meal was a significant occasion, a long-standing tradition with extended family and friends, and I felt honored to be included. "I love a holiday that has nothing to do with God," Addie would say. And then add breezily: "But I don't cook for more than ten."

She would spend time in the dining room on Wednesday night though, laying the table and "doing the cards." There was one year—our junior or senior—when she seated me next to a television producer who was doing a segment on female scientists and wanted to ask me some questions. Charlie sat beside the editor of a well-known literary journal. Even when we were undergraduates, Addie treated us not only as adults, but as women with a certain value to add, and I think we both strived to justify that confidence.

"Thanks for coming," I told Terrence as I turned off the car. "I know that was all kind of nerdy."

"It was different."

There was a light on in the living room, but otherwise Charlie's house was dark. "They'll be asleep, right?"

Terrence shrugged. "Doesn't matter. We don't really speak unless we're around Simmi."

"It's that bad?"

Terrence gave a short, unamused kind of laugh. I'd never noticed how far his brow extended over his very deep-set eyes; it made his profile even more striking than it would otherwise have been.

"Do you know why?" I asked.

"Same deal."

I had more questions, but it was unclear how much I could ask. Terrence made no move to get out of the car.

"About the letter she wrote her parents?"

"And where she got the drugs—yeah."

"Was it hard to get?"

He looked surprised. "The Seconal?"

"I didn't know what she used."

"Her doctor prescribed it for pain. We just hoarded it until she had enough. He knew, though. He once gave us the name of a doctor in Oregon, when she asked about it. But it wasn't like we were going to pick up and move Simmi, just so the death certificate would say something else."

"What would it have said?"

"Complications from lupus—that's what it *was*."

"What did it actually say?"

"'Acute overdose of Seconal. Took own life.' That's what they have to call it, everywhere except the aid-in-dying states."

"Oh."

"Who cares, though, right? She sure as hell didn't."

"But Addie does."

"She thinks someday Simmi will *look it up*." Terrence gestured dramatically with his right hand. "So she looks it up. And we tell her her mother was dying, and she was in pain. Simmi will be an adult then, and you know—she's already like her mother. They're not sentimental."

I laughed. "No. I would sometimes want to watch a stupid movie—like, a thriller or something, just to relax. But Charlie would want to analyze it."

"Right," Terrence said. "She could never just chill. Used to drive me nuts."

"And you think Simmi's like that."

But whatever reserve had lifted for a moment suddenly returned, and Terrence didn't answer. I probably should've stopped there, but I've always had trouble letting a question drop.

"But they couldn't think that you convinced her to do it that way?"

"Who knows what Carl or Addie thinks? They think somehow I got the drugs for her, from my brother, Ray—which is a joke. He's been clean thirty years. The doctor who gave it to us, you know where he went to school?"

Terrence didn't wait for me to guess.

"Tufts. The same diploma that's on the wall in there." Terrence looked toward the corner of the house, where Carl had his office with its own entrance. I knew exactly where Charlie's father's diplomas hung, above the leather couch where Charlie and I once sat drinking airline bottles of peach schnapps and Baileys Irish Cream, before sneaking out to the clubs on Lansdowne Street. Charlie sitting in the Eames chair, asking me questions in a sonorous voice:

What's the first word that comes to mind when I say the word "mother?"

"Father."

Hmm, interesting. What did you dream last night, Helen?

I don't remember my dreams.

Tell me about your earliest memories.

Watching two boys throw a cat back and forth in the alley behind our apartment. It was terrifying.

Charlie tipping her head back, taking another syrupy swig in the dark.

You are deeply fucked-up, Helen. I honestly don't know if I can help you.

And then the two of us laughing and shushing each other, in case her parents could hear us through the wall.

"Like I just got tired of taking care of her," Terrence said suddenly.

"That's absurd."

Terrence shook his head slowly. "No, it's not. I did get tired of it. She was all cheerful and fine in the mornings, before Simmi went to school. But then as soon as she left, she would barely talk. Just sleeping and reading all day. Like, you know you have a few months to live, and you're reading a *book*?"

"What was she reading?"

Terrence gave a frustrated sigh. "Who knows? The point is, I was there. But I could have been some health-aide robot. Until Simmi came home, and then she was all over her, kissing her, cuddling her. But if I tried to touch her—"

"Maybe it was too hard."

"To give me a hug?"

"Because she loved you."

"She didn't love me half as much as she loved Simmi."

"I'm sure that's not true."

Terrence didn't bother to respond to that. He took his phone out of his pocket. "You better get home to your sitter."

"I'm glad it's going to work out," I said. "With the apartment."

"Yup."

"I didn't expect the kids to get along so well. I mean, apart from the other night."

"He's a great kid."

"Thanks."

"He's his own little dude, you know—not a follower."

"I think he'd follow Simmi anywhere."

"I like him a lot better than those people tonight."

"You mean Neel and Roxy."

"She's cool," he said. "But that guy . . . I'm sorry, but I'm surprised you're still friends. No offense—but he kind of disrespects you."

"That's just his manner."

Terrence raised his eyebrows. "How long were you together?"

"Just a year, officially. Then we went to grad school in different cities. We worked together as postdocs and afterward, but we weren't dating then. And then it was mostly just email—a lot of email—until I had Jack."

"Uh huh."

"Also he was a little high tonight." Why did I feel the need to defend Neel to Terrence? I'd never had any doubt that Neel respected me as a scientist. But Terrence didn't know anything about science, and so that couldn't be what he was talking about.

"I can't picture him and Charlie hanging out."

"It was mostly just that time in Gloucester." If I thought that would prompt Terrence, I was mistaken. He remained stubbornly silent. What had she told him about that weekend? Had she told him it was when she'd given up on Oxford, decided to move to L.A.? Had she said what had forced that decision—that in a way, it was the reason they'd met?

"And Neel's not cool, if that's what you mean," I said. "Most of us have kind of given up on that."

"No kidding."

I couldn't help feeling a little offended. "The work's what's cool."

"Black holes are cool," Terrence admitted. "I just question the resources involved."

"That's fair," I said. "It's not efficient, at least economically."

"If you could do something with them, then maybe. Like put all the garbage in there."

For some reason this is an idea a lot of people have with regard to black holes, in spite of the glaring practical hurdles.

"I'm sure Charlie would agree—about it being sort of esoteric."

Terrence smiled. "No way. Charlie would love it."

"You mean LIGO?"

"Just the idea of a billion trillion suns. The chirp, and the—what do you call it—*ringdown*?"

I thought that in my twenties and thirties I would have defended pure science more vehemently. I certainly had none of the trouble arguing with men that some women I knew seemed to have. I didn't know what had changed as I'd gotten older—it might have had something to do with having Jack—but now I could see Terrence's point of view. What right did people like Neel and I have to spend our lives answering questions about the universe—questions that (at least so far) did nothing to alleviate suffering here on Earth?

"I can see how it seems expensive and useless."

Terrence nodded. "She loved expensive and useless." He gestured toward the house. "Look where she grew up."

I thought that wasn't quite fair. "The Boyces were really adamant about giving back, though. She said she spent her whole childhood volunteering."

"Community service," Terrence said drily. "We used to get some of that. Volunteers in the school. And presents at Christmas, one year. Secret Santa. We were supposed to send them a picture, so the rich people could be like, 'Look at the poor kids we helped.' But my mom just threw that stuff away. She might not have been rich, but she had dignity, you know? Next year we'd be off that list, and Ray and I would give her hell about it. Now I get why she did it."

"Carl still works at that shelter, though. And Addie's whole life is board meetings, after-school programs. They put their money where their mouth is. And their time."

Terrence didn't acknowledge that one way or the other. We sat there for a moment in silence.

"You're just here through Christmas," I ventured. "And then you'll have your own place, and I swear we won't bother you."

Terrence nodded slowly. "I'm going to have some stuff shipped, if that's okay."

"Yeah, of course."

"Not a ton—mostly Simmi's things. The L.A. toys have gotten really important. We talk about it all the time, you know, like, 'Is my stomp rocket still there? Is my play kitchen still there?' "

"That seems normal."

"Yeah, well, the stomp rocket is a lightweight plastic toy, but the play kitchen is this heavy wooden thing, and so I'm like, 'You don't play with that anymore.' And she just *looks* at me. And I remember that it's what she used to do when she was little, when Charlie still cooked sometimes. She'd stand there next to her, pretending—she loved that thing."

"It makes sense to let her keep it."

"Yeah?" He looked unsure, as if he really wanted my opinion, and also as if he might leap from the car at any moment. I thought of all the decisions he would have had to have made, as soon as they found out she was dying. How much should Simmi's regular routines be disrupted? When should a tantrum be calmed, and when encouraged? And what should she be allowed to save? Photos and jewelry, no question—but what about a T-shirt? A toothbrush? Hair from a comb?

Terrence's arm was resting on the passenger door and he was fiddling with the lock. "I was thinking, maybe we'll be able to help each other—watching them?"

I tried to sound casual when I agreed that exchanging childcare would be practical. It was further than I'd ever imagined he'd go. I thought we were admitting a particular vulnerability to each other, the one shared by all single parents asking for help, and it made me feel close enough to ask the other question I had, to which I was pretty sure I knew the answer.

"Did you ever find her phone?"

"No."

"Couldn't you explain to Addie that Charlie meant to write a letter, even if she didn't have time?"

"I think she did write one."

"To them?"

"Right. And if they want it, they should have their lawyer get it for them. It'd be the most useful thing that lawyer's ever done."

"But they won't do that."

"Because they don't believe me."

He had been staring straight ahead at the car parked in front of us—it was a Land Rover, with one of those decals that are supposed to represent their owners: two stick figure parents, three children with customized genders, a cat—but now he turned to me. His eyes were gray rather than green in the reflected light from the streetlamp outside.

"And none of us is really talking at the moment."

"I'm sorry."

Terrence shrugged.

I thought about the long Thanksgiving table, the garlands, and the bottles of wine. I thought of the producer seated to my left. I'd had an idea about Terrence—that Charlie had chosen him to piss her parents off a little. He represented, if not authentic black-ness—he had, after all, grown up in a household with a single par-ent who was white—at least the world outside the privileged bubble where she'd always lived. Authenticity had never been important to Charlie, though; she'd never wanted to be part of a group. I thought now that it was more likely exceptionality, the feeling of not quite fitting in anywhere, that had united them.

I wanted to say something reassuring about Addie and Carl—how they were in the worst stage of grief, and would eventually soften toward him—but I couldn't find the right way to frame it.

Terrence gave me a sort of pat on the arm. "Thanks for dis-tracting me tonight," he said. Then he got out and walked in his casual way, feet forward and shoulders thrown back, as if even his body were expressing its ambivalence, up the solid brick path to the house, his hands in his pockets.

6.

The last time I saw Charlie was a few days before Christmas in 2012. She, Terrence, and Simmi were in Brookline for the holidays; we had planned that she would bring Simmi to our house, where the nanny I employed then, Pema, would look after both children while Charlie and Terrence and I went out to dinner.

The fact that Charlie and I had landed in each other's hometowns was a coincidence, and it should have made it easy to see each other at least once a year. They always came to Boston for longer than Jack and I went to L.A., and so it made more sense for us to meet while they were in town. The Boyces were more demanding than my family, though, and much more socially active. When Charlie brought her family to Brookline for Christmas, there was always a slate of holiday visits and events on their calendar. Charlie had groaned about those obligations to me by text—once we were in the same time zone—but we often made plans that she canceled. When my phone rang that afternoon, I thought she was doing it again. Instead Charlie said that Simmi had a bad cold, and that she was going to leave her at her parents' with Terrence, while just the two of us had a night out.

That evening when I opened the door she did her customary shriek and grabbed me. We rocked back and forth, hugging each other, until I felt it was reasonable to detach myself. It had been four years since I'd seen her in L.A., and we'd been in only sporadic touch.

"I think it worked out for the best," she said, once she got inside. "I really wanted you to see Sims, but having Terrence at dinner would've changed the whole dynamic. My mom was dying to have you and Jack for the Christmas Eve party, but I told her you'd be in L.A."

Charlie looked around my living room, which I'd been seeing through her eyes all day, with misgivings.

"This is so Helen," she said. "It's perfect."

Charlie liked to read even more than I did, but she wouldn't have installed built-in bookshelves in the living room. I knew without having seen the inside of her house that the furniture would go together in a complicated way I wouldn't be able to articulate; that there would be a chandelier somewhere; and that at least one piece of furniture would be upholstered in toile. There would be a faux zebra rug, and especially nice bathrooms. She couldn't possibly have admired the midcentury modern living room set I'd purchased from a vintage warehouse in the South End—not because I especially liked that period, but because it seemed like what people bought these days—or my grandmother's threadbare Persian rug. Still, I felt that when she said "so Helen," her admiration was genuine.

"I love these old Victorians," she said, taking off her coat and hanging it over a wooden bench just inside the door. "I love that it's blue."

"It was blue when I bought it."

"It's cozy and whimsical." She was wearing a pink sweater and navy, wide-legged wool culottes that buttoned up the side. Her boots were knee-high and black leather, with a round toe, and she had a set of gold bangles on one arm. Her hair was still short, but it was straight, and a fringe of long, highlighted bangs fell over one eye. She pushed them behind her ear; only the diamond studs were unchanging. Even by her own high standards, Charlie was well-dressed.

She saw me noticing. "This morning Terrence said I save my best clothes for when we're at my parents, and I was kind of annoyed. But he's completely right. I still want to impress my mom more than anyone."

"I probably want to impress you more than anyone," I said. "And this is still what I'm wearing."

Charlie laughed. "You look great—you always look great. And thin."

"You're always thin."

"Yeah, but only because my meds are completely nauseating."

We could hear Jack and Pema playing in the bedroom. Charlie's face lit up. "Is he in there? Can I meet him?"

I nodded. I was filled with the same kind of anticipation I'd had when my parents came to see Jack and me in the hospital.

Charlie toned down her greeting for Jack, maybe sensing that he'd respond better to a more reserved approach. Even so, Jack was shy. He gave a barely audible "Hi," and scooted closer to Pema. They had built a zoo out of unit blocks, and were populating it with plastic animals.

Charlie got down on her knees, in spite of her outfit. "I have a little girl, and she loves these animals, too," she told Jack. "She especially loves horses."

"I love reptiles," Jack said, adding an alligator, but he didn't smile until Charlie reached into her capacious leather bag and pulled out a package in Christmas wrapping. "Sorry," she mouthed to me, and I soon saw why: it was a remote-controlled car, the kind of toy I rarely buy him. It lit up in rainbow colors, played music, and could even do stunts; when Jack pulled the toggle toward him, it turned a flip, landed on its rubber tires, and squealed off to a tinny, electronic pastiche of the *Star Wars* theme.

"Thank you!" Jack said, his face exploding into a natural smile. He was suddenly his best self, bubbly and polite, and let Charlie show him how to do a wheelie.

Charlie had taken a cab to our house, and so I drove to the restaurant. On the way Charlie said: "I knew I would only have a few minutes with him, so I wanted him to like me right away."

I didn't take that as anything more than a comment on our hectic holiday schedules at the time.

When Jack was in preschool and Pema was still with us, I would go out at night once a week. Sometimes these were work events, and other times just dinner with a few colleagues. I also socialized with the mothers I knew through Jack, especially Vicky and Eunice, and every few months I saw my old friend from Harvard, Elaine, now a professor of medical anthropology at Tufts. When I go out with any of these people, I know what the conversation is going to comprise. With Vicky and Eunice, I talk about the children; with other scientists, I gossip about MIT. With Elaine, who doesn't have children, I often have the most interesting conversations: about feminism and work, about politics and whatever each of us happens to be reading.

As Charlie and I drove to the restaurant, listening to the same station we'd often put on in college—they seemed to have given up on attracting new listeners, and were still playing the same R.E.M., U2, and Prince albums we loved back then—I thought about what was different from those other friendships. It was a level of intimacy that I'd never reached with another woman, not back then or once we became adults. I think that with most of our friends we choose how much of ourselves to reveal, and with a very select few it feels as if there is no choice.

We sat at a table against the wall, Charlie insisting that I take the banquette. We talked about the children for a while, eating some sort of special miso soup with mushrooms. Charlie told me a funny story about Simmi, who had asked Charlie innocently whether people had to "do sex" to have a baby. I made the joke I always make, that it's actually a lot easier to explain IUI birth with a C-section than it is a natural conception and birth.

Charlie laughed. "Does Jack ask about his donor?"

"A few months ago—he just came home from school and asked why he didn't have a dad."

"Oh god," Charlie said.

"Right. I started in on my whole spiel—I'd rehearsed it in my head a million times. At the end I asked him if he had any questions, and he said: 'Dylan's dad got him a light saber that really lights up.'"

Charlie laughed. "That's what dads are for. You can borrow Terrence anytime you need someone to buy Jack plastic weapons."

"How's it going, with his work and everything?"

Charlie shook her head disbelievingly. "It's amazing. I didn't think it would work—I didn't say it at the time, but I didn't really think Ray could pull it off. Then some of the pro surfers started buying the boards. They were actually in the *L.A. Times* style magazine last month, and now the store is going crazy. Online orders, too. Terrence does the online stuff, which used to be great, because he was home so much."

"But not anymore?"

We were sitting next to a large, tropical fish tank, presumably decorative, where fish we were not going to eat swam around: goldfish with swollen eyes, darting neon tetras, and an angry-looking lionfish, lurking against the multicolored pebbles at the bottom.

"Things are really hard with us right now. He almost didn't come to Boston."

Hearing about other people's troubles with their spouses sometimes made me glad to be single; other times it just made me think I'd never meet anyone.

"How come?"

"It's hard on him, me being sick. I decided I'm not doing staffing this year—that means competing for jobs on different shows. I had a flare at the end of the summer, and it was pretty bad. I'm a supervising producer now—that's basically two levels from the top. The idea is that I'm going to stay home and create my own show."

"The Manhattan Project show?"

Charlie nodded. "It's changed a little, though. I think I'm going to focus more on the workers in Oak Ridge, Tennessee. There were black nurses in the hospital, black laborers at the labs and the test sites. Did you know they segregated the female workers in a kind of barracks? I mean, you'd expect them to be racially segregated—but the women were even separated from the men, even the married ones. There was a curfew and guards outside the gate."

"I didn't know that."

"I feel like it's a kind of Buffalo Soldier story, but with women. And science."

"I'd love to watch that."

"Thanks. Unfortunately, you're not anyone's target audience. And even if I can write it and sell it—that's a big if—I don't know if I have it in me, being in the office or on set in the way it would take to make it happen."

"You look great," I told her.

"People always say that," Charlie said. "I mean, thank you, but that's one of the things with lupus. You can't always see it, so it's hard for people to understand how bad it is."

Charlie had ordered us some dumplings that arrived steaming in a basket. We were drinking sake from purposefully mismatched green-and-purple shot glasses.

"People keep telling me to stick it out another year, get the co-EP credit—that's co–executive producer, the next level—and then leave. But I'm just sick of it. You know about 'diversity staffing,' right?"

"I've heard of it."

"So basically all the networks have these programs for women and minority writers, where they'll subsidize the salaries of baby writers from those groups. That's what you're called when you're a staff writer—entry level. Most of the programs will only pay staff writer salaries, so there's no incentive for the showrunner to promote you. I know a woman who was at a show for three years, as a staff writer, and then they were like, 'Okay, we need some fresh diversity!' A lot of people from these diversity programs get fed up and leave."

"But that didn't happen to you."

"No," she said, "although my salary was paid by the network the first year. The showrunner said he would've hired me anyway—he was class of '92, and I knew him from the Signet, so that helped—but it would've been crazy for the studio to pay a salary they didn't have to pay. And then I was promoted after the first year, and I kept moving up. I had all the right connections, and so for me, it was easier. As usual. But then stuff still happens, even now."

"Like?"

Charlie rolled her eyes. "This guy Josh, who I know from that horrible CW show—we're kind of buddies. I can't talk to Terrence about work because he doesn't really get it. But Josh and I sometimes go out for a beer after work; he's this menschy guy, and we always joke that everybody sees us and thinks he's rich and I'm an actor." Even in the restaurant I'd noticed people turning and looking at us; in the clothes she was wearing, and especially in Boston, Charlie did look as if she had to be famous.

"We always go to the same dive on Highland," she said. "And then the other night he asks me if I'm staffing for fall shows, and I say I don't know. And he asks if I want to be his writing partner."

"What does that mean?"

"Well, you share the work, and the salary. Josh said he could deal with the pay cut, temporarily, because he wants to write a pilot at the same time. And I was thinking that it would actually be perfect for me right now—you know, to get the co-EP credit but do half the work. And there's this new Netflix show we're both really excited about, and we're talking about it. And then Josh says he thinks we would have a really good shot, because I would make us the 'high-level diversity' everyone's looking for." Charlie shook her head. "Do you know what that feels like?"

"No," I said. "But we have this program called 'Career Development.' Five of the female professors in the department are in it, and also the one African guy."

"Right," Charlie said. "Network shows are seventy-one percent male. And I'm one of the ones who made it, but I had a real leg up. And I just feel like such a fucking traitor sometimes—when we're in the room, and I laugh at a joke just because everyone's looked over to see if I'm going to laugh."

"What did you say to the guy—Josh?"

"I laid into him. I said I'd rather try for the seventy-one percent of spots that go to white men than for the twenty-nine percent that go to everyone else. And then when I got one, I'd like to enjoy the luxury of not having anyone say that I got it because I'm a black woman."

"What did he say?"

"He wrote me a lovely apology over email the next day. But I still don't want to be his writing partner."

"That's depressing."

Charlie sat up straight and shook her head. "It's way less depressing than the disease. I can handle Josh, and all the people who make Josh look like an angel—when I'm feeling good. I can even deal with the physical pain; my doctor says I actually have a high threshold." She smiled wryly: "A high threshold for a lupus patient. Which would be no threshold for anyone else. The disease basically rewires your neural pathways, so that your brain is getting messages that your body hurts when it really shouldn't."

"What are you taking?"

"I tried Lyrica, and now I'm on Cymbalta—the drugs all sound like women in Shakespeare."

"But they don't work."

"They work a *little*. You know what the worst thing is, though? They call it lupus brain fog. It actually cuts off some of the blood flow to parts of your brain. You can get confused, disoriented. You start forgetting things."

The waiter came and put the sushi in front of us. It was so pretty that it didn't look like food.

"Once Simmi came into my bedroom after school, and I got up to give her a hug. I said how happy I was to see her, asked her how school was and all that. And she's just looking at me like I'm crazy. I told her I hadn't heard her come in, and she says, 'Mama, I already came in.' I looked at the clock and it was four-thirty—she'd been home for an hour. I'd just *forgotten* that I'd already seen her."

I imagined not being sure whether my brain was functioning the way it should, and felt a visceral fear. Beneath that fear was something terrible I was ashamed to feel—a faint relief, that it was her and not me. I reached down to pick up my napkin, which had fallen to the floor. When I sat up, Charlie was looking right at me: I thought she had seen what I was thinking, but was pretending she hadn't.

"Has it been any better working at home?"

Charlie shrugged. "I've had good days. Like when I get to eleven without a migraine. And then other days Terrence takes Simmi to school, and I go into the bedroom and close the blinds and just lie there in the dark until the sitter brings her home."

"It's good you have the sitter."

"We didn't used to—Terrence used to pick her up most days. But he's been spending way more time at Zingaro or at Ray's place. He says it's because they're so busy—and they are. But I also think it's because he's afraid to come home."

"Afraid?"

"I'm no picnic when I'm sick."

"I'm sure you're not that bad."

"I am. I get really angry at myself when I can't work."

"But that's because you're sick."

"Sometimes it is. Sometimes it's because I can't see the point."

"The point of working?"

"It's a really long haul, Helen. This is my whole life. Balancing the meds, being exhausted. A great day is when I feel okay. I can't even remember what it was like to feel normal. My mom's like, 'You're a fighter.' But I don't know if I am."

"You are."

"You think? Because sometimes I think if it wasn't for Simmi, I'd just be done with it."

I didn't know what she meant, and then I saw it on her face. "Charlie!"

"Do me a favor and don't ask if I've thought about how I'd do it."

"Have you thought about how you'd do it?"

Charlie looked startled, and then she laughed. "I love you, Helen."

"I love you, too."

She sat back in her chair, poked at a piece of seaweed in a desultory way, then put the chopsticks down on a ceramic rest made to look like a fish. She didn't look at me, but her mouth was set in a way I recognized, refusing pity.

"But I am tired," she said.

7.

At some point that night, Charlie told me that she'd walked Terrence and Simmi through Harvard Yard, because they'd been in Cambridge for the afternoon, and her parents had suggested it. She had resisted opening "that can of worms" initially—since the difference in her education and Terrence's was such an issue for her parents—but both Terrence and Simmi had loved Harvard. Terrence had said that it was one of the few places that turned out to be just what you expected—in a good way. Simmi had liked the library steps; she had wanted to climb up and hop down again and again. It was only while Charlie was standing in front of that library, watching her daughter do an unwitting Shirley Temple routine on its marble steps, that she had realized Pope might actually be in there. She knew that several women, slightly younger than we were, had gotten together to make a complaint against him, and that they had been successful in ensuring that he no longer taught undergraduates.

"They called me to say they were writing a letter," Charlie said. "I think that woman, Trisha, might have given them my name— that pissed me off. I wanted to put the whole thing behind me, and so I said I didn't have anything definitive to say about him. Now I really wish I'd added my name."

Charlie hadn't been part of the official complaint, but she had looked Pope up more than once online, and seen that as a retired professor of such eminence—a professor whose retirement was quietly insisted upon, but might well have been voluntary considering his age—he retained an office, not in the Comparative Literature Department on Quincy Street, but in Widener Library itself. She told me she thought about going in and telling him what she was doing now, how much she earned as a supervising producer, and what she thought of the way he'd behaved.

She said she'd almost done it. She was going to tell Terrence and her parents that she was nostalgic, and wanted to go up and see the Francis Child Memorial Library on the third floor. But then she asked herself what would be the point. Someone like her friend Josh could learn, if she took the time to explain his mistake to him, and if he really cared to listen. But a seventy-year-old professor? She said it would be for herself that she was doing it, and she questioned why she still needed anything from a person like Professor Pope.

The first time I met Pope, I was looking for Charlie in that third-floor room where she liked to study. This was in the spring of our junior year, before cell phones, when you would guess where someone might be, and go try to find them. Once Charlie had dragged me up a little-used staircase, to show me the view of the star-shaped paths from above, and then forced me to read a poem she liked on the subject of the trees in Harvard Yard. I remember remarking that it didn't seem like a good poet would write a poem about Harvard, and Charlie had been impatient with me, told me that I knew nothing, that a great poet could write a poem about a comic strip or a shovel or her own ass and say something profoundly true.

This time Charlie wasn't there: I knew her schedule by heart, and when I looked at my watch, I realized she must be at her tutorial. I was so eager to tell her my news—I had gotten a summer internship at Fermilab outside Chicago, where the Tevatron particle accelerator was then operating—that I decided to go to Pope's office and wait for her. I asked a student, who directed me; when I reached the room number he'd given me, I could hear Charlie's voice coming from inside.

I sat down on the marble floor, my back against the wall opposite, and took out a paper I'd been meaning to read. I was forcing myself to confront Vilenkin's proposed boundary conditions in superspace as limits for solutions of the Wheeler-DeWitt equation, when I heard them approaching the door. I scrambled to my feet, since there was something childish and undignified about sitting on the floor in Widener. Charlie came out first. She was wearing a short gray wool skirt, black tights, and a blue-and-white striped collared shirt, with a sweater on top. It was preppy and a little dressier than your average student, the version of Charlie that had attended Choate Rosemary Hall. She saw me and started, as if I'd tricked her by appearing there. Because she was Charlie, her training overcame any surprise or disinclination to see me; she turned to her professor and introduced us.

"This is my roommate, Helen," she said.

You might have said that the professor looked at me "searchingly." He had blue eyes, along with the Roman nose and dark, wavy hair, with just a little gray at the temples, that had suggested our nickname for him. I'm not sure at that point in my life that I'd ever met anyone French, and I expected perhaps a cigarette, an accent; it turned out that Pope had grown up in Montreal, and done his celebrated early work at the Sorbonne, before moving to the University of Toronto, and then finally to Harvard. He was wearing a slim, dark suit with a white shirt, but it was open at the collar, as if he were eager to escape the formality of his surroundings. He frowned slightly and his voice was ostentatiously gentle, as if he'd just learned that I was suffering from some kind of injury.

"Ah, Helen—the physicist," he said.

Everything about him seemed mannered, which was, to be fair, something that people often said about Charlie, too. But where Charlie's affect was a defense that you had to wear away at little by little, Pope seemed to be able to turn his on and off at will. He wasn't tall or even especially handsome, but he had an obvious confidence in his own charisma that I disliked immediately.

"I hope so, eventually."

"Charlie says you're very talented. What's your area of interest?"

"Quantum cosmology, especially inflation theory." It was new for me, having an area of interest, and I couldn't help being proud of it.

"So you're a theorist." Pope looked from me to Charlie, and back to me. "You know, it's not actually all that different from what we do here, in our department. Charlotte has a brilliant critical mind, but my guess is that she's going to be a playwright. What the playwright does is to take voices—often those voices and that specific language that has been with him—or *her*—since birth, and employ them to communicate some truth that he hasn't determined in advance. Likewise you build a model that is a hypothetical solution to a problem, not yet observationally provable."

I privately thought that it was a foolish analogy, and if Charlie had said it I would have laughed. An equation had nothing to do with people saying words on a stage, apart from the fact that both could be written down. The relationships between the forces in our universe had an objective reality, and that universe had a discoverable history; I wasn't in the business of making things up.

"She's a superstar!" Charlie said, with typical hyperbole. And then to me, "Don't you have Glashow now?"

"It was canceled."

"I do need to excuse myself, however," Pope said. "I have the misfortune of having been chosen for a search committee, and so I'm off to spend two hours debating the merits of a candidate we've already decided won't be hired."

Charlie laughed, and he turned to her.

"Next week, Charlotte?"

He spoke in a different register, a continuation of whatever they'd been talking about before, and it was obvious—not only what Pope was doing, but that my friend was in some way enjoying it. He was brazen enough to touch her, just his fingertips on her elbow. I noticed that he wasn't wearing a wedding band, but there was an elaborately fluted gold and sapphire ring on the pinky finger of his right hand. He nodded gravely to me, before returning to the dim sanctuary of his office, shutting the door behind him.

"What are you doing here?" Charlie said.

"Waiting for you." I touched her arm, made my eyes wide. *"Charlotte."*

Charlie grinned. "He's intense—okay? But he's basically a genius. He actually won a MacArthur genius grant, after his last book was published."

"What was it about?"

"Pierre Choderlos de Laclos—who wrote *Dangerous Liaisons*. A biography of an eighteenth-century writer, which makes it even more incredible that people actually read it."

"Well, but the movies were so popular."

"But that was years ago. And he's not writing about the movies—he doesn't even like them. He writes about Laclos as a feminist, and also really a postmodernist, two hundred years before anyone even used that term."

"Is that crazy thing his wedding ring?"

"His mother's engagement ring—isn't it gorgeous? He told me it's vintage Boucheron."

"But he's not married?"

"No, he is. She's a professional dancer, or she was. She used to be with Paul Taylor in New York, if you can believe that."

I didn't know who Paul Taylor was, a fact I wasn't about to reveal. "So are you, like, having a liaison?"

Charlie gave me an exasperated look. "Helen, *please*."

This conversation happened in the spring of our junior year, before Pope had done anything more than compliment Charlie's intellect, and keep her in his office longer than their meetings were intended to last. There was a woman who warned Charlie about him, though. She was a senior named Trisha Young, whom Charlie knew from the Black Students Association meetings that she sometimes attended with Kwesi at the Student Center in the quad.

Trisha cornered Charlie in the dining hall at North House, where Kwesi lived, and told her that she should choose a different advisor, because two girls she knew (she wouldn't name them) had dropped Pope's seminar after rebuffing his advances. She described exactly how Charlie's association with Pope would go. The professor would begin with suggestive comments, would gradually start to touch her in a friendly way, would then one day confess his uncontrollable attraction—but only after making himself indispensable to her academic career. *You're his type,* Trisha had said.

Charlie related the conversation with Trisha when she got home that night. She told me she'd assured Trisha she could handle Pope, and that she didn't totally trust the older student, who she thought might have designs on Kwesi.

"You think she was lying about Pope?" I asked.

"No," she said.

"What did she say when you said you were going to apply for the tutorial with him anyway?"

"She said I'd go far."

We were in the living area of our room in Lowell House, smaller and less comfortable than the one we'd had the previous year but also older in feeling, with its scuffed wooden floor, low ceiling, and mullioned windows, the glass thicker at the bottom than the top. Charlie was on the green futon underneath the buzzing halogen lamp, sitting as she usually did, with her feet tucked under her.

"Was she being sarcastic?"

She got a funny smile on her face. "I don't think so," she said.

8.

I'd promised Vincenzo that I would make my last changes to our electroweak paper while I was traveling, but instead I spent my time taking notes for the possible book about kilonovas. Being alone in the modern hotel room in Pöllau, with its sleek wooden furniture and immaculate picture window, made me want to write. My window looked out on some ski slopes; I'd never learned, but I liked watching the old-fashioned double chair creeping up and down the mountain. The schedule for the conference was busy, a relentless series of mandatory lectures and panels, with social events at mealtimes. I rarely sleep much when I travel, and I got up early, even for Central European Time. Each of the three mornings I was there, I lay in bed until 5:30, then gave up and made coffee in the miniature espresso machine the hotel provided. I sat at the desk in front of the window, watching the winter sky lightening over the gingerbread roofs of the old village and the dome of the cathedral. The evergreens were blue under the snow. The sun came up, and the ski lifts jerked into action. The whole valley turned gold. It gave me a burst of confidence, as if for a moment you could see the precious stuff underground, which had been made inside colliding stars.

I got back to Boston a day later than I'd planned, because my connection from Frankfurt had been canceled. There was no snow on the ground when I arrived at Logan, only a cold, driving rain, and it took forever to get a cab. When I walked in the door, my mother and father were lying on the floor. My mother was on her stomach in what I believe is the scorpion pose, wearing a shiny blue unitard with a hood. My father was lying on his back, on the kitchen floor, his body protruding from the under-sink cabinet.

"Is that Helen?" My father's voice was muffled. "I'm rerouting your disposal pipe. I can't believe it's lasted this long."

"I'm so sorry about the flight being canceled. I couldn't believe it when I got to the airport."

"That kind of thing's happening more and more," my father said.

My mother took a deep, whistling breath. "He has a problem with catastrophic thinking—everything and the kitchen sink." I looked at my father, whose head was indeed hidden in that very spot. "This is especially good before or after a long flight, Helen. You should join me."

Most physicists have strange parents. The parents of future physicists must avoid imparting certain basic facts about the world, such as the fact that a person gifted in abstract numerical thinking might make a fortune in any number of financial jobs; the fact that most people are happier with money than without; and in some cases, the fact that women are vastly underrepresented in the field. When people ask what my parents did to encourage me toward a distinguished scientific career, I say that they simply didn't know any better. It's a joke, but with a lot of truth in it.

"Where's Jack?" I asked them.

"Downstairs, with your friends."

Andrea and I had made all the arrangements for the handoff of the apartment to Terrence before I left, but the full reality of their arrival this weekend had escaped me during the last twenty-four hours of travel. It was a relief not being immediately responsible for Jack's needs. I took my suitcase upstairs, dropped it in the bedroom, and washed my face. I'd developed a chest cold on the plane, and more than anything I wanted to lie down on the bed, take advantage of the fact that there were other adults who could be trusted to keep our small household running. A part of me wanted to ask my parents to stay even longer; my canceled flight had made them miss theirs, but I think they would have postponed it again, if I had asked. It wasn't only pride that kept me from doing so. I'd resolved when Jack was born that I would manage on my own. I had the idea that child-rearing, done in this intentionally challenging way, might be more interesting, less likely to fall into conventional patterns. I can see flaws in that theory now, but I wasn't ready to go back on it. And so I forced myself to go downstairs, where I found both my parents upright again, my father putting away his tools.

"You brought those with you, from L.A.?"

"Just the portable kit."

"I have tools, Dad."

My father ignored this statement. "I wouldn't have known the gasket needed replacing if there hadn't been a clog."

"Why was there a clog?"

My father glanced at my mother, who was now sitting in lotus position, her palms uplifted on her knees, her thumbs and first fingers forming little holes in space.

"Artichoke leaves," my father whispered.

My mother opened her eyes. "Now I eat an artichoke every day for lunch."

"Just an artichoke?"

"With Greek yogurt, cumin, and salt. I've been doing it for three weeks, and I can't tell you how different I feel. I've been trying to convince your father to try it."

My mother went back to college when Amy and I were in high school; when we were in college, she was getting her master's, and she eventually became a reading specialist for elementary school children. If there's one quality everyone in my family shares, it's a dogged persistence and a need to keep busy. Amy and I have discussed our mother's embrace of various wellness trends, and the possibility that she may have retired too soon.

"Artichokes," my father said. "So much mess, so little reward."

"Well, thanks," I told them both. "I would've missed the conference without you. Can you stay for dinner?"

"The flight's in four hours," my father said. "We want to leave in twenty minutes."

"I'll go down then and get Jack."

"He offered to have Jack stay with them yesterday," my mother said, standing up. "Your father didn't want to do it."

"We hardly knew Terrence before," my father said.

I was surprised. "Did you spend a lot of time with him?"

"Well, not exactly," my mother said. "But since the children were constantly together—"

"They were?"

My father made an irritated sound. He likes to arrive at the airport at least three hours in advance, even for a domestic flight.

"Oh yes," my mother said, ignoring him. "Poor little thing. And she's so pretty."

I thought this was something I might not have noticed, if I hadn't been friends with Charlie—the way that white people would compliment her in a manner that was designed to demonstrate their own aesthetic broad-mindedness. *That color looks great on you. I could never pull that off. I love your hair!* Charlie would dismiss people like that—"absurd"—I would agree, and in this way neither of us would have to think about whether or not I might have made similar comments if she hadn't been always subtly correcting me in advance.

"We weren't quite sure what to make of him."

"Terrence?"

"He's a little sullen, no?"

"Well, his wife just died."

"I meant his *attitude*," my mother said. "In general."

"I loved Charlie," my father said, with genuine feeling. Charlie, on the one spring break when she'd come out to visit me in L.A., had developed a teasing rapport with my father that had seemed to draw him out of the interior world where he lived most of his life.

"What does Terrence do for a living?" my mother asked.

"He and his brother have a business making wooden surfboards."

My father was interested. "They actually make them? You mean, by hand?"

I told him that they did, although I was pretty sure it was Ray who was the craftsman.

"Well, he's certainly handsome," my mother said. "I'll give him that."

When I went downstairs, I found Terrence and the children sitting at a glass coffee table playing Yahtzee. The table had an open, aluminum-alloy base, and Simmi had filled it with a miniature assemblage: key chains, a collection of molded plastic animals, tiny rubber erasers shaped like pieces of food, coloring books, markers, a puzzle featuring Noah's ark, a Slinky. Of Terrence's possessions, the only evidence was a pair of kettlebells, sitting in the empty brick fireplace, and a framed poster ("San Diego Surf Film Festival 2003") propped against one wall.

Jack ran to me. I took him in my arms, trying not to breathe on him too much—when both of us got sick, that was the worst. But he didn't let me hold him for long. He wiggled away after a moment, accusing me with his eyes.

"Why weren't you home yesterday?"

"My flight was canceled. Grandma must've told you."

"It didn't snow," Jack said, as if this was also my fault. "I told them it would."

"Last winter was brutal," I said. "This one's wimpy."

Terrence blew out his lips and gave a dramatic pretend shiver. It was rare to see him do anything silly, and Simmi laughed delightedly.

"We played fifty-eight games of Yahtzee," she told me.

"Not today?"

Terrence smiled. "Since we got here, she means."

"I didn't mean for you to have to . . ."

"It's fine," Terrence said. "We invited him." He'd been sitting cross-legged with the children, but now he jumped up lightly and went to check something on the stove.

"Grandpa just wanted to read to me." Jack experimented with a sort of adolescent tone. "It was so boring."

"You love reading."

"Their food is terrible."

"I like the green goddess dressing," Simmi put in.

Jack made a face.

"Well, we're getting pizza tonight," I told him. I looked at Terrence. "If you want—"

"We're already cooking. Vegan chili—you're welcome to join us."

"I love vegan chili!"

"Do you even know what vegan is?" I asked Jack.

"Chili from the planet Vega," Terrence said. "Taste it if you dare."

Vega is an AOV main sequence star in the constellation Lyra, but it seemed pedantic to point that out.

"I think we should give you guys a little peace. It sounds like Jack was down here all the time."

"He's cool," Terrence said.

Jack looked at Terrence as if he'd just offered a trip to Disney World, or maybe as if Terrence were Disney World. Then he turned to me:

"See? They love me."

I couldn't help laughing.

"Still," I said. "We're going to have to say goodbye. Just temporarily."

"After this game."

"Your grandparents are leaving in a half hour," I told him. "They want to see you before they go."

"That doesn't take a half hour."

"Jack!"

I'd been back for five minutes, and I was already scolding him.

"We'll finish later, little man," Terrence said.

Because Terrence had insisted, Jack followed me out of the apartment in a disgruntled way. On the carpeted stairs in between the two apartments, he started to cry.

"You never let me do anything fun. We always have to leave everything early, because of your stupid work!"

This was fairly standard, as a response to an out-of-town trip, and I wouldn't have minded if my parents and Terrence hadn't been within earshot. When I opened the door to our apartment, they were standing just behind it, fully dressed in their outerwear and peering at a printout of their reservation. They pretended not to notice Jack's expression.

"It says we arrive in Terminal Five," my father said. "But we left from Three."

"Why would that make a difference?"

"Five is under construction."

"Maybe it's only the departures that are under construction?"

"We'll need to ask while we're still on the ground," my father said. "We should have left earlier."

"It'll be fine," my mother said. Then she turned to Jack: "What was the score this time?"

"Her dad had one thirty-two and we had seventy-six. But then we had to stop."

"He doesn't let you win," my father said approvingly.

"Come here and give me a hug," my mother said. "How much does Grandma love you?"

"So much," Jack mumbled into her coat.

My father looked back at the printout and shook his head. "They charge you three hundred dollars to change the tickets now—even though we explained the situation."

"I'm so sorry," I said. "I'll pay for it."

My father shrugged. "It's not your fault. Nothing is predictable anymore."

My mother raised her eyebrows at me, and mouthed: "Catastrophic thinking."

My father hugged Jack the way he hugged everyone, as if he had made a careful study of the gesture and was attempting to reproduce it.

"Planning anything is ludicrous," he said.

9.

We ended up back downstairs for dinner. Jack wanted to help with the chili, but Simmi declined, and so she and I were left in the living room together.

Simmi looked at me for a moment, then casually extended one leg up above her head, cupping the arch of her foot in her hand.

"Wow."

"That's just a warm-up," she said. "I go to a gym here now."

"That's good."

"She can do everything!" Jack called from the kitchen. "Show her the back walkover."

A certain excitement manifested itself under Simmi's guarded expression.

"I'd love to see."

"We have to go in there," she said.

She took me to the back bedroom, the larger of the two, and it was immediately clear where Terrence had focused his decorating energy. Most of the floor was covered with a rainbow-colored sectional mat, and there was a small trampoline in one corner. Above her bed, he had drilled a toggle bolt into the joist, from which was suspended a net canopy edged with pink ribbon. Synthetic net is made of carbon fiber; the mat was probably vinyl and polyethylene foam. I often think about the oceanic gyres where so many of these materials will remain, long after all of us are gone.

"Could you stand against the wall?" Simmi asked politely. "I don't want to kick you."

I backed up and almost bumped into the small wooden play kitchen that Terrence had shipped from L.A. The kitchen had a range and control panel at the right height for a toddler, as well as an oven crammed with pots, cooking utensils, and wooden food. Simmi saw me looking at it.

"I don't play with that anymore," she said.

"Jack keeps some toys he used to play with, too."

"Uh huh. Okay, watch."

I watched her do a series of tricks; she did the walkover Jack admired, several cartwheel variations, and walked on her hands.

Then, to my alarm, she jumped on the trampoline and launched herself backward in the air, doing a full rotation before landing on the mat. She raised both arms in the air, Olympian-style.

"That's really something," I said.

Simmi dropped into a split. "My grandma doesn't like me to do it so much."

"How come?"

"She says I'm going to be too tall for gymnastics."

"I wouldn't worry about that now."

"She thinks I should do ballet instead."

"Well, if you like gymnastics . . ."

"That's what my mom used to say. But I think she really wanted me to be a scientist, like you."

"Really?"

"She was really into science. She wanted to write a show about it."

"She told me that."

Simmi nodded. "I don't know if I like science, though." She bent her front knee, drawing it toward her, and lifted her back foot, clasping it with both hands behind her head.

"Moms want their kids to do what makes them happy." It was the kind of platitude I try not to rely on too heavily, but it seemed best to go with safe and dull, under the circumstances.

Simmi trained her big eyes on me. "Did she tell you that?"

"Well, not exactly—we didn't talk on the phone too much."

"She hated talking on the phone," Simmi said.

"I don't like it either."

"But you know what?" Simmi rotated her hips into a straddle, then stretched forward, so her forehead was against the mat. "Sometimes when it rings, I think it's her. Isn't that weird?"

We ate at a small table in the kitchen downstairs, Terrence sitting on a stool because there were only three chairs. He held his plate on his lap, and reached down periodically to make sure we all had what we needed for the meal. There were no glasses—we drank water from mugs, but Terrence had found small bowls for various garnishes: sour cream, cheese, cilantro, and sriracha.

"This is amazing," I said.

Terrence was skeptical. "You just got back from Europe."

"Dessert in Austria is so great, but you'd think the rest of the food would be better than it is."

He turned to Simmi. "They fly Helen all the way to Europe to talk about physics."

"What is that, again?" Simmi said.

I looked at Jack, but he didn't seem interested in volunteering.

"Physics is the study of forces. We use math to describe the way things move."

"I hate math," Simmi said.

"Me, too," Jack said immediately.

"You don't hate math," Terrence said. There was a sort of pleading in his voice that surprised me.

"I do," Simmi said. "It's so boring."

"It is so boring," I said.

Both children looked at me, Jack in amazement, and Simmi with that same kind of wary interest.

"It's so boring until you get to higher math, which is one of the most fun things you can do."

"When is higher math?" Simmi asked.

"It can start in high school," I said. "Some people take two years of calculus in high school—I did."

"I'm not going to do that," Jack put in.

"But you have to do math, so you might as well work hard." I had an inspiration. "It's like gymnastics," I said. "Imagine if all you did was warm up. If you had to do warm-ups every day in practice, but you decided never to try the tumbling."

Simmi laughed. "That would be stupid."

"Or surfing," Terrence said. "What if you just practiced pop-ups on the sand and never got in the water?"

"Exactly," I said.

"But math isn't like gymnastics," Jack said.

"She says it is." Terrence gave me one of his disconcerting smiles.

"I could take you guys to see a real physics lab one day," I said. "We could have a private tour."

"Would we wear lab coats?"

I couldn't tell if lab coats were a draw. "Not coats, but definitely eye protection."

"Protection from what?"

"Lasers. We could go see a project called LIGO." If nothing else, Neel's presence would make this an easy promise to fulfill.

"Lasers are like light sabers," Jack explained.

"I know what they are," Simmi said. "May we be excused?"

I looked at their plates: both children had finished the chili, which substituted hominy and vegetables for meat, and was somewhat spicy. When they'd left the table, I complimented Terrence.

"He would never eat that at home—even if I knew how to make it."

"When they help cook, they always eat."

Terrence began gathering the plates. His T-shirt was short-sleeved, a brilliant blue, as if it were the middle of the summer, and it was clear that the kettlebells were in use. The tattoo on the inside of his arm that I hadn't been able to make out before was a sea creature—a stingray.

"I was thinking about the yard in the back," Terrence said. "Do you ever grow anything?"

"Besides the grass?"

"Simmi and I had a little garden in L.A.—peas, strawberries, Chinese cabbage, gigante beans. We even tried some corn."

"Really?"

"I wouldn't start with that here. But maybe some tomatoes and beans. Even summer squash would probably work." He picked up the stack of plates, and took them to the sink. I'd automatically agreed with Charlie's parents, when I'd first heard about Terrence from Charlie, that he was somehow beneath her—now I realized how stupid that was. What woman wouldn't want to be with a handsome surfer who cared about his daughter's education in math, and loved to cook? It was true that Terrence had gone to a two-year community college, did a job that had nothing to do with what he'd learned there. Wasn't the kind of education Charlie and I had received simply a set of words and references that connected you to a group of people like yourself? In physics we say that we do science for science's sake, and that there is value in that. Our knowledge of our universe itself, from its explosive early inflation to its current growth rate, has become exponentially more precise in my lifetime. We could all give a quote to a journalist, or end an undergraduate lecture with a few sentences about scientific think-ing as a key component of our humanity, and I think most of us really believe those words. When a practical application is avail-able, though—the ramifications of closing the freedom-of-choice loophole for cybersecurity, for example—we rush to emphasize it. While someone services our car, cooks our meal, or bathes our chil-dren, the sentences and paragraphs about our fundamental utility spin out like magic.

"That sounds great," I told Terrence. "Anything that makes him enthusiastic about food. He doesn't like being shorter than the other boys in his grade—I tell him he has to eat to grow."

"How tall was the guy?"

I wasn't used to anyone asking about Jack's origins. Even my closest friends tiptoed around it. I thought I might have behaved the same way in their places, and yet I always wanted to talk about it. Charlie, notably, had wanted to know all the details. She'd expressed remorse at the time that she hadn't been there to go through the bios with me, to help me choose.

"Tall," I said. "Six-two—most of them are. It seems like height is a lot of mothers' primary concern."

The kitchen was too small for me to be helpful without getting in Terrence's way, and so I went back to the table to get the mugs, the crumpled paper towels the kids had been using for napkins.

"I'm going to have to start going down to New York," he said. "Maybe every other weekend. We're opening a store in Williams-burg. I've been postponing it—you can do that, when you work for your brother—but it can't last forever."

I was hoping I knew what he was going to say, but I didn't want to guess and be wrong.

"She'll usually be with her grandparents, except this weekend they're going to a wedding. They said they could skip it, but I thought—"

"We'd love to have her."

"It's only two nights. And then the next time you go away—"

"It's no problem."

"I get you, you get me back." He looked up then, hopeful. "And I think it's good for them, too, since—"

"—they don't have siblings."

Terrence looked relieved. "Yeah."

We could hear the kids jumping around in Simmi's room; she had put on Taylor Swift.

"You know, I thought Addie would be so helpful. To have a woman in Simmi's life right now, and all that. My mom's—well, we're good now. But she's not anyone's idea of a role model."

I laughed. "Addie's definitely role model material."

Terrence nodded. "Charlie's 'issues' with her mom seemed like a lot of nonsense to me, honestly," he said. "She would go on about ballet and piano and church, and I would be like, uh huh. I mean, it sounded *ideal*."

"In some ways, I guess."

"But now I totally see it. I'm not even talking about Addie's whole thing with me. I could deal with that—temporarily—if it was good for Simmi. But I don't know anymore. She was asking the other day if it wouldn't be better to sign her up for ballet instead of gym." He shook his head. "And I'm like, yeah—let's change up the one thing she actually fucking likes—the one thing that makes her happy right now—so she can fit into your little vision of how everything's supposed to look."

"You want me to dry those?"

"They'll dry." He reached into the fridge and pulled out a dark brown bottle with an elaborate label. "It's kombucha," he said. "You want some?"

It was already past Jack's bedtime, and I knew I should take him upstairs. I was postponing it, not only because he would fight, but because it was comfortable here with Terrence and Simmi, the pop music playing in the other room. When we went up to our apartment, I would have to start all over again with the loud cheerfulness I often employ to make it feel as if there aren't only two of us there.

"I'll try it," I said.

Terrence poured the fizzy brown liquid into clean mugs. "Charlie thought this was a better place for kids to grow up," Terrence said. "She didn't always think that way, though, not when Simmi was born. She used to talk about how great Southern California was: the beach, and being outside year-round. But then the more successful she got, the more she'd complain—about the *values* out there. I was like, we don't have Hollywood values on the beach . . . but Charlie was just in the thick of it. She started to talk about Boston all the time—that's the main reason I thought we'd try it now."

"I guess we have our own set of problems."

Terrence laughed, and his expression showed his agreement a little more readily than I would have liked. "But I think Charlie thought everyone here was like you."

"Like me?"

Terrence nodded. "Because you don't care about all the nonsense that's such a big deal in L.A.—money and style and all that."

I was wearing a long sweater over leggings, which had taken me some time to select. I moved slightly, so that the lower half of my body was concealed by the kitchen counter.

From the bedroom, the children were shouting happily over the music. Five seconds, Simmi yelled, and Jack counted down: 5-4-3-2-1!

"And even the way you had him on your own—on purpose. She really admired that."

"Tons of women do it," I said. "More and more."

"Okay." Terrence leaned back against the counter, one leg crossed over the other. He took a drink of the sour, heavily carbonated tea, which I was getting down only a little at a time. "But your career, too. She said you'd given a lot up for it."

Where had they had this conversation? Sitting in traffic? Over dinner just the two of them, or just before they fell asleep at night?

"You don't give a fuck what people think," Terrence said.

"Thanks?"

"Yeah, man," he said. "It's a compliment."

10.

Terrence went to New York that Friday morning after dropping Simmi off at school. I skipped a department meeting in order to pick her up, but I had to put Jack in aftercare so that I could get to Simmi's school on time. I had considered asking Jack's sitter to do both pickups, but Simmi had only met Julia once or twice. I worried that she would be uncomfortable, and I wanted the first time she stayed with us to be perfect. The mania to perfect things that are by their nature imperfectible is one of those areas in which I most frequently make a wrong turn.

I just made it to Simmi's school by three, and I was waiting in the car on the school's circular drive when she came out. I had imagined that she might exit alone, even dejected: she'd been at the school only four months, and I remembered girls her age as especially nasty to newcomers. Instead she came out an alley alongside the brick building with two other girls, one with an arm draped over her shoulder, and the other trying to get her attention. Simmi was ignoring both of them; she was scanning the line of cars, looking for me.

I leaned out the window and waved, and she detached herself from her friends, came through the gate.

She came to the passenger window first, and smiled in at me. "Do you notice something different about me?"

She was wearing the silver parka, with hot pink trim, sweater leggings, and a popular brand of furry blue boots. Her mood seemed buoyant. Otherwise I couldn't see anything different, except maybe that the backs of her hands were covered with scrawled writing. The temperature was only in the twenties, but she wasn't wearing gloves.

"You wrote on your hands?"

Simmi got into the backseat and glanced at her hands, surprised. "I always do that. No—look!"

I pulled up a little, and then turned to face her. She had pushed her braids behind her ears to reveal a pair of earrings, gold studs with red rhinestone centers.

"Oh," I said. "Nice! It's going to be cold this weekend, though—do you have gloves, or a hat?"

"I can't because of my earrings—it hurts."

"Bye, Simmi!" a child called, a different girl than she'd come out with, and Simmi gave a casual wave out the window.

"I don't think they're supposed to hurt," I told her.

"They're infected," Simmi said. "So. I'm supposed to be putting stuff on them every night, but sometimes I forget."

I felt a moment of annoyance toward Terrence, who hadn't said anything to me about ear care.

"I'll remind you this weekend."

She looked up at me. "Yours aren't pierced."

"I played soccer when I was your age."

"You couldn't tape them?"

"You could, but it seemed like too much trouble."

"I've been asking forever, but my mom always said no. And then we were just walking by a place, weekend before last, and my dad surprised me. He's been wanting another tat—he had the design in his phone—and so we just went in and did both. It's three fish."

Simmi looked at me in her strange way—as if she could see me wondering where her father's new tattoo was located.

"It's because he's Pisces. And it's perfect, because of surfing."

"Cool," I said. "Well, let's go get Jack." I turned to check and saw that she'd fastened her seat belt without being reminded.

"Ready?"

"You didn't say the safety word."

"What?"

"We had to have a safety word, at my old school. You weren't supposed to go home with anyone unless they said it, even if you knew them."

"Oh," I said. "Well—I think that's a good system, but your dad didn't say anything about it. You want me to call him?"

Simmi considered. "No—I know I'm supposed to go with you."

I thought of asking what the word was, and didn't.

"Anyway, my mom's the one who made it up—it's in Latin," she added. "I'm probably the only person who remembers it."

We had quesadillas for dinner, and talked about Harry Potter. Jack and I had gotten only as far as volume three, and it annoyed me that the scenes Simmi was narrating came from later in the series. Jack looked so transfixed, though, that at first I didn't interrupt.

"The way to defeat a Boggart is to fight him with a partner," Simmi said. "It has to turn into its enemy's greatest fear, right? But if there are two people, it can't decide which fear it's going to become. It gets confused—sometimes it goes back and forth."

"I think J. K. Rowling might have gotten that from another writer, named George Orwell."

"Probably he got it from her," Simmi suggested. "She's really famous."

Jack turned to me. "Got what?" There was something heartbreaking in his expression, revealing his urgent desire to keep up with the conversation.

"The idea," I told him. "In one of Orwell's books there's a room where you find your greatest fear—whatever it is." I felt stupid the moment I'd said it. Room 101 was likely to be an interesting concept only if your greatest fear hadn't yet materialized in your life. But if Simmi made that connection, she didn't show it.

"It's just like that! Mine is spiders."

"Spiders eat mosquitoes, though," Jack said. "Mine is being locked in and not being able to get out."

"Jack once locked himself in a bathroom at his cousins' house," I explained.

"Hey!" Jack said, embarrassed, but Simmi wasn't paying attention.

"What's yours?" she asked me.

"What?"

But I was stalling. As I child it had seemed to me that most children (including my sister) worried about their parents dying, and I remember feeling guilty about my lack of concern in that department. It was my own death—not the dying itself but what came afterward, the complete and permanent cessation of my own consciousness—that terrified me.

Now that dread is magnified because of Jack, and eclipsed by an even greater one, of losing him.

"Clowns," I said.

Both Jack and Simmi giggled. *"Clowns?"*

"Don't make fun of me!"

"That can't be your biggest fear," said Jack, who knows me better than I sometimes like to admit.

"It is," I said. "I hate their makeup."

Jack picked up his plate from the table. "Can we go set up our sleeping bags?"

"You don't need a sleeping bag," I told him. "You have your bed."

"I want to sleep on the floor."

I hadn't been sure whether Simmi would want to sleep in Jack's room, or on the sofa bed in the living room. I offered her both options, while Jack watched her anxiously, clearly not having considered the possibility that Simmi might want her own space.

"I'll sleep in Jack's room."

Jack looked relieved.

"But if you're not going to use your bed, maybe I'll sleep in it?"

"Okay!"

I was annoyed again, although I tried not to show it. Had Simmi just manipulated my son out of his own bed, or was it natural that she should be dominant in their friendship? She was, after all, a year older than he was, and a girl, and it was nice that they got along so well. They went off to set up the sleeping bag while I half cleaned up the kitchen, and then got distracted by email.

At about eight, I suggested that they start getting themselves ready for bed. Simmi said that she needed a shower, and so I offered that she could use my bathroom while Jack took his shower downstairs. In the bathroom she asked if she could borrow a shower cap, moisturizer, and some cleanser for her face. I didn't know whether Charlie had introduced beauty products early, or if all eight-year-olds now required a separate facial cleanser, but I was able to locate all of these items. I handed them to her along with her towel.

"Do you need something for your ears, too?"

"Yes, please," Simmi said, and so I went downstairs again, to Jack's small bathroom, where I keep most of the medicine. I found him already on his bed in his pajamas, trying to read Harry Potter to himself, although we normally read it together. I thought he might have wanted Simmi to come upon him doing this; he gave me a wary look, as if he expected me to expose his ruse.

"Simmi needs some medicine for her ears," I told him. I couldn't find the antibiotic ointment, and so I googled "ear piercing care." The first blog that came up suggested witch hazel, something I had left over from when Jack had stitches on his eyebrow in kindergarten. I took this and some cotton rounds for Simmi. Jack followed me upstairs.

"Simmi," I said from outside the door. "I have something for your ears. Jack's here, too, but he can go downstairs if you want."

She opened the door. She was wearing shorts and a T-shirt

instead of pajamas, and I hoped Jack wasn't going to be embarrassed about his, which were a little too small for him, patterned with sporting equipment.

"He can come in."

"My dad used to use this when we scraped our knees." Simmi sat on the toilet seat, and pushed back her braids so that I could examine the piercings. The skin was red and maybe a little inflamed, but there was no pus or scabbing; it wasn't as bad as I expected.

"Witch hazel," Simmi read off the package.

"That sounds like Harry Potter," Jack said.

Simmi laughed.

"I am *Witch Hazel*," Jack declared, hamming it up.

"You can't be a witch. You have to be a wizard." Simmi gasped suddenly. "Ow—that stings!"

"Wizard Hazel zaps you with his Phoenix Wand!"

Simmi covered her ear with her hand. "That really hurt."

"I'm sorry."

Jack was overexcited, hopping up and down. "You need Hermione to mix you a potion!"

I touched his arm. "Go ahead," I told him. "You can wait for Simmi in your room."

When they were in bed, I got a beer from the fridge, thought about working on the electroweak paper, and instead watched the trailer for a French detective show that everyone in our department was suddenly crazy about. Then I watched a few more trailers, which I find is a good way of keeping up, without actually wasting time watching television shows. I was still doing it when Terrence texted to ask if Simmi wanted to talk. I said that we were having a great time, but that the kids were asleep and I was doing some work.

Great! Terrence texted back, *will call in AM,* and I thought I could hear his relief. Almost as soon as I'd sent it, Simmi appeared.

"Hi," I said. "Do you need anything?"

"Can I have some more of the witch hazel? My ears are hurting again."

"It didn't sting too much?"

"It stopped after a second."

I got her the solution and the cotton pads, and she disappeared into the bathroom. She came out a few minutes later, but instead of going back to the bedroom, she stood in the doorway, playing with the plastic package I'd given her.

"These are cool."

"The cotton rounds?"

"Can you use them for makeup?"

"You don't wear makeup, do you?"

Simmi looked sideways. "Sometimes my dad lets me play with it. At home."

In college Charlie had kept her cosmetics in a plastic case with separate compartments, like a makeup artist. I wondered if she had continued using it. Was that the makeup Simmi meant?

"Is Jack asleep?" I asked her.

She nodded. "For a while."

"He sometimes falls asleep before I'm out of the room."

Simmi gave me a knowing look, as if she were familiar with this quality in little boys. "I sometimes have trouble sleeping."

"Me, too."

"Women don't sleep as well as men."

"I don't know about that."

"My mom said it's because we're supposed to wake up when babies cry."

"You have a while before you have to worry about that."

"She said my dad used to be the one to get up and give me a bottle."

"You have a great dad."

Simmi looked at me from under long lashes: "But you had to do it yourself."

"Your mom told you that?"

Simmi shook her head. "No. But didn't you?"

"My mom stayed with us for two weeks after Jack was born. But yes, after that."

"Is that weird?"

"Getting up at night?"

"Not having a husband."

I looked at Simmi, and she looked innocently back.

"I've never had a husband, so it wasn't weird for me."

"What's Jack's dad's name?"

"I don't know."

"You don't know his *name*?"

"Nope."

"What if you just, like, ran into him? Like in Starbucks or something?"

"I don't think I'd recognize him. He certainly wouldn't recognize me."

Simmi shook her head. "*Super* weird."

I took the kind of deep, slow breath a therapist once recommended for challenging interpersonal situations. It had no immediate effect.

"Are you ready for me to take you back to bed?"

"I can go myself," she said. But she didn't. Instead she came farther into the room, leaned against the arm of the couch.

"Do you love him more?"

"I don't know him, so I can't love him," I said.

Simmi straightened her arms, pushing off the couch and lifting her feet in the air. Then she dropped back down.

"Not *him*. I mean Jack."

"Do I love Jack more than what?"

"Than if you had a husband," Simmi said.

"I love Jack more than anything."

"Why do parents always say that?"

"Because it's true," I told her. "Kids can't imagine how much we love them."

Simmi frowned. Then she sat down, not on the couch but on the armrest. Her back wasn't toward me, but she was sitting sideways, so I was looking more at her shoulder than her face.

"Parents have their own parents. And they have husbands and wives"—she glanced at me quickly—"sometimes. And their jobs and stuff. Kids just have parents."

"They have grandparents and other relatives. And school."

"That's not the same."

"You're right."

"Parents forget everything."

"We forget a lot."

Simmi lifted her knee so that her foot was lined up on the arm of the couch, like a balance beam. She picked at the last remains of some light blue polish on her big toenail. It was hard to hear her, because her chin was resting on her knee.

"They forget how much they used to love their own parents," she said, "when they were kids."

When Simmi had gone back to bed, I opened the electroweak paper to see if Vincenzo had added comments. He had, as usual, but I couldn't focus. I tried my sister; it was three hours earlier there, and she was making dinner. She said she could talk anyway and put the phone on speaker. I could hear her clattering around the kitchen.

I told Amy about my conversation with Simmi.

"Maybe she was trying to connect with you," Amy said.

"By interrogating me?"

"That must be a defense mechanism on her part," Amy said.

"Yeah, it's fine. It's just—what if she says something to Jack?"

"Like what?"

"About not having a father."

"Well, then he could ask her about her mother."

"Right—it would be a total disaster."

"Or exactly what they both need."

Amy said something to one of her daughters in a firm, maternal voice. I thought of how much better my sister would be at dealing with Simmi than I was. She seemed able to keep her feelings on an even keel, whereas I was always fluctuating between these poles of emotion, frustration and passionate attachment. Was that because I was the only parent, or because I was who I was? Had Charlie been more like Amy, or more like me?

"I haven't gotten one of those messages from Charlie's phone in a while."

"How long is a while?"

Like Jack, Amy requires precise answers, at least where numbers are concerned. "Almost a month."

"She's ghosting you."

"Ha ha."

"Sorry."

"I had to help Simmi with her ears. She said Charlie wouldn't let her pierce them, and then she did it with her dad. Now they're a little infected. She said her dad got another tattoo at the same time."

"I guess everyone has them now. Where is this additional tattoo?"

"I have no idea."

"I'm just getting the sense you might want to find out."

"He's my dead friend's *husband*."

"Yeah," Amy said, clanging metal on metal. "There's that."

I went in later that night to look at them. Jack was completely inside the sleeping bag, only a bit of his hair sticking out the top. As an infant, he'd liked being tightly swaddled, and even in his own bed, he would often sleep with the covers over his head. Simmi, on the other hand, had pushed off the quilt and the sheet, and was lying on her back, one arm draped over the side of the bed. I thought of rearranging it, but I was afraid of waking her. The expression on her face was an extreme version of the way she looked during the day, which I had taken for aloofness, even conceit. But it had been transformed by sleep. What I suddenly thought of, standing in the dark room, were the plaster casts from Pompeii: the lidded, alarmed eyes, mouth slightly open, chin tilted up, as if her face had been fixed in a moment of suffering. Suffering, but in four dimensions—what you might call yearning.

11.

It always took me a couple of weeks to catch up after a trip, and this one was no exception. From Pöllau, I'd gone on to see some of our colleagues at CERN in Geneva; those conversations had been useful, but I still had my own work to do on the electroweak paper, which I'd avoided in Pöllau because I'd wanted to think about the kilonova book. Vincenzo was furious about the delay on my end, with some justification; two of my grad students had completed theses over the holiday, and my postdoc Bence needed an extensive job recommendation. Jack's resentment about the trip also seemed of longer duration than usual. Whether this was because I hadn't let him come along, because he'd decided it was more fun downstairs with Terrence, or because it was the nature of seven-year-olds to be angry at their mothers, I had no idea.

It felt like the only person who wasn't fed up with me was Neel, who'd taken to coming to my office in the afternoons and attempting to drag me to the coffee shop on the other side of campus. One change in him since we'd last spent time together was his tolerance for luxuries like Italian coffee in the middle of the afternoon.

"They don't have coffee in Building 22?" I teased him, but I was always happy for the excuse to get out of the office, where the atmosphere that January had become less than congenial even before my trip. Most recently, Vincenzo and I had begun arguing about the temperature on our floor. I thought the office was overheated, whereas Vincenzo walked around with a martyred look, in scarves knitted for him by his most recent girlfriend. Before I went to Europe, my postdocs and graduate students had taken my side, while Vincenzo's had allied themselves with him, but on my return I found that both Srikanth and Bence had abandoned me. I'd initially been pleased that our preferences didn't line up with gender norms—wasn't it women in corporate offices who were always complaining about the air-conditioning?—but the problem got so bad that the plastic toggle on the thermostat actually snapped off, due to constant and vitriolic adjustment.

One night after Jack was asleep, I was catching up on email when I got a message from a graduate student in Vincenzo's group, a joke in the form of a graph. It was a spoof on our recent paper on luminosity correlations of gamma ray bursts: the most powerful electromagnetic explosions in the universe. The part of this "appendage" that was supposed to be especially clever was the addition of a temperature function to the graph, and the text underneath identifying it as a "Clapp correlation." The high-energy bursts as corresponded to temperature, of course, were supposed to be coming from me.

The email had been sent to my team of three postdocs and six graduate students, as well as to all of Vincenzo's. Of those nineteen people, three were female, including me, and the more I thought of the message's effect on my painfully shy grad student Chendong, or Vincenzo's outspoken (but primarily Italian-speaking) grad student Giulia, the angrier I got. I contemplated firing something back to the entire group, but resisted that very strong impulse. I waited until Vincenzo arrived in his office the next morning, his neck passive-aggressively wrapped in a multicolored balaclava.

"That was a bit disrespectful last night, no?" I tried to modulate my tone, so as not to be accused of creating "high-energy bursts."

Vincenzo glanced at his screen, as if to remind himself, but it was clear he'd been expecting my visit. He didn't get up. "Email," he said mournfully. "It has totally eroded the traditional relationship between teacher and student. When I was an undergraduate, at Sapienza, even the idea that we would've used a professor's Christian *name*—"

"But it needs to stop right now."

"Agreed."

"So, we leave the thermostat at sixty-eight—several degrees above what is necessary for human beings indoors. And your student comes to apologize."

Vincenzo waved his hand. "Done. That one's an idiot, anyway— I'm going to unload him on Nagy next year." He smiled at me. "My girlfriend tells me I'm more sensitive to temperature fluctuations in the early universe than I am to those naturally occurring in the women around me."

I stared at Vincenzo. Clearly I had missed the whole (not very skillfully delivered) point, which wasn't about cosmology but about me and my age—specifically the idea that I was having hot flashes connected to menopause. Never mind that I'm five to ten years from the average age at which women experience those symptoms; the whole office was now thinking about my menstrual cycle, and if I made more of an issue of it than I already had, it would be seen as evidence of my erratic, moody, essentially female behavior.

"It's not about the heat," I said.

"Of course not." Vincenzo expelled a puff of air from his mouth, and regarded me with what he must still consider his arresting black eyes. "And as for me, I'll simply put on another layer. The last thing I want to do is upset you, Helen."

It was a relief to walk to Mass Ave. for coffee with someone who wasn't a part of our group, and I took advantage of it as much as possible. It was also exciting to have an inside track on the events at LIGO, just before their big paper about the detection would be published. Now it wasn't only other scientists, but journalists and academics from non-science disciplines who were starting to hear about what they'd done. Neel said that a professor at Juilliard wanted to write a chamber piece for strings based on the data, and PBS was planning a documentary. All of this attention would become even more frantic when the chief scientists won the Nobel, a prize for which Neel could justifiably claim some credit. It killed me that he might think my idea for the book on kilonova was another attempt to piggyback on his success.

One afternoon in late January, because we were finishing a conversation, Neel accompanied me back from Building 22 to my office in Building 6. It had continued to rain instead of snow, and the cold was wet and biting. Neel was talking about gravity. As was typical with him, he wasn't talking about it in the abstract, but about a specific piece of equipment: a rotor that might be set up in proximity to one of the interferometers. The point would be to measure precisely the effects of gravity at distances we're familiar with here on Earth: what we call the meter scale. For Neel, LIGO had never been about the big news of a gravitational wave detection. The detection was nice, but his passion had always been the ways we could use—he liked to say "misuse"—these fantastic machines in the future. The rotor experiment was a perfect example. If he could get the money, he wanted to set up two of these rotors—the technical term was "dynamic field generators," or DFGs—one on either side of the laser. These would be rotating machines of extremely dense metal, like small windmills. They would be out of phase with each other, and would accordingly cancel out each other's influence on the laser inside the interferometers. Neel stopped, but I understood where he was going, and it was fantastically exciting. The LIGO scientists had always said that the interferometers could go beyond detecting gravitational waves, to probe our fundamental physical laws. If the rotors didn't cancel—if there was any disruption to the laser—that would change our understanding of the way gravity operates here on Earth. It would be nothing less than a refinement of relativity itself.

"I can make the rotor," Neel said. "I can even get the funding. For the rest, I'd need you." We had reached the plaza in front of the Center for Theoretical Physics, where my office was.

"I'm really busy these days," I told him.

"Too busy for a completely quixotic project that might change the world?"

"Obviously not."

Neel smiled. His hair was hidden underneath a dark red ski cap, and he'd shoved his hands into the pockets of his peacoat—possibly the same peacoat he'd owned in the days when we were meeting daily at the Hong Kong on Mass Ave., to work out the details of the Clapp-Jonnal. Neel liked even the worst Chinese food, and would always try the most unpromising dishes—Three Delights in a Nest, the Pu Pu Platter—just to see if he might discover a hidden treasure.

"It's not that quixotic," I said.

"Tilting at rotors," he said.

"That might be the nerdiest joke you've ever made. Is there even a chance we'd actually get permission to set up a rotor anywhere near one of the interferometers?"

Neel got serious. "It's a fairly slim chance. I wouldn't say it's impossible. We might have to set them up in the middle of the night, like those guys with the neutrino detector in Antarctica."

"I heard about that."

"They got in trouble, but they ended up getting funded in the end. NSF decided that if they wanted it that badly, they must be on to something."

"You're suggesting a midnight heist to revise non-Newtonian gravity?"

Neel smiled. "Let me just get through February."

"February's a big month for you." I hoped it sounded as if LIGO's triumphant announcement and Neel's wedding were just two events I was observing dispassionately from the outside. He bent down to tie his lace—he was wearing black construction boots, worn out at the toes—and I stopped to wait for him.

"Why did we break up?" he asked, standing up. "Do you remember?"

It was very cold, and it was possible that my shortness of breath had more to do with the weather than with the subject we were discussing.

"I think it had something to do with our disagreement over Einstein's fondness for Schopenhauer. You can *do* what you want—"

" 'But not *will* what you want,' " Neel finished. "Ugh. But was it really that, or was it the mind and the brain?"

"You certainly felt very strongly about that," I said.

"I still feel strongly that there's something we're talking about when we say 'human consciousness' that extends beyond the brain and the nervous system."

"And I still feel strongly that there isn't—but it's a ridiculous argument. It's not like we're going to change each other's minds."

Neel laughed and grabbed my elbow. "Change *what*?"

"The point is—we were absurdly self-important."

"We were twenty-two," Neel said. "And you were going off to Princeton."

"You were going to Chicago."

Neel released me, and we walked for several moments in silence down Albany Street, past the Pfizer building that was still under construction. In front of us the Kendall cogeneration plant released a sharply delineated white plume against the dingy sky.

"I'm going to Chicago next week, actually," Neel said. "Just for two days with my parents. They want to do a party for friends who can't make it to Mumbai for the wedding—I really can't spare the time this close to the press conference, but it means so much to my parents."

"Will the wedding be traditional?"

"It's going to be in Roxy's aunt's backyard—so no, not entirely. We are getting a priest, though."

"A Parsi or a Hindu priest?"

"One of each—for good measure. For the Parsi we had to find a sort of renegade. Women aren't supposed to marry outside the faith, because their children aren't considered Parsi. I think the rules are less stringent for men."

"Surprise."

"Yeah, but cut them a little slack. It's one of the oldest religions in the world—the Parsis have been at monotheism longer than anyone except the Jews. And the ceremonies are very pretty. The priests wear translucent white robes and white hats and they burn incense. And there are a lot of eggs involved—I'm not sure what's up with that. Roxy says that some of the priests are also magicians. For an extra tip, they'll do some tricks after the ceremony."

"Parsis believe in magic?"

"I think they just enjoy it. They're known for being fun-loving—the heaviest drinkers in India."

"It sounds like a great wedding."

"I wish you were coming."

"Me, too—if it wasn't so far. And if I hadn't just gotten back from Europe."

He looked at me in a knowing way, and I was sure he'd figured out the secondary motivation for my trip.

"What?" I asked.

"You remember how I asked you to be my second wife?"

It was a joke he used to make a lot, but it seemed to have acquired an entirely different meaning in the twenty-plus years since we'd been a couple.

"You're starting a little late for that, aren't you?" I said. "I think you should focus on just the one marriage."

"Right," Neel said, but he didn't take his eyes off mine. "That's what I'm planning to do."

12.

Neel and I had done our problem sets together for Arty; as undergrads, we'd studied in the Cabot Science Library, and sat around his room at the Grossmans' arguing and gossiping—but we didn't actually become a couple until the beginning of our senior year. A brief, depressing relationship of mine had just ended. On our first date, the young man in question confided in me gleefully about a bet he had going with his three roommates—members of the same all-male social club, with weekend binge-drinking habits and investment banking aspirations—about who among them was going to make the first million.

More significantly, Charlie's long-term boyfriend, Kwesi, had graduated, won a Rhodes, and gone off to Oxford; she'd been the one to insist that they separate, very much against the advice of her parents. This was while she was still planning to complete her thesis and apply for the Henry Fellowship at Oxford herself, so it was possibly more of a hiatus than a break. Charlie said that she didn't want Kwesi to feel tied down by an undergraduate girlfriend during his time in England, but I thought she broke things off also because Kwesi was so exactly what her parents had always hoped for her. Like everyone, I liked Kwesi—but I couldn't help being grateful that Charlie and I were single at the same time.

Somehow I had put off fulfilling my Moral Reasoning requirement, and was taking Michael Sandel's blockbuster course, Justice. I found myself debating with freshmen in our TF-led sections questions like, "Is it right to lie, if doing so might save the life of a friend?" and "Is patriotism a form of racism?" The class seemed so easy, compared with the work I was doing for my thesis with Professor Aksoy, on effective field theory calculations of the W and Z masses, that I spent very little time on it, often writing the response papers during the lectures. Charlie and I now lived off campus, and we had plans for after graduation. In addition to the work on my own thesis, I had a job with Arty as a faculty aide and was applying to PhD programs; Charlie was just as busy, writing her thesis on Laclos, rehearsing her role as Mme. de Merteuil, and applying for the Henry.

By the time I heard about them, that fall of our senior year, Pope's overtures to Charlie had become impossible for her to ignore. Sometimes he would stop in the middle of their tutorial, say that he couldn't continue because Charlie's presence was too distracting. She kept him up at night. Yes, there had been other girls, but he'd never felt anything like this before. He knew she didn't feel the same way, but he had to be honest with her; he couldn't pretend their relationship was purely pedagogical anymore. I noticed that she was often sicker than usual on Thursdays, and occasionally spent that day in bed, skipping not only her tutorial but her other classes as well.

When I asked her what she was going to do about Pope, Charlie usually made a joke and brushed it off. But she did once ask me if I knew what actually happened when students reported a teacher for that type of offense: that they had to testify in front of a board of other students and faculty, who would then hear the tenured professor's side and make a decision. She said that if she'd learned anything from her mother, it was that there was always more than one solution to any problem. She was a big girl, and she could handle it on her own. Many times I resolved to press her to do something—I fantasized about ways I might help. Charlie and I both felt very adult that last year of college, very experienced; I think we believed that what we'd achieved academically was akin to growing up, rather than something we might have done in place of it.

One Friday night I had planned to get Chinese food with Charlie after her rehearsal. I was taking a shortcut diagonally through the Yard after a lecture entitled, "Is Torture Always Wrong?," heading home, when I ran into Neel. As always happened when another romance ended, we'd been spending more time together, and I was glad to hear him calling my name. He told me he'd spent most of the day at the college observatory on Garden Street, and was meeting some mutual friends for a beer. Did I want to come?

I don't think I worried about alerting Charlie to my change of plans. "The problem with you," she once told me, "is that you go out with the people who ask you; you never take the initiative with anyone you like." Now the person I liked had asked, and I knew she would want me to go. Anyway, it was early.

Neel and I passed through the wrought-iron gate and started down the brick sidewalk, under the double-globe streetlamps. I asked him about the observatory, and we talked about the program he was organizing for at-risk teenagers to visit at night and view the comet, Swift-Tuttle.

"My parents were confused—my father asked me what risk I meant. He didn't understand that the program was for poor kids, and I realized it was because I hadn't made it clear. Because *I* was uncomfortable saying it. What is it about Americans that makes it so hard for us to say what we mean?"

We developed a theory about our national addiction to euphemism as we walked to the bar: we also disliked "hooked up" and "passed away." Our friends Chris and Vlatko were already there when we arrived, along with Vlatko's girlfriend, a computer science concentrator whose name I can't remember now. We finished two pitchers talking about people we knew in common, and when I said that I had to go home because I had a research fellowship application to finish, Neel offered to walk me.

Up until that point, the evening had been like any other, but the offer to walk me home felt like a romantic gesture, and both of us became unusually quiet as we got closer to the house on Brewer Street, where Charlie and I rented an apartment on the second floor. What was so exciting for me was the feeling of being with someone—not smarter, necessarily, because I knew I was better than Neel at grasping an abstract idea and proving it mathematically—but so committed to the precise articulation of ideas. It wasn't true what Charlie said about me, or not entirely: I might have tended to allow other people to choose me, but once I was in a relationship, I was usually the one in control. My conversations with Neel, on the other hand, felt more equal, or even as if I were going to have to prove myself, if I wanted to hold his attention. I wanted to prolong the potential of a real relationship as long as possible, not take any step that would propel Neel and me in one direction or the other. I couldn't imagine anything better than imagining myself with Neel.

We stopped just outside the light from the fixture over the porch. I was shivering in a dark green cashmere coat that I'd bought with Charlie at a thrift store in Porter Square, more for style than for warmth. Neel was looking at me with his unique brand of curious detachment.

"So see you," I said.

He kept his hands in his pockets. "Is that a euphemism?"

"We deplore euphemism," I said. "Remember?"

"Too bad for me, then," he said. He lingered for a second—I thought he was going to kiss me—but only squeezed my hand, before he turned and went. I watched him go, thinking how strange it was that the buoyant feeling in my chest could be produced from so little.

The people who lived below Charlie and me in that apartment house on Brewer Street had a small child, and seemed often to be screaming at each other; that night the commotion struck me as somehow touching, part of what my Justice professor had just referred to as the "rich pageant of human experience." I ran up the stairs, eager to tell Charlie about my spontaneous date with Neel.

But the apartment was dark. I turned on the lights, threw my stuff on the couch. Then I went into the kitchen to look for something I could eat—our refrigerator was almost always empty. I was rooting around in the cabinet for my Pringles, or even Charlie's Smartfood, when I heard a sound from her room.

"Charlie?"

Her door was half-open, but because the lights were off and she hadn't said anything, I'd assumed the room was empty.

"I thought you weren't here!" I said.

She was lying in her bed, the covers pulled up to her chin.

"Are you okay?"

I turned on the light. The magazines that were always lying around her room had gone from a mess to something more alarming. They covered the floor like a carpet: *Vogue* and *Elle*, *Essence* and *Vibe*, as well as *Daily Variety* and *Vanity Fair*. Charlie didn't drink more than the average Harvard student, and she didn't like weed. Her drugs of choice were ibuprofen and caffeine; when she had a migraine, she went to the campus health center for something stronger. The night table was crowded with empty plastic bottles of Diet Coke—I could smell the saccharine sludge at the bottom—and there was an economy-sized bottle of Advil on the base of the lamp, from which she would take five or six tablets at a time. I'm embarrassed to think I once suggested she try to wean herself off it.

"He was here," she said.

"Who?"

"Pope. I left our door unlocked, but I still don't know how he got in downstairs." She was wearing plaid pajama pants and a worn gray T-shirt that said *Choate Lacrosse* in yellow.

"Pope followed you home?"

"No—he was watching rehearsal again. He found me afterward, and said he wanted to apologize for being 'badly behaved.' I said I was meeting you at home, and I had to go, but he said it would just take a minute. I said we could talk at the theater, but he said we couldn't. He asked if he could walk me home."

"What did you say?"

Charlie shrugged. "I said okay. And he was actually very polite and nice, at least while we were walking. He said he shouldn't have said those things to me—of course it was confusing for me—even if he felt them. He said my thesis was the best one he'd advised in years, and he really wanted to continue. He promised he wouldn't talk about his feelings, or even touch me anymore."

"He touches you?"

"Well, not—you know. But yeah. His hand on my arm or my back all the time, once on my thigh. He promised not to do it anymore, as long as I don't drop the tutorial. He said he'd never forgive himself if I quit—and that he didn't want to give me an incomplete."

"An incomplete—Charlie, that's a threat!"

"Well, I mean, I have thought about it."

"You can't quit your thesis—no matter what. You'd graduate without honors, and you wouldn't be able to apply for the Henry—or any other fellowship. What did you *say* to him?"

I didn't mean it as any kind of reproach, but Charlie was defensive.

"I said, okay—I mean, what am I supposed to say? I don't want an incomplete either. It's not like I was *taken in*."

"Of course not."

Charlie hesitated. "I mean, I'm sure he doesn't think it's the best."

I started to argue—or did I only think of arguing? I didn't really believe that she would sacrifice her thesis and her honors designation in order to be free of him.

"So then he says, 'So see you Thursday?' And I wasn't sure but I said I would, just to get rid of him, you know. And then I came in. Louise downstairs was having trouble with her stroller, and the kids were running around, and so I held the door for her, and maybe it didn't close all the way."

"Oh god, Charlie—what happened?"

"Nothing," she said. "Nothing like that. I was sitting on the couch, reading. He just came in and—" I was sitting next to her on the bed, and Charlie turned and demonstrated, putting her palms on the wall behind me, trapping me in the half circle of her arms.

"What did you do?"

Charlie took her arms away, releasing me. She leaned back limply against the wall behind the bed.

"I mean, did you scream?"

"No," she said.

"Louise would've heard you."

"I know."

"She would've come up."

"Yeah, but I would've been so embarrassed."

"That he was attacking you?"

"He didn't do anything."

"He pinned you to the couch!"

Charlie put her head down on her knees for a moment. I rubbed her back uselessly. I thought she was crying—we cried all the time at that point in our lives, over boys, midterm exams, the incomprehensible preoccupations of our parents—but when Charlie looked up, her eyes were dry.

"He didn't touch me. He didn't even say anything. He just stayed there looking at me."

"Ugh, Charlie. If I'd just come straight—"

She shrugged, tired of speculating. "That girl warned me—Trisha. I didn't listen."

"You shouldn't have to be *warned*."

Charlie got up suddenly. "Just come with me to look."

I didn't know what she meant, but I followed her to my bedroom in the front of the apartment. I reached for the light, but she shook her head.

"Leave it off. Can you see him?"

"Pope?"

"He was walking up and down the block."

"In front of the *house*?"

She shook her head. "No, over on Mount Auburn. Is he still there?"

I looked out to the main street, where people were passing under the streetlamps. Students with backpacks, but also people unconnected to the university, hurrying home after work. It was hard to distinguish faces.

"I don't see him."

Charlie turned on the light, looking visibly relieved. My room wasn't exactly a model of tidiness either. Papers, problem sets, empty cups, and diskettes littered my small desk. My bed was covered with clothing, and the wooden seat in the bay window was serving as a home for anything I didn't know what to do with, including the telescope my parents had given me as a gift, before I left home. It made me feel guilty to think of the money they'd spent on it, now that I had access to the much more sophisticated instruments at the Center for Astrophysics. Charlie moved it unceremoniously to the floor and sat down.

"Jesus, Charlie—we have to call the police."

"The police?"

"At least the Harvard police."

"And tell them that the Elmer Blakely Professor of Comparative Literature is walking down Mount Auburn Street? Was walking down Mount Auburn, but has now gone home to his wife of fifteen years for dinner?"

"Tell them what happened."

"Do you know who Elmer Blakely was?"

"A writer?"

"I bet that's what he called himself. Class of '02. Taught eighteenth-century poetry here, then went on to Illinois. A noted anti-suffragist."

"Anti–women's suffrage?"

"He published a book of essays—all by women, except for his introduction. Why the vote is too big a responsibility for women because of their 'natural' responsibilities; why 'stay-at-home' voters would make bad government; how states with male suffrage actually made better laws *protecting* women than the equal-suffrage states."

"How do you know all this?"

Charlie gave me a rueful smile. "Pope told me. Or at least he said Blakely was a fraud—that's the word he used—and so I was curious. I went to the library and found the book. It was incredibly weird, reading those essays."

"Weird how?"

"Weird like looking at your own twat in the mirror."

I laughed, but Charlie was serious:

"So ugly."

"But Pope didn't argue when they gave him the chair in Blakely's name," I said.

"Of course not."

"It's amazing they haven't changed the name."

"Not really. They still have Agassiz Theatre, too—Louis Agassiz was a big creationist. And also into polygenism."

"What is that?"

"All races have different origins, different *purposes,* so slavery's okay."

"They should rename it."

"The theater?"

"And the chair."

"They'd have to rename a lot of shit."

I remembered this conversation the spring after Charlie died, when I read that Harvard Law School was changing its crest in response to student protests. The original design came from the coat of arms of one of the school's initial benefactors, a brutal Antiguan slaveowner. Within a week of that decision, the college also did away with the designation "Master" for the heads of its residential houses. They kept Mather House, named for another of the university's slave-owning patrons, as well as Agassiz House, Agassiz Theatre, and the Louis Agassiz Museum of Comparative Zoology.

Peering out the window of my college bedroom that night, I didn't know any of those facts. I was just processing new information about the school I'd been so proud to attend, of which I'd been so anxious to prove myself worthy. It was one of those moments when I knew Charlie was giving me a chance to catch up.

"So what do you want to do?"

"Right now?"

"About this—Pope. I mean, he broke into our house and threatened you."

"The doors were open, so technically he didn't break in. And he didn't say a word, at least after he came inside."

"But with his body?"

"He didn't touch me."

"He trapped you on the couch."

"And I just sat there."

"Well, I mean, he's a man."

"An old man."

"He's not that old."

Charlie opened her eyes wide and shook her head. I could tell she wanted me to stop talking, but I couldn't let it go.

"How long did it last?"

"A minute or two." She hesitated. "Or longer?"

"So what now? If we're not going to call the police."

I was sitting on the floor, leaning against the wall. Charlie was still on the window seat, her long body folded in three parts, her chin resting on her knees. Her eyes were very bright.

"Let's go somewhere," she said.

13.

We arranged to borrow Charlie's friend Brian's old VW Jetta, and first thing the next morning we set out for Aunt Penny's house in Gloucester. Penny was Carl's sister, and Charlie's favorite aunt. During the week, she shared an apartment with another teacher near the high school in Roslindale, where she taught history, but Gloucester was her real home. Charlie kept a key to the house on her ring, and said we were welcome whether or not Penny was going to be there. But when Charlie called that night, it turned out that Penny was staying in the city for the weekend; she encouraged Charlie to use the house.

Charlie drove at her breakneck, Boston pace, even once we were outside the city. In the car we alternated between *Automatic for the People* and *3 Years, 5 Months and 2 Days in the Life Of . . .* and didn't talk about Pope. We didn't talk about how the university might have made it easier for students to report unwanted sexual advances from other students or faculty. We didn't talk about what Trisha might have meant, when she said Charlie was Pope's type, and we certainly didn't talk about whether Charlie was going to tell her parents what had happened. I don't think it ever occurred to either of us that she would.

Maybe today black girls and brown girls and white girls, lesbians and bisexual and trans people sit in their dorm rooms talking about privilege and adjacency and intersectionality. It's just that it wasn't like that then. Talking about it would have violated every unspoken rule of our friendship, which was like that game, popular in the nineties, in which you removed rectangular blocks from the base of a tower, adding them to the top. Charlie had the theater, I had the lab; Charlie had her social club, I played intramural soccer; Charlie had a "summer place" in Gloucester, I had a work-study job; Charlie was black, I was white. When that last binary came up, we dismissed it with a kind of eye roll. It was uncool, sort of embarrassing and outdated, to make a big deal about it.

Instead, on the way up, Charlie asked me about Neel.

"You have to call him," Charlie said.

"And say what?"

"Invite him up."

"You mean another weekend?"

"Tonight," Charlie said. "As soon as we get there. He could take the commuter line to Gloucester."

"Isn't that a little—"

"Yeah," Charlie said. "It's ballsy."

"Not this weekend, though. You need to recover."

"Oh, spare me the therapy session—it was no big deal."

I didn't think that; I didn't think Charlie thought it either, but there was a tone I recognized, just a little louder and more flippant than the situation warranted: a warning to back off.

"If there were a bunch of people, maybe."

Charlie sighed. "I don't want a bunch of people."

"Neither do I!"

She looked at me sideways, one hand resting only very casually on the wheel. "But you want *him*."

"I don't know."

"Yes," Charlie said. "You do."

I left a message with Neel's roommate with the phone number at the house, and then Charlie and I went to the grocery store. When we got back it was noon; the sun was pale and very far away, and the gulls called frantically to each other. The air was surprisingly cold and you could smell the ocean. We ran from the car to the house without our coats, bringing in the bags; when we got inside, we pushed Aunt Penny's plaid draft-catchers against the gap at the bottom of the door and blew on our hands to warm them.

"We'll have a fire tonight," Charlie said, as we brought the groceries into the kitchen. "And hot toddies—ooh, look!" She indicated the phone, where a red light was flashing. Neel had left a very brief message, letting me know when I should call to reach him.

Charlie wrote the number on a pad, and handed me the phone.

"I can't."

"C'mon," she said. "It'll be fun."

"No," I said. "Honestly. It's too obvious."

"What about that comet?" Charlie said.

"What?"

"Isn't it streaking across the sky, or whatever, this weekend? You said we could see it from here."

"Swift-Tuttle. I thought so, but look out the window—it's too cloudy."

"It might clear up."

"It's probably still too close to the sun."

"The sun's not going to be out at night!"

"I mean, too close in its orbit. I don't think the conditions are ideal."

"But the conditions *are* ideal for you to get it on with Neel."

"Did you seriously just say, 'Get it on'?"

"You're impossible," Charlie said, glancing at the number on the pad. "And yeah, I sure did. I'm calling."

"You better not."

Charlie keyed in the number and held it over my head, out of reach.

"Charlie!"

Charlie widened her eyes and pointed at the receiver; it was ringing. She put the phone to her ear, and when she spoke, she sounded perfectly serious and slightly exasperated, as if she'd been interrupted in the middle of something important.

"Yes, hi—I just got a call from this number."

In spite of the fact that Neel couldn't see her, Charlie frowned—as if she really weren't sure who was on the other end.

"Oh hey, Neel," she said. It sounded as if she were surprised, as if she hadn't heard his name for months. It was the kind of thing Charlie pulled off better than anyone.

"She is, but she went for a run on the beach. Yeah, I know—it's like, arctic down there—she's crazy. Anyway, I think she was going to ask if you wanted to come up to see—a comet or something?

You guys would know better than I do." Charlie winked at me. "The town is Gloucester. You can take the commuter line from North Station."

Neel said something, and Charlie started to laugh silently. She looked at me, straightening her face with effort, and then nodded gravely.

"I definitely think you should bring it," she said. "We have an attic bedroom with a very high window."

I listened in disbelief as she reassured Neel about his welcome—he was really coming—and gave specific directions about where we would pick him up outside the station. She managed to encourage him without sounding as if she cared much either way. When she hung up, she looked at me.

"He wants to bring his *telescope*," she said. "The two of you are going to stargaze."

"People confuse comets and meteoroids with stars—but they're different. They're just balls of ice and rock; they get close to the sun and then they heat up. Comets have more ammonia and gases than other space rocks, and that's why they have the coma—sort of like a halo around a rock. The evaporating gas is what makes the glowing tail."

"Mmm," said Charlie. "Fascinating. I told him he could set his *instrument* up in the attic room. Do you think you're going to *see it?*"

"No," I said. "I don't. Because it's way too cloudy."

"Oh," Charlie said. "That's too bad. So what are you guys going to do up there?"

Whether it was because Neel was coming, or just because we were away from school, the weekend seemed especially exciting. It was an adventure to stock the kitchen, an adventure to get firewood from the pile behind the house. Charlie had said she was going to make boeuf bourguignon, and she delivered; she cooked without a recipe, a skill she'd learned from watching cooking shows with her nanny while her parents were at work. Like me, my mother was indifferent to food—you ate, and then you moved on to more important business—but my father loved being in the kitchen.

One of the first things he and Charlie had bonded over, when Charlie came home with me for spring break junior year, was a recipe for homemade chocolate truffles. In my father's case, cooking was a kind of tinkering: the more complicated and esoteric the recipe, the better. For Charlie it was about pleasure, her own and other people's, as generous as the smell of meat and oil and herbs saturating every room of the house.

While she cooked, I explored. The house had wooden siding rather than shingles, and was painted brick red. A yellow tin star decorated the narrow front door. There was a living room with a low, beamed ceiling and a fireplace, furniture in dark green plush. There were lace curtains. From the living room, a steep, narrow staircase ascended to the second floor, past a photo wall with pictures of the family in Baltimore, where Carl and his younger sister had grown up. I recognized Carl in a group of young people, elegantly dressed and crowded at a zinc bar in front of a wall of felt pennants, and as a child on the sidewalk outside a church, holding the hand of a little girl who must've been Aunt Penny, in a full-skirted short dress and white gloves, carrying a bouquet. These would have been taken in Baltimore in the fifties and sixties.

A more contemporary photograph showed Penny with her graduating seniors at the school in Roslindale. From Memorial Day until Labor Day weekend, she was always in Gloucester. Charlie and her brother had come to stay for most of every summer, while their parents worked in the city. There was a photo of the two of them playing on the beach with Penny, and another of the whole family, including Carl and Addie and the dogs—a pair of the small white terriers that the Boyces had always kept. There were school pictures of Charlie and William, and a snapshot of their parents, much younger, with their arms around each other, standing on a dock with boats in the background. Carl was grinning, perfectly relaxed, but Addie's expression was more guarded, as if she had considered the photograph's long life on her sister-in-law's wall, and all of the people who might someday look at it. She was beautiful but impossible to read.

Charlie had a theory about her parents' marriage. She said that when they first met, her mother, by virtue of her class, her education, and her beauty, had all the power in the relationship. It took

Carl four years to convince her to marry him, and most of their courtship was epistolary, since she was in New York, and he was using his G.I. Bill benefits for college in North Carolina. It was after the children were born, when Carl's career had taken off—when he was offered the chair of his department as well as the lucrative television gigs—that the ground shifted, and Addie found herself at a disadvantage.

Charlie said that her father had had an affair with a young stylist on one of those shows, and that her parents had almost split up over it. Her mother had taken her and William to live with a cousin in Paris for a year. When they got back, William had gone to college and Charlie had gone to Choate, where she spent her last two years of high school while her parents figured out their marriage. In a certain mood, Charlie would rail against them for "exiling her" at Choate; in another, she would wax nostalgic about "Deerfield Day," or something called the "Last Hurrah." When Charlie talked about the crisis in her parents' marriage—in a breezier way than she might have if I'd known her while it was happening—she'd described it as a "necessary correction." Her father had had to prove himself to her mother all over again. Charlie said that this dynamic was what reanimated her parents' relationship, since it restored the conditions under which they'd first fallen in love—but added that if the guy she eventually married ever did that to her, she'd leave him in a second.

Charlie had instructed me to put my bag in the second-floor guest bedroom, where her parents always stayed when they came up on summer weekends. We'd turned up the thermostat; you could hear the radiators clanking, but it was still cold, and the house had a musty, unused smell. There was a queen-sized bed with a patchwork quilt, and a large wooden armoire with a heart cut out of the door. In the hallway outside the bathroom, a ladder led to an attic room under the steeply gabled roof, where Charlie had joked about Neel putting his telescope. I used the bathroom, where the toilet sat on a raised wooden platform to conceal the plumbing, and the copper content of the water (bracing, from a well) was evident from brilliant aqua stains on the porcelain sink. I looked into the spotted mirror above the sink—my hair a little wild, my cheeks still pink—and thought of the emotional toast I would make about Charlie's role in our courtship, if Neel and I someday got married.

14.

We were almost twenty minutes late to pick up Neel, and I had been worried during the short drive from Aunt Penny's that he would have gotten on a train back to Boston. But when we arrived at the quaint Gloucester rail station, with its round sign for the T Commuter Rail, there he was. The temperature had dropped and we were using the heat and the defrost inside the car, but Neel wasn't taking advantage of the station's enclosed passenger waiting area. He was standing outside where the light was better, under an antique, bell-shaped streetlamp, reading a book. The red digital numbers on the station's display board read 6:47, but he seemed unconcerned by our delay. As soon as I saw him, I had a different worry. What if it was too awkward, just the three of us?

Charlie pulled into a space across the street from the station.

"There he is," I said.

"So cute he's reading," Charlie said. "Look how serious he is. Also, I like the peacoat."

"He doesn't normally wear glasses."

"What's wrong with glasses?"

"Nothing—should we honk or something?"

"What do you think he's reading?"

"History of science, maybe?"

"That's hot."

"Shut up."

"No, really—I buy his act, and I like it." (This was a joke between us, with several variations. We might say, "I like her act, but I don't buy it," or, "I don't like his act and I don't buy it either.") "Are you ready?"

"No."

Charlie honked and Neel looked up; I rolled down the window, letting in some of the cold air, and waved. Neel put his book away in the backpack, picked up something at his feet—it was the telescope, in its black nylon case—and jogged across the street, his breath steaming in front of him.

"Sorry we're late," Charlie said when he got in. "We were making dinner."

"Dinner sounds great," Neel said. "Thanks for inviting me."

"It was all her," I said. "She's a great cook."

"I like cooking, too," Neel said. "My mom taught me, after my sister disappointed her forever."

Charlie made an illegal U-turn in front of a stone church with Gothic windows, its white spire rising in the dark. "Really? Disappointed her how?"

"Moving away," Neel said. "Not going to graduate school. Becoming a midwife instead of a doctor. Not saying who she's dating."

Charlie looked in the rearview mirror. Other people's families always interested her.

"Are you going to cook for us this weekend, then?" she asked.

"Probably not," he said. "I can only do Indian, and it's almost impossible unless you're in an Indian kitchen. But I did bring us something to drink." He handed me a bottle in a paper bag; it was bourbon, and I could see that Charlie, glancing over, approved.

"Ooh," she said. "You know what we should do?"

The heater in the Jetta worked only intermittently, and we could see our breath inside the car. Charlie zigzagged easily through the village, with its narrow, irregular streets, and then took Bass Avenue east out of town, toward the Atlantic. The beach was surrounded by a preserve; on one side of the road were simple cottages—most looked shut up for the winter—and on the other were scraggly, maritime woods. The road ended at Good Harbor Beach, where the small parking lot was empty. Charlie found a flashlight in the glove compartment and we put on hats; when we got out it was cold but not unpleasant, somewhere in the high thirties. Charlie led the way to a narrow, sandy path that took us between the dunes to the beach. The beach was very dark; the houses with access seemed to be at least a mile in each direction down the coast. Small waves slapped against the sand, and the sky was overcast. In the breaks between the clouds, you could see a few stars.

"Maybe it'll clear up for you guys later tonight," Charlie said, trying to make me laugh. I elbowed her, but if Neel noticed, he didn't give any sign of it.

"I haven't been to the beach in years," he said.

"We should stay off the dunes," Charlie said. "My aunt is obsessed with shoreline preservation. But if we sit just in front of them, we'll be out of the wind."

We sat close together, me in the middle, and passed the paper bag back and forth. The dunes did provide a little shelter, or maybe it was just the whiskey making us warm. In the dark the salt smell was intense.

Charlie told Neel about Penny: how she'd never married, how it had been her dream to buy this place, and then how Charlie and William had spent summers here.

Neel said that the extent of his childhood beach-going was Lee Street, on the lake in Chicago, where his parents had taken him and his younger brother once each summer, always packing a cooler full of food. "For a long time I thought that the point of going to the beach was to eat."

"We did that, too," Charlie said. "But Helen had the real experience in L.A."

"Not really," I said. "It was a good forty-five minutes from where we lived, and my parents were always complaining about what it cost to park. We went in the summer. But none of us really liked it."

"You lived in L.A. and you didn't like the beach?"

"I like this beach," I said. "The ones in L.A. are so exposed. And I used to be scared of going in the water." The whiskey was making me more comfortable.

"Sharks?" Charlie said.

"Waves. I'd read some book about a tsunami. Once I was being such a pain in the ass that my parents actually packed up the car and pulled out into the street—pretended like they were going to leave without me—just to make me get in."

"Look," Neel said, pointing to a gap in the clouds.

"Is that the comet?" Charlie asked.

"No—good eyes, though. I thought it was the International Space Station, but it's just a weather satellite. The comet wouldn't look as if it were moving like that."

Suddenly a section of the water lit up, a green-and-white cone.

"What is that?"

"From the parking lot," Charlie said. "It's so lame—sitting in your car to look at the water."

"It's not even that cold," Neel said.

"Have you guys heard of polar bear clubs?" Charlie turned to me. "My aunt's in a women's one. They run down here in the winter and get in—all these ladies in bathing caps. Then they go to someone's house and eat pancakes."

"I forgot my bathing cap," Neel said.

"I think we should go for it," Charlie said.

"The water's probably warmer than the air," Neel speculated. "But what about afterward?"

"It's just to the car," Charlie said. "I'd love to hear what those people in the parking lot say, when they see three naked butts in their headlights."

"Are you kidding?" I asked.

"I'm game," Neel said.

Charlie laughed. "Come on. I polar bear dare you."

If not for Charlie, we never would have done it. In retrospect I think we were lucky neither of us suffered hypothermia. I say neither of us, because I made a point of not looking as we undressed, and then as we started to run, the headlights switched off. Whether Charlie was right, and some old couple was horrified, or the car just left at that moment by coincidence was unclear, but because it was so dark, I believed it was the three of us running screaming to the water. The water was so cold that for a moment there was nothing but a burning sensation. I made it only to my waist before turning around, but Neel dunked his head, made a great bellowing sound, and was ahead of me as we ran back dripping toward the parking lot. I saw his body then, thin and light gray in the dark, and—I don't think this is fabricated—made myself remember exactly how I felt, preserving it, in case I never was that happy again.

Charlie was already sitting in the driver's seat, fully clothed. She had started the engine and managed to get the heat blowing. She was blasting Prince's "Thieves in the Temple," our new favorite.

I tried to talk, but I couldn't make my mouth move.

"Traitor," Neel said.

"Are you kidding?" Charlie said. "Who was going to get your clothes?" She passed each of us a bundle.

I struggled into my sweater and jeans, then turned around and looked at Neel. His hair was wet and there were actual, tiny ice crystals in it. He'd gotten his cords and T-shirt on, and was pulling a sweater over his head.

"Who stayed in longer?" he asked Charlie, pulling his sweater over his head.

"I did," I answered for her. "You couldn't take it."

"You didn't even dunk," Neel said, reaching out to touch my hair.

15.

After dinner we sat in the living room and finished the whiskey. Charlie was on the couch, and Neel and I sat in the worn armchairs closest to the fire.

"This is a great place," he said, looking admiringly around Aunt Penny's living room. He wasn't the type of young person who disparaged his elders' taste; I thought he was likely to prefer the family of china ducks on the brick mantelpiece, the multicolored braided rag rug, to anything sleeker or more refined. I could see his appreciation for Charlie deepening, too, because this was a place she clearly loved.

"Thanks," Charlie said. "Whatever's going on, it's always a good place to escape."

"We could use a place like that in my family," Neel said.

Charlie looked at Neel curiously. "What's the deal with your sister?" she asked. "Who's she dating that your parents don't like?"

"A doctor," Neel said. "Super nice guy."

"So?" Charlie said.

"He's Jamaican," Neel said.

"Indian Jamaican?" Charlie said. "Are there Indians in Jamaica?"

"There are Indians everywhere. But he's a black guy."

Neel didn't talk a mile a minute to cover up the fact that he'd just referred to someone's color, nor did he rush to clarify that he didn't feel as his parents did.

"I once saw a movie where this Indian guy in New York had to go back to India to choose a bride," Charlie said.

"I'll get my ticket as a graduation present," Neel deadpanned.

"Your parents don't care who you marry?"

"It's not that they don't care." Neel had stood up and was stoking the coals; now he replaced the iron poker and turned to face us. "They'd like her to be Indian. But they're not hoping to arrange it or anything—they're pretty assimilated."

Charlie held up her hands. "Just wondering."

"What about you?" Neel said. "What do your parents have in mind?"

"An extremely successful black guy," Charlie said. "Failing that, an extremely successful white guy will be okay."

Neel laughed. "I think our parents are on a similar trip, just with slightly different parameters."

"Kids?" Charlie said. In a group she often liked to throw out a topic and then listen to everyone respond. She already understood back then how much people like to talk about themselves.

"No, thanks," Neel said.

"Helen? Are you still in the 'no' column on munchkins?"

"I didn't say that."

"You said you weren't sure."

"I just feel like there are enough people already," I said. "If I really wanted a kid, I guess I'd adopt one."

"But then you don't know what you get," Neel suggested.

"You don't know what you get either way. Plus you can be older and adopt. It takes forever to get established in science."

"Helen knows exactly what she wants," Charlie said. She pulled a red wool blanket off the back of the couch, and tucked it around her knees. She was wearing a thick white turtleneck sweater that made her wrists look especially delicate, emerging from the sleeves, her fingers especially long. No one disagreed about Charlie's beauty; it was an incontrovertible fact.

"Penny didn't have kids?" I asked.

"No," Charlie said. "She was married, when she was young—but he was supposedly horrible. Now she's with this really nice guy my mother calls 'Penny's gentleman friend.' Gerald. But I think she's sad about the no-kids thing."

I had a sudden realization. "Aunt Penny's the one who made that Winnie-the-Pooh sampler."

Charlie nodded. "She did it when I was born. We've always been really close."

"Winnie-the-Pooh?" Neel asked.

"She embroidered one of those nonsense rhymes," Charlie said. "'Cottleston Pie.' My mom says it took her a year."

"'A fly can't bird but a bird can fly,'" Neel said.

Charlie looked pleased. "He knows it!" She winked at me. "I like him, Helen."

"Phew," Neel said. "And it's all thanks to my parents' British-colonial taste in children's literature." He got up and went to the window, parting one of the curtains. "Hey, it looks a little clearer out now—if you guys want to give the comet a shot?"

"You know what," Charlie said, jumping up. "I should call Penny—just to tell her everything's okay with the house."

I was suddenly frantically nervous. "I'm sure it's still too cloudy."

Charlie winked at me. "You kids go on up and see. I'll be there in a sec."

I climbed the ladder to the loft bedroom first; Neel followed me. There were two single beds fitted with yellow-flowered spreads. The bedspreads were some sort of synthetic fabric with thick piping, more like dust covers than blankets, as if the room weren't often used. The blue-and-white patterned wallpaper was sun-faded on one side, and an aged craft project, two wooden sticks wrapped in yellow and orange yarn, a God's Eye, was nailed above one of the narrow beds.

Neel moved the optical tube to the side to crack the window. "You know we're not going to see anything."

I thought I'd never liked someone's face so much for no special reason. There was something about the big eyes, shaggy hair, and slightly crooked nose that had appealed to me immediately. His shoulders were broader than you would expect for someone as thin as he was.

"It doesn't reach perihelion until December," I told him.

"We'd still be able to see it—if it were clear."

"Did you check the weather before you came?"

He raised his eyebrows at me. There was a faint stubble on his upper lip. "Did you check before you invited me?"

"It was Charlie's idea. I think she wanted some company."

I had often been indiscreet with Neel, but I couldn't tell him why I thought Charlie had been so insistent about him coming up this weekend. She hadn't wanted to come to Penny's house alone, but she also didn't want to spend the weekend talking with me about what had happened.

I glanced at the door, which we'd left open.

"Do you think she'll come up?" Neel asked.

"No," I said. "She's going to give us a lot of time."

"No faith?"

"She doesn't think you can close the deal."

"Why am I the closer?" As he said it, he stepped toward the telescope. There was just about a foot between the two of us, and another between me and the bed. From downstairs I heard Charlie's voice—I wondered if she had called Kwesi long-distance.

I sometimes think that the words "electric" and "magnetic" have been taken over by their colloquial usage, so that they hardly retain their scientific meanings at all. When Neel kissed me, I felt nothing related to charge or its movement through a field. What I felt was a slow, spreading pleasure. Neel and I had been building to this for three years, and if not perfect—the kiss definitely included some fumbling—it left me short of breath.

Neel stopped. "Did you want this?"

"Doesn't it seem like I do?"

Neel shook his head. "I mean before—when we were first-years."

"Did you?"

Neel nodded, acknowledging that this was an interesting question. "Sometimes I did—definitely. But then I made this sort of promise to myself, that I was going to date nonscientists."

I felt a little hurt. "Why?"

"The lab gets kind of insular, don't you think? I wanted an outside life, and I thought the most efficient way to do that was to date a Visual and Environmental Studies concentrator or something."

"I've never understood what VES actually is."

Neel shook his head. "Something to do with film? I don't think they know themselves."

We started talking about a class—I think it was Georgi's Lie Algebras—and the people we knew who were also taking it. There was a romantic drama between two of the teaching fellows, and we covered that, too. We were talking a little too loudly, with a little too much animation.

"I liked what you said before."

"About what?"

"Adopting a kid. If I wanted one, I'd do the same. I bet very few women say that."

"Men either."

"Yeah, but guys my age don't talk about kids."

"We hardly ever do."

"You're reasonable, is all I'm saying."

"Wow, thanks."

Neel laughed.

"I was about to compliment you on your organizational skills," I told him. "But I didn't want to be too forward."

"What with your rationality and my systematic thinking, we would probably have amazing sex."

Of course it's only when I let go of my rationality and systematic thinking that I can have amazing sex. Neel smelled and tasted like salt, and he really looked at me; he wasn't one of those people who close their eyes and go somewhere else during sex. He held my arms over my head and said, "Do you like this? And this?" He got up once and found a sheet in the closet, to put over Aunt Penny's narrow attic bed. He insisted we keep the light on. There was a lot of talking. He said that I seemed younger than other girls he'd been with.

"I'm not talking about your mind," he added, before I could protest. He ran his hand down my body, admiringly, put his hand between my legs and left it there. "Not your body either, but everything else."

I didn't know what he meant—what was there, besides my mind (my brain) and my body?—but I could barely think while he was touching me. He was patient and made me wait a long time. We came together, incredibly, the first time.

Later we crept down the ladder shivering in our T-shirts and underwear. I took the sheet with me, and hoped I would be able to find the washing machine without asking Charlie. The house was quiet, and I assumed she had gone to bed downstairs. We climbed into the bed I was supposed to sleep in—I realized Charlie hadn't given Neel a room—and got undressed again, but we didn't touch each other again right away. Instead we talked: first Neel about his parents, who had left their lives and their families in Hyderabad when they were the same age we were, because his father had been accepted to medical school in Chicago. He said that his mother had told him recently that she'd cried every day for the first fifteen months they lived there.

"What happened at fifteen months?"

"She got pregnant with me," he said.

I told Neel about my parents' conscientious objection to Vietnam, the fabricated epilepsy diagnosis that kept my father out of the war. I might have overemphasized my parents' counterculture ideals to make them seem more compelling. I said that they hadn't been married when they had us.

Neel was interested in that. "Really?"

"They did it later, when we were kids. But it wasn't any different from marriage, not calling it that."

Neel nodded. "I guess it's my Indian heritage showing, but I do want to get married."

"I think it's a little soon."

He smiled at me. His teeth were very clean and white. "I'm thinking I want to marry you the second time around."

"*What?*"

"After your adopted waif is out of the way, and we're established as a theoretical-experimental physics power couple. The Ivies will have to duke it out for us—we'll demand extremely generous terms, and only go somewhere with great weather."

"I always liked the idea of MIT."

"I could do MIT," Neel conceded. "But the University of Hawaii also has its appeal."

"Don't think I'm not insulted." We were sitting against the headboard of the bed, and I pulled the sheet up over my chest. I was playing, but not entirely. He wanted me to be his *second wife*? Or was he joking, too?

Neel tugged gently at the sheet.

"Please don't cover those up," he said. "They're perfect."

I could tell I was blushing, and I was glad the room was dim. The only light came from a small bedside lamp, with a low-wattage, flame-shaped bulb.

"Don't you think the really happy old people you meet are the ones who haven't been together that long?"

"Your parents aren't happy?"

"Who knows? They would never split up, though."

"How come?"

"It's not part of their culture—all that. But also because they did this huge thing together. Immigration was the great experience of their lives."

Our legs were touching under the quilt, but we weren't looking at each other directly. I could see a shadowy version of him in the mosaic-tiled mirror on the wall next to Aunt Penny's armoire. He tended to gesture when he talked.

"They have a whole Indian community in Chicago now—all these couples came here around the same time, but I think each experience was very individual. Only the two of them really know what theirs was like. I don't think they'd feel at home with anyone else."

"Mine, too, for more banal reasons, I think. They're just set in their ways."

"But there's not a lot of romance," Neel suggested, turning to look at me directly. His mouth was beautiful, too, the generous lower lip. Between the sex and the talking, we stayed awake most of the night. We agreed that we should have as much sex as possible now, since that wasn't the kind of thing that was going to improve by the time we were ready for our second marriages.

16.

When we went downstairs late the next morning, Charlie was already up. She had made coffee, and there was even a *Globe* and a bag of fresh doughnuts on the counter.

"Gloucester has the best powdered-sugar doughnuts on the planet," she said. "Little-known fact."

She didn't tease us or make a big deal out of what had clearly happened, for which I was grateful. Because of her long relationship with Kwesi, there had been a lot of mornings when I was the third wheel; being a part of every aspect of each other's lives felt natural to us then.

Sun streamed into the kitchen, but frigid air seeped in around the kitchen door. A thermometer mounted on the window frame outside read seventeen degrees. We sat at Aunt Penny's kitchen table, where a wooden boat held a stack of paper napkins folded to form a sail.

"Penny loves all this kitschy stuff," Charlie said, moving the boat to the counter to make room for our mugs of coffee and the paper.

"I used to be so embarrassed about my mom's things," Neel said. "She loved stuff like that boat, but she also had a lot of religious knickknacks. She used to have a shrine in the corner of their bedroom, when I was little: just a framed poster with a brass bell and a couple of candles. Sometimes she would put flowers in front of it, or a rice ball or some ghee. I always used to close the door before my brother and I had playdates—I was worried our friends would see it."

"Does she still have it?"

"No," Neel said. "And I kind of miss it. I get the feeling the temple is more of a social thing for them now."

"It's the same with my parents," Charlie said.

"They had a shrine to the goddess Lakshmi in the bedroom?"

Charlie giggled. "I mean with church. Except my dad was the one who started out more religious."

I liked the way they were joking together. In my mind I'd already moved ahead to the stage in which Neel spent enough time in our apartment that Charlie would feel comfortable wearing her pajamas in front of him. That morning she was fully dressed in a sweater and jeans, and even wearing a little makeup. It was her public self she was presenting; at first I thought that was only because she and Neel didn't yet know each other well.

Charlie cupped her hands around her mug, warming them, and leaned forward in a conspiratorial way.

"I have an announcement to make."

"Uh oh," I said. I thought she was still joking.

"I'm giving up my thesis."

"Charlie!"

"No, listen. I thought about it a ton last night. I'm totally decided."

"What were you writing about?" Neel asked.

"Choderlos de Laclos."

"He wrote *Dangerous Liaisons*," I told him, but Neel wasn't familiar even with the movie.

"See?" Charlie said. "Laclos is totally irrelevant."

"I wouldn't go by me," Neel said, and for a moment I was distracted by the way he looked that morning, his hair still wild from the salt water and the night we'd just spent, the line of his jaw, his pale fingernails—all these parts of him were suddenly known to me in a way they hadn't been before.

"I'll tell you one thing," Charlie said. "Ask anyone in L.A. how a twenty-one-year-old Harvard student should spend her last year of absolute freedom—finishing an undergraduate-level paper about an eighteenth-century French novelist, or writing a spec script for *Law & Order*—and I know what they'd tell you."

"Do you want to act, or write?" Neel asked.

"Both, I hope." Charlie pulled her bare feet up to the seat of Aunt Penny's Shaker chair, and looked suddenly younger than usual. "I don't really know. But you're supposed to go out there with something finished."

"Maybe you should go 'out there' for a little longer than a spring break, before you up and move," I said.

"I loved L.A. even *before* I visited you there," Charlie said. "Maybe because it seems like the total opposite of Boston. In any case, it has to be better than clawing my way up in academia, toward the aspirational goal of a living wage."

"Best case," Neel agreed. "Not that you'd be doing it for the money."

I felt suddenly annoyed. "Her tutor thinks her thesis is the best one he's advised in years," I told him.

Charlie gave me a look. "For what that's worth."

"You'll graduate without honors if you don't turn in the thesis."

Charlie put on an expression of mock horror. "I didn't think of that—how am I going to survive out there in the *real world* without two or three Latin words on my diploma?" She turned to Neel, as if she expected him to be more sensible. "I even talked to Penny about it last night. My parents are going to flip, but she'll support me. And I know it's the right decision."

This must happen to everyone who loses someone too early: sentences stand out with sudden clarity, take on retrospective meaning. There are turning points that might have been taken, but weren't. Of course there was no guarantee that an Oxford fellowship would have led to an academic career—Charlie could just as easily have ended up in the cutthroat world of London or New York theater. And it was only magical thinking to imagine that her disease would have manifested itself differently in a different life. But I can't help picturing her now in a book-lined university office somewhere on the East Coast, where the sun shines at a safe, wintry distance for many months of the year, cloistered with her poetry and plays—insulated, underpaid—alive.

I couldn't have had any of those thoughts then. Maybe my feeling of foreboding was due to the idea that we would be separated, that I wouldn't be there to look out for her, or her for me.

"You should still think about it a little," I said. "Don't do anything right away."

But it was Charlie's style to do things right away, to completion, with very little looking back.

UNCERTAINTY

1.

A few days after Neel had walked me back to my office, talking about the rotor experiment and his wedding plans, I got a call from a Chicago number. This was in the dreary middle of January, when everyone was harried because of the resumption of classes. My sabbatical had started, but I was in the office anyway, reading Jim's thesis on magnetic fields in the early universe, and how they might have influenced the ultraviolet Lyman-alpha radiation our satellites observe today. I knew Neel was in Chicago for his parents' party; when the phone rang from that area code, I thought for a moment it might be him.

Instead it was a woman's voice. She gave me her name, said I didn't know her, but that she was class of '92, and she'd been asked to write an article for *Harvard Magazine* about my friend Charlotte Boyce. Her name—Patricia Young—sounded familiar, although I couldn't place it at first.

"The magazine ran an obituary when it happened. This is different—more of a profile." The woman sounded tentative. "I should talk to her family as well."

"I can connect you."

"That would be great. Or, you know, 'great.' I think I'm the last person she would have wanted. I told them they should look for someone out in L.A., but they said they needed it right away. Do you know Kwesi? He suggested me."

"I'm sure she'd be glad you were doing it."

"Really?"

I googled Patricia while we were talking: she was a professor in the History Department at U of C.

I told her the kind of things I thought might be appropriate for an article in a university magazine: about the show Charlie wanted to create, and her frustrations with the diversity-staffing programs in Hollywood. I told her what Charlie had said about having more women in positions of power.

Patricia sighed. "That's right—that's what I tell my students, too. Maybe you do the same thing in your field. But then, do you ever feel like you're selling them a bill of goods?"

"Sometimes."

"I want them to be ambitious. But then you get here—the University of Chicago, Berkeley, or MIT, or wherever—and you're the go-to person. An accomplished black woman has died? I write about her. Someone needs to speak to lawyers, or bankers, or tech company executives about the history of affirmative action? That's me. You should see the shelf of awards I've collected. And then there's this low-level resentment from my colleagues, right? Who also, by the way, want to co-create courses with me, because there are a lot of popular courses these days that need a black faculty member in order to have any kind of credibility. I'm the only black woman with tenure in this department."

"We have three tenured women in my department, total."

"Any black women?"

"No—two are white and one's Indian."

"Black men?"

"One. He's in the 'career development' program, with the five nontenured women."

Patricia laughed. "Right. And you know how many recommendation letters I'm supposed to be writing right now? *Eighteen.* I'm doing mine, and the letters for one of my colleagues—I insisted on doing hers, because she's on bed rest for anxiety and exhaustion. We actually do have a lot of young black women who want to go to graduate school in this field—which is terrific. I've got to do a great job on those letters for them, because the only answer is more of us. But the question is, what am I signing them up for?"

That was when I remembered: "You're *Trisha* Young."

"Oh—yeah. I went by Trisha then."

"You were friends with Kwesi, and you knew Charlie from the BSA."

She laughed. "You just remembered me."

"It took me a minute." I hesitated. "Charlie told me you warned her about—" I used his real name.

Patricia got serious. "Oh god, yes," she said. "He's not still around?"

"Not teaching," I said. "But he still has his office. Did you have problems with him, too?"

"No," Patricia said. "No, but I didn't look like Charlie, either.

I had friends, though. And then later I heard those younger girls were trying to get him out."

"Charlie told me about that." I didn't say that she'd been angry at Trisha for giving those girls her name. "She said later that she was sorry she hadn't joined them. But this part's off the record, right?"

"By its very nature," Patricia said. She paused for a long moment, and I thought that maybe she was going to revise what she'd said; maybe something had actually happened to her, with Pope.

"She must have told you what I said?"

"About him?"

"Yes, but I mean what I said years ago—to her."

"She said you told her she'd go far."

Patricia laughed bitterly. "What I said was, 'You're going to go far, because you're the type of black person white people like.'"

I wasn't sure what to say to that.

"She didn't tell you that part?"

"No."

"I guess she wouldn't have. Anyway, I've always felt bad about it. My radical period—but that's no excuse."

"I think Charlie might have wondered if she should've stuck it out, gone into academia after all," I said.

"I wish I could've relieved her mind about that."

There was a silence, in which I thought that we had gotten deeper into this conversation than either of us had expected, and were now unsure how to extricate ourselves.

"I think there was a lot I didn't understand about the pressure she was under," I said.

"No," Patricia said. She was generous but definitive. "You couldn't."

2.

On a Wednesday afternoon at the very end of January, I went to Harvard. The purpose was ostensibly to meet a fellow in Laura Bergstrom's lab, who was interested in collaborating with my post-doc Bence. I'd scheduled the meeting at two o'clock on purpose, and I excused myself a little before three, leaving Bence and Peter talking excitedly in Hungarian about a home-built scanning probe microscope.

I walked from Laura's lab to the yard, past Memorial Church, just as the bells were ringing. It was overcast and cold. A group of prospective undergraduates were huddled together in front of the library's neoclassical façade, listening to a chipper student guide telling the story of the unfortunate Harry Elkins Widener, a member of the class of '07 who had perished on the *Titanic*. In her grief, his mother had commissioned the famous library in his name.

My MIT faculty ID was sufficient for the guard at the desk. We had interlibrary privileges, but I was pretty sure I hadn't been in Widener since I was an undergraduate myself. I made my way up the marble staircase to the third floor, where everything was exactly as I remembered it. Even the massive wooden card catalogs were still there, each topped with a cardboard placard—something that would have to be replaced periodically—signposting its contents: H–J, K–M, etc. Was it possible that anyone still used them?

Once you were out of sight of the staircase, the marble flooring became brown linoleum. The linoleum was very clean, reflecting the light from an unnecessary number of globular ceiling fixtures, so the effect was of a beam traveling down a narrow passage. The silence and the absence of people, the symmetrical pairs of doors, gave the corridor a dreamlike quality. The doors didn't seem to have nameplates—possibly they were shared, or changed hands frequently—and I might have missed Pope's office if he hadn't affixed his own name, neatly typed on a folded square of paper, underneath a window of reinforced chicken-wire glass. The window was obscured by a shirred white cotton curtain, and the door was slightly ajar. You couldn't see whether anyone was inside.

But Pope had heard me. "Come in," he instructed, as if he'd been waiting.

He looked, sitting at his desk, less aged than he had in the church. He was wearing a casual, dark gray Oxford shirt without a jacket, and his thick white hair was styled in the way I remembered, curling around his collar.

"You're not Catherine," he said. "Are you?"

I introduced myself, and Pope's whole manner changed. From

a slightly aggravated professor conducting mandatory office hours, he became an eager student himself, almost boyish. He stood up and took my hand.

"I read your book on black holes last year—wonderful! So much science writing is either overwrought or relentlessly technical. I actually thought of getting in touch at the time. Are you still at MIT?"

I said that I was, and that I'd been an undergraduate at Harvard in the early nineties, then returned as a postdoc four years later. Did he remember me?

"I was especially interested in the historical component—the idea that black holes were just too radical for early twentieth-century physicists to countenance."

I was momentarily taken aback. A conversation about the history of science was the last thing I'd expected.

"I hadn't realized that even Einstein doubted their existence."

"He didn't doubt their existence mathematically, only that such an object could be an observable reality. Now we can see them—or rather the marks they leave on the rest of the universe—all the time. I hope I made that clear."

"You did." Pope smiled at me. "It really is such a pleasure to meet you, Helen. I guess it's too much to hope that you have a burning question about the French Enlightenment?"

"I'm specifically interested in Choderlos de Laclos."

"Really! I never tire of him myself. I'm teaching *Dangerous Liaisons* through the SorbonneX program. A surprising number of people are interested in studying literature digitally."

The office was interior, not large, with an oaken desk and bookshelf, a green banker's lamp. There were a few family photographs: one of him and his wife on a hiking trail, Pope with a wooden walking stick, and another that might have been his son, in the ocean holding a small child. On the facing wall was a framed pencil drawing of a man in seventeenth- or eighteenth-century dress.

"Is that him?"

Pope glanced up. "Oh—that's Rousseau. Laclos's contemporary, and one of the earliest critics of modernity. Rousseau saw the problem from the beginning. He says that the ancients talked about morals and virtue, while all we talk about is business and money.

This was in reference to his own time—can you imagine what he'd think of ours?"

"No."

"Laclos was in many ways a more practical man, an army general and a military engineer. He perfected Vauban's geometric fortifications—those might interest you, a pattern of intersecting fractals—and so they sent him to fortify the Île d'Aix. He was there for a year, but it was never attacked. He was bored, and so he came up with *Dangerous Liaisons*—the only novel he ever wrote."

"There was a production of the play when I was an undergraduate here."

"It's a perennial favorite. I don't mean to be a curmudgeon, but I have a quarrel with almost all of the adaptations, stage or film. It's an impossible book to dramatize, precisely because of how brilliantly Laclos structures it—I'm talking about the letters, of course. He absolutely *refuses* to let us know what the characters really think, because we have only their written words. Performing it on the stage or the screen, you lose that moral ambiguity."

"My friend might have said that that's the actor's job. She played Madame de Merteuil."

"I don't know much about acting," Pope said. "But it seems to me that the actor would have to know his, or her, character's motivation. I'm not sure that Laclos intends them to be knowable in that way. What are we supposed to make of the ending? Valmont is killed, or perhaps allows himself to be killed, by Danceny. Merteuil suffers smallpox and loses her beauty, a great part of her capital. But she escapes to Amsterdam with a box of valuable jewels, whereas Cécile is shut up in a convent, and Tourvel dies there."

I thought: *He doesn't recognize me.*

"Tourvel is the only purely moral character, in spite of her transgression with Valmont. She's the only one who loves unreservedly, against her own self-interest, and we see what happens to her. I found that the book baffled my undergraduates—when I was teaching undergraduates. It's astonishing for someone of my generation to see how uncritically young people today believe in romantic love. They've exploded gender, race, class, all the old shibboleths. But for some reason love is unassailable."

"You don't believe in it."

Pope sighed. "I'm saying that the ambiguity in Laclos serves a purpose, namely to respond to Aristotle's question about tragedy. Why do we enjoy watching *Antigone,* or *Hamlet* for that matter? What do we get out of entering into other people's suffering in art, when we often avoid it in life?"

"But what's his answer?"

"He won't answer it. And that's the genius of this novel, because he rejects the notion that either the characters' pain or their romantic passions can be used to illustrate the author's ideas. It's disconcerting for us, because we expect a novel to possess some sort of underlying moral structure. What Laclos suggests—and this is just my opinion—is that you would have to step outside of conventional society in order to negate some of the power relations that corrupt love. To achieve reciprocity between men and women. Even more than Rousseau, Laclos was a feminist; he left a long, unfinished essay at his death about the position of women in society. Incidentally, he himself had a long, happy marriage—none of the intrigues he writes about in *Les Liaisons.*"

"That's interesting," I admitted. What had I thought it would be like? I would come in here and find a sad old man, accuse him of a twenty-year-old offense, and inspire—what? Some kind of remorse or repentance?

"My friend loved the play," I said. "I don't think it baffled her."

"Your friend who played Merteuil?" Pope asked.

"In '92, our senior year. Her name was Charlotte Boyce."

He didn't catch his breath, or sit down, or make any other sort of dramatic gesture. It was only that his attention was suddenly fully engaged.

"That's it," he said. "At the memorial. I thought I recognized you, but out of context . . ."

"She was my best friend."

"Ah. I'm very sorry."

"You and I met here once before, when Charlie and I were undergraduates."

"That would've been a different office, around the corner," Pope said. "I appreciated what you said about her."

"It was just one story."

"An illustrative one. *Je suis mon ouvrage.*"

"What?"

"I am my own piece of work. I remember how well your friend Charlotte said that line—Merteuil's credo."

"She wanted to go to Oxford, continue studying."

Pope looked at me, and put a hand on his massive desk. "As I remember it, I encouraged her to persist with a fellowship."

"But you'd already made that impossible."

"Those fellowships are very difficult to get."

"You told her she would get it, though."

Pope looked politely perplexed by this. "How could I have helped her, if she didn't even bother to apply?" He sat down, crossed one leg over his knee, and indicated the chair opposite.

I didn't want to sit. "She was twenty-one."

"She was brilliant. I was quite taken with her."

Pope was watching me with his intelligent blue eyes. I thought that Charlie had been right not to come back.

"She moved to L.A.," I said. "She was very successful there, in television. But then she got pregnant and her disease flared."

He raised his hands in front of his chest. "You can hardly blame me for that."

"Hollywood wasn't good for her. There was a lot of bias and stress." I was speaking faster than usual: "Sunlight is apparently a trigger—her mother thinks L.A. was a death sentence for her."

Pope gave me a distasteful look. "That seems somewhat un-scientific."

"I didn't think you were still on campus. Then I saw you at the memorial."

"And so you decided to drop in." He looked me over, then tapped his right hand impatiently on a leather blotter; I saw that he still wore his mother's ornate sapphire ring. "To discuss Laclos. And your best friend." There was just a slight emphasis on the last two words, which made them sound juvenile.

"She changed her whole life because of you."

He paused and leaned back in his chair. "Isn't that what you all come here for?"

A current of pure rage—it seemed, for a moment, to short-circuit my heart.

"There should have been more about her career at the memorial." My hands were shaking, but my voice was even. "She went out at the very top."

Pope met my stare, but remained silent.

"So few people can say that."

"It's rare," Pope said drily.

There were footsteps in the corridor, and then a knock.

"Come in," he said.

A woman stepped into the office. She was perhaps in her mid-sixties, wearing Birkenstocks and carrying a backpack, gray hair tucked behind her ears.

"Catherine?" Pope confirmed. He turned to me with a hard little smile. "Catherine is one of my wonderful correspondence students, who's been kind enough to drive all the way from Woburn."

Catherine beamed. "It's such an inspiring class. I have some questions about Molière, but I don't want to interrupt."

"Professor Clapp was just leaving," Pope said. "We were discussing moral ambiguity in Laclos."

"I've seen both movies," Catherine said. "I'm so eager to read the book."

"It resists every reductive explanation," he told Catherine. Then he turned to me: "Like its subject."

"What is its subject?" I asked.

Pope exaggerated his surprise. "Love," he said. "It's a book about love."

3.

The first weekend in February, Jack was invited to a slumber party. On the way to Miles's house, we talked about kidnapping. It wasn't the first time we'd discussed the subject. When I was pregnant, other single parents told me that our bond would be profound in both positive and negative ways, and that Jack might suffer more separation anxiety at school or camp than the average child. That hasn't been the case, maybe because the scope of my childcare needs got Jack used to a variety of different environments early. I did notice that he had certain fears which might have been more intense than those of children in two-parent families.

"What if a stranger says, 'Do you want some candy?' and you say no in a loud voice, and you run the other way, but the stranger runs after you and grabs you and puts you in his car?"

"Kidnapping is very rare," I told him.

"But I mean, *if?*"

"Even when it does happen, in most cases the kidnapper is someone the child already knows."

This piece of information seemed to intensify Jack's anxiety rather than comfort him. "Why would someone you know kidnap you?"

"Usually it's the other parent. For example, if the parents are divorced, and one parent wants more time with the child than they're allowed in their agreement. And so maybe they take the child and go somewhere for a while, just because they miss them."

"Like Stella in my class?"

I wondered if I'd gotten myself into more complicated territory than I'd realized, in my attempt to reassure him, "I'm sure neither of Stella's parents would kidnap her. I just meant that you don't have to worry about it, because it's just you and me."

I couldn't look back, because I was turning, but I could tell from the silence in the backseat that Jack wasn't buying it. I had an inspiration. "If you want, we could make up a safety word."

Jack was interested immediately. "What's that?"

"It's something only the parent and the kid know. If someone other than the parent is supposed to pick up the kid, the kid can say, 'Do you know the safety word?' And if the person knows it, then the kid knows it's okay to go with them."

"Because the parent told them the safety word?"

"Right. It's like a code."

Jack didn't hesitate. "I want to do it."

"Okay," I said. "You choose. It can be any word."

" 'Jack,' " Jack said.

"Maybe something harder to guess than that."

" 'Ninja'?" he suggested.

" 'Ninja' is fine."

"Okay!"

"Then we're all set."

Jack was quiet for a few minutes. I thought I'd handled the situation well, and that he was just processing the conversation. When we stopped at the light, I glanced back at him: he was staring out the window, holding his backpack on his lap. He was thinking hard, but he waited until we were moving again, perhaps intentionally, to ask his next question:

"Do donors ever kidnap kids?"

"No, never."

"Why not?"

"Our donor doesn't have any information about us. He couldn't find us, even if he wanted to."

I pulled up in front of Miles's family's large, Colonial house in Somerville. Miles's three siblings would be there in addition to the guests, and you could hear the noise inside already. Another child was getting out of the car in front of us.

"There's Graham," Jack said excitedly.

"Jack," I said. "Do you have any more questions before we go in?"

He hesitated. I could see his desire for information warring with his eagerness to get to the party.

"Do the kids who get kidnapped ever want to be kidnapped?" His eyes darted to mine, then away again. "I mean the ones whose other parent kidnaps them. Who isn't a stranger."

There was an expression on his face I'd never seen before, a more mature kind of empathy than he'd so far demonstrated. I realized that he was concerned about my feelings.

The other boy bounded up the front walk, where a bunch of red and gold balloons were tied to the porch railing. He was followed more slowly by his father, a balding man in his forties, encumbered by a sleeping bag and a wrapped gift. Jack watched them expectantly, one hand on the door.

"I don't know," I said.

4.

On my way home I realized that I had the evening free, and could've made plans to meet a friend. Instead I picked up a burrito and ate it standing at the kitchen counter, which reminded me of being a student in a pleasurable way. I decided I would use the opportunity to do some work.

This was the Saturday night before Neel's team was slated to make their big announcement. The press conference would happen on Thursday, the same day the paper would finally be published in *Physical Review Letters* and go up on the open-access server. In four pages, the paper would announce the first detection of a gravitational wave and the first direct observation of a pair of black holes merging. Neel had sent it to me under strict confidence in January, and I had to admit it was beautiful: revelatory, concise, and comprehensible. It would make history, but as the LIGO scientists (who would have to continue justifying their funding) were quick to point out, it was only a beginning. Now that LIGO's interferometers had detected two black holes merging, they would start to look for other cosmic events powerful enough to create gravitational waves they could measure. Most of all, they would want to see a kilonova, a collision of two neutron stars.

Binaries of living stars were known to astronomers by the beginning of the nineteenth century; it was William Herschel who first understood the relationship between Mizar and a companion in Ursa Major. Objects that were more difficult or impossible to observe directly took longer, but even before John Wheeler coined the term "black hole," in the late sixties, the Soviet physicists Zel'dovich and Novikov had proposed a search for these mysterious objects in binary relationships with stars. LIGO's scientists had expected that the first detection would be a gravitational wave produced by a black hole–black hole binary, simply because the colossal mass of such objects allowed them to collide with more force than anything since the Big Bang.

Black holes merge in absolute darkness; when an especially big star dies, the resulting supernova explosion produces light across the electromagnetic spectrum. Neutron stars are somewhere in between: they are dead stars that flicker like embers until they spiral into each other in a brilliant burst of color. What would be so exciting about detecting a kilonova with LIGO's interferometers is that traditional astronomers could immediately point their telescopes in the same direction; it would be the first time we could hear the "chirp" of the gravitational wave and see the burst of light at the same time.

There are two windows in my office, but the desk faces a wall, a strategy for concentration Arty once suggested to me. Nothing else about my setup at home is very considered. Mostly the desk is full of paperwork: bills, school forms, second-grade artwork, a large number of Post-it notes reminding me to pick up Jack's allergy medication, email Vincenzo, buy toothpaste, and finish Bence's recommendation letter by February 12. I was adding a note about the connection between primordial black holes and LIGO's new findings—about the possibility of using the interferometers to search for dark matter—when it occurred to me that I had the ringer off and that Miles's parents had no way to reach me if Jack were to get homesick or need something. I went downstairs and found the phone in my jacket pocket. At first I thought the message on the home screen was from Amy, since she often sends me pictures of my nieces.

But there was an alert with the thumbnail: "Charlie's iPhone would like to share a photo." It had been almost two months since I'd gotten a message; our last exchange—in which I'd threatened to report the phone as stolen—had occurred just before Neel's engagement party, at the beginning of December. Amy joked about "ghosting," but the fact was that Charlie ghosted even while she was alive, even before that practice had a name. She wouldn't answer an email or a phone message for months, even half a year; I would be hurt and swear that I'd given up on her. Then, out of the blue, she'd send me something—a picture of Simmi, usually—and I'd write back right away. It occurred to me, as I typed, that I'd managed to develop the same type of relationship with whoever was using her phone.

I tapped "accept," and the image opened on my screen. It was me and Charlie, on the day I'd been to visit her at their first house in L.A. Maybe we'd taken it when we went outside to drink coffee by the pool, or in front of the house before I left? At first I thought the poor resolution was due to the older device's early-model camera, but even that didn't explain how out-of-focus it was. I turned the phone horizontally to accommodate the photo's orientation, and saw that it was a picture of a picture, taken on a table or desk (you could see the wood around the edges of the print). Part of my face, including one eye, was washed out by glare. If Charlie had reproduced it, she'd focused on herself, as well anyone might—it was an especially beautiful picture of her, vamping for the camera with her arm around my neck. My smile looked strained, the way it always does when I know I'm being photographed. The best pictures of you are the serious ones, Charlie once observed, but I only look good when I'm smiling. That was untrue: it was hard to take a bad picture of Charlie, regardless of her expression.

Where did you get that picture?

The oven.

The answer startled me, and I almost dropped the phone. There was only one time I'd held human remains in my hands. My paternal grandmother's ashes had gone into a plot in a churchyard in Kenosha, Wisconsin, where she was born. I had been surprised by how coarse they were, more rock than ash. I thought then of the physical process that had occurred: the temperature inside a cremator can reach two thousand degrees—about a fifth as hot as the surface temperature of the sun.

I didn't understand, and I sent back a question mark. The gray dots appeared, then disappeared, then appeared again. It took forever and I thought maybe the person on the other end was typing a detailed answer. But when it finally appeared, it was only four words long:

Cottleston, Cottleston, Cottleston Pie.

I stared at them; my chest hurt. People all over the world knew that rhyme, but how many people knew what it meant to Charlie?

A fly can't bird but a bird can fly.

The person on the end seemed to be waiting. A minute passed, and then another. Were they still there? I tapped out the next line, experimentally:

Ask me a riddle and I reply.

The response came immediately:

Cottleston, Cottleston, Cottleston Pie.

I heard a noise, or imagined it. I was standing in the front hall with my back to the door. I felt the walls contract around me; the person, whoever they were, had suddenly seemed to come much closer: from the generic symbols, to the scientific inquiries, to the hiatus when I hadn't heard anything at all—was that planned, so I would let down my guard?—to the photograph and this poem, more intimate than anything I'd yet received.

Unlike my sister, I've always been afraid in a house alone. But our father instilled in us both a mania for saving electricity, and all my lights were off downstairs. I turned them on one at a time as I went through the living room and into the kitchen, to look out the window at the empty yard. I put my head into the small bathroom in the hall between the kitchen and Jack's bedroom. It was unusual for his door to be closed, and I felt my pulse in my ears as I pushed it open.

Clothing, Legos, and a game of Battleship littered the rug, and Jack's unmade bed was crowded with plush animals. I told myself I was being foolish. I stood there waiting for the phone to ping, and when it didn't, I began cleaning up. I wanted to be doing something. Dust had been among the primary triggers for Jack's asthma, and he still wasn't supposed to sleep with more than one stuffed toy. They tended to accumulate, though, and so I started to put them away. Their glass eyes were strangely animate, a trick of the light.

I heard the noise again, now clearly the television coming from Terrence and Simmi's apartment downstairs. At first the voices were reassuring. They were here; I wasn't alone. And then I understood. The answer was so simple that I was ashamed I hadn't thought of it. *How is it possible*, was what my parents used to say, on the frequent occasions when I failed to assimilate some piece of obvious practical information—*someone as smart as you?*

I picked up the phone from Jack's bed, and typed out her name:

Simmi?

I waited for several minutes, but there was nothing more. I felt frantic: we both knew now, and so there was nothing to hide. I thought of calling the phone, but of course it couldn't take voice calls. Maybe her father had said something to her from the living room, where he was watching television; maybe Simmi was stashing the phone in whatever hiding place, or series of places, she'd been using for the past eight months. I went to my door and listened; when there was nothing, I went down the interior stairs and stood just inside the front door, where I could pretend I was on my way out if Terrence were to open the apartment door. I could hear the TV more clearly here; it was a popular political drama, not anything that would interest Simmi. Where was she now?

I thought back to last June, the day after Charlie died. Simmi had been watching television while her father made call after call, alerting their friends—was it possible that she'd wanted to call someone, too? And what had she thought when I immediately called back—just as if her mother were alive? Was that what had prompted her to send the tiny pictures by email? Once the phone service was turned off, she'd had to use the Wi-Fi to send email, and then text. The first message was nonsensical, perhaps in imitation of a greeting Charlie would have used with tongue firmly planted in her cheek ("luvya lady"), but once Simmi actually met me, science would have seemed like a natural topic. The questions had been simple not because the person on the other end was unbalanced, but because she was eight years old.

Could she have written to multiple people, and I was the only one to respond? It was possible that she hadn't considered the fact that her messages would appear under the name "Charlie"—that in fact she hadn't been playing any kind of trick. Instead she had simply been asking the same type of question she'd asked the first day she came to the house, about stars. Both her father and I had immediately shut that down, and so it made sense that Simmi had taken the conversation to another medium. Maybe it was less about a need for answers, and more about the connection—about getting to know a person who had been important to her mother before anything terrible had happened, in the radiant but increasingly insubstantial past.

The front hall had been painted robin's egg blue by the previous owners, and I had left it that color. There was an anodyne watercolor of a sailboat in a wooden frame. I stood in front of it, and felt a creeping guilt. I'd been using all my adult faculties to try to outsmart a child—*Charlie's* child, who had wanted something from me. Whatever it was, I'd failed to give it to her. I thought of the arch tone I'd adopted: *Are you interested in physics?* Did it say something about me, that I had immediately suspected some kind of intentional provocation or foul play? Was I especially suspicious, liable to take offense, unapproachable? Was that the reason Simmi had adopted this strategy in the first place?

Even if all of those things were true, I couldn't understand why the messages had stopped suddenly, or why they'd started again tonight. Had she sent me something so personal, something only family and close friends would recognize, because she was finally ready to reveal herself? And if so, why now?

Across from the sailboat was a row of hooks with Simmi's silver parka hanging at the end of it, rainbow-striped knit gloves spilling out of the pocket, her scooter parked underneath it with an iridescent green helmet hanging off the T-bar. The other hooks held a collection of sweatshirts, canvas tote bags, and Terrence's down vest and leather jacket. I couldn't say anything to Terrence until I'd talked to Simmi; whatever I did, I had to let her know, now, that she could trust me. I allowed myself to think that it might not be too late, that there might be something I could do for her. She had come up with an ingenious way for us to talk, and I had to find a way to use it, before I was obliged to tell her father what I'd figured out.

I scrolled through my own photos, the ones I'd collected of Charlie, but I was worried about making Simmi sad. Instead I sent one I'd taken of her and Jack in his room, in a fort they'd constructed from the sheets and pillows on his bed. They had called me to come see. It was a long, thin structure, a tunnel, and they had used it to create an optical illusion. Simmi's head was sticking out the front and Jack's legs out the back—as if they were one child, stretched in two directions.

I wasn't wearing my coat, but I didn't want to go back upstairs. I took my sweatshirt from a peg in the hall and went out. It was forty-five degrees: warm for February—I thought I would walk just to the river and back to clear my head. I hurried past the quiet side streets, the rows of shabbily genteel, hundred-year-old houses, most of them filled with people like myself, obsessively committed to one obscure subject or another, the importance of which we communicated in books we passed among ourselves. It was exactly that insularity that Charlie had been eager to escape when she'd left home for L.A.

I knew Charlie didn't want to talk about being sick, but what if I had insisted? I had respected the boundaries she put up around her disease so carefully that our friendship had been squeezed out into the shrinking margins of her life. There was the body and there was the brain. Eventually there had been nothing but the body to talk about, and so we'd stopped talking. And I'd been self-involved enough, stupid enough, to take that as a rejection of me.

The thoughts were painful, but there was something freeing about having them, as it is when you're working on a difficult calculation and suddenly realize why your method is wrong. Charlie loved me, but it was too late; it was too late, but Charlie loved me. I felt closer to her than at any time since she'd died. It was almost as if a real ghost was nearby. When I heard someone behind me, I didn't turn around. I was alone on the sidewalk, but I wasn't afraid anymore. Our two sets of footsteps made a staccato rhythm on the cold pavement. *Ask me a riddle, and I reply.*

Come on, I thought, and it was as if someone else was talking inside my head: If you're going to come, *come now.*

A man in a dress coat and shiny shoes passed me on the sidewalk, walking fast. A stranger.

"Excuse me," he murmured, before crossing the street toward a waiting car.

I had come to the river. It was a clear night, but the skyline gave off too much light to see stars. I crossed the new pedestrian bridge over Memorial Drive, clogged with red and yellow taillights, but didn't descend on the other side. From up here I could see the river. Jagged floes of gray ice clung to the shore, but out in the middle the office towers dropped their inverted reflections in still, black water.

Automatically I reached for my phone. But what did I want to say, and to whom? The object had lost its special power because there was now no chance that something would come from "Charlie." There was no chance, because there was no Charlie anymore. My friend was gone.

5.

I picked Jack up from Miles's house the following morning. It was a crisp, bright day, and I had the idea I might take him downtown to the aquarium. I hoped Terrence and Simmi would agree to join us. I thought there would be a moment when the children would want to split up and see different exhibits. I could offer to take her wherever she wanted to go—the Pacific Reef, or the touch tank—and use that opportunity to talk with her alone. I'd texted Terrence early to suggest it; I hadn't heard back, but when we came in the front door we could hear them in the apartment.

"They're home!" Jack said, and knocked.

There were thumping feet, and then a female voice:

"Just a sec!"

Jack gave me a questioning look.

The door was opened by a young woman. Simmi was behind her in the kitchen, and Terrence was nowhere to be seen.

"Hey!" Simmi said. "I'm making pancakes by myself. You want some?"

"Yeah!" Familiar with Terrence's house rules, Jack slipped out of his shoes without being told, and hurried into the apartment. He barely looked at the stranger who'd opened the door.

Her hair was dyed an artificial jet-black, cut short in a jagged style. She was wearing black jeans, ripped across the thigh, and a purple tank top, no bra; over the tank top was Terrence's blue sweatshirt with the Japanese logo. She was wearing too much eye makeup for 9:00 a.m. on a Sunday, she was very pretty, and there was no way she was older than twenty-five.

"Hi," she said. "I'm Nicki."

"Is Terrence—"

"He went surfing. I stayed over so he could leave last night." She imparted this information in a helpful way, without suggesting that there might be anything disturbing about it.

"Surfing where?"

"Rhode Island? I don't exactly know. I've only done it a couple of times—but I've dated surfers before? They get up *really* early. That was mostly when I lived in the Bay Area." She spoke in a familiar way; it wasn't only teenagers anymore. You heard it from parents pushing strollers in the supermarket, and podcasts on NPR: over-whelmingly interrogative and laden with pauses, confident in its carelessness, as if each sentence came as surprise—though not an unpleasant one—to its speaker.

"You're babysitting?"

Nicki glanced in the kitchen, where Simmi was balanced on a kitchen stool, in order to be at the right height for the stove. "Yeah? We're hanging out."

"Can I stay for pancakes?" Jack asked.

"We're going to the aquarium."

"Can Simmi come?"

I looked at Simmi, who was dribbling batter from a plastic ladle onto the griddle. She finished one and looked back: not unfriendly, but a little wary. She acknowledged what we both now knew, but wanted to be sure I wouldn't say anything in front of Jack and Nicki.

"Not today, honey. Terrence wouldn't know where we were."

"You could text him," Jack suggested.

Simmi made an effort to flip a pancake that wasn't ready. It fell apart.

I went over to the stove. "You need some help?"

Simmi glanced at me anxiously. She was standing on one of those collapsible kitchen step stools—I thought Andrea and Günter must've left it behind—and I imagined her toppling forward, her hand landing on the sizzling griddle. I decided that Nicki had no idea how to take care of children, that that was the reason I was suddenly furious with Terrence.

"Can I jump on the trampoline?" Jack asked, and I gave him permission. I put my hand on Simmi's back.

"Careful on this stool, okay?"

Simmi looked up uncertainly. "You're not mad?" she said in a low voice.

"What?"

"About the—" She glanced at Nicki, who had sat down on the couch and was looking at her phone.

"No," I said. "Of course not."

"You're not going to call the police?"

"What?"

"You said Daddy would call the police."

"Oh, honey—oh no. No, I didn't mean—"

"You *said.*"

"But I didn't know it was you then! I didn't know until last night."

Simmi picked up the spatula again; this time the pancake turned, but ended up on the burner instead of on the griddle. She started to cry, silently. I put my arm around her and took the spatula in the other hand. I flipped a pancake, which was now burnt almost black on the other side. Simmi laughed at the terrible pancake, but when she looked up at me, her eyes were full of tears. I remembered Terrence saying that Simmi didn't cry when her mother died, only when they couldn't find the phone. Had she been struggling with that guilt, on top of everything else? And then instead of helping, I'd frightened her with the notion of the police. I wondered if Terrence's absence last night had been the reason she'd risked taking out the phone and contacting me again.

At that moment Nicki looked up and noticed her charge's expression. "Simmi?"

"We're having some trouble with the pancakes," I said. "It's frustrating."

"Pancakes aren't good for you anyway," Nicki said cheerfully. "How about if we go out for smoothies, Simmi?"

Jack came out of the bedroom. "Can you please text her dad and just *ask* about the aquarium?"

"He's surfing," Nicki said. "He won't see his texts. Unless he has one of those watches." She fixed her round blue eyes on me: "Does he, do you know?"

"No idea. But we'll do it another day."

Jack groaned, but my tone prevented him from arguing. I turned off the stove for Simmi, and held her hand unnecessarily as she stepped down from the stool. Then I folded it and put it away in the broom closet. Simmi came with me to the door, where Jack began slowly putting on his shoes.

Nicki stood up from the couch.

"How do you know Terrence?" I asked her.

"We met her at the coffee shop," Simmi offered. "Nicki works there."

"I go to BU," Nicki said. "I'm getting my master's."

"In what field?"

"Art history. Abstract expressionism?"

"What are you going to do with that?"

I don't think I've ever asked that question of anyone, and I was a little ashamed. I didn't know where it had come from. Nicki, though, seemed accustomed to answering it.

"I don't know yet? I'm also in a band, so we'll see."

Jack finally stood up.

"Good luck with that," I told Nicki. "Nice to meet you." Then I turned to Simmi, who had the end of one braid in her mouth. "We'll be out," I said. "But you know how to reach me, if you need me?"

Simmi nodded, but she wasn't looking at me.

6.

Jack said he was too tired to go to the aquarium, now that Simmi wasn't coming along. I heard Terrence come in, around eleven, and then I heard Nicki leaving. About an hour later he came up and knocked. There was nothing unusual in his manner, and I was struck by how relaxed he looked, as if he'd slept well for the first time in months. I didn't know whether to attribute that to Nicki or the surfing, but the dark shadows under his eyes were gone. He asked Jack if he wanted to help with a project this afternoon, and Jack, who had been moping in his room most of the morning, eagerly agreed. I said that I had to prepare for a colloquium, but Terrence asked if I could come down for just a minute. There was something he wanted to show me.

We followed Terrence downstairs, through the apartment, and out the back door, which opens onto a narrow porch. There are a few steps down into the yard, the grass yellow and patchy at this time of year. On my porch were two simple cedar planters, rectangular and at least three feet deep, four bags of potting soil, and two bags of mulch. Jack peered into the planters.

"Did you get seeds?"

"It's too late to plant," Terrence said. "The ground is frozen. But we can put in bulbs this fall."

"I want hibiscus," Simmi said.

"We can have those in the summer," Terrence told her, then turned back to me. "And I'm going to put some herbs in the planters this spring, if that's okay with you? Maybe some sungold tomatoes later on?"

"Great," I said.

He had even bought two spades with colorful, enameled handles, and two small sets of gardening gloves.

"We'll get started with the mulch this afternoon," Terrence said, and looked over at Jack. "Your mom can help if she wants."

"You don't want my help," I said quickly. "Any plant I touch dies immediately."

Terrence smiled. "You're a scientist. You can't be that bad."

"Different science."

"She says she does science," Jack said glumly. "But it's really just boring old math."

Simmi was standing by the brick wall at the back of the yard, where there's a rotting wooden table covered with old toys: shovels, a bucket, a rusty Tonka truck. She had found a pinwheel left over from the summer, and was blowing to make it turn. Jack went over to look.

"We met your friend," I said to Terrence.

He crossed his arms over his chest, but didn't turn around. He was wearing a down vest over a flannel shirt and a black watch cap. There was a white rectangle on the back pocket of his jeans, where he kept his wallet. I thought he might not respond, and when he did, it was in the same laconic tone he'd used the first time Simmi came over to play, as if he'd rather be anywhere else. "She was just watching Simmi. I needed a little time."

"You could've asked me."

"Simmi told me Jack was on a sleepover."

"Still."

"I'm not going to dump another kid on you the one morning you can sleep."

He took a step down, toward the children, and I noticed the back of his neck, the neat line of the barber's clippers. He was still keeping his hair very short.

"But I mean, who is she?"

Terrence turned sharply to face me. "We met her at the coffee place. We *chatted.* She offered to babysit. Do you need any more information?"

"Sorry. It's just—she was wearing your sweatshirt."

Terrence sighed. "Look, I can't help whatever trip she's on. We've hung out once or twice. Sometimes it's nice to talk to someone who just keeps it light, you know?"

I felt stung by this comment, and also reassured.

Terrence modulated his voice a little for the kids. "We left Addie's because I couldn't deal with her questions, okay? I can't stay here either, if you're going to be investigating me."

The children had found an old Wiffle bat and were, for some reason, taking turns banging it against the brick wall. The sky was gray and heavy; it looked like it was going to snow.

"Sorry," I said again.

"It's fine," Terrence said tightly.

We were silent for a moment. This wasn't the scenario in which I'd imagined telling him about the phone, but it would be worse the longer I waited. I sat down on the porch railing.

"I think I figured out the mystery of the phone." It felt wrong, too casual, possibly because I was attempting to sound like someone who could keep it light.

"Charlie's phone?"

"I've been getting more messages."

"*What?*"

"I mean, not many. A couple."

Terrence was squinting at me, his lips drawn in, as if he suspected some brutal joke.

"Since it happened," I continued nervously. "Or since we talked about it."

"What did they *say?*"

"Random stuff. About science mostly. But then—last night—I got a picture of me and Charlie. A picture of a picture really, of me and her. And then that rhyme—'Cottleston Pie.'"

Terrence was startled. We both turned at the same moment to look at the children, who were crouching down now, their heads together, examining something in the dirt.

"Sims," he said quietly, almost as if he were talking to her.

"I didn't understand it was her—until last night."

"You didn't *tell* me?" Terrence spoke in a lower register than normal, as if he were trying to control himself.

"I didn't know! And then I came down to tell you—" *And Nicki was here,* I was about to say. "And you were out."

Terrence shook his head. "I mean, about the messages before that."

"I did! You told me it was a spammer."

Terrence closed his eyes for a moment. "Okay—that first one. But after that?"

"I thought it would—be painful for you."

Terrence gave me a look, and I hurried on. "And you guys were moving in—I mean, I wanted you to," I admitted. "And what would have been the point? You weren't going to report it."

"I might have, if I thought someone was using it."

"I thought of that. But I mean, the police don't get people's phones back. And I thought maybe I could convince the person—before I knew who it was."

"You thought you'd do a better job than the police."

"Well—maybe. I would definitely be more focused on it."

Terrence shook his head: "You guys are really something."

Did he mean me and Jack, or me and the Boyces? Or people like me in general—people who thought they were smart?

The children had stood up, and were cupping something in their palms.

"Look," Jack called. He held out his hand, but I couldn't see anything at this distance. "Roly polys!"

"He calls them roly polys, but in L.A. we say pill bugs," Simmi added. "Right, Daddy?"

"My sister and I used to say 'potato bugs,'" I told her. "I think they go by a lot of different names." I started down the steps to join them, mostly to separate myself from Terrence, but he stopped me. We were so close that I could see the gray flecks in his eyes. His irises had dark rings around them.

"Hey," he said. "Where is it?"

I shook my head.

He looked toward the door. "But it's here."

It was as if the phone's full potential was hitting him only now, as if the months it had been missing had somehow decreased the possibility of finding it: he couldn't quite believe it was really happening. The letter that promised to vindicate him with Charlie's parents wasn't even the majority of the device's significance. It was instead the simple fact that those words she'd written had to be close, steps from where he was standing. The essence of magical thinking, that it could be stripped of its magic—that this time, the beloved will actually walk in the door—was visible on Terrence's face. It was almost as if he and Charlie had a future together again, of whatever brief duration.

He turned back to me reluctantly. "She must've hidden it in the play kitchen. Right?"

The oven, I thought—of course that was the oven Simmi had meant. I looked at him. "How would you know that?"

Terrence stepped back, and smiled faintly. "If I'd known she had it, I would have found it right away," he said. "It's not rocket science."

My hands were trembling a little when Jack and I got upstairs, either from the cold or from the conversation. I worried that I'd somehow betrayed Simmi in the way I'd told Terrence about the phone—would it have been better to encourage her to tell him? That of course would have been difficult to do this morning, in front of Jack and Nicki. I regretted bringing up Nicki with Terrence at all, although in the moment it hadn't felt so far out of line. Terrence was my dead friend's husband, and he was living in my house. On the other hand, I wasn't sure whether it was loyalty or jealousy that had made me react to Nicki the way that I did.

I had thought the plans for the garden might improve Jack's mood, but he clearly hadn't gotten enough sleep. As soon as we were back in our apartment, he began a familiar argument about how much less fun I am than other parents. Leo had a bowl of M&Ms in his room; Dylan had an iPad mini, loaded with all kinds of games—*not* math games, he clarified; and Miles, as we had often discussed, had three siblings. I had little patience for the fight he was trying to pick. I told him I was going to make some coffee, and that he could play in his room, or read, or even lie down and take a nap.

"Can I watch a movie?"

"Didn't you watch movies all last night?"

"*So?*"

"So it's enough."

Jack was suddenly tearful. "I bet every other kid on the whole planet is watching a movie right now. I'm tired. It's not going to rot my brain or something—just watching one movie."

"Jack, I love you. But you're being very difficult right now." I was proud of myself for remaining calm.

"Oh, so now you think I'm *difficult?* That's nice. That's very nice. Everyone in my class except me has a phone."

"I know that's not true."

"It is true."

We had been standing in the entryway, and now, instead of going toward his own room, Jack ran up a few steps toward mine, then stopped and turned around.

"Simmi has one."

I hesitated for a moment. "Her iPad, do you mean?"

"*No,*" Jack said. "You think I don't know the difference? You're stupid!"

"Jack! You don't talk to me like that."

"She has a phone *and* an iPad. She has everything."

I was filled with a kind of furious rage. I climbed the stairs to him, grabbed his shoulders.

"'*She has everything?*' How can you say that?" I wasn't screaming, but I wasn't in control any longer. I was right in his face. I could see that he was scared, but I couldn't stop. "She lost her *mother.*"

Jack broke free of me and ran up the stairs. He slammed the door, but the walls are so thin that I could still hear him.

"I wish I could lose you!"

.   .   .

I went down to the kitchen and made coffee. I was thinking about my parents, who had spanked me only once or twice, with little conviction. I had never hit Jack, but sometimes I wondered if what I did was worse. I got angry, then apologized and tried to take it back. And what had been the point of it? Technology? My restrictions and his access to it? What other kids were allowed to do? Did it really have to do with the devices, in all their seductive power, or was it Terrence he wanted—a father?

I drank half a cup of coffee, then went upstairs and found Jack where I knew he'd be, in the closet. He was holding a porcupine quill that my parents had brought back from a trip they took to Kenya, a photographic safari in 1979. It had been their biggest splurge, the only time they'd ever left us with our grandparents and gone somewhere together. They were both passionate about animals, and especially touched by any suffering creature; growing up, my sister and I had cared for abused dogs and cats, as well as rabbits, guinea pigs, and a pair of rats from the school's science lab. My father would help my sister and me design mazes for them out of blocks.

Jack was frowning, using the quill to draw a pattern in the wall-to-wall carpeting that I'd always meant to tear out. There were nice wooden floors underneath it.

"I don't want to talk," he warned me.

"Okay." I sat down and he glared at me. "I just wanted to tell you sorry for getting upset."

Jack didn't say anything.

"Are you still angry about the phone?"

I waited, but he remained silent.

"What do you want a phone for?"

"To play Minecraft."

"You can play that on the computer."

"You never let me!"

I was about to argue, and reconsidered. "And Terrence does?"

Jack hesitated. "He doesn't know."

"That Simmi likes Minecraft?"

Jack sighed. "She doesn't. I mean, he doesn't know that she has a phone." He stopped suddenly, put his head on his knees.

"Jack?"

He mumbled something.

"What?"

"Don't tell him." He looked up fiercely. "Promise you won't. She told me not to tell *anyone*. She'll hate me."

"Okay," I said. "I promise. But I already knew she had a phone."

Jack's sullenness returned. "You did?"

"She told me." I thought this was essentially true.

"But do you know what she uses it for?"

I was pretty sure Simmi hadn't told Jack about our correspondence, and her behavior this morning had seemed to confirm it. Other possibilities occurred to me: shopping, pornography. There had been an incident in the third grade at Jack's school last year.

"No, what?"

He got a little smile on his face, like when he's going to try to sell me on something. "She doesn't need the metamorphosis typewriter."

"Metaphase. Why not?"

Now Jack had rolled up his sleeve, and was using the quill to scratch thin white lines on his arm.

"Careful."

"She can talk to her mom on the phone."

"I don't think so, Bug."

Jack nodded vigorously, contradicting me. "She showed me." He was tugging on his ear.

"Maybe she was writing to someone else?"

"No," he said, but he seemed to have gotten control of himself. It was only when someone refused to listen that he got really upset. "She wouldn't let me see what she was writing, but she showed me the messages. It said, 'Mom' at the top."

" 'Mom'?"

"Yes."

Something occurred to me, and my stomach curdled.

"And she showed me pictures."

"Of her mom?"

Jack shrugged. "Most are just her. Or her and her dad. One is even of you." Jack looked up at me, gauging my reaction.

"Me and Simmi's mom."

He nodded. "Yeah. But that was a really long time ago."

7.

Charlie died in June. Terrence and Simmi arrived in July, just before the memorial. In the middle of September, early one Monday morning, Gravitational Wave 150914 hit the machine in Livingston, Louisiana. Ten milliseconds later, it hit LIGO's other machine, in Hanford, Washington. The wave stretched one arm of the L-shaped machine about one ten-thousandth of the width of a proton, and shrank the other arm by a corresponding amount. Its shape exactly matched the geometry for gravity that Einstein had described a century earlier, in November 1915.

Einstein showed us that space bends time, and Schwarzschild gave us the math to prove it. He wrote down the first exact solution to what we call Einstein's field equations of general relativity in a letter to Einstein in 1915. Schwarzschild was at that time serving in the German army, and most biographies have it that he wrote the solution from a wet and frigid trench on the Russian front, and sent it to Einstein by diplomatic pouch: *As you see, the war treated me kindly enough, in spite of the heavy gunfire, to allow me to get away from it all and take this walk in the land of your ideas.* The letter itself was probably written from Mulhouse, in Alsace, although Schwarzschild may well have done the math on the front lines. The trenches were also where he contracted the rare skin disease pemphigus, which led to his death the following year. There is a crater named for him on the northern part of the far side of the moon.

Black holes were a consequence of Schwarzschild's calculations, but neither he nor Einstein believed that they really existed. The wave Neel's team recorded shows the last four rotations of two enormous black holes, just before they collided. The first was twenty-nine times the mass of our sun; the second, thirty-two. This happened more than a billion years ago, 1.4 billion light-years away, and so it's just a coincidence that the technology Neel's team built was ready to record it during a test run last September. The shape of the wave matches the theoreticians' descriptions of such an event so perfectly that there is only a 1 in 3.5 million chance that they could be wrong.

Physicists knew that gravity could stretch matter. We knew that a collision between enormously dense objects—black holes or neutron stars—was the most likely way we would be able to hear it. One scientist came up with a good Hollywood analogy—that the universe had finally "produced a talkie." Actually, the universe has always produced talkies; it was only that we didn't have the ears to hear them. Neel's interferometers became the ears.

You can hear about something for a lifetime, though, even something you know is happening all around you, and still not really believe it—until it happens close enough to feel yourself.

8.

I called Addie and asked if we could have a cup of coffee. She suggested that I come over to the house the following Thursday, and I rescheduled a talk I was giving. This was early February, just after the LIGO press conferences. Neel had attended the most important of them, at the National Press Club in D.C. I had watched it in my office with Vincenzo and several of our postdocs. At one point I thought I recognized the back of Neel's head in the audience, but I later learned that he'd been in another room, watching on a monitor with members of his team. The next day he left for India, to get married.

I turned into the Boyces' driveway that Thursday a few minutes early. It took Addie some time to come to the door. Her face was exhausted, much more so than when I'd run into her outside the sandwich shop in September, but she was still beautifully dressed, in a dark orange cardigan, a brown wool skirt, and leather boots. The current set of terriers yapped around her feet.

"George, off!" She moved one of the dogs out of my way with her boot. "We'll be informal and have coffee in the kitchen."

I followed her down the hall, past two valuable pieces of art. One was a Kara Walker silhouette of a woman in a highly ornamented costume, beautiful and technically virtuosic. Charlie had once told me that her mother bought it while Walker was still studying at RISD. I knew without being told that Addie wouldn't have hung any of Walker's more violent images in her home, even if she was likely to admire them. The other was a triptych of tall, rectangular photographs meant to recall Chinese scroll paintings: one fresh peony, one fading, and one covered with frost. They looked real until you got up close and saw that the blooms themselves were actually made of raw meat. I had a residual feeling of excitement, entering Charlie's house, as if I were still a student, eager to prove to her parents that I was worldly enough to have a place at their table.

The hallway opened up into the kitchen, a long, rectangular room with a bow window opening to the backyard. Somewhere was the faint but steady drone of television news. The kitchen I remembered had white cabinets with blue-and-white china knobs, a tiled countertop, and the same mottled white appliances my parents had owned. At some point in the last twenty-three years, the Boyces had replaced those with stainless steel, the counters with granite. The cabinets had glass fronts and you could see the orderly towers of china inside, the wineglasses hanging upside down from their stems. I complimented Addie.

"I've always liked glass," she said. "When the children were young, I needed to hide the mess, but now it's much easier to stay organized." She offered me coffee and I accepted. The television in the other room switched off, and Carl emerged from his office. There was a dark *V* on the front of his T-shirt, and he was wiping his face with a towel.

"Helen!" he said. "It's wonderful to see you. I won't hug you."

"I bought him a Peloton bike," Addie said. "He pretends not to like it."

"I don't pretend," Carl said. He turned to his wife. "You look beautiful—are you two going out?"

It had been many years since Carl's infidelity, and the year Addie had spent in Paris with the children, but there was still a note of deference in the way Carl spoke to his wife. He sounded more like a newlywed than a husband of nearly half a century. Addie didn't dismiss this attention; nor did she really seem to notice it. Charlie once said that what her mother had gotten in exchange for taking him back was absolute confidence in his loyalty, not only sexual but in every other matter as well. That might have been true, but there was nothing pragmatic or dutiful about the way he looked at her. I wondered if a betrayal would be so much to pay, if you could have someone who loved you like that.

"Later," Addie said. "Helen and I are going to chat first."

Carl turned to me. "I saw the news last week. Are you involved with LIGO?"

"Not directly, but I have some good friends there."

"What is LIGO?" Addie asked.

Carl explained about the detection. He described the black hole inspiral and merger, the rippling effect of the waves, and the basic mechanism of the interferometers. He even knew where they were located. Then he turned to me. "I'm ninety-nine percent sure I have all that wrong."

"No," I said. "That's exactly right."

"Ripples in spacetime," Addie said. "I'm afraid that's beyond me."

"It's beyond pretty much everyone," I said. "Most people don't understand as well as Carl does."

"She's being kind to an old man," Carl said, patting my arm. He wasn't handsome, or even especially distinguished-looking, but I could understand why women might have responded to him. He had a way of really looking at you while he was talking, as if he were choosing each word based on subtle shifts in your expression. I was sorry when he declined coffee and said he was going upstairs to shower. It might have been a trick of his profession, but it seemed more difficult to talk as soon as he left the room.

Addie put some cookies on a flowered plate. We sat on stools on either side of the marble-topped island.

"I have to apologize for not having you here sooner," Addie said matter-of-factly. "Things have been very hard."

"No, of course."

"But it sounds like you're doing well," Addie said.

"Well—"

"I hear from Terrence that Jack and Simmi are becoming close."

"They are," I said. "It's wonderful." But this conversational line seemed unlikely to lead to where I wanted it to go. I needed to ask whether Addie had been receiving the same kinds of messages I had. Did she know their source?

I turned on my stool, and noticed an elaborate wooden tree-house, prefabricated and almost certainly new, in an old elm near the fence.

"Carl ordered that for Simmi," Addie said. "He thought he could put it together himself—happily there are people you can hire through Amazon to redo it."

I laughed. "I would've loved that as a kid." Actually, I thought that I would love it now: the rope ladder, the walkway around the perimeter, between the leaves, the enclosed cabin into which no one on the ground would be able to see.

"She did," Addie said. "She does, although she doesn't get to use it as much now that they're at your house."

"That's part of what I wanted to talk—" I began, but Addie held up one hand, ringed and manicured, and shook her head.

"We couldn't be happier about them renting from you. It was never going to work with Terrence living here. Just Simmi, yes—but not the two of them. Frankly I was surprised it lasted as long as it did."

"But things are better between you and Terrence, now that—" I stopped, because I didn't know for sure what Terrence had found on Charlie's phone, nor what he'd shared with Addie.

"Now that we have the letter," Addie finished.

I nodded. I couldn't ask about the contents of the letter. If she wanted to tell me, she would. Addie paused and touched the woven gold choker resting against her clavicle.

"It's a difficult letter to read," she said. "To write, too—she didn't finish it."

"I'm sorry."

Addie took a breath and steadied herself on her stool, but she maintained her composure. "What Carl says—it shows that she wanted to explain, and that she loved us. He thinks that's all that's important."

I was going to agree with that, but I could see that Charlie's intentions weren't enough for Addie. She wanted information, an explanation. She wanted to know how a catastrophe like this could have happened at all.

"Terrence said she left other unfinished communication in her drafts. Part of that was her illness, of course," Addie continued. "She had trouble focusing, and her mind wandered. The letter's evidence of that."

The letter I had been imagining was an excruciating goodbye. Or maybe it was a set of instructions—but it wasn't any further mystery. If Charlie's mind had wandered during her last weeks on Earth, where had it gone?

Addie passed a plate across the island. "Have one."

She seemed to be trying to shift the conversation to safer territory, but I couldn't make myself eat, even to be polite. The cookies sat untouched on the plate between us.

"Carl and I are so glad you've become friends with Terrence. We would never want to put you in an awkward position, or jeopardize an arrangement that has clearly been beneficial for Simmi."

"It's been beneficial for Jack and me, too. I've explained to him that it isn't permanent—but I think he'll be devastated when they eventually go back to L.A."

"You never know," Addie said.

I was surprised by how hopeful it made me to hear her say it.

"For now we want to make Simmi's life here as stable as possible," she continued. "That's why Carl and I are sending her to school. And her cousins from New York—William's family—may come up here for the summer. We thought they could all go to camp together."

I thought about the L.A. I'd seen in pictures, Terrence's surfing and his family there. "Do you think he might really want to stay in Boston?"

"I don't think he knows what shape his life is going to take—he's still quite young. You are all still quite young."

"I don't feel it."

"But you are. So much happens." Addie tilted her head slightly to one side. "I don't doubt that he loved our daughter. I think he was destroyed by this. You can't understand the power of people's emotional needs. At my age I've seen it again and again: divorce, illness. A person loses a partner—this is especially true of men who lose their wives—and they become like ducklings, imprinting on the first person who is kind to them. I want to be prepared for whatever happens—though of course it could be someone wonderful."

Did I imagine the way she looked at me? But I thought even Addie knew she couldn't go so far as to make her son-in-law fall in love with someone she chose.

"But if it was someone we thought was inappropriate in any way—" Her voice descended suddenly in pitch: "we'd fight with *everything* we have."

This burst of passion was followed by an uncomfortable silence, in which I examined the blue flecks in the Boyces' granite countertop. What I'd come to do was even more delicate than I'd expected.

"I think Simmi's been—reaching out a little." The canned phrase sounded absurd, even to me. "I've been getting some messages."

Addie's whole demeanor changed suddenly. She was completely attentive. "What kind of messages?"

"Texts."

Addie put both hands on the countertop, as if to steady herself. "From?" she said.

"From Simmi, I think. I think she's been using Charlie's phone."

"Simmi!"

It was the only time I'd ever seen Addie struggle to keep up. Ordinarily she seemed to be several steps ahead of everyone else.

"It shocked me," I said. "Terrence told me the phone was lost. I thought what kind of crazy person would—"

Addie was nodding slowly. "That's exactly what Carl said! *What kind of crazy person . . .*"

"You've been getting them, too?" I tried not to sound as if I'd suspected it.

Addie nodded mutely.

"Do you remember when they started?"

Addie got up and went to her purse in the hall. She was of a generation that didn't keep the phone in arm's reach at all times. I realized what I'd been hoping: that Addie had begun receiving messages right after Charlie's death, at the same time I had. That what Jack had suggested to me in the closet was wrong—that Simmi had simply been writing to her grandmother in the same way she'd been writing to me.

Adelaide came back into the room. "The first one was in November," she said. "Just before Thanksgiving."

Of course Thanksgiving was exactly when we had found Jack and Simmi in the closet, building a machine to talk to ghosts.

"Was that when you started getting them, too?" Addie asked.

"A little earlier," I said.

Addie nodded. "I showed those to Carl, too, of course—he's very forgiving, but he said that if someone was doing this to me . . . well, I thought if he found out who it was, he would have killed them. He thought we might be able to trace it. I talked to Robert, our lawyer, about that as well. Carl wanted to know if there was a way to prosecute a hacker like that." Addie laughed miserably. "If only we'd known whom we were hoping to prosecute."

"I didn't know either. And the messages didn't suggest a child—at first. They were about science. They were simple, but not so different from the questions many adults ask. I thought maybe an unsophisticated person . . . someone who'd seen my name somewhere."

Addie nodded slowly. "But why didn't she just come to me? She's my granddaughter."

"Maybe this was easier for her?"

Addie considered that. "They say the technology is having all kinds of negative effects on kids, with bullying and sexting and all of that. But I have a friend with a teenage son—she thinks he's able to express himself better on his phone than in person. He and his friends talk about their feelings in a way that boys never would have done, when she and I were young."

Addie had been looking out the window at the treehouse while she spoke, and for a moment she lost focus in the same way she had that day outside Darwin's. Then she turned back to me.

"Carl told me not to reply to those messages—because it was a hacker. Who else could it be? But it's the middle of the night, and I get a message with my daughter's name on it. It says, 'Dear Mama'—did you know Charlie called me that? Not William—he started with 'Mom' as soon as he was out of diapers. But her—it was always 'Mama.' 'Dear Mama—I miss you.' Addie frowned and pressed her lips together. She didn't cry, or there were no tears, but her brow and her upper lip contracted into dry furrows. 'Dear Mama, Where are you?'" She covered her face with her hands.

Charlie's mother had never been someone who succumbed to ordinary pressures and reversals. She was almost supernaturally strong, and it felt wrong, almost presumptuous, to try to console her now.

"Why would she do it?" Addie said, looking up. "Why would she *pretend*?"

There was the sound of footsteps upstairs: Carl had finished his shower, and was talking on the phone. I could hear his voice very faintly.

"Jack loves to play with my phone. It's a sort of talisman." I tried to introduce the idea I had gently. It was the kind of idea that anyone would resist. "Sometimes he doesn't completely understand that there's a person on the other end."

Addie looked blank.

"Does Simmi call you 'Mama,' too?"

"No," she said. "That's why I was confused. She always called me 'Nana'—'Mama' is what she called Charlie." Addie hesitated, then took a sharp breath, realizing. "Oh. Oh, Helen."

I didn't know if I'd ever seen true shock on someone's face before. Her eyes were wet, and her mouth had dropped open in a kind of wondering agony. It was in frightening contrast to the way she normally presented herself.

"We can't be sure what Simmi was thinking," I began. "Maybe she knew she was really writing to you, but she wanted to imagine something more—metaphysical."

Addie didn't say anything.

"But Jack did say something to me—that's why I wanted to talk to you."

Addie's makeup had smudged, but not run. She was sitting up straight in her chair. "What did he say?"

I thought it was best to be plain. "That she used the phone to talk to her mother."

Carl seemed to have stopped talking on the phone upstairs. The only sounds were the hum of the appliances, a blue jay calling raspily from the feeder outside the kitchen door.

"And I responded." Addie's voice was very low. "I said—" But she broke off. She didn't tell me what she'd written back, or whom she believed she was writing to, in the middle of the night. She looked at me now with new alarm. "I have to talk to Simmi."

I thought about it for a moment. "Do you think it would be better for Terrence to do that?"

Addie looked surprised, then she nodded slowly. "I'll have to talk to him."

"I could do that."

Addie's relief was apparent. "Would you, Helen?"

"Sweetheart?" Carl was in the hall. "I'm seeing someone at three-forty and then four-thirty. I should be back in—" He came into the kitchen, stopped. He was dressed in a purple-and-white button-down checked shirt and trousers, and his bald head was smooth and shiny from the shower. His voice changed from the one people use only with their most intimate relations to another, more social register:

"Helen—I didn't know you were still here." He smiled at me. "You had a nice, long chat."

"I should go, actually. I have a meeting at four."

Addie was still sitting on the stool, but her posture had changed radically. Even at the memorial, her straightness had been notable, early training that she'd never forgotten. But now it was as if gravity had suddenly taken a more powerful hold on her. She didn't look at either one of us when she spoke.

"We've all been a bit confused. Helen has clarified things."

Carl smiled at me. "Well, yes. That's her strong suit."

9.

I had promised Addie I would talk to Terrence, and I wanted to do it when I was sure he would be alone. That night I put Jack to bed, and waited until I thought Simmi would also be asleep. Then I went downstairs. I knocked quietly, so I wouldn't wake her, and again with a little more force. I stepped back; there was a space under the doorframe, and I could see that at least the lights in the living room were off. It would be unusual for Terrence to keep his daughter out past nine on a school night, but the apartment was very still.

I rang the bell, to be sure, but no one came. The key to Terrence's apartment was silver, distinct from the other brass keys on my ring. The apartment was dark, except for a low light over the stove. The kitchen didn't look as if it had been used that evening: everything was scrupulously neat, except for a piece of paper on the counter. For a moment, I thought they'd left me some kind of note. I imagined Terrence deciding he'd had it—with Boston, with Carl and Addie, with me. I imagined him and Simmi taking off for some remote surfable location: Hawaii, Indonesia, Peru. I thought that if the house in L.A. had sold, they could disappear for years on the proceeds from that alone.

But when I got closer, I saw it was only a piece of mail for Andrea. Terrence must've saved it for me to forward; no one left paper notes anymore. If you wanted to leave something for someone to find, you did it digitally—*other unfinished communication,* Addie had called it. Terrence hadn't told her what kind of communication, but I thought it had to be personal. Notes to family members, and friends. It was only the events of recent months that made me think it was possible Charlie could've written to me as well. Sometimes you could hope for an outcome so intensely that it led you to break your own rules in order to produce it; even very distinguished scientists sometimes saw a meaningful pattern in what turned out to be simply noise.

Terrence had probably taken Charlie's phone from Simmi once he found it. If that were the case, I would leave immediately; I wasn't prepared to search his bedroom. There was a small chance, though, that he might have gotten what he needed from the phone, and then put it back wherever Simmi had hidden it, for whatever comfort it might supply her. I remembered that once, when he was in preschool, Jack had asked if I could leave my phone with him during the day. Only later had I had the unsettling realization that it must have seemed to him like a way of guaranteeing my return.

Terrence had recognized the phone's significance in the first conversation we'd had about it: a twenty-first-century transitional object, for a transition no one wanted their child to have to make. I looked now toward Simmi's room, the door slightly ajar. I did think about what would happen if they came back while I was inside—but even then there were explanations I could give. I'd smelled gas, or heard a noise. I was the landlord as well as a friend, and Terrence knew that I kept a key.

I went into Simmi's room. This was less tidy, with clothing on the floor and books (the same type of graphic novels Jack preferred) in a pile by the bed. The nightstand was cluttered with the detritus of childhood: coins, a crystal rabbit, hairbands, pencils, a pink rubber caterpillar, a deck of UNO. There was a trophy with a golden gymnast balanced on her hands, legs scissored above her head; the lamp was decorated with satin award ribbons.

But the wooden kitchen was gone. I looked around—maybe she'd finally gotten rid of it, now that it was no longer useful as a hiding place? As I was standing there, the room lit up suddenly; I whirled around, but it was only a car passing. Its brights swung across the ceiling and down the wall, illuminating for a second the little gold figure, the foil printing on the ribbons.

I should have left then, but instead some instinct made me open the closet door. The kitchen was there in the back corner, shoved underneath a row of dresses. The hems rested on the four burners, with their rings of painted blue flame. I opened the oven door, and there was a shoebox full of old papers, schoolwork, drawings, a rubber-band bracelet; at the bottom, I felt it, the size and shape immediately recognizable. As a last layer of defense, she'd stowed the phone inside a sock—not her own, but a woman's trouser sock: thin gray silk.

The phone had been charged recently and had sixty-eight percent of its battery; the photo on the home screen was of Simmi when she was four or five, looking very seriously at something in her hand—a shell. The date and time were correct, February 25, at 10:20 p.m., but the top left-hand corner said "No Service." The Wi-Fi, however, was connected.

I put in the passcode—1234—and opened Charlie's messages. The ones between Simmi and me I knew almost by heart, stretching back from "Luvya lady" to the most recent, just her name and a question mark, to which there had been no response. Above my name, the first one in the queue, was Addie, identified on the phone as "Mom." The beginning of the message showed up on the next line: *Dear Mama, It is the night time here . . .* That was all I could see without opening the thread. It seemed wrong to read

Addie's responses—although it occurred to me these scruples were somewhat beside the point, when you were crouched on the floor of a child's closet snooping in her dead mother's phone.

I opened Charlie's email. There were four messages from today, all from mailing lists that hadn't yet registered her as deceased. The previous days were similar; I had to scroll down to another page before I found one that looked like it was from an actual person. I hadn't known (but might have guessed) that Charlie never bothered to erase email; she had 9,560 messages in her inbox. I clicked to the drafts, and it was the same: there were 595 messages Charlie had begun and failed to send. I put my name into the Search function, but it was as I'd expected—all my efforts produced zero results.

That was when I heard them. They were coming in the first door from the street. I put the phone back inside the sock, shoved the sock where I'd found it, and closed the oven door. I came out of the closet as quietly as I could, and went into the living room. Then I switched on the light and hurried to the front door.

"Oh," Terrence said. "Hi. What—?"

"Hi—I'm so sorry," I said. "I thought I smelled gas. But it's nothing . . . it's fine."

"Christ," he said. "Okay—are you sure?"

"It had to be from the street. There's no smell in here. I'm really sorry."

Terrence's expression shifted from alarm to something more watchful. "*Nuestra casa es su casa*—right, Simmi?" he said, but kept his eyes on me.

"It's Daddy's birthday!"

"It is?"

"Yeah."

"You should have told us."

"I forgot," Terrence said, in a tone that could have convinced only an eight-year-old.

"Can you believe it?" Simmi exclaimed. "We didn't realize until Grandma called!"

I glanced at Terrence.

"My mother," he clarified. "Simmi wanted to celebrate. So we went for sushi and *Zootopia*."

"We were defrosting veggie burgers! Then we just threw them away and went out!" She was clearly thrilled by the spontaneity of it all.

"And now it's way too late for you," Terrence said. "You better be in PJs in no more than seven seconds."

Simmi giggled and disappeared into her room, where I hoped I'd left no sign of my intrusion.

"You're sure there's no gas," Terrence said.

"Positive."

"Okay."

He didn't seem thrilled by my presence, but neither did he seem as antagonistic as he had been the last time I'd seen him.

"Do you have a second? Or I could come back after you put her to bed."

"Yeah," Terrence said. "Hang on." He disappeared into Simmi's room, and I sat down on one of the stools at the counter. I looked at the email on my own phone to distract myself: a message from Vincenzo about visits from the accepted PhD candidates, who toured the department every February. This year five were from mainland China; five from the rest of the world; and five from the U.S. Everyone seemed most excited about a young man from Hefei working on astrophysical plasmas.

Terrence returned after a few minutes, closing the door behind him.

"Happy birthday," I said. "You didn't really forget, did you?"

"No. But I'm not a big celebrator. Plus, you know, we have Charlie's birthday coming up, and then the anniversary in June. So I was trying not to make an event out of it."

I hadn't thought about the anniversary.

Terrence had gone around to the other side of the counter. He took out a lunch box—a fancy metal one, with different compartments for different items. He was wearing the same thing he'd worn to Neel and Roxy's party, a close-fitting black Henley shirt with two buttons at the neck. He pushed the sleeves up to his elbows and started to take food from the refrigerator for his daughter's lunch: tomatoes, carrots, a block of tofu, a mesh bag of individually wrapped cheeses.

"What did you want to talk about?" he said, without looking up.

"I talked to Addie."

"Yeah?"

"Did you know Simmi was writing to her, too?"

"Not until you gave me the heads-up about the phone," he said. "But, yeah." He hesitated. "You think they're rational—and then they do something like this. I think she saw 'Mom' and just—"

I'd expected that he would have seen the messages, but I hadn't known if he would understand what Simmi had been trying to do. I'd underestimated him, though. What it had taken Addie and me months to comprehend, he'd gotten right away.

I watched him slice a kiwi, wash the knife, and then cut smoked tofu into neat squares. The veins on the back of his hands stood out prominently, and there were dry patches on the skin of his knuckles.

"Addie said you sent them something."

"Of course." He looked up. "But not to prove anything—I don't care what they think."

"I think they think—"

"I'm a pusher—a monster. Yeah, I know. Who got her the drugs so she could die without her parents there. That's why I'm here in Boston, three thousand miles from *my* family, five hours from the only passable surf break on the East Coast, packing a lunch box."

"That's not what I was going to say. I think they're just worried about keeping up their relationship with Simmi."

"Why wouldn't Simmi have a relationship with them?"

"I think Addie thinks you might meet someone, eventually."

Terrence looked up sharply. "You didn't tell her about seeing Nicki here?"

"No," I said. "Of course not."

He seemed to relax.

"She thinks you're grieving, and it's hard to be alone."

"Yeah, well . . ."

"And she's going to miss Simmi so much if—when you guys go back to L.A. I think she wants to keep you guys close as long as possible. I think the letter helped."

"Did she show it to you?"

"She just said it was unfinished."

Terrence looked frustrated. "Nothing satisfies that woman!"

"Maybe nothing could, in this case?"

He looked at me. "They were *all* unfinished."

"Were there—a lot of them?" How many friends had Charlie written to, to say goodbye? There could be a kind of jockeying for position around a tragedy, and I didn't want Terrence to think I was doing that. I tried to keep the hurt out of my voice, but he could see it on my face.

Terrence was watching me steadily. "You didn't smell gas," he said.

"No," I admitted. I felt my neck getting hot.

"Did you look for it?"

"For what?"

"A letter, for you."

"No." I met Terrence's eyes. "Yes," I admitted. "But there wasn't anything."

He latched the lunch box, then bent down to rearrange something in the fridge to make room for it overnight. Then he stood up. "You have to search in Sent. I sent it to myself."

"You mean, she did write to me?"

Terrence indicated his computer, which was sitting on the counter next to a roll of paper towels and his keys.

"Not to you," he said. "But she mentions you, in her note to them."

"To Carl and Addie?"

Instead of answering, Terrence opened the laptop and tapped a few keys. Then he turned it to face me.

"Read it if you want," he said.

"Are you sure?"

"I wouldn't be," Terrence said. "If you weren't in it."

"But Addie didn't say anything."

"Addie doesn't know who Iphigenia is." Terrence's face came close to a smile, without actually arriving there. "She asked me, after I sent them the letter, and I said I didn't know. But the other day I remembered Charlie referring to you that way, near the end. There were a couple of other things like that, words and names that she'd mix up, especially to do with the past. I wouldn't point it out—I didn't want to make her self-conscious."

Then he half turned away, giving both of us our privacy.

Dear Mama and Daddy:

I know you're not going to be able to forgive me for this. And I'm so sorry. There's so much I want to say to you, and I know you wanted to be here. It's just—if you're here, I can't do it the way I want to do it. I have to wait to have it done to me. And I can't stand that.

They called them "ruby slippers" in the '70s—maybe you remember? That's because Judy Garland is supposed to have used them, but so did Dinah Washington. Did you know the first song she ever sang in public was Billie Holliday's "I Can't Face the Music"? Isn't that amazing? It's like she knew what would happen to her from the beginning.

I think this way is better for Simmi. I do it after we've had a good night, so she can remember that later. I choose.

One request. I didn't want to ask this of Terrence—I don't want to make things any sadder than they already are. But I'd like there to be a photo of me at her graduation. A real one on paper, if possible. If it seems like you might not be around at that point either, could you pass this request on to Iphigenia? I have her in mind specifically, not just because I trust her to carry it out (even if she won't approve) but because I'd like her to be there that day, if I can't.

I say "if" because Terrence and I have been reading this book. The author thinks that our consciousness must live on after we die, because all we are is consciousness anyway. And so the photo is my own take on it. I have this crackpot notion that it could be a kind of window, that I could look out and see her.

I've started and stopped this note so many times. Today I'm going to finish it. I love you. I am terrified of

I scrolled down, and then panicked. Had I somehow erased a part of it?

"Where's the—"

"That's what she meant," Terrence said. "Unfinished."

I read it through again, as if something might change, and again.

"Terrified of—"

"Not the actual dying," he said. "Just not being here."

There was a catch in my throat. As far as I could remember, Charlie and I had never talked about that fear. "Yeah," I said. "I know."

"Simmi used to look at our wedding pictures a lot before it happened. When she was little she would ask where she was, why weren't there any pictures of her? Then one day Simmi said: 'That was when I was dead.' Very matter-of-fact. We tried to explain to her the difference—that not being born yet isn't the same as being dead—but she couldn't understand."

We were quiet for a moment.

"Could you forward this to me?" I asked him.

"Yeah. I would have anyway—you didn't need to break in."

"I'm really sorry."

Terrence shrugged. He had picked up a pink rubber ball from the kitchen counter and was squeezing it, first one hand and then the other. His forearms tensed and relaxed.

"I should go back upstairs," I said. "Jack never wakes up, but if he did and I wasn't there, he'd freak out." I stopped, because I thought it sounded insensitive to Terrence's situation, but he just nodded. I picked up my keys from the counter. I was almost at the door when he spoke.

"You wrote back."

"What?"

"To Simmi."

"Once or twice."

"Four times." His voice was matter-of-fact: "Email and text. But you didn't know it was her."

"Not until she sent me 'Cottleston Pie.' Then I knew."

"Who'd you think it was before that?"

"The thief," I said.

"Not a ghost."

"No."

"Because you don't believe in them."

"I'm a scientist."

Terrence shrugged. "Yeah, okay."

"Why—do you?"

"It's not *believing*," Terrence said slowly. "It's a physical thing."

"Your memories."

Terrence let out a breath.

"Terrence, I—"

He was suddenly fierce. "It's knees—okay?"

"Knees?"

"In my back. She had really long legs, right? She liked to sleep all curled up. Sometimes they're there when I wake up, sometimes not. Just like before."

"Like phantom limb syndrome. There's a lot of research on that—it's well documented."

Terrence shook his head. "Not like that." He came around the counter suddenly, and pressed his fist against my back. "Like this."

His knuckles rolled off my vertebrae. Then he took his hand away, but we were still only a few inches apart. I was scared that if I looked at him, he would know how I felt when he touched me. I was scared he knew already.

"You don't have to believe me."

I tried to answer carefully. "It's confusing enough for adults," I said. "For kids—"

"No kidding." Terrence was leaning back against the kitchen counter. The sleeves of his shirt were still pushed up to his elbow, and I saw the new tattoo for the first time: three elaborate green-and-orange goldfish, like a Chinese painting, in a wheel on the inside of his right forearm.

"Did they really believe in ghosts?" Terrence asked. "Those scientists?"

I didn't know what he meant at first. "Which ones?"

"You know," he said. "The ones who made the typewriter."

"Enough to build at least three machines."

He leaned forward, his forearms on the counter. "And these were real scientists?"

"Some people think they were the best of their generation. That they saved physics."

"Saved it from what?"

"Relentless calculation."

Terrence smiled suddenly.

"You mean boring old math," he said.

10.

Terrence and Simmi went to L.A. for spring break, two weeks at the end of March. I worked the first week, and hired Julia to take care of Jack. The second week I took Jack on a real vacation: we went to Costa Rica to see olive ridley turtles nesting on a black sand beach on the Nicoya Peninsula. Our guide let Jack, wearing rubber gloves, assist a newly hatched turtle down the beach and deposit it carefully into the Pacific.

Jack and I got back on the Friday before school was to start up again. Terrence and Simmi had returned midweek, and Terrence had gone down to spend a few days at the new Brooklyn Zingaro, leaving Simmi with her grandparents. He texted me from the train on Saturday; Simmi's grandparents were bringing her home at six, and he was running late. Would it be possible for me to give her dinner with Jack, since Carl and Addie had plans in the evening? I said yes and Jack was delighted. He wanted to make lasagna, and so we went to Trader Joe's for the ingredients.

I had been expecting Addie, but it was Carl who dropped Simmi off.

"I saw turtles!" Jack exclaimed as soon as I opened the door for them. "I held one!"

Simmi looked tanned from her trip, a little sunburned under her eyes; clearly they'd spent a lot of their time in L.A. at the beach.

"We saw seals," she said. "Way out."

"I can't compete with that," Carl said to me. "We saw a couple of squirrels in the backyard, but that was about it."

Simmi and Jack wanted to go into our backyard before dinner, and so I sent them around the side of the house; I felt funny now about using my spare key to the downstairs apartment. I stepped out onto the porch with Carl, closing the front door behind me. The sun was going down, and although the days were getting more spring-like, the nights were still cold. Carl was wearing a brown suede jacket, a newsboy cap, and a plaid wool scarf.

"Would you like to come in for a drink?" I asked him.

"I could use one, but Addie made me promise to be back by seven. We're going out to dinner with friends."

"How is Addie?"

Carl listened for a moment: we could hear the children faintly in the backyard. There was the repetitive whoosh of the Stomp Rocket, as they sent it flying again and again.

"Not so good this week," he said. "It varies. Thanks for asking."

However excruciating these months had been for Addie, the letter would have made it even worse. I wondered for the first time if she could've denied its reality in part out of apprehension—now justified. The familiar voice, alive for the thirty seconds it took to read. Then gone forever. The word "terrified," then nothing more. The crying Terrence had heard through the wall, then a pill her husband prescribed, then the slow agony of waking up. Then her public face again. And again and again and again.

Did I imagine it, or did Carl's mouth tremble? He had one of those mouths that had settled downward in the corners, but not in a way that had ever made him appear sad in the past. Now he looked as if he were suppressing an unexpected wave of emotion.

"Addie said something to me the other day. She said I'd been 'working through it'—not in the sense of processing it, but that I had immediately 'gone to work' after it happened. I've been taking care of her, and my son, too—to some extent—telling them the same kinds of things I tell my patients." Carl stopped, adjusted his cap to cover his ears.

"I always talk about a scar: that the wound never goes away, but that it gets covered by some protective tissue, more and more each year. And then one woman says to me, 'Yes, and then the tissue grows so thick you can't see out.'" He looked at me: "You have some people who absorb everything you say, as if it's all wise and useful. And then there are others who argue all the time—those patients are exhausting, but I think you learn more from them."

"It's the same with students of physics."

Carl smiled for the first time. "Yes," he said. "I imagine it would be."

As we were talking, a white taxi pulled up at the curb outside the house. We both watched as a light went on inside, and Terrence paid the driver. I saw him notice us both standing on the porch, and his reluctance was apparent as he got out of the car. As usual, he wasn't wearing warm-enough clothes: the black down vest, with only a T-shirt underneath.

"Boy doesn't get dressed in the morning," Carl said, under his breath. His tone surprised me a little, and I remembered what Terrence had said about Carl being the one to make them sign the pre-nup agreement. He seemed to make an effort to shift his affect, as his son-in-law came up the walk to us. "How'd it go down there?" he asked.

Terrence nodded. "Good. They've had a great couple of weeks. People are gearing up for the season in Montauk. We have to see how it goes in the fall; it's hard to keep a surf shop open year-round on this coast."

Carl made a sound demonstrating his agreement with that skeptical assessment.

"How's Simmi?"

"I was working, but she and Addie had a great time. They went to afternoon tea one day, did some shopping."

"I hope not for clothes," Terrence said stiffly.

"Addie needed some distraction."

"Don't we all," Terrence said.

"The kids are in the yard," I said. The atmosphere was tense, and I tried to defuse it. I turned to Terrence. "We didn't expect you back so soon—I haven't even fed them."

"We can all eat, if you want," Terrence said. "Pizza?"

"Jack and I made lasagna."

Carl looked from me to Terrence. "I'll leave you kids to it. And we'll see you Thursday for dinner," he confirmed with Terrence. He touched his son-in-law's back in place of a hug. Then he kissed my cheek.

"It's always nice to see you, Helen," he said, before he made his way down the steps. From behind he looked older, his shoulders slightly rounded, his midsection heavier than before. He paused to let some slow-moving evening traffic go by, before crossing our narrow street to his car.

Terrence and I went into the front hall and closed the door. I could feel his relief now that the interaction with his father-in-law was over, at least for the time being.

"Does it ever get warm here?" he said.

"This was a warm winter," I told him. "You were lucky. I remember one year it snowed in April—and that was before the climate went nuts." I was aware that I was talking too fast; it was so nice to see him. "I can't promise the lasagna's going to be amazing," I said. "But it's ready—if you want to call the kids?"

"Yeah," he said. "Okay."

"It's good to have you guys back."

"Yeah, no—it's good to be back. L.A. was pretty intense." He looked at me, and I thought he was going to say something else. I waited, halfway up the stairs.

"I'll see you in a sec," he said, and disappeared into the apartment. I could hear the children's voices, shouting in the gloom. I knew they would come in sweaty from running around in the cold, their faces flushed. The lasagna had come out well, and I secretly hoped Terrence might be impressed. I felt suddenly surprisingly happy, the way I sometimes do in my office, when I get a new and especially promising idea.

11.

The kids complained at dinner that we'd never made it to the aquarium, and Terrence offered to take them himself the next morning, if I had work to do. I did have some papers Neel had emailed me, related to the rotor project we'd been talking about in January, asking for my thoughts. It was the first time he'd written since returning from his honeymoon—a trip to some islands I'd never heard of, off the coast of southern India—as if nothing unusual had happened in his personal or professional life since we'd last spoken. After considering for a moment, I decided to go with everyone to the aquarium.

I think the pleasure of aquariums has almost nothing to do with science, just like planetariums aren't really about astrophysics. One moment you're in the bright exterior world, and the next you've been transported to a dim blue one. The children felt it the minute we went inside; they ran toward the Giant Ocean Tank, and pressed their faces to the glass. Jack wanted to start at the top, with the coral reef, and so we took the elevator to Level Four. We descended slowly, from tropical to freshwater to temperate, and then to the marine mammals. I didn't supply any facts about the rapid and probably unstoppable murder of the planet's coral reef ecologies; I let us all just enjoy it in peace. The rays especially awed the children, gliding along like knives in the water, then suddenly tilting upward, revealing rhomboid swaths of white flesh.

"Whoa," Jack breathed.

"Like Daddy's tattoo," Simmi said.

I thought that made it okay to ask. "Why the stingray?"

"It's for my brother," Terrence said.

"And you have fish," Jack said.

"Those are for me and Simmi."

"And Mama," Simmi added.

I glanced at Terrence, who didn't break his focus on the tank. "Yep."

That was why there were three.

"You have so many sea animals on you, you could be a giant poster for the aquarium!" Jack said.

"Are rays actually fish?" I asked, inanely.

"Yeah," Terrence said. "We sometimes see them in warmer water—when Ray and I went down to Nicaragua there were a ton of them. You have to sort of shuffle, getting into the water."

"What happens if they sting you?" Jack asked.

Terrence ruffled his hair. "You don't want them to sting you, dude."

"Hey," Simmi said. "Do they really have a touch tank here with *sharks?*"

"That's my favorite thing," Jack said excitedly. "Can I show her?"

I nodded. It was Sunday and the aquarium was crowded. Terrence and I had to pay attention to keep the kids in view. When we got to the touch tank, Jack and Simmi waited their turn for a place among the small children and their parents at the edge of the exhibit. The tank hosted Atlantic and cownose rays along with the small grayish-green epaulette sharks. Terrence and I stood back a little from the crowd.

"I wanted to say sorry again about the phone," I told him. "I don't know what I was thinking."

"We're cool on that front," Terrence said.

"But I should have told you right away. I was worried that it would be one more thing for you to deal with. And I also really wanted you to take the apartment. I thought it would be good for Jack," I added quickly.

"I think it was good for both of them," Terrence said.

"They just seem to get closer," I agreed. We watched them jockeying for a place in the midst of the other children, rolling up their sleeves. The lights in the ceiling were like spotlights, picking up the shine in their hair.

"The house is finally in contract," Terrence said. He was leaning against the wall, hands in the pockets of a pair of loose, dark jeans. Today he was wearing an actual down coat, over a green T-shirt that said *Dogtown*.

"In L.A.? That must be a relief."

"It is for me."

"Is Simmi doing okay with that?"

"She wanted to go back and see it," he said. "I tried to talk her out of it, but . . ."

"Oh, no."

"Yeah," he said. "It was awful. Our furniture's still there, but the brokers had brought in all this stuff to make it easier to sell. The room we used for a den they turned into another bedroom—a nursery, with a crib and everything. And then in our room, there was a different cover on the bed." He stopped for a minute. All those people in the enclosed space made the voices reverberate, as if we were underground. Everyone seemed to be shouting, but from far away.

"It was like—I don't know—a museum or something. A museum where everything's for sale. We didn't stay very long."

"That sounds really hard."

"Otherwise, we saw my brother, and hung with a bunch of his friends in Venice—that was great. The kids all go to the beach before school every day."

"Really?"

"I saw some apartments there."

I was glad we were in the dark because I needed a moment to adjust my expression. I'd thought we were having a different conversation—not necessarily that they planned to stay in my house forever, but that the sale of the house in L.A. indicated their intention to put down stronger roots here in Boston.

"For you two?"

Terrence looked at me. "I wanted to tell you first, but you and Jack were away. I already talked to Carl and Addie. They aren't happy, but I think Carl at least gets it. All that stuff with the phone made me realize what I've been doing wrong." He turned toward me earnestly. "I thought I was bringing her here to, you know, be together in all this—a family. But it was super confusing for her to just up and leave."

"I don't think you were doing anything wrong," I said. "It's an impossible situation."

"But I think that if we'd been home—in L.A.—she wouldn't have been able to . . . fantasize like that. Carl said that made sense." Terrence sounded proud that his father-in-law, an expert, had agreed with him. "Until we went home, it was almost like she still thought there was a way around it."

"She might have thought that anyway."

Terrence shrugged. "Maybe."

Jack turned around and waved at me, pointing into the tank.

"I think it would be good to be out there for the anniversary, anyway. There, but in a new place. I might even try to buy before we get there, now that we'll have the cash. Save her having to move twice."

"That sounds wise."

"She can go back to her old school, her friends. And I can surf every morning, which will make me a seriously nicer person."

"You're pretty nice." I felt the blood rushing to my face, that same uncomfortable separation between my thoughts and my physical self. I wanted to excuse myself and hurry to the bathroom, lock myself in a stall, and put my forehead against the cool metal of the door. But Terrence didn't seem to notice.

"You know how there's one thing you do that makes you feel like you're ten years old? Like you're just completely yourself while you're doing it—no bullshit?" There was a note of pleading in Terrence's voice; he really wanted me to tell him he was making the right decision.

"Yes," I admitted. "I know exactly what you mean."

The kids were making their way back toward us.

"I hope it's going to be okay for you," Terrence said, "finding someone else."

"What?"

"We can pay rent until you do."

"Oh," I said. "It shouldn't be a problem. I can probably find a tenant through the housing office at MIT, even. People are always cycling in and out of this zip code."

"Great," Terrence said, with relief.

The children reached us. "I'm so hungry," Jack said.

"Can we get snacks now?" Simmi asked.

"Can we get astronaut ice cream from the shop?"

"And a souvenir? I want to remember this place." Simmi smiled at her father, and then at me. "After we get home."

That night I called my sister.

"It's so late there," Amy said when she picked up.

"I wanted to wait until your kids were asleep."

"Almost," Amy said. "In a minute Bess is going to call out that she can't sleep, and then I say, 'You don't have to sleep, you only have to rest.' We go through the same routine every night. Then she goes to sleep."

"Kids are so perverse."

"But predictable," Amy said.

"Terrence and Simmi are leaving—they're moving back to L.A."

Amy was quiet for a moment. "Helen, I'm sorry."

"It was never going to work long-term. I mean, I knew that. It was a fantasy—Addie's fantasy, really."

"But yours, too, kind of."

"But not like that!"

"I read this article about how you can have anything going on in your head, as long as it doesn't manifest itself. Like a reflection."

I waited for my sister to expand on that, but she remained quiet.

"Like a reflection that's different from what's doing the reflecting," I suggested.

"Exactly—hang on." In a wearily cheerful voice, Amy called out: "You don't have to sleep, Bess—you just have to rest!"

"They're moving to Venice," I said. "Or back to Santa Monica."

"Now that sounds nice," Amy said.

"They're going to surf before school."

"Don't we all."

"You do?"

"I still live in Pasadena, Helen, remember? Before school we pack lunches, argue about clothing, and then sit in traffic for forty minutes gnawing on toaster waffles."

I laughed. There was a shuffle of papers in the background. Maybe Amy had been grading when I called.

"I think I know what the Swedish flag means," my sister said.

"I think it was just random."

"Charlie wants you to win the Nobel Prize. Wanted, I mean."

"Yeah, right. You know who is going to win the Nobel?" I didn't wait for her to guess. "Neel."

"Neel Jonnal? Really?"

"Not him, specifically—but the chief scientists on his project."

"Seriously?" Amy said. "Wow!" Then she tried to modulate her tone: "That's really something. I read some of the press about the detection, but I didn't know it was that big a deal."

"Yep."

"What are you working on these days?"

"Neel and I are thinking of starting a new project together. It would be a way of using Advanced LIGO—the same detectors, with the improvements Neel's team is working on now—to investigate gravity at regular, Earth-sized distances. Meters and kilometers. We'd use these rotors—dynamic field generators, we call them—small, incredibly dense machines that turn around and around. The universe doesn't usually make very small, very heavy things."

"I don't get it."

"General Relativity is a perfect description of reality when you're talking about very large masses—stars and black holes. And quantum mechanics describes the tiniest pieces of matter equally well. It's the middle that's tricky. But LIGO could be used to test gravity at those shorter, familiar distances, with much greater precision than we've ever done before. We could actually find deviations from General Relativity—modifications."

"That's really exciting."

I thought Amy knew me well enough to guess how I was feeling, and that she was enthusiastic about the new project for that reason, more than any genuine interest. It disappointed me for a second, until I realized it was the whole reason I had called my sister.

"I'm going to be so sad when they leave," I told her.

"I know you are," Amy said.

12.

They left three days after school let out. Simmi came up that morning to say goodbye to us. She was dressed in her leopard-print leggings, a black hoodie—airplane clothes—and there was an almost manic excitement about her. She repeated information I already knew from Terrence: that they were in contract for an apartment five minutes from the beach; that they would stay with her uncle Ray until it was ready; that she was having a sleepover with her best friend, Clover, the night after they got back.

Jack didn't understand that her behavior could be defensive, and so he was hurt by it. He said "bye" in a small voice, and remained inert while Simmi hugged him.

I bent down to give Simmi a hug. She smelled like whatever she put in her hair, a little like sunscreen. Her mother had always been delicate, bony almost, but Simmi felt solid and healthy in my arms. I told her I hoped we could come visit soon.

"Yes, come! We can go to Disneyland," she said. She glanced back at Jack, a question on her face. "Are you afraid of roller coasters?"

Jack looked offended. *"No."*

"Good—me neither!" Then she pounded down the carpeted stairs the way Jack does, making enough noise for someone twice her weight. Her father came out of the apartment.

"The car's here in three minutes," he told her.

"I'll watch for it," Simmi said. She went out the front door without looking back. Terrence was locking the apartment door. I went down, but Jack stayed on the landing.

"It's clean," Terrence said. "You could show it anytime."

"I'm sure." I tried to keep my voice even. "I hope you guys have an easy trip."

Terrence had knelt down and was binding the suitcase's zippers with a miniature padlock, something my father always encouraged me to do.

He straightened up. I realized we'd never hugged or kissed each other casually in any kind of greeting. There was nothing casual about the way I felt while we were doing it now. My arms were around his neck, his around my waist, and for just one second I was in that other world, the reflection. Then I pulled away. I didn't know what Terrence was feeling; he didn't meet my eyes. Instead he looked up at Jack, who was watching us steadily.

"Hey—you want to come down here?"

Jack shook his head.

Terrence nodded. "Yeah, I hear you. I hate this goodbye stuff, too."

He lifted the larger of the two suitcases, and I started to open the door for him, but Simmi was standing right outside. "Let me do it," she said. She held the door while Terrence came back for the other suitcase.

"Take it easy, little man," he said to Jack. "See you soon, okay?"

Simmi smiled unexpectedly at me and mouthed something so her father couldn't hear. Then she closed the door.

Only then did Jack come down the stairs. He leaned back against me, and allowed me to put my arms around his chest. We watched Terrence and Simmi get into the waiting car. Their shapes were distorted by the mottled stained-glass panel in the door.

"What did she say?"

"Luv ya," I said. "I think."

Jack made a skeptical noise. "Girls are dumb," he pronounced, before opening the door himself, so that he could better see the car disappearing around the corner.

13.

It was almost as if Charlie died again. I went to my office at MIT, but I hardly got anything done. I brought the photograph of us at her wedding from my desk at home, and I looked at it more and more. My teeth hurt. I thought it was all the coffee I was drinking—but I'd always drunk too much coffee. One day a white balloon floated by the window, and I watched it, transfixed. Where had it come from? It seemed impossible that it had originated from anywhere around Building 6. Vincenzo's wind chimes—a source of conflict in the past—were beautiful in a way I'd never noticed. Differently sized metal cylinders struck a clay disk, producing a pentatonic scale. Next to those otherworldly sounds, the work in front of me was gray scratches on paper.

Jack and I didn't talk much about Terrence and Simmi that summer after they left, but I knew Jack thought about them. Periodically he would drag me outside to weed the garden, according to Terrence's detailed instructions. Neither of us was good at distinguishing between the weeds and the vegetables he had planted. Once he said, out of nowhere, but as if we'd just been talking about them:

"Terrence didn't have a dad either."

It was a hot July morning, and we were on our hands and knees, raking a dry bed that Jack swore contained carrots. The shoots coming up looked like chickweed to me, but I pulled out the grass around each plant anyway. Jack used the watering can.

"He *had* a dad, but his dad didn't live with them."

"Did he tell you that, or Simmi?"

"He did."

"When they were living here?"

"When we were making chili that time."

"How did he feel about that—I mean, having his dad live somewhere else?"

"He missed him," Jack said. "But then he saw him, when he was grown-up."

I waited.

"It wasn't like he expected."

"Oh," I said. "What did he expect?"

Jack nodded, as if that had been his question, too. "He thought they would know each other already."

"But they didn't."

Jack shook his head. "They were strangers."

14.

Jack turned eight and started the third grade. Vincenzo and I finally published the electroweak paper, which was prominently cited right away, pleasing our department chair and our students. I had a full teaching load again that fall, but my busy schedule didn't seem to upset Jack the way it had a year earlier; he was more self-possessed and more cheerful than he'd been when he was seven.

Early in December, Addie emailed me to say that Simmi was coming to visit. She was flying on her own, without her father, and Addie wondered if I'd like to set up a time when she and Jack could see each other. It seemed like the perfect opportunity to make good on the promise I'd made them last winter, and take the kids on a lab tour. For me it was also about the political events of that year, which made science education feel more crucial than ever. As I expected, Addie was enthusiastic about the idea, and so I arranged for her to bring Simmi to LIGO's office on Albany Street, next door to the lab, a little more than a week before Christmas.

It was a cold, gray Tuesday afternoon, and the air had a wet bite that suggested snow. On Albany Street the telephone poles punctuated at regular intervals the brick façades of the labs, formerly warehouse and factory buildings. We waited for Simmi in the courtyard of Building 22, where there was a wooden bench and a few trees, just planted in the spring and now bare. Jack ran up the ramp to the entrance, then gave me an embarrassed smile, returning to the bench via the stairs. I could see him deciding that running up and down ramps was childish.

Simmi and Addie were late, and so we decided to wait in the lobby, where it was warmer. Jack admired the wall-sized posters of the interferometers, and I told him where they were located.

"Which is which?"

"Guess."

Jack thought for a moment. "I guess that's Louisiana and that's Washington."

"The other way around."

Jack looked disheartened. "I thought the desert would be in the south."

"That's logical. But it's the southwest where we have desert in this country; Louisiana is very green. Hanford is more barren, and still pretty contaminated—it was a nuclear facility before LIGO was there. The Department of Energy was working on cleaning it up."

I thought about the recent changes at DOE, and decided not to mention them. In the past few months Jack has become exasperated with my talking back to the radio. *You have to cheer up,* he'll say, or: *You can't be like this for four years!* And so I've been trying to keep most of my feelings about the news to myself. I'm grateful for the trust and sanguinity Jack displays these days, which makes me feel I've done something right. It's only that, as the world seems to become an increasingly dangerous place, I wonder if happiness is the point. Maybe passion, something that can keep you satisfied inside your own head, independent of other people, is going to be worth more in Jack's lifetime.

"Contaminated with what?" Jack asked.

"Well—nuclear waste, mostly. You remember I told you about the Manhattan Project? Those scientists made the plutonium at Hanford for the bomb we dropped on Nagasaki."

"Fat Man or Little Boy?"

"That was Fat Man."

"Pyoo, pyoo," Jack whistled, under his breath. Then he stopped making bomb sounds and put both fists in the pockets of his sweatshirt, stretching it out.

I glanced through the glass doors to the street, and saw Simmi and her grandmother turning into the courtyard. Simmi was looking at the ground as they walked, listening to something Addie was saying. She was wearing the same silver parka from last year, a little small now—she wouldn't have needed a new one in L.A.—and her hair was shoulder length, styled in tight ringlets, more grown-up.

I opened the door for them, and Adelaide kissed me once on each cheek. I hugged Simmi, who hugged back a little shyly. She was still taller than Jack, but only just barely now.

"Hey," she said, punching Jack gently on the arm.

"That's the way you say hello, after half a year?" her grandmother said.

Simmi glanced at her grandmother, opened her eyes wide at Jack, then dropped a curtsy, holding out an imaginary gown. Jack laughed, but I marveled: it was so perfectly Charlie. Simmi had taken off her coat and was wearing black jeans and a gray sweater, along with patent leather Doc Marten boots.

Addie shook her head. "We have ascended several degrees on the fresh-o-meter since we saw each other last," she said, but her expression was wistful, not scolding. If Simmi had stayed in Boston, I thought it would have been much easier for her grandparents, seeing her on a daily or weekly basis, to think of her as her own person. After a hiatus of several months, they could hardly help but be struck by the similarities, the moments of uncanny synchronicity in Simmi's looks and manner, which would only increase as she grew into a woman both like and unlike her mother.

The children had wandered across the lobby to look at the photographs of the interferometers.

"How are you?" I asked Addie.

She was wearing a dark red coat, black leather gloves, and a round, vaguely Russian fur hat. We exchanged the kind of despairing remarks about the election that were standard that winter in Cambridge.

"The bright spot is that William and Caroline and the boys spent the summer with us." She glanced at Simmi, who had gotten very close to the Livingston photo, as if she were trying to see the individual pixels. "I wish we could've had all three of the grandchildren in one place, of course. But very few modern families get that."

"My parents say the same thing."

Addie nodded. "And so there are good days, and very bad ones. People used to ask me, when I had the gallery, whether I had ever wanted to be an artist—and I always said, Oh, no—that wasn't my inclination at all. I confess that this is the only time I've ever wished to have that talent. So there would be somewhere to put all of this." She gestured to her chest, where a black cashmere scarf was expertly draped. "If someone had described art to me in those terms then, I would have dismissed them out of hand. Art isn't therapy, I would have said."

I drew in a breath. "I've sometimes found science a little therapeutic," I suggested.

"I can imagine," Addie said. "A whole other world."

"If you'd like to join us for the tour—"

Addie glanced at her watch. "Will you promise me a rain check? I'm meeting a friend nearby. And then I thought I could come back for Simmi whenever you're ready."

We arranged for me to call her when we were finished. After she left, I buzzed the keypad on the second set of doors and the department secretary let us in. We walked through the recently renovated common area, with peripheral glassed-in offices. I pointed out Rainer Weiss's office to the kids.

"Rai built the first version of those machines in the pictures. That was in the seventies, when I was a baby." Jack was distracted by Simmi's presence, and both children only nodded. I might as well have said that Rai had built his prototype during the Crusades. "Hardly anyone thought that detecting gravitational waves was possible back then. But now everyone thinks Rai's going to win the Nobel Prize."

"Oh," Jack said. Then he turned to Simmi. "What were you for Halloween this year?"

Rai wasn't in, but we found Neel on his computer around the corner. He had just changed offices, and this was the first time I'd seen it. The new space was almost empty, dusty sunlight pouring in from two rectangular windows just below the ceiling. There was a whiteboard on the wall behind his desk, covered with notes in red, a couch with metal arms, and a coat tree in one corner. Neel and I had been working steadily on the rotor project since the spring, making progress, but most of our communication was over email or on the phone. When we met, it was usually in my office. There was something slightly different about our interactions since his marriage; I had expected it, but the change seemed to take Neel by surprise. Sometimes I would find him looking at me in a strange way, as if I were the one who'd done something that had caught him off guard.

This new office was nothing like Arty's—like most of MIT, it felt efficient and intentionally unadorned compared to Harvard—but I could remember coming upon him just this way in the past, when he was concentrating, one hand resting on the keyboard, the other twisting a piece of his hair between thumb and forefinger. He tended to rock very slightly back and forth in his chair, as if to some rhythm in his own thought.

He heard us at the door and looked up.

"Jack!" he said. "Hey!" They hadn't seen each other since the spring, when Jack had spent an afternoon in my office on a day off from school.

"And this is Simmi," I told him.

Neel got up and high-fived each kid. Then he indicated his screen. "Want to see something funny?"

The children stepped closer to see the screen. It was a cartoon of Santa Claus in space, throwing down the sort of warped net we sometimes use to represent gravitational waves. *Oops, I almost forgot LIGO,* Santa was saying.

Simmi made a questioning face at Jack, who clearly didn't understand either.

"You might have to explain," I told Neel. "To me, too—because if the rumors are right, Santa's definitely not going to forget LIGO next year."

Neel grinned at me. "Roxy says the prize will only count if I get an invitation to Stockholm myself—and even if LIGO wins, I'm not important enough to go. So you and I are going to have to hit it big with the rotor project." Then he turned to the kids. "The machines 'heard' gravitational waves for the second time around Christmas," he said, "so the joke is that the new waves were a present from Santa. The reindeer are being knocked around by the waves. That's silly, since you wouldn't be able to feel gravitational waves unless you were right up close to the source."

Jack smiled uncertainly.

"But I also think it's funny because there are a lot of people who thought gravitational waves were about as real as Santa Claus. It's been a while since you guys were into Santa, right?"

"Jack hasn't believed since he was three," I said. "I had to remind him not to spoil it for the other kids."

"Oh yeah, me, too." Simmi suddenly sounded young, in her eagerness to appear the opposite.

"You have to wonder about those kids who believe in him," Neel said, pleasing both children. "But I like the cartoon. What we do here does sometimes feel like magic, at least inside the lab." He looked from one to the other. "So do you guys want to go in?"

15.

We left the offices in NW-22 through a side door, descending a few iron steps where there had once been a loading dock. We crossed the parking lot and went up another set to the adjacent building that contained the lab.

"Are there real lasers in here?" Simmi asked.

Neel nodded. "Very cool infrared lasers, actually."

"Can we see them?" Jack asked.

I started to explain why that wouldn't be a good idea, but Neel looked down at Jack and smiled: "Let's pull out all the stops," he said. "Why not?"

"Awesome," Jack said.

"You're just going to have to pay attention," Neel said. "Really follow instructions, because the lasers could be dangerous."

Both kids nodded solemnly. "What could they do?" Simmi asked.

"They could burn your skin, or your eyes," Neel said. "Not where we'll be standing, though. We'll be looking at them through a little round window, like the porthole of a ship. But we'll wear glasses, just to be absolutely safe."

We followed Neel down to the basement level, where he used his ID to open another locked door into a hallway. Posters describing different elements of LIGO's operation hung under fluorescent lights, giving the stuffy, underground passageway the feeling of a high school corridor. Neel guided us past the restrooms, which the children assured me they didn't need, and around a corner to the small control room that led to the lab. The control room was narrow inside, only about six by ten feet, with a row of computers on three walls. To the right of where we'd come in was a second door—heavy, steel, and plastered with cautionary signage—which led directly into the lab. I saw Jack noticing the black-and-yellow

"Danger" sign, as Neel passed us the safety glasses, along with paper shoe protectors and elasticized white surgical caps.

"Are these to keep us safe from the lasers, too?" Simmi asked, tucking her hair into the cap. She wasn't wearing earrings, but I saw that her piercings had closed neatly, without any visible irritation.

"Those are actually to protect the machines, not you," Neel said. "Same with the booties over our shoes. You'll see that almost everything inside the lab is covered with foil or plastic; even just a few specks of dust inside the interferometer, and the experiment stops working the way it should."

He indicated the red light above the entrance. "When that light is red, it means the lasers in the lab are on."

Jack and Simmi were suitably impressed, and even more so when we actually entered the lab. There was the steady hum of the equipment; our feet in their paper shoes made no sound on the concrete floor. I saw the children taking in the colored wiring, the pneumatic tubing, the surrounding installations of shiny auxiliary equipment; this was what science was supposed to look like. We turned a corner, and there was the massive steel beam pipe right at eye level, almost four feet wide. The two silo-shaped vacuum chambers at either end of the pipe rose higher, almost to the skylit, triple-height ceiling.

"Whoa," Jack said, looking up.

I had been wondering if Neel was going to be able to boil his description of gravitational wave detection down to the kids' level, but he was remarkably patient. He explained that the beam pipe represented just a small segment of the enormous machines in the photos they'd seen outside. Neel pointed to the vacuum chambers at either end of the pipe.

"Each one of those chambers has mirrors in it. The laser light bounces back and forth between the mirrors, making a pattern we can study. We know that our machines have heard a gravitational wave when the pattern changes. That's because space actually curves when the gravitational wave rolls through it. Of course you know you have to walk farther on a curved path than you do if you walk in a straight line. The same thing happens to the laser, if a gravitational wave curves the space it's traveling through—only with a gravitational wave, that extra distance is tinier than anything you can imagine."

"Like an atom," Jack said, glancing slyly at me.

"Like if you divided the tiniest piece of an atom into ten thousand parts," Neel said. "That's what we have to measure. And that's why we have to make the beam so perfectly empty and quiet—because we don't want anything except a gravitational wave to get in the laser's way as it goes back and forth between the mirrors. We pump everything out of the beam, to make what scientists call a vacuum."

"Vacuums are usually loud," Jack pointed out.

"Loud when they're taking air in," Neel said. "Sucking things up. Quiet when they're closed off, because sound can't travel without air—does that make sense to you guys?"

"Do *we* have to be quiet?" Simmi asked.

"Well, I wouldn't yell," Neel said. "But we've already figured out how to block out the noise people make. Now we're working on much smaller noises. Like the noise the light makes when it hits the mirror. That's why we have to squeeze it before it goes into the machine."

"Squeeze *light?*" Jack said.

"I know," Neel said. "It's weird. But have you heard of photons? Those are the smallest pieces of light. They travel together, in little groups."

"Like the girls at my school," Simmi said knowingly.

Neel smiled. "Exactly. When each clique of photons hits the mirror, they make a noise—let's call it a squeal. We're trying to get rid of the squeal, without getting rid of the girls."

Apart from the four of us, there were only two other people in the lab, a postdoc working at a computer, and a technician sweeping the floor underneath one of the vacuum chambers, behind plastic sheeting. The children seemed especially interested in the technician, who was completely swaddled in a loose-fitting white suit, made of the same paper as our booties. He wore a cap like ours, as well as a surgical mask and yellow plastic gloves; even his eyes were barely visible behind the amber lenses of his glasses.

Neel called to the postdoc, and he left his station across the lab to join us.

"Meet Vlad," Neel said, "our Optical Parametric Oscillator specialist. That's the actual light-squeezing tool."

When Neel told him who I was, Vlad became excited; he was interested in the electroweak paper my group had published in the summer, and had several questions. While we were talking, the technician shouldered past us, carrying a blue plastic cleaning bucket filled with water bottles wrapped in aluminum foil. There was plenty of room, even with the group of us, but he came unnecessarily close, as if we were in his way.

"Hey, Eddie. Have you seen a step stool?" Neel asked.

Eddie pulled down his paper mask in annoyance and pointed toward the lab's south wall, but didn't offer to get the stool, possibly because he didn't like taking orders from Neel. "Getting some of this shit out of here," he said, indicating the cleaning bucket. The children gave each other a look: profanity delighted them.

"Charming guy," I said to Neel.

"Eddie's all right," Neel said. "Just a little misanthropic."

"I'll grab it," Vlad said. He disappeared behind one of the steel towers, and came back with a step stool, also covered in foil. The children would need it to look through the viewport, which was at adult height.

"We're going to see the lasers, right?" Simmi asked.

"And the mirrors," Neel promised. He was carrying an undistinguished-looking gray plastic case; now he put it down on a steel table next to the vacuum chamber, and removed a black metal viewing tube, mounted on a pistol-like grip.

"This is called a monocular. It's like half a set of binoculars," Neel said, "only for infrared light."

"Like binoculars for a Cyclops," Jack said.

"Cyclopular," Simmi replied, without thinking. That playing with words, I thought—that was Charlie, too.

Neel led us over to one of the metal silos that housed the vacuum chamber. He lifted the plastic, and we walked around its cylindrical base to the viewport, a round window at the height of the beam pipe. Vlad positioned the stool so that the children would be able to see inside, and removed a Plexiglas cap that protected the round glass window.

"Take a look," Neel said. "What you're going to see first are the most expensive mirrors in the world. Then I'll give you the monocular, and you can check out the laser."

Vlad excused himself to go back to work, and Simmi stepped up to look into the window.

"Oh," she gasped. "It's so pretty!"

She looked for longer than I would have expected, and Jack waited patiently until she'd had her fill. Then he took his turn.

"You've got to see this, Mom," he told me seriously, when he'd finished.

I was very familiar with the LIGO setup from all the lectures I'd attended, the schematic drawings in innumerable papers, but I'd never actually seen the interior of an interferometer in person. I found myself looking into the steel cavity of the vacuum chamber, a space maybe ten feet in diameter. In the center, between me and the dark opening to the beam pipe, were two mirrors: the size of a stack of dinner plates, but clear and fantastically strong. Each one was like a glass lozenge, or a gem. They hung suspended inside steel scaffolding, connected by pure glass threads. The penultimate mirror had a diamond clarity, but the optical coating on the lowest-hanging mirror—what made it so extraordinarily reflective—also lent the glass an opalescent, dark pink cast.

"The laser is bouncing off the mirror right now?" Jack confirmed.

Neel nodded. "It is. But to see an infrared beam, you need your Cyclops eye. Get on the stool first, and then I'll hand it to you."

He handed Simmi the monocular, and the children took turns looking at the laser. They asked smart questions: Why did the air look green around the red beam? If the laser was so powerful, why didn't it burn the mirror?

When they'd both had a turn, Simmi wanted to look again. Jack obligingly returned the monocular, but as Simmi stepped up and put her eye to the instrument, we heard the sharp crack of the metal tube hitting the window.

Before I could react, Neel grabbed Simmi, swinging her violently to the floor. "Careful!" he barked, pushing the children out of the way; we stumbled backward, through the plastic, and I dragged the kids underneath the steel table, crouching with them there and instinctively trying to protect their faces. I braced myself for an explosion: breaking glass and the roar of the machine. But nothing happened. They cowered against me, pressed against my sides, but after a few moments they looked up, trying to determine from my expression whether they were safe.

"Neel?" Vlad called out from across the lab. "Everything okay?"

Neel was checking the glass viewport, shaking his head. When he was satisfied, he replaced the protective cover. "All good," he called back to Vlad. Simmi and Jack and I crawled out, and climbed unsteadily to our feet.

"What happened?" Jack said.

"Nothing," Neel said. "No problem." But he looked over their heads at me, and mimed wiping sweat from his brow.

"Did I break it?" Simmi asked in a small voice.

Neel put his hand on her shoulder. "No," he said. "No—but I was actually more worried about you than the machine. If the viewport were to crack, the glass would implode. The pipe would start sucking in everything around it, like a giant vacuum cleaner. It would suck you right in with it."

"And then the lasers would burn you up," Jack concluded.

"Well, no," Neel said. "The laser would shut off automatically. But your head wouldn't be in very good shape with all that broken glass."

I still had my arm around Simmi, and I hugged her to me. "You okay?"

"Yeah," she said. "I'm fine." But her voice was shaky.

"I'm so sorry," Neel said. "I didn't mean to scare you."

"It was kind of exciting," Jack said. "Right? Has the porthole ever actually broken?"

"The viewport," Neel corrected automatically. "It happened once in Italy, at the VIRGO detector. No one got hurt, but the experiment shut down for a year."

Simmi's eyes darted around the lab, as if anticipating danger from another source. "Is the tour finished?" she asked.

"If you want it to be," Neel said. He looked at me guiltily, and I understood: it had been going so well. "There's more we could see—" he ventured, but the kids' faces made it clear that they were finished with the lab. Neel changed his tack. "I wanted to talk to

Helen about something. We have a computer with a really fast connection that you guys could use in the control room, if you want to play a game or something?"

Simmi turned to Jack. "Do you like Fruit Smash?"

"Oh yeah," he said. "I play it all the time."

Neel took the kids back to the control room to set them up at the computer. "They're having a great time in there, mutilating digital fruit," he said when he returned, a few minutes later. "They won't be able to reenter the lab without an ID card. But I told them to knock loudly if they need something."

"I'm sure they'll be fine."

Neel had exchanged the safety goggles for his regular glasses, and taken off his cap, and so I took mine off as well. I noticed he was wearing the same sweater he'd worn to his engagement party.

"That was completely my fault, by the way," he said. "I should have warned them to be careful of the monocular hitting the viewport. I probably should have held it for them."

"You've never given a tour for children."

But that didn't seem to reassure Neel. He looked even more upset than I would have expected, given that no harm had been done. "I'm not very good with kids."

"Come on," I said. "It's like anything else—you just haven't had any practice."

"I guess. But that's about to change." Neel looked down at his hands, and in the instant before he said it, I knew.

"Roxy's pregnant."

I pulled my sweater around myself; the inside of the lab was several degrees colder than the offices had been. Neel's expression was questioning, waiting for my reaction, and I had to look away. I focused on the oscillator bench across the lab, where Vlad's outline was just visible behind hanging strips of plastic. It is often impossible to understand a concept in physics without an analogy, and used in that way I have no problem with them. What I dislike are scientific analogies for emotional states. Squeezing light from a filter cavity, for example, has nothing to do with what I felt in my chest, when Neel told me this piece of news.

"You're having a baby?"

"I know," Neel said. "I didn't think I'd do it myself."

You're not going to do it yourself, I thought.

"That's wonderful," I said instead. "Congratulations."

Ever since Neel had come back into my life, I'd been determined to keep my feelings under control—but they had never gone away. They were like the polished piece of glass inside the vacuum chamber, both powerful and contained. Now it was as if the chamber had in fact imploded, dropping its glittering cargo onto the metal floor. Scientific analogies for emotional states are imprecise, but recently I've been finding them difficult to avoid.

"But that actually isn't what I wanted to talk to you about," Neel said. "I have some great news about the rotor."

"The rotor?" I asked.

"Someone just proposed installing DFGs for calibration, which could be great for our project. That means we wouldn't have to get funding for our own rotor—we could just use LIGO's."

"You're not going to have a lot of time for extracurricular projects," I said.

"Don't try to back out now," he said. "We'll make the time."

"I'm sure you'll find any number of people to help you with it."

"People," Neel said dismissively, and I had to admire the fact that LIGO's success hadn't gone to his head. He was just curious to see what he could do with it. "I can set up the experiment, but you're the one who's going to have to do the math."

"We would definitely have to do the math together. Probably with other people helping us."

"Granted. But you're the only one who's going to be able to explain it in a way that makes people understand how important it is," Neel said.

We were quiet for a moment. "When is the baby due?"

"Beginning of June," Neel said.

At the beginning of June, I thought, Charlie will have been dead two years. That blank fact seemed impossible.

"I'm not telling anyone about our project, at least not yet," Neel said.

"Our project," I repeated dumbly, but I wasn't there. Time contracted, and I was running over wet leaves, an equation on a scrap of paper in my armband, to tell Neel what I'd discovered. I was stripping off my clothes, racing with him from the sand into the freezing sea. Then I was standing outside Aunt Penny's house, watching through the window as Neel fed a log to the fire.

I rapped on the glass, but there was no sound. The night was wet and dark. Then there were footsteps, sharp, unmuffled ones, and the click of the lock on the inside of the door. The door opened, but instead of Neel standing there, it was Charlie. Her whole body was wrapped in a sort of long red cloak. *Come in,* she said to me. *Poor thing, come in, it's so cold.* She took my hand and brought me in. We sat down in front of the fire and covered ourselves with the cloak, which turned out to be a blanket—Aunt Penny's red wool blanket. The blanket was endless, less a covering than her body itself, unspooling. I looked up and saw the source of that terrible cold: the roof was gone and there were only stars above our heads. *Are you warm,* she said. *Are you?* I lied and said yes, even though my teeth were chattering. But she could see right through me. She took my chin in her hand and turned my face toward hers, made me look into her eyes. *Because that's all that matters, in the end.*

I have to be very clear. I don't mean that I stood in the lab with Neel and remembered something about my friend. What I remembered couldn't have happened, because Charlie and I didn't talk to each other that way at that time. Such an honest and tender exchange was impossible, but I remembered it so clearly that even now, it has a different quality than my actual memories of her, as if it happened under floodlights, perhaps in a theater, where I was a character in a play and a member of the audience at the same time. It was something that had never happened, but felt more true than almost all the things that had.

And then it was finished. Neel was still talking to me. He had moved on to the specifications for the rotor, a titanium and tungsten disc sixty centimeters in diameter, and the effects it would have on the lasers inside LIGO's interferometers. "If we're really installing rotors to calibrate the lasers, I think it'll be no problem to get permission to use one of them for our experiment—as long as I time it right."

"Okay," I said.

He started to tell me the ideal position for such a rotor, exactly where it would be located in relation to the laser. At one point he left to get a pencil and a pad of paper from Vlad's workstation on the other side of the lab, so that he could draw it for me. He had been talking passionately for nearly fifteen minutes, engaged by the profound implications of the rotor's gravitational effects on the laser, when I heard Jack calling me. Strangely, his voice seemed to be coming not from the control room, where Neel had left the kids, but from inside the lab.

Neel looked startled. "How'd he get back in here?"

We hurried around the corner, and found Jack standing just inside the metal door.

"Can you come talk to Simmi?" he asked me.

"How did you open the door?" Neel asked, but Jack was tugging his ears.

"Mom, please—Simmi's really upset."

"Upset about what happened before, with the interferometer?" I asked.

Jack shook his head. "I don't think so. She was fine, until a few seconds ago. We were just playing on the computer. But then she put her head down, and she wouldn't answer me."

I thought then that I understood: Simmi had been frightened by what happened in the lab, and it was only hitting her now. It was a normal reaction to such an unusual event.

"Okay," I said. "Let me talk to her."

"You go ahead," Neel said, unlocking the door for us. "I'll come in a second—I have to go find Vlad."

"You think he's the one who let Jack in?"

Neel made a skeptical face. "I doubt it. That would be against all our protocol."

Jack and I found Simmi sitting at one of the computers in the control room. When we came in, she swiveled around to face us and rubbed her eyes. Then she smiled.

"I guess I took a nap," she said.

Jack looked incredulous, and I hoped he wouldn't argue, especially since everything seemed fine.

"See," I said, running my hand over the back of his head. "She's okay."

Jack still had too much reverence for Simmi to contradict her, but I could tell that her account of the ten or so minutes we'd left them alone in the control room didn't coincide with his version of events. And I had to admit that it was hard to believe—a nine-year-old falling asleep in an unfamiliar environment, in the middle of the day.

"I'm fine," Simmi assured us. "But I need some water."

"I have a water bottle," I said, feeling around in my bag for it. "I think it's empty, but I can fill it up for you in the bathroom."

"I can do it," Simmi said.

I didn't want to let either one of them out of my sight again. "I'll go with you," I said.

"I can go by myself," Simmi said calmly, taking the bottle from my hand. "Really—I remember where it is."

I gave in, but I opened the door to the corridor and pointed her in the right direction, just in case.

"She wasn't asleep," Jack said urgently, as soon as Simmi was gone. His face was determinedly flushed: it was important to him that I understand. "She put her head down, like this—" He demonstrated, sitting on the chair Simmi had recently vacated, hugging his knees and putting his forehead against them.

"Okay," I said. "Maybe she was just recovering. That was pretty scary in there for a second."

Jack shook his head, clasping the armrests of his chair and tapping a rhythm with his sneakers on the hard floor. "I asked her what was wrong, but she wouldn't talk to me. She was all curled up. That's why I came to get you."

"Did Vlad let you in?"

"No—the door was open."

"It couldn't have been—you need an ID."

Jack shrugged. "It was."

"Maybe the tech—Eddie—let you in?"

Jack screwed up his face, considering. "I didn't see anyone. I pushed the door and it opened—I was just looking for you."

I thought it was possible that Eddie could have heard Jack knocking and opened the door from the inside. Jack, in his hurry to find me, might not have noticed him. But I couldn't understand why the tech would let Jack into the lab—a child, alone—without alerting us. I was going to ask Jack to start again and explain from the beginning, but just then Neel came back into the control room. He looked perplexed.

"Vlad's checking the vacuum pump," he told me. "I asked him to do it, just to be sure everything's working the way it should be."

"And it's okay?"

"Everything's fine," Neel said. "But he didn't let Jack in."

"It must've been someone else."

"I didn't see Vlad," Jack agreed.

Neel glanced down at him. "Vlad's the only one here, apart from us."

"And Eddie," I reminded him.

"No," Neel said. "Eddie went home. He was on his way out when we saw him."

"Is there another tech?"

"Not today," Neel said. He looked around the room, alarmed. "Where's Simmi now?"

"She went to the bathroom for some water," I said.

Neel raised his eyebrows at me. "Please, no more excitement."

"No excitement. I'll just go check on her."

"I can stay here with Jack," Neel offered.

"He can come with me."

"Hey, you'll stay and hang out with me—right, buddy?" Neel insisted, and a part of me rebelled—was he trying to practice parenting? But then I saw the pleasure on Jack's face.

"Do you like Fruit Smash?" he asked Neel.

"I don't know," Neel said. "I've never played."

"I can teach you," Jack said eagerly. "It's really easy. The different fruits are worth different amounts of points. I can play against you—but maybe we should do one game together first?" He looked up, waiting for Neel to decide.

Neel pulled another chair up to the computer, and rested one arm on the back of Jack's. "Together, definitely," he said, and Jack beamed. "I'm a novice, though," he continued. "So you'll have to start from the beginning."

.　　.　　.

Simmi was sitting on the floor of the corridor with her back against the wall. Her hair had sprung out around her head, mussed from the cap, and her cheeks were very pink.

"Hi," I said. "There you are. You okay?"

"I was just waiting for you guys."

I didn't say that we were the ones waiting for her. I still thought she must've needed a moment to herself, in the control room and again here in the hallway. She didn't make a move to get up, and so I slid down the wall, sat on the floor next to her. Simmi was playing with a green rubber band bracelet she'd taken off her wrist, stretching it between her fingers.

"I didn't think I was that tired," she said suddenly.

"Tired enough to fall asleep, you mean? It might be the traveling—sometimes that can be exhausting. And the time difference from California."

Simmi shrugged, reminding me of her father. She worked both wrists into the rubber bracelet. "I had a dream."

There was a metallic taste in my mouth; I'd been biting the inside of my cheek without realizing. "A daydream?"

"No." Simmi was decisive. "A real dream."

She was looking at me directly, waiting for my reaction, but I couldn't say anything.

"It was too weird to be a daydream," she insisted.

"You can have a weird daydream," I said, but I sounded weak, unconvincing even to myself. Of course I knew exactly what she meant about the difference.

Simmi unfolded her legs and stretched them across the empty corridor, the toes of her boots turning outward on the linoleum. One of her laces had come undone.

"What was the dream about?"

"About my mom picking me up from school."

I waited, as I do with Jack, and after a few moments, she continued.

"The weird part was, it wasn't my school in L.A."

"No?"

"It was BB&N—here. I usually don't even think about that school."

"Maybe it was in your dream because you're in Boston right now," I said. "Sometimes dreams mix things up that way."

"It was like—" Simmi looked at me sideways, as if debating how much to reveal. "I mean, I wasn't surprised to see her."

"Just like you weren't surprised to be in Boston."

"Yeah. But then she said our word."

I was confused. "Which word?"

Simmi smiled a little. "You know, our safety word—in Latin."

"The one you said was your mom's idea?"

"Right—but that's what was weird. You don't need a code word, when it's a parent."

I hesitated. "Sometimes people say things in dreams that they wouldn't say in real life."

Simmi nodded. "But this wasn't exactly like she said it."

"No?"

"More like I read it . . . on a screen."

Simmi's expression was serious, but she didn't seem on the brink of any strong emotion. We sat with our backs against the wall, staring up at a poster-sized graph entitled: "Measured Noise Relative to Shot Noise as a Function of Sideband Frequency and Readout Quadrature."

"I think I might have had a dream about her, too," I said.

Simmi looked down, picked at a frayed place in the leg of her jeans. She didn't say anything but she seemed to be waiting for me to continue.

"We were just sitting and talking in a room. By a fire. She asked me if I was cold."

Now Simmi looked up at me and frowned. Her thick brows contracted, almost meeting in the middle. "Was *she* cold?"

"No," I said quickly. "No—she had a blanket."

Simmi took a deep breath: "The room, with the fire—where was it?"

"Not far from here," I said. "Near Boston—although that's not weird in my case. Most of the time your mom and I spent together was in Boston."

Simmi nodded slowly. Then she put one finger on the linoleum and traced a curving path between us, back and forth.

"When you were young," she said.

16.

I went back into the control room, where Neel and Jack were playing the game.

"The pineapple!" Jack cried. "Get the pineapple!"

"Thanks for keeping an eye on him," I told Neel. "We'll get out of your hair now."

"I'll come out and say goodbye," Neel said. He looked toward the door. "Is she okay? I hope that drama in the lab didn't freak her out too much."

"I don't think so," I said.

"Good." Neel smiled at Jack. "And I hope these guys got something out of it. I know I'm definitely not going to forget this visit."

Jack touched Neel's sleeve familiarly. "Tell her about the log."

I looked at Neel.

"Oh," Neel said. "Right—the data log. We'll have to ask Simmi if she made an entry."

I didn't follow. "Simmi made an entry in your data log?"

"I had the log open on this machine," Neel explained. He indicated the computer next to the one he and Jack had been using.

"It couldn't have been Simmi," Jack said. "I was here with her."

"But maybe when you came back into the lab to get us, when you were worried about her?" Neel suggested.

Jack shook his head, and I had to agree with him. "I doubt Simmi would touch any of the other computers," I told Neel. "Especially after what happened in the lab."

"It's no problem," Neel said. "I just didn't get why our data log was suddenly in Latin."

"Latin?"

"More likely it was just random letters—someone must've leaned on the keyboard."

"Random letters." Jack was looking at me steadily. "Like the metaphase typewriter."

"What nonsense are you feeding him?" Neel asked mildly.

"Which letters?" I asked.

"*E-X-*" But Jack couldn't remember any more of it. "Maybe it's a code word."

"Can I see?"

Neel indulged me, scrolling up the log and pointing at the screen.

"*E-X-E-U-N-T,*" Jack read, leaning over his shoulder. Then he turned back to me.

"What does that mean?"

17.

The three chief scientists on the LIGO collaboration won the Nobel Prize in October 2017. Two weeks later, they announced the first detection of a neutron star collision. It was what I'd been hoping would happen, but I didn't end up writing a book about kilonova after all. When I sat down to try, I found that what I started writing had moved further and further away from my original idea about the cosmic origins of precious metals, into what is for me entirely new territory.

I have been thinking, in particular, of Neel's and my old argument about the mind and the brain. I still refuse to accept that there's some ineffable essence hovering between our brains and the outside world—at least not something we'll ever be able to study with scientific tools. We can know what's possible only in the universe we've observed. But if LIGO has done anything, it has reminded us how little of what's out there we've actually seen. To understand more of our cosmology, we're going to have to admit that there may be laws so different from the ones we know, so seemingly counterintuitive, that it will take all our imagination to uncover them.

In 1979, in honor of the centennial of Einstein's birth, John Wheeler delivered his famous lecture "Beyond the Black Hole" for an elite audience of scientists at Princeton's Institute of Advanced Study. He began with an analogy about the "Iron Duke" Arthur Wellesley, who, among his many other military victories, was famous for defeating Napoleon at Waterloo. When he grew old, the duke liked to go for drives with a friend in his carriage, especially when they could visit countryside that wasn't familiar to either of them. He would propose a game in which he and his companion each had to guess what kind of landscape lay over the next hill; not surprisingly, the duke nearly always won the game. He claimed that his strategy was to identify "strangenesses" in the terrain, surprising features; it was whatever was unfamiliar or irregular in the scenery that allowed him to predict what was coming next. Einstein, Wheeler proposed, used scientific strangenesses the same way. By studying paradoxes in our knowledge of the physical world, he was able to intuit startling new truths about the nature of light and gravity. Wheeler believed that it was the job of each generation of physicists to use the paradoxes in the physics they inherited to take the work even further.

Sometimes I have a feeling that Neel and I are getting close to a breakthrough with the rotor project. But it isn't the same as it was when we first worked together. This work is harder than the modeling we did early in our careers, and it's messier, too; it requires more guesswork, and more faith. Charlie was skeptical by nature, but I think she would have agreed with what her brother said at the memorial: that loss is different for each of us. A person dies, and a whole crowd goes out—not exit, but *exeunt*. And, if that is the case, then it must be possible for those essences (ideas, let's call them) to return. To circle back around like Neel's and my rotor: a pair of heavy things at a fixed distance, turning and turning forever.

This isn't just analogy. Physicists know that if you and I are sitting in a room together, you exert a gravitational force on me. It's almost nothing—I can't feel it—but it's the same force that binds our planet to our star. That's the very simple, very elegant purpose of the rotor: to hold a pair of tiny stars. Each time one of them swings toward the laser, spacetime bends just slightly; the laser must travel a slightly longer path to reach the mirror; a line spikes on one of LIGO's screens. Even that silent signal could be enough to let us reimagine gravity, and the way it moves us on the human scale.

ACKNOWLEDGMENTS

When I started writing this book, science felt more foreign to me than any country I'd ever visited. I'm deeply grateful to the patient guides I met there, including the authors of the following wonderful books: *The Universe*, edited by John Brockman; Harry Collins's *Gravity's Kiss;* Louisa Gilder's *The Age of Entanglement;* Walter Isaacson's *Einstein: His Life and Universe;* David Kaiser's *How the Hippies Saved Physics;* Janna Levin's *Black Hole Blues;* Lisa Randall's *Warped Passages, Knocking on Heaven's Door, Higgs Discovery,* and *Dark Matter and the Dinosaurs;* Kip Thorne's *Black Holes and Time Warps;* Steven Weinberg's *To Explain the World.* It's great that curious outsiders can read the important physics being published today on the e-print archive (arXiv.org), without even registering a password.

No book can really give you the texture of what it's like to work in a particular field of study, and so I'm especially grateful to the physicists who talked to me during this process. LIGO physicist Imre Bartos sat with me for hours in his office, and once walked through Riverside Park with a voice recorder in his pocket, trying to explain gravitational wave science to a former English major. Lisa Barsotti took me on a tour of the Green Lab at MIT, one of the most fascinating places I've ever been. On a conference call from the LIGO detector in Livingston, Louisiana, she and Matthew Evans solved a plot problem for me off the top of their heads (in spite of what the narrator of this book might claim, physicists are actually smarter than other people). Which brings me to David Kaiser, an extremely busy person who gave me more of his time than I had any right to expect, patiently answering my questions about quantum entanglement, the Fundamental Fysiks Group, and life in a university physics department. I'm especially grateful to him for his early scientific read of this book; any mistakes are my own.

Outside of the physical sciences, I relied on Pankaj Mishra's *Age of Anger* for its brilliant argument about the Enlightenment in Europe and its political repercussions today. I'm indebted to Paul Beatty, Brit Bennett, Ta-Nehisi Coates, Reni Eddo-Lodge, Margo Jefferson, Claudia Rankine, Tracy K. Smith, and Colson Whitehead for work that helped me think

ACKNOWLEDGMENTS

about what race means and doesn't mean to the characters I was trying to create.

Emma Freudenberger, Amy Waldman, Cathy Park Hong, Jasanna Britton, Alison Markovitz, and Vanessa Reisen read early drafts of this book quickly and critically when I most needed help—thank you so much. I'm very grateful for my generous and talented community of local writers: Kiran Desai, Monica Ferrell, Eliza Griswold, Katie Kitamura, Idra Novey, Meghan O'Rourke, Julie Orringer, Amanda Stern, Jen Vanderbes, and Monica Youn. I owe more thanks than I can express to Allyson Hobbs, for her comments and gentle criticism, for our ongoing discussions, and for being awake and on her phone when no one else is.

I've said it before, but Binky Urban is the best agent a writer could have: responsive, direct, and thorough. At Knopf, I'm grateful to Erinn Hartman, Julianne Clancy, and Rachel Fershleiser for all of their help and faith in this book, and to Susan VanOmmeren for an especially meticulous proofread. Annie Bishai went far beyond assistant editing, offering rigorous insight on subjects as varied as contemporary race and gender, iPhone technology, and the proper way to graph temperature. My most significant thank-you is to Robin Desser, for her tough editorial love. I am overwhelmingly thankful for the talent and wisdom she gave to this book.

Thank you to my dad, Daniel Freudenberger, for a helpful final read, and to him and his wife, Ruth Bloch, for Thursday afternoons at my desk. Thanks to my mom, Carol Hofmann, for all the other time, and for once even staying over during a snowstorm so that I could meet a deadline. Thank you to my children for the sign they posted outside my office door, telling themselves to go away, and for the Post-it on my computer encouraging me to persevere. Thank you to my husband, Paul, for being so loving and supportive, always, and for encouraging me to try something new this time.

A NOTE ABOUT THE AUTHOR

Nell Freudenberger is the author of the novels *The Newlyweds* and *The Dissident*, and of the story collection *Lucky Girls*, which won the PEN/Malamud Award and the Sue Kaufman Prize for First Fiction from the American Academy of Arts and Letters. Named one of *The New Yorker*'s "20 Under 40" in 2010, she is a recipient of a Guggenheim Fellowship, a Whiting Award, and a Cullman Fellowship from the New York Public Library. She lives in Brooklyn with her family.

A NOTE ON THE TYPE

This book was set in Adobe Garamond. Designed for the Adobe Corporation by Robert Slimbach, the fonts are based on types first cut by Claude Garamond (c. 1480–1561). Garamond was a pupil of Geoffroy Tory and is believed to have followed the Venetian models, although he introduced a number of important differences, and it is to him that we owe the letter we now know as "old style."

Typeset by Scribe, Philadelphia, Pennsylvania

Printed and bound by Berryville Graphics, Berryville, Virginia

Designed by Iris Weinstein